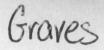

The Friends We Keep

Books by Holly Chamberlin

LIVING SINGLE

THE SUMMER OF US

BABYLAND

BACK IN THE GAME

THE FRIENDS WE KEEP

Published by Kensington Publishing Corporation

The Friends We Keep

Holly Chamberlin

KENSINGTON BOOKS
http://www.kensingtonbooks.com

KENSINGTON BOOKS are published by

Kensington Publishing Corp.
850 Third Avenue
New York, NY 10022

ISBN-13: 978-0-7582-1401-0
ISBN-10: 0-7582-1401-4

First Kensington Trade Paperback Printing: July 2007
10 9 8 7 6 5 4 3 2 1

Printed in the United States of America

As always, for Stephen
And this time, also for Peggy

Acknowledgments

Once again, I extend my deep appreciation to my editor, John Scognamiglio. I offer thanks to Joan Donner, from whom I get what talent I have, for her editorial input in an early and difficult stage of the book. Last, but never least, thanks to my husband for creating our lovely home.

* 1 *

*It's vitally important that men continue to keep se-
crets from women, and that women continue to keep
secrets from men. The entire male/female dynamic
relies on misrepresentation and misunderstanding.
Why tamper with a good thing?*
                    —Men, Women, and Secrets: It's All Good

EVA

My name is Eva Fitzpatrick. I was born Eve but changed
my name to Eva around the time I turned thirty. It seemed to
suit me better.

I grew up in a largely nonpracticing Catholic family of
Irish and German ancestry and was raised in a very American-
ized or culturally neutral way. I know nothing of my family's
European roots. My parents didn't speak a word of German.
In spite of our last name we never celebrated St. Patrick's Day.
We did not go to church unless it was to a relative's wedding
or funeral.

Neither of my parents was particularly demonstrative. As
the older of two children—my sister, Maura, was born when
I was ten—I was expected to be mature almost from the
start. I have been working since I was fourteen (I babysat
until I could get working papers) and was always a good student. This was partly because I loved learning and partly be-

cause it was expected of me. I did not want to disappoint my parents.

My parents died of cancer—first my father, followed a few months later by my mother—when I was just out of college and looking forward to graduate school. My plan was to earn a PhD in English literature and then to teach and write. Because my parents had nothing to leave their children but the house and a small insurance policy, I gave up my graduate career, sold the house for the cash, and went to work to support my younger sister. In spite of my urging—or maybe, because of it—Maura dropped out of college in her junior year.

Two years after that Maura married a man twenty-five years her senior. A few years later, when his cocaine habit had bankrupted them, she divorced him. Now Maura lives in a small town in Michigan with her second, high school–educated husband and their four kids, all girls: Brooke, Britney, Angelina, and Jessica. On occasion Maura hints at needing money. Her husband, Trevor, works at a gas station as a mechanic and she is a night cashier in a local grocery chain. I send a check to a post office box, as Trevor doesn't accept "charity." I don't know how Maura explains the extra cash.

In spite of the years of financial support, my sister and I aren't close. On occasion, Maura, who is a nice enough person, invites me to visit, but I never do. The thought of staying in my sister's cramped and kid-friendly home (I've seen pictures; there are plastic toys everywhere.) isn't at all appealing and there are no decent hotels nearby. So except for solitary trips to the islands once a year I stay on the East Coast. I hardly ever think of my nieces. Sometimes, I realize that I've temporarily forgotten their names.

I am the senior vice president of the most important advertising agency in the Northeast. I say that without a shred of modesty. I worked my way up from secretary; I learned the business the hard way, which is often the best way. I'm successful and I'm proud of my success. I see no sense in hiding my light under a bushel.

I dress the part of an executive in suits and separates. I am fond of heels and not in the least bit uncomfortable being taller than a man, which does happen, given my height of five feet eight inches.

I carry my clothes well, especially the sleek, tailored pieces I favor. I choose neutrals: black, gray, brown, taupe, and white. I haven't owned a pair of jeans since college, when I dressed in whatever was clean and available. These days, I don't do casual; I am always what my mother called "put together." People remember a woman with a signature look; she makes an impression.

My hair is professionally colored ultrablonde. I wear it closely cropped in a face-flattering style. My eyes are brown. The contrast between my bright hair and dark eyes is arresting.

I prefer an oversized leather bag to a more traditional briefcase. Into that bag I stuff any combination of the following: my PDA/cell phone of the moment, an extra pair of stockings (in case of runs), a makeup bag, a potboiler novel of the sort I wouldn't dream of admitting to reading, an iPod, my laptop, the latest issues of *W* and *Vogue,* the latest issues of my industry's trade publications, the *New York Times* (I read the *Wall Street Journal* and the Boston papers online.), and a bottle of fortified water (You can never be too hydrated.).

I go to the gym five days a week. For years I worked with a trainer but, having learned a thing or two, now I work out on my own. Currently, at the age of forty-two, I'm in the best shape of my life.

I am not married, nor am I involved in a long-term, committed relationship. I don't date. I have a lover, someone with whom I have regular sex. We're not friends; lover is even too intimate a term to describe who Sam is to me or who I am to him. On occasion I have sex with other men. None of them are ever invited to my apartment.

At this point in my life, I have no one to answer to but myself. Everything, I am pleased to report, is in place.

✳ 2 ✳

Dear Answer Lady:

I'm seventeen and lied to my boyfriend about being a virgin when we met. The truth is I've been having sex (protected) since I was fourteen. I really like this guy and now I'm wondering if I should tell him about my past. Is our relationship doomed because I lied to him at the start?

Dear Poor Little Thing:

You are under no obligation to tell your boyfriend a thing about your past sex life. Has he told you about his? How do you know he hasn't left something out, like the underage girl he got pregnant? How do you know he isn't lying, for example, about never having had an STD? Everyone lies or withholds information about their sex life. It's normal. So keep your past to yourself and don't give up on the condoms.

JOHN

My name is John Alfredo Felitti. My parents came to this country from a small town just north of Naples, Italy, when they were still in their teens and unknown to each other. Each joined family already in Windhill, a suburb of Boston.

Within a year of their separate arrivals they were married. Five years later I was born. During the interim between the wedding and my birth my father established a decent business as a tailor.

Two years later my sister Theresa was born. We call her Teri. Today she works as manager of a successful clothing store in the Prudential Mall and is married to a guy named Frank. Frank is midlevel management with the electric company. They have three kids: a four-year-old girl named Jean Marie and twin boys, Andrew and Scott, age twelve. Every summer they go to Cape Cod for a week. In the past few years they've offered to take along our parents but Mom and Dad aren't interested in the beach.

A year after Teri came along, my youngest sibling was born, Christina. Chrissy is married to a guy named Mike, who is in construction. Chrissy works part-time as a salesclerk. The rest of her days and nights are spent being a parent to ten-year-old Lucy (after our mother, Lucia) and eight-year-old Paul (after our father, Paolo). Both Teri and Chrissy are active in our parish church, St. Boniface. Much to my parents' dismay, I haven't graced the door of a church since high school graduation, except, of course, when performing a family duty.

Teri and her family, Chrissy and hers, and my parents all still live in Windhill in houses only minutes from one another. Our family is a close one, with few if any smoldering resentments and rare displays of outright anger. Unless, of course, someone "acts up." Then my mother lets fly with dramatic gestures and pleas to God to take her to his side, etc., etc., until the offender apologizes profusely, at which point Mom blesses herself with the sign of the cross and shuts up. Hey, it works for her. We all find our strengths and play to them.

I have been told that I have a commanding presence. I'm six feet two inches. My shoulders are broad. My body is in shape, thanks to almost daily workouts. My face, which still retains something of youth, is made to seem more serious and mature by my glasses—I have several pairs, with stylish designer frames. (I wear contacts only while exercising.) My hair has thinned only slightly. I'm an anomaly in my family. My parents and my sisters are short and have much darker complexions than I do. My father used to joke that I was the milkman's son (My mother would giggle and smack his arm.), but in truth I take after my father's older brother, long dead (I know him only from pictures.), who towered over the rest of the family. (Maybe he was the milkman's son.)

From childhood, I've had a sense of my own importance. I was the firstborn, the only son of very old-fashioned people. It was a struggle at first but over time it became a habit—not to indulge that sense of importance, but to choose to believe that I'm in this world for a purpose, and that purpose is to do good for others. Since as far back as I can remember I've been the go-to guy for just about everybody I've ever known. If I'm going to command attention, then I'm going to use that power for the good. No one likes a self-important asshole. The last thing I want to be considered is stuck-up, full of myself, arrogant. I work hard to be humble. It hasn't always been easy, when other people see you as something special.

Poor me. I'm teetering on the brink of sounding like a self-pitying wretch, and no one likes one of those, either.

* 3 *

Maybe she can't see you this weekend because her mother really is coming to town for an antique doll convention. Maybe he's late coming home every Tuesday because he really is taking lute lessons. The unlikely does occur; the unusual does take place. Don't automatically dismiss an excuse because it sounds "creative."
—Recognizing a Lie: It's Not as Easy as You Think

SOPHIE

I was born Sophia Jimenez. I am an only child. My mother doesn't like to talk about "such things" but over the years I gathered that though she and my father tried hard (how hard I don't know) to have another baby, it just didn't happen.

Growing up I didn't mind not having a brother or sister. I guess I still don't. You know, they say you don't miss what you've never had.

My paternal grandparents were Cuban. They came to the United States when my father was four years old. They were very Catholic. When my father eventually married, he chose a woman who had been raised in the Episcopal Church. My grandparents were uneasy about this until my mother agreed to raise the children Catholic. They couldn't do anything about my mother's not being Cuban, though. But my mother won them over. She's a very big-hearted person; people take to her right away. Besides, her own family was never a close one. My mother was happy to have in-laws who showed so much interest in her—far more than her parents ever did.

I had a smooth childhood. I did well in school and had plenty of playmates. When I was in college my grandfather died. That was the first really bad thing that happened to me. My grandmother lived another ten years, and though the last three of those years were spent in a nursing home, she never complained.

In my freshman year of college I met Eve Fitzpatrick and John Felitti. Eve became my first real best friend; in high school I was part of a loosely knit group of girls but not one of them had become a real confidante.

John was the first male friend I ever had. In our sophomore year we sort of went out for a few weeks but it was a mistake and due to too much beer at a party. We were both relieved when the "relationship" ran out of steam (not that it had had much steam to begin with) and we could go back to being just friends. We never told Eve about it; she hadn't been to the party—it was a campus thing John and I sort of wandered into. I don't know why but we felt the "relationship" should remain our little secret.

When I was a senior, I met Brad Holmes. He impressed me because he knew exactly what he wanted to do after school: make money. He was a whiz in economics and math, in all the subjects that left me cold even when I could figure out what was going on. He treated me nicely, holding doors and buying me dinner, all that old-fashioned stuff my parents had taught me was important. When at Christmas he asked me to marry him after graduation, I immediately said yes. My parents were pleased. Brad's parents were less so. They wanted him to finish graduate school before settling down with a wife. But I won them over, just like my mother won over her prospective in-laws.

Brad and I were married the summer after graduation. Eve and John weren't at the wedding. It was held on an island in the Caribbean—Brad's parents' choice—and neither of my friends could afford the price of airfare and accommodations. I was disappointed they couldn't be there for my "big day," but at the same time I was so giddy with excitement— the dress, the ring, the reception, the exotic location!—I almost didn't notice their absence once the festivities began.

It wasn't long before I was pregnant. Jacob Michael Holmes was almost nine pounds at birth and delivered by a C-section. Jake was a healthy and a happy baby. I doted on him and so did Brad, to the best of his ability. Brad knew how to do all the right things but he wasn't, still isn't, an affectionate man.

When Jake turned three we relocated to Los Angeles. Brad got an offer he couldn't refuse—for the sake, of course, of his wife and son—from one of the big studios. Brad's career flourished and the three of us lived very comfortably. For the first few years I was lonely for my hometown of Boston, but eventually, I adjusted. Twice a year I traveled back East with Jake, and sometimes Brad came along. His parents, who were fairly well-off, came to see us whenever their busy social life allowed, but they never stayed in our home, preferring instead a luxury hotel. My parents, solidly lower-middle class (at the time there was such a thing), did stay with us when they visited, which was usually in February or March, months that are often dreary and depressing in New England.

Over time our parents traveled less frequently. Age took its inevitable toll on their mobility and their desire to be far from home. When Jake was twelve, his paternal grandfather died. After that, his paternal grandmother went to live with Brad's older brother, Gary, in a suburb of Chicago; her last trip to LA, with Gary, was for Jake's college graduation not more than a year ago. She looked terribly frail and, not to be morbid, but I suspect that the next time I see her will be at her funeral. Gary confided that Mrs. Holmes has cancer and that she'd decided not to undergo a long and painful treatment.

And my parents? Now they divide their time between their modest house in Freeham, Massachusetts, and their modest condo in an over-55 development in New Smyrna Beach, Florida. They seem content and their health is good but for the usual, annoying ailments that come with advancing age.

Anyway, back to my life in LA. When Jake reached high school, I found myself with time on my hands so on a whim I took a real estate course and got my real estate license. Honestly, the job was always more of a hobby than a career. We didn't really need my income, but I enjoyed the social aspects of the job, meeting new people and having someplace to be every day. Everyone wants to feel needed.

And with no close friends, a son who was growing more independent every day, and a husband who spent most of his time with his colleagues, I did need to feel needed. Until, I don't know, I just sort of lost interest—and quit.

So where was Eve all this time? Back East—and out of touch. Over the past twenty years or so my friendship with Eve, once so strong, gradually slipped away. There were no bad feelings, simply two lives diverging. I've often asked myself why.

Maybe the answer is that after college our lives took such different paths. My life played out pretty much as I'd wanted it to, but Eve's did not. For one thing, Eve never married. She'd intended to, and had planned on having two or three children.

I can't help but think that Eve's not marrying and her not having a child alienated her from me, and me from her. Maybe if she'd shown an interest in Jake our friendship might have survived. Eve could have been a sort of aunt to Jake; I would have liked that. But Eve rejected every attempt I made to involve her with my new family. I know she was upset about her parents' deaths and about having to postpone graduate school indefinitely. Not that she ever admitted to feeling sad or angry or depressed. But she must have been and maybe that was part of the reason she rejected a relationship with Jake . . . and part of the reason she chose to abandon a friendship with me.

Maybe it doesn't make much sense but it's all I can come up with. I'm not sure I'd ever have the nerve to ask Eve why she didn't want to spend time with Jake and me. I'm not at all confrontational. Maybe, someday, she'll tell me on her own. Maybe she'll open up about those years just after her parents died and her life was thrown so wildly off course.

I hope so.

* 4 *

Dear Answer Lady:

A few months ago I met this really great guy. We started dating and have even talked about getting married. My friends think he's adorable. Anyway, this past weekend we visited his mother's house (his father is dead). I was coming back from the bathroom when I overheard his aunt and mother saying: "Should we tell her about him?" and "No, he's different now, everything will be okay." They shut up when I came into the kitchen. Since then, I've been wondering if they were talking about me and if the "he" was my boyfriend and if so, what are they not telling me? Should I confront my boyfriend? What if he's hiding something awful about his past? Or should I just forget what I heard and go ahead with our relationship, which, as I said, is really great?

Dear Person-Who-Needs-to-Know-That-Ignorance-Is-Not-Always-Bliss:

Ordinarily, I advise against the need for full disclosure. Everyone has a right to his or her past. But in this case, I advise you to get to the heart of the matter before you wind up in several bloody pieces strewn throughout the house. This supposedly great boyfriend could, in fact, have a criminal record and be guilty of

*anything from embezzlement to murder. And be sure
to bring reinforcements when you confront this supposedly great boyfriend. A large man armed with a
semiautomatic weapon is a wise choice of backup.*

EVA

Where the hell was my assistant? On the fifth ring I picked
up the phone.

"Eva Fitzpatrick."

"Oh. Is this Eve Fitzpatrick?"

"This is Eva Fitzpatrick. Who is this?"

"I'm sorry," the voice said. "I was looking for an old
friend from college, someone named Eve Fitzpatrick."

"I didn't catch your name?"

"Oh, I'm sorry, it's Sophie Holmes. It used to be Jimenez."

I had a strong urge to disconnect the call. I shook off the
urge and said, "Sophie, this is Eve. Except that I changed my
name to Eva."

The voice, the woman, Sophie laughed with relief. "Oh,
my gosh, it is you! Hello!"

I sat heavily in my desk chair. "Well. Hello. It's been a long
time."

"I know, too long."

"So, why—I mean, where are you living these days?"

"That's why I'm calling. I'm back in Boston. Brad and I,
well, we're divorced."

I had never much liked Brad. Very full of himself. "Oh," I
said.

"Yes. Anyway, my son's in school here now so I thought,
why not come back East? Plus, I'd be close to my parents and
it would give me an opportunity to look up some old
friends."

"Yes, well." Oh, I thought, here we go. I was going to kill

my assistant for this. It was easy not to return a call. It wasn't as easy to reject a person face-to-face, as it were.

"So," Sophie went on, "I was wondering, would you, you know, want to get together some time?"

Why, I thought, can't people leave the past alone? It was past for a reason—it was over.

"Eve? I mean, Eva?"

"Yes," I said resignedly, "okay. I could meet for a drink."

I suggested one of my favorite restaurant bars. If I was going to allow myself to be hauled down memory lane, at least I could be eating oysters while at it.

* 5 *

If you gain a deserved reputation as a keeper of se-crets, your social value will soar. Everyone wants a friend to whom he can spill his ugly guts without fear of those ugly guts being publicly displayed. Plus, you'll probably get a lot of free meals being such a cherished friend.
—The Social Value of Keeping Secrets

JOHN

My keeper of the gate, my right-hand woman, and, though this might be unusual, my friend, is a woman named Ellen Mara. She's been with me, with the firm, for almost five years now and I hope she's with me—wherever I am—for the next fifteen at least. Why Ellen didn't go to law school I'll never understand; she's one of the keenest minds I know. She claims she was too lazy to get her law degree but I'm not buying it.

Ellen is fifty. I know this because she told me. I hope I'm not breaching professional ethics by saying that she has a great body—what I've seen of it, of course. She often wears fitted skirt suits, but tweaks the sophisticated look with one-of-a-kind jewelry she buys at craft shows.

Ellen's husband, a guy named Austin who I've met on a few occasions, is in finance at one of the major firms in town. They have a small vacation home on a lake somewhere in

Maine; they keep the exact location a secret to avoid pop-ins and never invite friends or family to stay with them. Ellen has told me they feel it's important for a couple to have a place entirely their own. I suppose she's right but I can't imagine ever trying to keep my family from barging in on my vacation house when I settle down enough to buy one. They'd track me down like bloodhounds. Besides, the guilt would kill me. In my family, what belongs to one person belongs (potentially) to every person. This is one reason why I chose to live in town rather than in Windhill, where Teri, Chrissy, and my parents all live. Some buffer zone is required if I'm to live any sort of independent life.

I was on my second cup of coffee, which means it was about ten-thirty, when Ellen buzzed me. (I know "buzzed" is no longer an accurate way to describe this function, but I like it.)

"John," Ellen said. "There's a Sophie Holmes on the phone."

The name didn't register at first. I hear what seems like thousands of names a week, some I recognize, some I don't. And then the image of a young, laughing woman with long dark hair and half-dorky glasses popped into my head. Could it be?

"Thanks, Ellen," I said. "I'll take it."

* 6 *

Dear Answer Lady:

I work in the produce department at this super-market. The pay isn't great but the hours are okay. Besides, I'm studying for my GED and until I get my high school diploma I don't have much choice as far as jobs go. The thing is, almost everyone I work with in produce takes home fruit and vegetables. I mean, without actually paying for them. Not a lot, like maybe a couple of bananas or a head of lettuce at a time. They've been doing it for years. Until last week I refused to join in but then, one of the guys started ribbing me about being a wimp so I took home a bunch of grapes. Nobody found out and since then I've taken home more grapes and am thinking about going for a bag of tomatoes next. It's not hurting anybody, right?

Dear Thief:

I've heard that you can study for the GED while serving time in prison. Hey, I bet it helps wile away the hours. Are you a religious person? If so you might remember the Commandment that forbids the act of stealing. Unless you have a starving wife and child at home and the grapes (and possibly tomatoes) are their only source of nutrition, stop STEALING from the business that employs you.

SOPHIE

John seemed genuinely pleased to hear from me. Eve—Eva—on the other hand, didn't. But maybe I'd caught her at a bad time.

Oh, well, I thought, what's done is done. I was to meet Eve—Eva (that would take some getting used to)—for drinks. John was all booked up until the following week but promised to call then.

Eva had asked me, well, in fact she'd told me, to meet her at Churchill on Tremont Street across from the Common. This, I read in the paper, was a popular new place with a "power clientele." With these intimidating words in mind I ventured to my closet. It didn't take long to realize that I had nothing appropriate to wear.

Over the years I'd cared less and less about my appearance. I'd let the gray in my hair show through and as for clothes, well, though I wasn't much heavier than I was in college, I'd taken to wearing clothes meant to deemphasize my figure. Loose tops and flowing skirts were comfortable and easy to care for, but now, about to meet someone I hadn't seen in almost twenty years they seemed . . . dull.

I closed the closet door and decided to treat myself to an afternoon of shopping at the Prudential Mall. I wasn't at all sure what I was looking for but for the first time in years the notion of new clothes seemed exciting. New clothes, a new life, and renewed friendships. What could be bad?

* 7 *

For the select few, lying is more than just an occasional indulgence. It's a way of life, constituting both a need and a desire. For such an individual born to live a life of deception—deception of others as well as of the self—it's important that he believe the words he speaks. If the dedicated liar begins to doubt his own falsehoods, then what peace of mind can he ever know? And isn't the natural-born liar as deserving of happiness as the truthful man?
> —It's the Truth If You Believe It, or Life as a Sincere Liar

EVA

I was surprised to hear from Sophie Holmes. The last time I saw her was when her son, Jake, was a toddler, just before Sophie moved to the West Coast so that Brad could take an important job he'd been offered by one of the big studios. Her parents threw "the kids" a going-away party, and though it meant I had to take a night off my job as a waitress—one of several jobs I was working at to support my sister and me—I went.

I didn't have much to say to Sophie by then; our lives had taken such incredibly different directions. I vaguely remember us hugging awkwardly when I left to catch a train back into the city. I don't remember Jake at all; maybe he was asleep somewhere. I do remember John sailing in with his latest girlfriend in tow; I'm not sure we said more than a word that evening. John had finished law school, Sophie was married and a mother. I was the only one not doing what I thought I would be doing at the age of twenty-four.

For a while after Sophie moved to the West Coast we sent each other birthday and Christmas cards. Sometimes they included dashed-off notes about what was going on in our lives; Sophie often included wallet-sized department-store portraits or school photos of Jake. I have no idea where those photos are now. I suspect I tossed them at some point, probably after the cards stopped coming—or I stopped sending them. Who forgot a birthday first? Who was too exhausted from holiday shopping to send a Christmas card? I couldn't remember.

I also couldn't remember much about our friendship during the four years of college. This wasn't terribly surprising. I learned early on, right after my parents' untimely deaths, that dwelling on the past is simply unproductive. And every moment of life should be productive. If the past has to be let go in order to ensure the future, then so be it. Repression or willed forgetfulness can be powerful tools on the road to success. Recovered memory? Not for me. What I've forgotten I believe I've forgotten for a very good reason: it was inconsequential.

And yet, I found myself willing to meet Sophie for a drink. I wouldn't commit to dinner; I wasn't prepared to spend an entire evening with her. But I was willing to see how things would go, maybe out of simple curiosity. How had Sophie fared since I'd last seen her? Did she look older than her forty-two years, or younger? And how would I compare?

Stranger still, I found myself wondering if whatever it was that had drawn us together in college, whatever it was that had made us friends, would be there again, after all this time.

And if it was there, I wondered if I would care.

* 8 *

Dear Answer Lady:
  My wife just dyed her hair a shade of red I find repulsive. Should I tell her that every time she walks into a room I want to vomit?

Dear Incredibly Stupid Husband:
  Keep your incredibly stupid mouth shut.

JOHN

I'd been thinking a lot about my personal relationships, even before Sophie's call. And I'd come to the realization that other than my father and brothers-in-law, I didn't have any male friends—and I wasn't sure I could properly call family members friends. Sure, there were a few colleagues with whom I occasionally had a drink or caught a ball game when someone scored free tickets. And although I work out almost every day at a local gym, I avoid getting into locker room conversations. I'm there to do a job—keep my body in some semblance of order—and once the job is done for the day, I'm gone.

Maybe, I thought, having no guy friends wasn't a problem.

There is one guy at my office who deserves a mention in this context. His name is Gene Patton. He's thirty-three and a rat of a guy, a real sleaze. He regularly cheats on his doting, stay-at-home wife, a sweet woman named Marie. I met her at last year's company Christmas party, at which Gene completely ignored her, compelling me to spend an entire half hour chatting with her. She's not a great conversationalist but short of dragging her bum of a husband to her side by his ear, I wasn't going to let her stand there all alone in her not-so-fine finery, looking like a scared rabbit.

I meet so many women in the course of my work who've wound up with such disgusting specimens of my sex and always I ask myself: How and why did this happen? There are all sorts of answers, of course, from the economic to the personal, from social strictures to family pressures. But even when I learn the specifics of a particular story I'm still left wondering. I still feel unsettled.

But back to Gene. Not only is he a slime in his personal life, he's also a pimple on the butt of society in that he's a major tax evader. Understandably, I'm uncomfortable with this knowledge but my personal code of ethics forbids me from ratting on a buddy. Gene might not be a friend but he is in a way a companion and while I can advise him never again to mention his illegal activities to me, as I am, in fact, an attorney, I also won't turn him in to the IRS. So sue me.

As if cheating the government isn't bad enough, this guy never picks up the tab when a few of us from the firm go out for a drink after work. We're wise to this habit and have devised several schemes to leave Gene stuck with the bill whenever the tab is particularly high.

Still, I tolerate this guy's presence. And sometimes it keeps me awake at night wondering why.

It's pretty clear to me that a lot of Gene's hanging around my office is due to a rabid desire to get in good with one of the firm's partners. I'm no fool—I'm not going to award Gene anything he doesn't deserve—but the fact is I'm a bit of a lonely guy these days. I'm not proud of it, but sometimes I find that spending an hour with a creep is better than spending an hour by myself. And Gene does understand some of my professional pressures. In spite of his severe character defects, he is a pretty good attorney. Okay, some might say that his professional skills are a direct result of his defects as a human being. Suit yourself.

As long as I'm confessing, I'll go further and admit that on occasion, I'm amused by Gene's antics—the ones that cause no real harm to anyone but himself, of course, like when he's forced to give a report at a staff meeting while nursing a hangover.

That said, I have counseled Gene on his appalling behavior as a husband, but I know that my words fall on deaf ears. If Gene's going to undergo a personal epiphany, it won't be a result of my influence. My ego isn't so big that I believe I can make a real difference in his life for the better.

There's one more thing I want to say regarding my troublesome colleague. In my more harried moments—I should say, in my most harried moments—I wish that I could be a bit less concerned with other people's problems and a bit more concerned with my own happiness. I wonder what it would be like to be a little like Gene, a self-serving person instead of a giver.

Of course, it's impossible that I would ever morph into a Gene, even for an hour. It's simply not in my nature to be . . . to be what I'm not. I'm not bragging; I'm fully aware that I'm no saint. And I'm not seeking pity; my life is a pretty damn good one.

In fact, it seems to me that my entire life has been charmed.

School came easy for me, right from the start. My mother tells me that I was reading before I got to kindergarten. I don't remember a time when I wasn't reading, so maybe she's telling the truth and not exaggerating, something she tends to do when talking about her children's finer points.

I went to a private high school on an academic scholarship, then graduated from college at the top of my class. After that, it was law school, where I made law review even while maintaining a very active nightlife.

I've been told I'm a good-looking guy, and I have plenty of evidence that I'm personable (for that, I thank my father, who could charm a smile out of a corpse). Yeah, I use my looks and personality to meet women—why not? But the game stops there. I don't lie to women; I don't promise anything I can't deliver. That doesn't mean that some women haven't accused me of leading them on, of toying with their feelings. I've never made a promise of forever or of exclusivity, but some people hear what they want to hear.

At the age of thirty-five, I made partner in my firm. For a while I felt as if I was on top of the world. And then the loneliness began to seep in through the cracks of my bright-and-shiny life. "Bright and shiny" usually implies a quality of brittleness. Time causes stress, stress causes cracks, and in through those cracks trickles grim reality.

Still, I did nothing about the loneliness except to let it continue to seep in and crowd me. I was busy. That was my excuse for ignoring the ultimately more important aspects of my life.

And then I hit forty, and realized that I was the only single man of my professional or personal acquaintance. Even those guys who were divorced were actively in the process of signing up another wife while spending fun-filled weekends with their kids from the first one. No man in the firm, gay or hetero, was going home to an empty apartment except me.

The loneliness had become loud and insistent, a giant wave rather than seepage. Something had to be done. But what?

Here's what I came up with, the grand plan. Step One: No more casual sex. I'd come to realize that a lot of the thrill in casual sexual encounters had worn away. Not all of it—my libido is as high as any guy's—but somehow, the effort, which was, admittedly, minimal, just didn't seem worth it. Most times. Okay, so I expected some trouble adjusting to this new rule of delayed gratification but I was confident I could adopt new habits.

Step Two presented itself to me in the form of a phone call from Sophie Holmes, Sophie Jimenez back when I knew her in college. After years in Los Angeles she'd moved back to Boston and was hoping to reconnect with me and another of our college friends, a woman named Eve Fitzpatrick.

Step Three would have been Step Two if Sophie hadn't emerged from the past. Step Three was to begin to look in a serious way for Ms. Right.

I'm a guy. I identify a problem and I go about solving it in a methodical fashion. Which is not to say that love was ignored in the project. I knew myself well enough to know that without genuine love I'd never be able to pull off a trip to the altar.

I'll admit I wondered if the newly divorced Sophie might be looking for a husband. It might, I thought, be easier to rekindle a friendship—and have it build to a romance—than to start from scratch. I'm not lazy, but the notion of dating with intention was daunting.

And what about Eve as a candidate for the role of loving life partner? The answer to that would be a big fat *no*.

Back in college I had a crush on Eve but I never pursued it. I'm not stupid, nor am I a masochist. Eve never gave me the slightest clue that she might be interested in me. In fact, she spent a good deal of time berating me for being self-important and overly fond of pretty but stupid women.

Besides, after a failed fling with Sophie, which, thankfully, ended with our friendship intact, I was hesitant to risk another friendship with a woman I admired. Sure, Eve seemed to find me morally repulsive, but she also continued to count me as a friend. Go figure.

Anyway, a few years ago I ran into Eve at a big fund-raiser. At first, she didn't recognize me, which I found a bit surprising, as I've been told I haven't changed all that much since college. But maybe I shouldn't always believe my mother.

I introduced myself and from that moment the conversation, if it could be called that, was all about the guy she was seeing and how fantastic he was. I remember being suspicious about the whole thing. In my experience, when one member of a couple (or worse, both) claims that everything is perfect, the relationship is just about to tank.

I also remember being struck by how much Eve had changed. For one thing, what was with the name change? The tall, superblonde, stylishly dressed woman I met at that fund-raiser was a carbon copy of the kind of woman I regularly dated, the kind of woman I had grown tired of: fast talking and self-absorbed. The Eve I had known back in college was the antithesis of that woman—deliberate in her speech, and almost entirely other-focused.

I'm not saying that Eve—Eva—didn't look great, she did. But looks aside, I wasn't happy about the transformation. At the time I wondered if the change in her personality was due to the influence of her mystery man. And, I considered, maybe the change wasn't really all that deep; maybe my surprise was largely due to the unexpected nature of our meeting. Finally, I thought, maybe when she was at home Eve was her old self. We all play a role when we're out in the world. Maybe Eve was just acting—as Eva.

Still, I looked forward to seeing Eva again, and Sophie. I was curious to see what further changes time had wrought, on all of us.

And I was curious to see what our future might be, together.

* 9 *

In spite of what most organized religions would have their cowardly, superstitious members believe, shame is an outdated notion that you are under no obligation to experience (as in, "I'm so ashamed of what I've done."), and are in no way granted permission to instill (as in, "You should be ashamed of yourself.").
                                                    —Shame on You!

EVA

She hasn't changed a bit.

This was my immediate impression when Sophie walked into Churchill. The sense of familiarity was powerful, far more than I'd anticipated. There was the thick dark hair. There were the gold-framed eyeglasses. It was only as Sophie started to walk toward me that I noticed the changes: a visible strand of gray; glasses more stylish than those she'd worn in college; and, something new, clothes that had the distinct, somewhat matronly look of Clearwater Creek.

I must, I thought, get her to dress her age. She's a good ten to fifteen years too young for midcalf skirts and tunics, even if they're expensive, and especially if she's hoping to meet a man. I'll introduce her to my colorist. I'll inquire about contacts.

I stood as Sophie approached the bar, a look of tempered excitement on her face.

"Eva?" she asked. "My gosh, I hardly recognized you with your hair so short—and so blonde!"

"Yes, well," I said.

I put out my hand at the same time Sophie attempted to give me a hug. It was an awkward moment. I'm not one for affectionate gestures.

We each took a seat at the bar. When the bartender had taken Sophie's drink order, a Cosmo, our reunion began.

"So, what have you been up to for the past twenty years or so?" I asked. I delivered the question in a jaunty tone, expecting an answer on the order of *"Rotting away, and you?"*

"Well, there's Jake, of course," Sophie said seriously. "Raising him took up almost all of my time, especially with Brad so involved with his job. Which was fine because, honestly, I enjoyed every minute of being a stay-at-home mom."

I looked for an indication of quiet desperation in Sophie's eyes, and found none. Maybe, I thought, I'm just not looking hard enough.

"Wasn't it ever . . . dull?" I asked.

Sophie laughed. "Oh, no, never dull! There's always some excitement cropping up. Sometimes, though, it was a bit . . . lonely."

I nodded.

"You know," she continued, as if I'd asked her to explain, "if Jake was in bed and Brad was working late . . . Come to think of it, I spent a lot of time by myself over the years."

"Another baby might have kept you company, stretch marks be damned."

I can't describe the expression on Sophie's face right then except to say that it combined sorrow and anger in a distinctly uncomfortable way. Shit, I thought. What crazy impulse had made me say that?

I watched Sophie struggle to regain her formerly pleasant demeanor. "It still upsets me to think about it," she said after a moment.

"I shouldn't have—"

Sophie waved her hand dismissively. "No, no, it's okay. It's just that Brad wasn't thrilled about my trying to get pregnant after Jake. I don't know why but he just didn't want more kids. But when Jake was three I finally convinced him that a sibling would be a good thing for Jake—and that another baby was what I really, really wanted."

"But Jake's an only child?"

"Yes. The thing was, I just couldn't get pregnant. After about a year of trying on our own, I went for tests and . . . And I found out there were problems that would make another pregnancy difficult to achieve."

"Oh," I said. I have little knowledge of the intricacies of the female reproductive system. I know enough not to get pregnant and that's about all.

"Anyway," Sophie went on, "it was a very painful thing to hear. I was told there were plenty of fertility treatments available and Brad said fine. By then, he was resigned to the idea of another baby. But in the end I decided against the treatments. The process was long and expensive, and there was no guarantee I'd actually get pregnant."

Brad, I thought, must have been thrilled.

"And," Sophie added, with a slight air of apology, "I have a problem with the idea of extensive fertility therapy. Maybe it's a holdover from my Catholic childhood, I don't know. Of course, I would never tell anyone else what to do with her body."

"Of course," I agreed. But what did I really know about Sophie? Anyway, it seemed expected of me to continue the topic I, after all, had so stupidly started. "But what about your desire for a baby?"

"Oh, I didn't give up the idea of another baby entirely. I began to research adoption, foreign adoption, specifically."

"A popular course. I can think of the three people in my firm who've adopted from Asia."

"Yes," Sophie said. "I thought that if I presented Brad with all my research from various agencies he might actually consider adopting a baby, maybe from Eastern Europe. Brad's great-grandparents came from Poland, you know."

"But no luck?"

Sophie raised her eyebrows in that way that says bingo.

"He shot down the idea without even looking at the information. Brad said that if we were going to have another child it would have to be our own. He suggested I change my mind about fertility treatments."

"Well," I said, "did you explain to him your . . . moral . . . hesitations?"

"I tried to. But Brad thought I was just being stubborn. He didn't understand me and, frankly, I'm not sure he even tried to understand."

"Wait a minute," I said. "Why was Brad suddenly all gung ho about the fertility option? I thought he didn't want another baby, period."

Sophie laughed ruefully. "I don't think he did. I think he just wanted me to put the adoption issue to rest. And suggesting I get all caught up in fertility treatments was one way of getting me out of his hair. If another baby was going to give me something to do—so that I wouldn't have the time to pester him—fine, he'd deal with another baby."

I hadn't spoken to Sophie in years. I had no idea what sort of rights I had. So, I asked. "Am I allowed to make a negative comment about your ex-husband?"

Sophie thought about this for a moment before saying, "Yes. You can say what you want."

"Brad sounds like an ass. I never was a big fan, even back in college when you started bringing him around in our senior year. Then, again, from what I can remember, which isn't much, I got the impression he didn't quite care for me, either. Or for John."

"Brad was jealous of John. He thought something had gone on between us." Sophie paused and then added hastily, "He thought that about every guy who even looked my way."

"Ah, an ass and jealous. Lucky you."

"He wasn't always an ass," Sophie corrected. "There were times when he was really sweet. And his possessiveness seemed to die away when Jake was born."

Right around the time you began to fade into his background, I surmised.

"But the whole thing about another baby," Sophie said, almost as if she was speaking to herself. "I was so angry with Brad for such a long time after that. When he finally told me he was leaving, I realized that things had started to fall apart years ago. The whole experience—trying to get pregnant, wanting to adopt—drove a wedge between Brad and me. Eventually, we just split apart."

All those years, wasted, I thought.

"Maybe if we'd gone to counseling," she went on, "to talk about Brad's resistance to adoption and my resistance to the therapies, I don't know, maybe we could have had a happier life together."

Maybe, but I doubted it. A happy life, in my opinion, rarely involved anyone other than the self. Another one of my opinions is that sacrifice of anything more important than the last cookie on the plate is rarely, if ever, worth it.

"You gave up what you really wanted," I said bluntly, "so that your husband could have what he wanted."

"I know. Sometimes I wonder why I didn't find a way to get what was so important to me."

"It might not be too late. If you're more open to science playing a part in conception, you could still have another baby."

"No," Sophie said emphatically. "No. It's far too late."

I could have asked Sophie to explain why she felt it was too late. She would probably have told me. But I didn't ask. Instead I wondered how I had stumbled into a conversation of such a personal nature with someone I hadn't seen or spoken to in almost twenty years.

I wasn't sure I wanted, or needed, a friendship—at least, this particular friendship. I'd been on my own for so many years, utterly self-reliant. Being there with Sophie, once a friend, was disquieting. I'd left my old life and old self behind, even changed my name, in order to survive on my own—and eventually to thrive. And that was what I was doing, wasn't I? Thriving, without the intrusion of old friends.

"So, you didn't work all those years Jake was growing up?" I asked somewhat meanly. "I mean, at a job with pay and health benefits and business trips and a pension?"

Sophie didn't seem to take offense. "Well," she said, "once Jake was in high school there wasn't much for me to do at home—Brad insisted we have a housekeeper. So, I decided to get a real estate license."

"Interesting," I said, though real estate doesn't interest me in the slightest. Aside from my own apartment, which I bought primarily as an investment on the advice of my accountant, I have little interest in the buying and selling of property. But in women earning their own money—that's a topic I consider of great importance.

"It was fun," Sophie said. "But I didn't stick with it for long. I guess . . . I guess without the financial incentive I just couldn't make myself focus like I should have. Brad's income was very good . . ." Sophie shook her head, as if tossing off a piece of unpleasant self-knowledge—perhaps that she was lazy?

It was really none of my business but I found myself asking Sophie how she was situated. In other words, had Brad done right by her in the settlement?

"It was an uncontested divorce," she said a bit defiantly. "We didn't need lawyers. We came to an agreement on our own."

I didn't quite know what to do with this bit of information, other than to say, "Oh." Only an enormous expenditure of self-control prevented me from adding, "Are you insane?"

"Yes," she went on, fiddling with her napkin, "I'm fine. Brad is an honest man."

Ah, the questions that were crowding my mind! Such as: How can you be sure Brad hasn't hidden hundreds of thousands of dollars under the proverbial mattress?

I asked instead, "So, what do you do with yourself all day? Really, I don't know what I'd do if I didn't get out to an office every morning. Kill myself, most likely."

"Oh, Eve—Eva—don't say something like that!"

I made a face as if to say, "*Whatever.*" Since turning forty, I try not to use that expression, but I'm not past implying it. "Well," I repeated, "what do you do?"

"Well, unpacking and setting up the apartment took some time. But I'm almost finished. So, I don't know. I'm thinking of going for my real estate license here in Massachusetts. I was thinking that working in real estate might be a good way to meet people."

"Yes," I said. "And by people, do you mean men?"

Sophie laughed. "I mean all people, but yes, men, too."

"So, you're ready to get back in the game?"

"Yes. I think so. Why?" Sophie asked eagerly. "Do you know anyone for me?"

Assist the rival? Not that I considered Sophie much of a rival. "No," I said. "I'm afraid you'll have to find your own dates."

"Oh." Sophie looked downright crestfallen. "I was hoping . . . It would be nice to meet someone through a friend, someone I can trust. You know?"

So, Sophie considered me a friend and not simply an old, dusted-off acquaintance. She considered me someone she could trust. Was Sophie someone I could trust? How was I to know? Besides, I thought, I'm not in the market for a trust buddy.

I nodded, offering neither a yes nor a no.

"I want to get married again," Sophie explained. "But I want to take the dating thing slowly. I don't want to make a mistake and it's been so long. I really don't know what I'm doing."

"Taking things slowly makes sense. Though you'd better not wait too long before making a move. Forty might be the new thirty but there are an awful lot of men out there who prefer the actual to the 'as if.' "

"I know, I know. The whole thing is so daunting."

"And yet you still want to try again. Even after going through a divorce you feel positive about marriage."

Some people, I realized long ago, are gluttons for punishment.

"I do, yes. Marriage worked for me, for a long time. A new marriage would be different, of course. Well, obviously."

"Obviously."

"For example, this time I'd like . . ." Sophie hesitated.

"You'd like what?" I asked.

"Well," she said, after a quick glance to her left to assure she couldn't be overheard, "I'd like a more passionate marriage. I'd like to know what it feels like to really . . . to really want someone."

"A marriage with passion? Good luck finding the impossible."

"Even in the beginning," she went on, ignoring my remark, "Brad and I weren't—I don't know, wild. We were in love but it was more like . . . more like friends who love each other. I'm not saying that was bad. Our marriage worked for a long time. Still . . ."

"This time you want orgasms that cause the neighbors to pound on the wall."

Sophie's eyes widened. "Well, I don't want to be fined for disturbing the peace, but I wouldn't mind some fireworks! And I know—at least, I've read—that you can't manufacture real passion. You have to let it find you."

"So," I said, "since your wedding day, no sex with anyone other than Brad?"

"Certainly not."

"And Brad?" I asked, casually. "Was he faithful, too?"

"Of course," she replied in a slightly insulted tone.

I didn't believe her for a second, but everyone has her pride.

"What about since the divorce? Please don't tell me you've been celibate."

"I did have one minor sexual . . . encounter," Sophie confided, again with a glance to determine possible eavesdroppers. "It was before I moved back East. I met this man at a museum and he asked me out for dinner the next night. We had a nice time and then we went back to his house and, well, we fooled around a bit, but . . . I just couldn't go through with it. It was too soon after the divorce."

"And you never heard from him again."

"Of course. But I don't feel bad that things didn't work out. He wasn't really my type, for a relationship, I mean. But I do wish I'd had the nerve to go, you know, all the way."

All the way? I refrained from laughing at the use of such a quaint turn of phrase. "Well," I said, with as much sympathy as I could muster, "there's always another man. You'll get your chance."

Sophie looked doubtful. "I hope so. There are so many attractive women in this city and they're all so much younger than I am. Then again, Southern California was even more crowded with starlet types."

"You'll do okay," I said. "Your clothes could use some work and you need to get rid of that gray, but your skin is good. You maintained your figure. What I can see of it, anyway, under that floppy jacket. Have you considered contacts?"

Sophie shook her head.

"Well, think about it. I'll give you the name of my colorist, too."

"Oh. Thanks." Sophie busied herself with her napkin, wiping an invisible spot of dirt off the bar.

Realizing I hadn't exactly been encouraging I introduced a topic Sophie would find of interest. See? I do have some social graces.

"Jake—that's your son's name, isn't it?"

Sophie's head shot up and she smiled. "Yes. Jacob Michael. Michael is my father's name."

"How nice," I said. What else? And then I remembered that mothers and grandmothers carried photos in their wallets. Mine had, anyway. I thought again about the photos Sophie had once been in the habit of sending me—Jake on a department-store Santa's lap; Jake at his graduation from kindergarten; Jake in a school play.

"Do you have any recent pictures with you?" I asked.

Sophie reached for her purse, a sort of backpack, the kind used for, I'm told, hiking. "I'm embarrassed to admit that I don't!" she said. "I used to be much better at that sort of thing. I could show you a picture taken when he was in third grade?"

"No, no, that's fine," I said. "Really. Next time."

Sophie put her cumbersome bag back on the floor. I was relieved. I know I had asked to see the photos but I am terribly unskilled at oooohing and aaaahing.

"You know," Sophie said then, "I've been wondering about something. Back in college you used to talk about writing children's books."

"I did?" I asked. "You're kidding."

"No, really. But I guess that answers my question. You haven't written a book?"

A bit of memory flickered to light. "No," I said firmly. "And if I did write a book it certainly wouldn't be for children."

"I remember like it was yesterday, how you used to talk about wanting to write a novel that would become a children's classic."

A little overambitious of me, I thought. "Well," I said with some impatience, "we all 'used to' do and say a lot of things we don't do or say today. Things change, people change, you can't go home again, the past is the past, period, the end."

And yet, I thought, here I am with Sophie, the closest friend I'd ever had. My protestations sounded ridiculous even to my own ears. Something had made me say yes to Sophie's invitation, something other than mere curiosity, and if it wasn't partly nostalgia, then I was fooling myself.

"I'm going to order some oysters," I said.

* 10 *

Dear Answer Lady:
I get terribly seasick. Even the sight of a body of water makes me nauseous. My girlfriend has been pestering me to go on a cruise with her. She doesn't know about my problem and I'm embarrassed to tell her. What should I do?

Dear Idiot:
Tell her about your problem. No woman wants to spend seven days on the high seas with a man while his head is in the toilet.

SOPHIE

"I've been going on about me this whole time! I'm sorry, Eva. I guess I'm just excited seeing you after all these years."

Eva smiled a bit. "Oh, that's all right. There's not really much to tell about me."

I didn't believe it for a minute. No woman carrying a Gucci bag (the bartender had raved about it, that's how I knew it was a real Gucci) lived a boring life. "Oh, come on," I said. "I'm sure your life is very exciting, at least, compared to mine. So, tell me, are you seeing anyone special?"

"No," she said flatly.

Undaunted, I asked: "Are you looking?"

Eva gave me a look of studied blankness. "Why?" she asked. "Should I be?"

"No, no," I replied hurriedly, fearing I'd been rude, "of course not, not if you don't want to be looking."

Eva's expression remained unchanged. "I don't really have the time right now for a relationship."

"Oh, sure," I said with a nod. "I understand. What with your job and all."

"Right. What with my job."

Eva looked away and busied herself with the oysters she'd ordered. (I don't like oysters.)

"Was there ever someone special," I ventured, "you know, after we fell out of touch?"

Eva put down the skinny little oyster fork and seemed to consider before answering.

"Well," she said, "I dated, of course. But nobody struck me as good enough to marry, if that's what you're asking."

"Oh," I said. "I'm sorry. Maybe—"

"Actually, there was one exception, a few years back. I thought for a while that he was worth the effort of a serious relationship."

Eva took a sip of her drink—a martini—and left me to consider that tantalizing nugget of information. "What happened?" I asked.

Eva carefully replaced her drink on the bar before replying.

"What happened," she said, "was that he left me."

"Oh, Eva, I'm sorry."

I reached for her left hand on the bar but Eva moved it away. I remembered then how awkward my greeting kiss had made her and vowed to avoid unnecessary physical contact until we got better reacquainted.

"There was another woman," Eva said. "He denied it but I knew better."

I nodded. Didn't most men cheat on their wives and girlfriends? At least in my limited experience they did. My son, I was sure, was not "most men." I'd tried very hard to teach him the importance of fidelity.

"Look," Eva went on, her expression hard, "what else could it have been but another woman? I'm successful, I'm smart, I'm attractive. Why would a man in his right mind leave me unless another woman had gotten her hands on him?"

For a moment I thought that Eva was joking, mocking herself and her own faults in the relationship, and then, looking carefully at her face, I realized that she was dead serious.

"Of course," I said soothingly. "You're a wonderful woman. Any man would be crazy to leave you."

"I know. Anyway, everything was just fine between us. We spent a part of each weekend together and we text messaged during the week. It was all perfect, not a glitch."

"Oh, he lived out of town?" I asked.

"No. Right here in the city."

"But you said you didn't see each other during the week. Did he travel for business?"

"No. But do you know how crazy my schedule is?"

"No, I guess I don't."

"Believe me," she said—beckoning to the bartender for another drink (I declined)—"I have very little free time. At first, he complained. He wanted to be with me almost every night. He even wanted to talk on the phone every day and I just have no time for empty conversations. I have a very demanding job; I just can't be available to everyone. He didn't get that about me at first."

"At first," I repeated. "So, he understood eventually?"

Eva shrugged. "He came around. And everything was going just fine until he met that other woman. For weeks after he broke things off with me I watched his apartment. I was dying to catch him red-handed."

I took another small sip of my Cosmo and thought: *You had the time to stalk him after the relationship but not the time to see him during the relationship.* But I would never say anything so confrontational.

"So," I said, "did you ever see him with a woman?"

"Unfortunately, no. He always came and went alone."

I thought: What was the point of the stalking? Just because he came and went from his apartment alone didn't mean he hadn't been seeing someone during his relationship with Eva. Anyway, by that time he was single again and perfectly free to date other women. Poor Eva. She must have been terribly distressed to act so strangely.

"So," I said gently, "what happened next?"

"I called him, of course. Several times. I wanted an explanation for why he ended the relationship."

"He never gave you an explanation?" Well, I thought, that can be very frustrating.

"Oh, sure," Eva said, waving her hand dismissively, "some nonsense about our not being compatible for the long run, about each of us wanting different things out of the relationship, ridiculous excuses."

Well, Brad had said similar things to me—and he'd been right. "So, what did he say when you called him?"

Eva took a sip of her second drink before answering. "Nothing, really. He refused to talk back, which I knew meant he had a guilty conscience. He would just listen to me call him a liar and worse, and then he would say, very calmly, 'Goodbye, Eva,' and hang up."

"Huh," I said.

"I tried to get him to meet me face-to-face but for some reason he kept refusing."

I thought: *Because he was afraid of you, and maybe rightly so.* And then I felt bad for the disloyal thought. Eva was my friend and there I was taking the side of some man I didn't even know.

"He said," Eva went on, "he thought it best to just cut the cord and walk away. It was extremely frustrating for me."

"Oh, I'm sure it was. Everyone needs closure." Even Brad and I, though I wondered if we'd ever achieve complete closure, given the fact of our child.

"Exactly. But he just couldn't give me that."

"So," I said tentatively, "since then?"

"No one," she said. "For the past few years I've just been a wreck."

If what was sitting next to me at the bar was the personification of a wreck, I thought, I, too, want to be a wreck. Eva looked marvelous. Her skin glowed. She was impeccably dressed and looked toned and fit. Suddenly, I was acutely aware of my own unpolished appearance and flabby upper arms. Right there I determined to buy a set of hand weights and take a subscription to one of those fitness magazines.

But maybe, I thought, Eva is a wreck on the inside. Maybe she's just skilled at hiding her real feelings. Maybe, I thought, I should have sympathy for her.

"Of course," Eva went on, "I have sex whenever I want, so I'm not lonely."

"Oh," I said, my voice unnaturally high with surprise.

Maybe it was my imagination but I found Eva's tone challenging, and the sympathy I'd felt for her a moment earlier wavered.

Eva looked at me, and again, I thought I sensed challenge. "Does that shock you, that I have sex without being in a relationship?"

"No," I said quickly, "it doesn't shock me." I thought: *Your tone shocked me, as you intended.* "It's just that I'm not used to hearing that sort of thing from other women."

"Your friends are all married, I suppose."

"Well, yes," I admitted, thinking of the acquaintances I'd left behind in California. "Except for those who are divorced, and they're all dating, hoping to meet someone to marry. They're not just sleeping around. Not that I mean to imply that's what you're doing!"

Eva laughed. "Poor Sophie. I don't take offense all that easily. Anyway, it's not like I go to bars and pick up strangers. That's stupid, not to mention dangerous."

"Of course," I said.

Eva went on airily. "I have this friend—well, he's not really a friend. We have sex and we go our separate ways. And sometimes I'll have a quick fling with someone, no one who works in my industry, of course. That's just bad policy. Anyway, I've decided that relationships are simply too risky. Look at you and Brad. The perfect couple, or so everyone thought."

Who was everyone? And how little Eva knew about the later years of my marriage! I wondered if she'd even be interested in finding out. Maybe, I thought, I shouldn't have told her about the baby we never had. Maybe I shouldn't have let her call Brad an ass.

"But life is all about risk, Eva," I said. "I'm sure you take risks in your professional life."

"Calculated ones. You can't take a calculated risk in matters of the heart so you're bound to lose."

"Not necessarily," I argued. "Even if a relationship doesn't last forever, you can still gain a lot from the good parts of it."

Eva shook her head. "Not interested. I'll stick to sex without commitment to anything other than pleasure. My pleasure, to be precise."

The bartender removed Eva's appetizer plate. I was sure by the tiny grin on her face that she'd heard Eva's last statement.

"Do you like your . . . friend?" I asked in a whisper. "The one you sleep with?"

"Sure," Eva said, "he's nice enough. He's a bit younger than I am, a bit naive in some ways, but he's good at providing what I need from him."

I was trying, really, but I just couldn't get my head around this idea. "But what do you talk about when you're together?" I asked. "I mean, there has to be some conversation."

"Why? I'm not interested in his life outside the room we're occupying at the moment. And he's not interested in mine. Well, not entirely. He does tend to ask me questions like how's work going and have I seen any good movies lately, that sort of thing."

Friendly chitchat I could understand. That . . . humanized things a bit for me. "So, you answer his questions?"

"Of course. I say 'fine' to the first question and 'no' to the second."

"Eva," I said with a shake of my head, "you're unbelievable. Seriously, I don't know if you're pulling my leg or what!"

"Why would I do that? Look, if my life shocks you—"

"No, no," I lied. "I'm just unused to hearing about—that sort of relationship. That's all. I certainly don't condemn you for it."

"Well," Eva said with a drawl, "that's big of you."

I reached out to give her arm a little squeeze but quickly withdrew my hand. "Oh, Eva," I said, "you know what I mean. There's nothing wrong with having sex without a relationship. In fact, I don't know, maybe it's something I should consider, at least before starting to date seriously."

"It's not you, Sophie," Eva said with conviction. "It wasn't you back in college and it's not you now."

I felt almost insulted by Eva's pronouncement. A moment earlier, I'd been judgmental of her behavior. And now I wanted to be considered capable of it myself. Eva, I realized, was unsettling to be around.

"How can you be sure it's not me now?" I asked. "It wasn't you, either, back in college. You were so serious and sincere, but you changed. Maybe I have, too. In fact, I know I have."

"Are you saying I'm not sincere now?" Eva gave me a grim little smile.

"No, no," I said hurriedly. "What I mean is that you were very earnest back then, very into finding causes to support, very conscious of doing the right thing. You seemed to have no time for people you saw as—I don't know—casual or uncommitted." I smiled. "I remember how you used to berate John for wanting to make lots of money, for being so in-

volved with campus politics—really, for just about everything he did!"

Eva shrugged. "He could be a jerk."

"I never saw him as a jerk," I said. "I always felt you were
being a bit unfair about him."

"You're entitled to your opinion. Anyway, I don't really
remember much about college. That was a long time ago and
so much has happened to me since then."

"To us all."

"Of course," she said. "And, as I already mentioned, I
can't stand to dwell on the past or on what might have been.
I only think about how what I do today is going to affect tomorrow and the day after that. I stay very focused and keep
my eyes straight ahead. No nostalgia for me."

"Not even a little?" And then I dared to say: "I'm curious
to know why you agreed to get together after all this time."

Eva didn't answer my question.

Instead, she asked for the check and I left our first meeting
doubting the wisdom of trying to resurrect an old friendship.
But my natural optimism had been dampened, not entirely
drowned. By the next morning I was looking forward to seeing Eva again. The question remained: Was Eva looking forward to seeing me?

* 11 *

Contrary to popular belief, lying will not result in your pants catching fire or in your nose growing to outrageously long proportions. These are myths meant to frighten children away from the largely adult pleasures of telling falsehoods. This writer's advice? Enjoy yourself and lie away.

—Liar, Liar, Pants on Fire, and Other Harmful Nonsense

EVA

I'd never told anyone about Ben. Who was there to tell? At the age of forty-two I had no close friends, maybe no friends of any description—until the reemergence of Sophie. And I wasn't sure that I could call her a friend and mean it.

And yet, I'd blabbed to her about my failed relationship with Ben. Worse, I hadn't presented an entirely accurate picture of what had happened between Ben and me, or about how upset I was when he left. The truth was that I hadn't been half as devastated as I'd let on. So, why the exaggeration?

See, this is what I was discovering: When you're self-sufficient for a length of time, you fall out of the habit of trading personal information. So, when you find yourself in a rare position to talk, you either say too little or say too much and one way or the other, the other person is left with an erroneous impression of you.

Someone with an active social network, someone with friends and confidantes, doesn't have this problem of balance. Someone like me, with no friends or confidantes, does.

How does an adult go about making friends, anyway? I don't consider colleagues candidates for friendship. I'm convinced it's impossible to be friends with someone in a subordinate position and I'm uncomfortable with the notion of office chatter, even if it's among people at the same professional level. I don't want to waste my time standing around the coffee machine sharing anecdotes about my dog or my kid; well, I can't, really, can I? I'm not interested in the domestic details of people with whom I have a professional relationship. And I refuse to show anyone the cracks in my armor; rivals can arise from anywhere.

Some people, of course, consider family members friends. But I hadn't called my sister, Maura, in months. Neither had she called me, but her neglect was to be expected. I'd set the tone of our adult relationship years ago, after Maura moved to the Midwest, married, and started having kids.

Even growing up we weren't close. There are ten years between Maura and me, too large a gap to bridge in the early years. How could I tell a five-year-old about my first French kiss? Maura could come to me with her little-girl troubles— after all, I'd been there, I knew the terrain. I didn't mind being the big sister back then. It gave me another way to identify myself: big sister, first child, good student.

No, it wasn't until college that I knew what it was like to have a confidante—and to be one. But then . . .

I wondered what Sophie must think of me, a pitiful wreck of a woman, washed up on the rocky shores of love.

I realized I would have to erase that erroneous impression. The truth was I'd almost forgotten about the pain that the breakup with Ben had caused me. What buried memories of hurt feelings still existed had been coaxed into emergence by the unexpected presence of a sympathetic ear. But those memories could easily be stuffed back into forgetfulness. And the next time I was with Sophie—because I did want to see her again—I would watch my words more carefully.

12

Dear Answer Lady:

My conscience is killing me. I just got engaged to this wonderful man. But with every day that goes by since he gave me his grandmother's engagement ring (!) the guilt gets worse. Sometimes I think I'm going to crack up. Sometimes I just want to blurt out the truth about my past. Sometimes I try to convince myself that it's better to keep my first marriage a deep, dark secret. I'm divorced and there were no children. I don't even know if the guy is alive or dead; his drug habit ended things in a very ugly way. No one else knows about this early disaster (I was nineteen) except my sister and she would never break the family silence. Still, I hate keeping a secret from my future husband. Please, help me!

Dear Woman Seeped in Guilt:

First, let me congratulate you on your desire to be honest with your soon-to-be spouse. Second, let me say that given the circumstances of your first marriage, I believe that you are under no moral obligation to dredge up this old and painful information and share it with your fiancé. However, if the secret is indeed weighing on you so unbearably, speak up. If this fiancé is as wonderful as you say he is he'll un-

derstand your reluctance to divulge an embarrassing past and appreciate your desire to open up to the man with whom you are pledging to spend the rest of your life. Keep in mind, however, that many people have a tendency to react badly to the news of prior lovers, let alone to prior spouses. Think carefully before you act. Forget about yourself and consider the feelings of your fiancé. You are in a tough situation and only you, knowing this man, can make the right decision. (I'll expect a full report and, if things go well, an invitation to the wedding.)

SOPHIE

What was there for me in California after Jake came East for graduate school? Certainly not Brad. If anything, the proximity of my ex-husband, especially once he began to date women young enough to be his daughters, was a big negative.

And as for friends, well, there were no friends to leave. I had acquaintances but I knew that within a few weeks of my leaving I'd be almost entirely forgotten. Acquaintanceships rely on frequent face-to-face interaction. Friendships, I believed, could survive even great distances.

I suppose it was only postdivorce that I realized that in all the years I'd lived in California, I hadn't made one close friend. Sure, I'd socialized with women I met through Jake's involvement in school activities. The strongest thing we had in common was our children; conversation was about soccer teams and yoga classes; bake sales and SUVs; what movies were kid-friendly and what movies were not. Once our children graduated into different middle schools and then high schools, once our children needed us less and less, we mothers drifted apart. At the time I didn't much miss their presence in my life. Girls' night once a month gave some structure to

my social life, but none of the "girls" ever meant anything
to me.

Maybe that was my fault. Maybe I just didn't try to get to
know anyone well. Maybe I was just too lazy. Like with my
weak attempt at a career in real estate, maybe I'd failed to
find an incentive. Why did I need friends when I had my husband and my son?

Anyway, after that first, somewhat disappointing evening
with Eva, I began to worry that I'd set myself up for a major
disappointment by coming back East.

In reality, I knew I wouldn't see my parents all that often.
For several months each year they took off for the condo in
New Smyrna Beach, and when they were here, at their home
in Freeham, they enjoyed a busy social life. The last thing I
wanted to do was tag along with my parents, the newly single third wheel, to be pitied by the smug married women and
ogled by the regretful married men.

My parents didn't need me in any tangible way; they were
healthy and had pensions and health insurance. I was glad
for that, of course. Someday, when the end approached, I
might be of actual service to them, but not now, not yet.

And Jake. Well, of course, Jake still needed me, even if he
protested that he didn't. I know my own child. He had already made it a habit to stop by for dinner once a week, and
that said something.

Yes, I would still have Jake for a few more years, at least
until he finished his graduate program. And I consoled myself
with the thought that Jake might not marry until thirty,
maybe even later. That he would someday "settle down" and
have a family I had no doubt. But for my own, selfish sake, I
hoped that day was far in the future.

Although, it would be nice to have grandchildren. I could
be of great help to Jake and his wife; I could be there whenever they needed me.

Because if no one needs you, who are you? And what's the point of your life?

I realized with some alarm that I would have to shake off my complacency. I would have to make myself needed. At the very least, I would have to make a friend. Maybe, that friend would be Eva.

* 13 *

Say, for example, that you lifted a couple of twenties from your friend's bag when she went to the ladies' room. Act horrified when she tells you that she was robbed. Vow to hunt down the culprit and demand restitution. Before long you'll completely forget that you are to blame.
— Just Forget It Ever Happened: How to Repress an Unpleasant Truth

EVA

"Want to grab something to eat? I'm starved."

I turned from the mirror and looked hard at Sam. Why did he have to do this again? He really was good in bed. Why did he have to ruin things out of bed?

"What?" he asked, and his voice squeaked just a bit. "What's with the look?"

"You are unbelievable. You know our deal: sex and no other involvement."

Sam sighed and continued to button his shirt. "Eva, I'm not talking about a marriage. I'm talking about a sandwich."

I turned back to the mirror. "Still involvement."

"You have to eat lunch."

"I'll grab something on the way back to the office," I said. And I will eat my lunch in peace.

"Why not grab it with me? There's a good coffee place just down the block. They have great paninis."

"Sam, no!" I swung around to face him again. He was entirely dressed now, all buttoned into his beautiful suit. "What do I have to do to make myself heard? No lunch, no dinner, no coffee, and definitely no drinks. Ever. Look, if you have a problem with this arrangement—"

Sam looked away. "No, no, I'm fine with it. Don't go crazy, I'm fine. So, same time next week?"

"Can we do it on Tuesday, instead? I've got a meeting Wednesday and timing might be a little tight."

We each reached for our Blackberry.

"Tuesday's no good," Sam said after a moment. "How about Thursday?"

"No. It's Friday or we skip the week. No big deal."

"Man. I've got a lunch on Friday . . . Look, I'll cancel it." Sam slipped his Blackberry into the breast pocket of his suit jacket and looked back at me with an expression that hovered between resignation and bemusement. "I'm not stupid. I know what a good deal I've got with you. Sex with no strings? It's every man's dream."

"Let me tell you," I said as I grabbed my bag, "it's a working woman's dream, too. I'm off. See you next Friday. Your turn to pay for the room."

My hand was on the doorknob when Sam spoke again.

"I don't know why we can't just go to your apartment. It's so close to both of our offices. Why does one of us have to lay out all this money every week?"

I sighed. Really, I wondered, was the sex worth this misery?

"You know, Sam," I said, still facing the door, "I think you're getting early-onset Alzheimer's. I told you why I don't want you in my apartment. It's my territory, it's my refuge, and I don't want you getting the wrong idea. If I take you to my apartment, the next thing I know you'll be asking for a key and popping in whenever you feel like it."

"No, I wouldn't. I'd respect your privacy, I swear. Could you face me when we talk?"

I looked at Sam over my shoulder. "Anyway, it's a hotel or nothing and if you can't afford the hotel, then—"

Sam waved his hand dismissively. "No, no, I can afford it. Sex with you is well worth the money, you know that."

"I do know that," I said carefully. "Now, don't you forget it."

And I left. As was our deal, Sam waited five minutes before following.

* 14 *

Dear Answer Lady:

A *few weeks ago I saw one of my son's classmates smoking pot in the parking lot of the mall. (He's my son's age, twelve.) I know the "social code" says that I should tell his mother (his father skipped out years ago) what I saw so that she can intervene and try to save him from a life of dissipation. But here's the thing. I hate this woman. She's got her eye on every husband in town, including mine, and insists on wearing skintight clothes and wearing her hair like, I don't know, a movie star. Did I mention that she owns her own business, a private gym? I would just love to see her perfect life go up in flames when her son gets caught doing something much worse than smoking pot (I've read that pot leads to all sorts of bad things, like heroin and serial killing). Legally speaking, I'm under no obligation to tell her what I saw, right? I mean, I suppose I could go to the police now and rat on her kid but I don't think he'd get much time for such a small offense, what with him being a minor and all. Right?*

Dear Deeply Disturbed Individual:

You don't really expect me to condone your jealous, small-minded, and downright irresponsible be-

haviors, do you? Here's my advice: See a therapist for your tendency toward cruelty; get your son into counseling (Clearly, with a mother like you he lacks all sense of ethics.); lose weight and get a haircut so that your poor husband doesn't flinch every time he walks in the door; and, finally, get a hobby or, better yet, a job so that you don't have time to waste on plotting revenge for imagined offenses. One more note: I've contacted the owner of the private gym regarding her son and she was very thankful for my concern. In fact, she offered me a full year's membership for free! See you around!

EVA

I sat next to Sophie in her latest-model Saab as we winged our way to the suburbs to watch her son's baseball game before driving back into Boston to meet John for dinner. "Winged" is the exact word I want here. Interestingly, given her mild nature, Sophie drove with a lead foot. All those years sitting in backed-up LA traffic must have been terribly frustrating.

Really, I thought, I have no clear idea of why I'm here. I have no interest in baseball, in sports of any kind, for that matter. I could have used this time to finish the book I was currently reading, a juicy adventure novel by one of today's top-selling writers. (The name stays with me.) I could have gone to the Armani Exchange store and bought that jacket I'd been considering.

I sighed.

"What?" Sophie asked, her eyes shifting to look at me.

"Nothing. Keep your eyes on the road."

"I'm an excellent driver," she said. "I've never gotten a ticket."

"Maybe because the police haven't been able to catch

you," I muttered as we whizzed past a string of fast food giants with colorful names like Timmy's Tub o' Lard and Duke Danny's Donuts.

We arrived eventually at the field, a big, square plot of grass and dirt punctuated only by a high fence and two sets of rickety, unpainted wooden bleachers. Nice, I thought. I'll get a snag in these pants and they'll be ruined. Two hundred bucks down the drain for a charitable act of so-called friendship.

Sophie and I took seats halfway up one set of bleachers. Sophie seemed extraordinarily happy to be there. But already I was bored silly and very aware of the stares I was getting from some of the people scattered across the ancient bleachers. Fine, I thought, let them stare. The sweatpants-wearing public is no concern of mine. I will die, I thought, before I plunk a hot-pink sun visor on my head.

But I wasn't bored for long. For some crazy reason I'd been thinking that we were on our way to watch a bunch of pimply preteens. But the players trotting out onto the field were men. Young men.

Of course. The three-year-old boy I vaguely remembered would be an adult now. Kids. They're tricky.

I let my eyes roam over the players taking positions and discussing, no doubt, vitally important strategic matters. It was quite a display. One player in particular caught my attention: a tall, well-built guy with thick, wavy dark hair and a butt for which a woman would kill to have access. As if reading my lascivious thoughts, the guy turned and looked right at me.

There it was, the spark that sizzled and burned. I felt overwhelmed with lust, almost sick with it.

Suddenly, Sophie grabbed my arm. I didn't even have the presence of mind to shake off her touch. "Eva, look," she said excitedly, "there's Jake!"

Sophie let go of my arm and waved wildly toward the playing field. "Jake, over here!"

And then the guy with the amazing butt was ambling toward us, a slow grin dawning on his very beautiful face.

"Oh, shit." The words escaped my lips and Sophie turned to me with a frown.

"Are you okay?" she asked.

"Fine," I squeaked. "Just . . . just a splinter from the bench."

And then Jake was climbing up the bleachers, his muscular thighs outlined nicely beneath his formfitting pants.

"Mom, hey," he said. Sophie leapt to her feet and threw her arms around Jake's neck. I sat, transfixed. Over her shoulder, Jake gave me a wink.

"Are you glad I came to see you?" Sophie asked when she'd let her son go.

Jake smiled. "More than you know, Mom."

Oh, shit, I said, this time to myself.

"Oh, where are my manners!" Sophie turned to me and said, "This is my friend Eva. Eva, you remember Jake, don't you? Though he doesn't look anything like he looked when we moved West!"

Jake extended his hand. I put out mine as I searched for an appropriate greeting. "*I want to have sex with you immediately*" probably wouldn't cut it.

"Hey," Jake said. "It's nice to meet you."

His eyes held mine. Yeah, I know that's a trite expression but how else to describe the "moment"?

"Hey," I said back. "The pleasure is mine."

The moment the words were out I thought I'd blown it. Had Sophie heard the implication there? I released Jake's hand quickly (though reluctantly), but the happy smile on my friend's face put my mind at ease.

Sophie told Jake that we were having dinner in Boston after the game with our college friend John.

Jake put his arm around Sophie's shoulders. "Hey, maybe I'll come with you, no? After I clean up."

I imagined Jake in the shower. He looked at me and I'm sure he knew what I was thinking.

Sophie playfully patted her son's chest. She was killing me and had no idea. "Don't be silly," she said. "You'd just be bored. All we'll be doing is reminiscing."

Jake squeezed her shoulder and then released her. "Okay, well, maybe some other time. I'd better get back to the field. The game's about to start."

I smiled pleasantly, but my heart—rather, the seat of my libido—sunk. With a wave and another smoldering look (yes, smoldering, and very daring, too), Jake loped off to join his teammates.

Sophie sat down next to me and beamed. "Isn't he wonderful?" she asked.

"Yes," I said weakly, "wonderful."

* 15 *

The best lies sound perfectly ordinary and often make good sense. You suspect you smell of another woman's perfume? The first thing to do when you walk through the door that night is complain loudly about the overperfumed woman who squeezed in next to you on the train. Your wife will have no good reason to suspect you of foul play.
    —Covering a Lie: It's Easier Than You Think

EVA

God, what a beautiful man.

These were the words that came to my mind when John walked into the restaurant that evening. The thought was dispassionate. There was no sexual chemistry like there'd been with Jake earlier that afternoon. My appreciation of John was of a different sort. Nevertheless, I skillfully squashed it.

John had suggested Marino's for dinner, a mom-and-pop Italian place in the North End, a little downscale for my taste. Sophie, however, loved it, proclaiming it so "warm and friendly." John said he ate there once a week, as he loved the puttanesca sauce.

Sophie leapt to her feet and embraced John. He hugged her back with enthusiasm. I remained seated and offered my hand. He took it and we shook briefly and firmly.

"It's so good to see you!" Sophie gushed. "You look wonderful!"

They took their seats and engaged in a meeting of the mutual admiration society while I waited. Finally, John turned to me.

"You look well, Eve," he said.

"Eva."

"Of course. You haven't changed a bit since I ran into you at that event a few years back."

I had a vague memory of that night. Ben. I remembered going on about Ben. I stifled a shudder. "Yes," I said, hoping John wouldn't ask about my ex-boyfriend. "I take care of myself."

John gave me a half-smile and asked nothing more.

When the wine arrived, a bold red that John had selected, he proposed a toast. "To us," he said. "The old crowd."

Sophie raised her glass and beamed. "It'll be great being friends again. It'll be just like old times!"

How could I be expected not to betray my native skepticism? "It's been said that you can't go home again."

John frowned at me. "Whatever happens," he said soothingly, "I'm glad that Sophie got us all together."

I took a sip of the wine (which was really very good) so that I wouldn't speak my thought: that I still wasn't sure I was glad Sophie had hunted us down.

Before the first course, talk turned to our professional lives. Sophie asked me if I enjoyed working at Caldwell and Company.

"My career is everything to me," I said, and then I wondered: What, exactly, do I mean by that? My career is everything because there is nothing else? There is nothing else because my career is everything? I took another few sips of wine and thought, so what if I get drunk? There's no one at home to yell at me.

"I'm doing exactly what I'm supposed to be doing," John

was saying when I tuned back in. "I can't imagine not working in the law. But who knows? Maybe five, ten years from now I'll feel the need for some sort of change. Burnout happens. So does boredom. If I don't feel challenged, I'll move on, expand, something."

Sophie smiled. "You're lucky. I mean, how many people can say they like their jobs?"

"Not many," I said abruptly—not if you listened to my staff.

"I'm not saying that my job can't be stressful," John added. "Some nights I'm so wiped I can hardly muster the energy to get on the T for home. And pretty much on a daily basis I have to contend with a variety of idiots, creeps, and bureaucrats. Still, on the whole, I'm happy."

"At least you're not digging ditches," I said, for no reason at all.

John looked at me curiously. "How did you know about that?"

"About what?"

"The summer I did a volunteer gig in Africa. Mostly we dug trenches for irrigation."

"Really?" I asked. "How socially conscious of you."

Sophie laughed. "John," she said, "I can't believe you're not married! You're perfect!"

I thought I saw John wince but I probably imagined it. John never did have any real modesty. He just pretended to be humble. It got him more adoring, empty-headed girls.

"Hardly," he said, lightly. "But thanks, Sophie. It's nice to have fans."

"You never did make a big deal of your accomplishments," Sophie went on. "I remember when you were elected into Phi Beta Kappa in our junior year you just shrugged and said something like, 'Oh, it was just luck.'"

Ah, now John pretended to blush! Really, I thought, why didn't he take up acting or politics instead of the law? His considerable talent was being wasted.

I made a bit of a choking sound. John looked at me. I smiled and said, "It's a bit thick in here, don't you think? The air, I mean."

"I'm surprised you don't have kids, Eva," John said abruptly.

"Why are you surprised?" I replied with a casual lift of my shoulder. "Lots of people don't have kids. You, for example. Unless you've got an illegitimate son or daughter stashed away somewhere."

"No children that I know of," he said evenly. "And do people really use the term 'illegitimate' anymore?"

"I'm surprised, too, Eva," Sophie said, turning to me. "Back in college you used to talk about having two or three children. You were sure you'd marry an artist, maybe a sculptor, and live in a big loft with all handmade furniture and a big dog. Remember?"

A dog? Did I drop acid in college? "No," I stated firmly. "I don't remember."

"Do you think about having kids someday?" Sophie asked John. "I think you'd make a wonderful father."

"I'm not opposed to the idea," he said carefully.

"Ah, I can see it now," I said. "He'll play around until he's sixty, then marry some thirty-year-old to bear the children he won't live long enough to see graduate college. I suppose you think that teenagers will be a comfort to you in your old age?"

Sophie looked uncomfortable. She took too big a sip of her wine, reached for her napkin, and coughed politely into it.

"Where is your sister these days, Eve?" John asked, pointedly ignoring my comment.

"Eva."

"Eva," he said, and I thought I detected a bit of amusement at my expense in his tone.

"Maura lives in Michigan. She's on husband number two. She has four kids, a tiny house, a lousy job as a cashier, and yet she's happy. At least, she claims to be."

Sophie, recovered, looked puzzled. "Why would you doubt her?"

Because it's hardly the kind of life I would want for myself, I thought. Call it supreme self-centeredness but it was hard for me to imagine my own sister being content with what I considered to be such a crabbed life. It made me angry somehow that she didn't want more, that she was so entirely different from me. But I wasn't sure why I needed her to be someone she was not.

I shrugged in reply to Sophie's last question.

"Do you see her much?" she asked.

"No," I said, wondering suddenly when it was I had last ventured to Michigan. Three years ago? Four? It had only been for a night, anyway; I'd gone to Ann Arbor to visit a potential client. I'd stayed at a Hampton Suites. Maura, who'd come into town to meet me for dinner, saw the little kitchenette and pronounced it paradise. "In fact, I've never met her youngest. I think she's about two now."

"Oh," Sophie said. "That's too bad."

"There's nothing to do out there in the sticks," I said by way of explanation, "so visiting has no appeal. And they can't afford to come here unless I put them up in a hotel, and Maura's husband won't allow that, something about his manly pride, so . . ." I shrugged. "It doesn't matter. We were never close. Probably due to the age difference."

"Age matters less when you're an adult," Sophie said. "I mean, I don't have siblings of my own but I can imagine."

"I'm surprised you're not more involved with your sister's kids," John remarked then. "I can't get enough of my nieces and nephews. I do my best to visit every week. I don't want to just be the guy who shows up at graduations with a check."

"Well," I stated flatly, "I'm not you."

Sophie put her hand on John's arm. "John, Eva doesn't remember wanting to write children's books. Can you believe that?"

"I can believe most things," John replied with a grin. To me, he said: "I remember you kept notebooks of story ideas. And sketches, which, by the way, were really lousy."

"You read my private notebooks?" I demanded. Suddenly, I had a vision of the ratty, paisley-print satchel in which I'd carried my school stuff. I wouldn't be caught dead with that satchel now.

"I looked over your shoulder from time to time," John said, with absolutely no shame. "Now that I think about it, I remember one story idea. Something about a sculptor, a woman, sort of a twist on the Pygmalion thing."

I had absolutely no memory of that story, or of any others. Where, I wondered, were those notebooks? I imagined I'd thrown them out at some point. Without my parents' basement for storage—of course, I'd had to sell the house immediately after their deaths—I'd had little room for childhood memorabilia. Dolls, games, most had gone out in the trash. Anything of any value, like a small desk painted white with yellow daisies, had gone to a resale shop. But the notebooks?

"You would have made a good writer," Sophie said.

Would I have? "Things change," I said, dismissively. "We were kids then, young and naive."

"Young, maybe," John replied, "but not naive. At least, when it came to a career path. I knew I wanted to be a lawyer ever since high school and I've never regretted that decision."

"And I knew I wanted to have a family," Sophie said. "I've never regretted having my son."

"What about having married Brad?" I asked. "Do you ever regret that?" It seemed a reasonable question but John raised an eyebrow at me.

Sophie didn't answer immediately. "No," she said finally. "I don't regret marrying Brad. He's the father of my child and he's basically a good person. Things just didn't . . . last. Besides, I don't understand how any woman could regret marrying the father of her child!"

John took a slow sip of his wine before he said: "If you'd

met the number of abused women I have, you might understand. Especially when your jaw has been broken and the child support is late because your ex-husband has spent all his money on drugs. You might very well regret ever having met the father of your child."

"You've been lucky, Sophie," I said.

"I'm sure Sophie earned what good things she has in her life," John said with a pointed look in my direction.

"Oh, I know what Eva means," Sophie said. "But I'd say blessed rather than lucky."

I laughed. "Then I suppose I could say I've been damned. My parents dying suddenly, my having to give up the graduate program to support my sister—that is, until she took off with some idiot twenty-five years her senior. Of course, after the divorce she was destitute so I supported her again until she met her current husband, who works in a gas station."

"I've had my share of hardships, too," Sophie said, defensively. "My life hasn't been a bed of roses. I'm divorced. I'm living alone for the first time ever. I'm studying for my real estate license and it's not easy, there's a lot to learn."

"Of course," John said soothingly. "I'm sure Eve didn't mean to imply that you've had a free ride. Did you, Eve? I mean, Eva."

I looked at my old friends, teamed up against me. "Is anyone having coffee?" I asked, suddenly eager to get the hell out of there.

* 16 *

Dear Answer Lady:

I'm getting married next spring in an awesome ceremony after which there's going to be a really amazing reception. The whole thing is costing my father, like, thousands of dollars and believe me, I'm spending a lot of my own money, like on a personal trainer, visits to a tanning salon, a stylist, and a honeymoon wardrobe to die for. There's only one problem and it's a big one. See, my three girlfriends from high school are still my best friends. Naturally, they expect to be my bridesmaids and I have no problem with two of them. Like me, they're in shape, tall, and blonde. They'll look awesome on either side of me! (I'm thinking of spring green for their dresses. Well, my stylist is thinking. She's amazing.) But the third girl is kind of fat and she's much shorter than the rest of us and her hair is really dark brown. I mean, this stuff never bothered me before. She's really funny and let's face it, next to me (and my other two friends) she's no threat! But if she's in my wedding party, she's going to ruin everything! What should I do? She's destroying what is supposed to be the most awesome time of my life!

Dear Most-Shallow-Woman-Alive:
You must do the right thing and ask all three of your friends to be bridesmaids. Under no circumstances are you to suggest that your short, plump, dark friend wear five-inch heels, go on a diet, or color her hair. But before you do anything related to this sickening display of self-indulgence you call a wedding, you are to get out your checkbook and write a hefty check to one of the following charities. (See below.) Try thinking about someone other than your pampered self for once and maybe, just maybe, you'll discover how awesome it is to be a human being.

SOPHIE

In the kitchen, Jake perched on a stool at the counter while I made a salad. I'd bought the raspberry dressing he liked.

Jake claimed to be eating well but I know my son. He can barely boil an egg without it resulting in disaster. Maybe his lack of culinary skills is my fault. After all, he never even had to make a sandwich for himself. I was always there. Anyway, I'd asked him over to my apartment on the pretext of giving him a packet of new socks. I knew that once he smelled my famous roast chicken and mashies, he'd stay on for dinner.

"I talked to Dad yesterday," Jake said, as if he'd just remembered.

I looked up from chopping a Vidalia onion. "Oh? How is he?" I wondered if I really wanted to know. It was hard to say.

"He's good," Jake said.

Why do women have to drag information out of men? "Is he still seeing that bimbo, what's her name, Kara?" I asked.

"Carly. Yeah, he's still seeing her." Jake looked at me curiously. "Mom, when was the last time you talked to Dad?"

"Oh, maybe about two weeks ago. Why? Is everything all right?"

Jake grabbed a tomato from the counter and began to toss it from hand to hand. "Everything's fine."

"Then, what?" I asked, grabbing the tomato midtoss. Hadn't I taught Jake not to play with his food? "There's something you're not telling me, Jake. What is it?"

"Nothing!"

"Jacob Michael. I'm your mother, I know when you're lying."

Jake sighed. "Mom," he said, "I'm not sure it's my place to tell you, okay? I don't want to get involved any more than I already am."

"Involved with what?" I asked, somewhat disingenuously. "I'm not trying to play you off your father, Jake. And if there's something you promised not to tell me, fine. But—"

"Dad's thinking of asking Carly to marry him," Jake blurted. "Okay? That's the big secret although he didn't actually tell me not to say anything."

I laid the knife on the counter; my hand shook ever so slightly. "Oh," I said. "But he's only known her for, well, for less than a year."

"I know. Like six months, tops. Look, it's not a done deal, he's not a hundred percent sure he's going to ask her. He's just thinking about it. I shouldn't have said anything."

"No, that's okay," I said. "I kind of forced you to tell me." I brought the finished salad to the table before saying: "Are you okay with this?"

Jake half-laughed. "With the idea of having a stepmother only four years older than me? It's a bit unusual but it's not the end of the world. I guess I don't really care. Dad can do what he wants."

"He always has." My tone was bitter; it surprised me.

"Well, it is his life."

I'm sure I looked a bit stricken. Jake and I rarely argued, about anything.

"Sorry, Mom," Jake said. "I just really don't want to hear

anything bad about Dad from you or anything bad about you from Dad."

"I didn't mean to sound like I was criticizing your father," I said, contrite. "But I know I did. I'm sorry, Jake."

Jake smiled. "It's okay, Mom. I'm just looking out for myself, you know. Setting boundaries."

"Change the subject?"

"Gladly. I'll be right back."

Jake loped off to the bathroom and I finished setting the table.

As I laid out forks, knives, and spoons, the shock Jake's news had induced began to wear off and in its place was embarrassment, as if Brad's choice of a much younger, much more beautiful woman (She had to be more beautiful, I was sure of it.) somehow devalued me in my son's eyes. It certainly devalued me in my own.

But it's not in my nature to wallow in self-pity. Before the plates were in their places I felt a flash of that "I'll show him!" spirit burning inside me. The same spirit that helped me to fight back when I lost the presidency of the PTA to a particularly obnoxious woman, the mother of a boy who'd bullied Jake for an entire school year. Let's just say that a little voting fraud was uncovered (I can be very tenacious when on a mission.) and within weeks, I was the newly elected president of that fine organization.

I'll get back out there, I swore, bringing the salt and pepper to the table, and I'll find a guy so much better than Brad could ever be and I'll marry him and we'll live happily ever after!

So what that I was a single woman approaching middle age? There was a man out there for me. There just had to be.

Jake loped back into the kitchen. "So," he said abruptly, "your friend, what was her name, Eva?"

"You mean the woman you met at the game?"

"Yeah, her."

"Oh. Well, actually, her name used to be Eve but somewhere along the line she changed it. I don't know why. I think Eve is such a pretty name and—"

"Does she work here in town?"

"Oh," I said. "Yes, in fact, she's senior vice president of Caldwell and Company. It's the biggest ad firm in New England. Well, that's what Eva tells me."

"So, you guys were pretty tight back in college? You, Eva, and what's that guy's name?"

"John," I said. "Yes, we were. There was a kind of loose group of friends in the scholarship program, but for whatever reason John, Eve, and I became close. Close in the way of students, I mean. Close in the way young people are. I used to think we'd be friends forever. It never even occurred to me that we might lose track of each other."

"But you're glad you got back in touch with Eva?" Jake asked. "And John?"

"Oh, yes," I said, pouring a glass of a nice Sauvignon Blanc. "I mean, things are different now, we're different. At least, Eva seems to be. I'm not so sure I've changed all that much since college and John, well—he just seems more of himself, if that makes sense."

"So, you guys weren't exactly wild and crazy?"

I laughed. "Hardly! We were all on academic scholarships. Our parents couldn't afford to send us to college without financial help. If our grades slipped, then the money slipped away, too. Some kids were tossed out of the program—and maybe they had to leave school, I don't know—but not us."

"But you must have had some fun, Mom," Jake prodded. "Spring break? Summer vacation?"

"Oh, sure," I said automatically. But then I thought about it. "Well, during spring break I'd usually go and visit my grandparents. I loved them and I always had a nice time but Grandpa was getting sick so it wasn't exactly what I'd describe as fun."

"But what about the summer?"

"I worked every summer to help pay for expenses during

the school year. All of us did. But Eve—Eva—and I did manage a few trips to the Cape. I remember one year we stayed in this horrible little motel. The shower floor was covered in ants and the sheets were full of teeny holes, like something had been chewing on them."

Jake made a face. "I have a hard time imagining you, my scrupulously clean mother, staying in such a place."

"It was horrible. Eva didn't seem to mind it, though. She was very laid-back in those days."

"What about when you guys were in Boston?" Jake asked. "Did you hang out at clubs, dance to all that insipid New Wave stuff?"

What had brought on this sudden interest in my past? I wondered. "It was not insipid," I protested, though I remembered Eva calling it much worse, which is one of the reasons we never went out to clubs. "Saturday nights," I said, "Eva and I would sometimes go to see a movie. John was usually out on a date. We didn't see much of him during the summers, come to think of it. I remember one year he went to Italy with his sisters. They visited family, I think."

"Uh-huh. What about Eva? Did she date a lot?"

"Oh, no!" I laughed at the memories. "She thought the whole idea of formal 'dating' was ridiculous. When she did get involved with someone it was usually more . . . organic, I guess. You know, first she'd be friends with a guy and then they'd get romantically involved. But honestly, I only remember her having two boyfriends through all of four years of college, though Eva never considered them 'boyfriends' in the usual sense."

"What do you mean?" Jake asked, leaning forward on the island between us.

"I don't know how to explain it," I said. "You'd have to ask Eva. She always was very much her own person."

"A character?" Jake suggested.

"I wouldn't use that term, no. Maybe . . . strong-willed.

Definite in her opinions. But never flamboyant or eccentric. Not a character."

Jake went to the fridge and got himself a beer. He's into something called boutique breweries and weekly gives me a list of favorites for when I go shopping. I've never been a beer drinker and Brad was always a vodka man. Who, I wondered, introduced Jake to good beer? I hated not knowing every little thing about my son's life.

"So, before you met Dad," Jake said, as he poured the beer into a special glass (I bought it for him; it's supposed to help the beer taste good or something.), "did you have a serious boyfriend?"

"No, no one serious. Well, maybe except for . . . Never mind."

"No, what were you going to say?"

"It's nothing," I protested.

"Do you know how annoying it is when someone starts to say something and then changes her mind?"

"Yes," I admitted.

"So, spill."

Really, what could be the harm of Jake knowing? "Well," I said, "if you must know, John and I were involved. Very briefly," I added, as if that changed the fact of the relationship.

Jake smirked. "Details, details."

I swatted him with a dish towel. "You're not getting details. Frankly, I don't remember much about our little—whatever it was."

But I did remember that when I was with Eva the other night I'd almost let slip the fact that John and I had been briefly involved. I don't know why I thought it important she not know about it. But I'd—well, I hadn't lied, I'd just omitted to tell the truth.

"Please don't say anything to anyone, Jake, okay? Promise me."

"Who would I tell?" Jake asked. "Anyway, I know I asked about boyfriends, but, well, I have to say I'm not really comfortable with the idea of you being with anyone other than Dad."

"But Dad's being with another woman doesn't bother you?" I asked.

Jake laughed. "Well, that's a lot easier for me to take."

"Jake, that's so old-fashioned!"

"I know," he said. "It's stupid, but hey, it's how I feel. And feelings can't be judged. Only actions."

"How smart you are!" I teased. "Jealous of the men in my life, but smart enough to admit it."

"Jealous! I'm not jealous. Mom, that's . . . weird."

"Oh, I don't mean anything weird by it, you know that. Just that—you know you've always come before your father with me, but how can you be sure another man might not take your place someday?"

"Have you been reading Freud in your free time?"

"Not since college, no. Anyway, I'm proud to say that I've never been jealous of your girlfriends."

Jake raised an eyebrow at me. "Uh-huh."

"No, really," I protested, "I haven't."

"Maybe not jealous, but, Mom, you never liked anyone I brought home. Ever. And you weren't exactly nice to a few of them."

"That's because no woman is ever going to be good enough for my son."

"Oh, boy, here we go. Can we change the subject, please?"

"Oh, okay," I said. "If you insist. Anyway, it's time to eat."

"Good, I'm starved. I missed lunch."

"See!" I said. "I knew you weren't eating right!"

"Mom!"

"Sit. I made those brownies you like for dessert, the ones with the walnuts."

Jake pulled out a chair at the kitchen table and plopped

into it. "Are you trying to give me heart disease before I'm twenty-five?"

"You're skin and bone! You could stand to put on a few pounds."

"My body mass index is right where it should be, Mom. And I work at keeping it that way."

I put the roast chicken on the table. "Does that mean you won't have a brownie?"

"No, Mom. I'm sure one little brownie won't kill me." Jake grinned. "Maybe two."

I beamed. Brad could have his twenty-four-year-old girl-friend. I had Jake.

* 17 *

Remember: The mind is a sacred space. No thought or feeling is wrong. Guard your thoughts well; respect your feelings. Learn to choose wisely what you would share with friends (for example, the fact that you enjoy vanilla ice cream) and what you would not (for example, that you harbor a fantasy of murdering your former second-grade teacher).
— The Mind Is a Sacred Space

JOHN

"Is it my imagination or are we getting a lot of calls today?" I asked Ellen.

"No, it's not your imagination. I finally told Eric to only put through the calls from men. My time is too precious to waste."

"What?" I asked.

Ellen perched on the edge of my desk. "Counselor," she said, "the town is abuzz with the news. One of the most eligible bachelors in Boston is looking to settle down."

"What?" I repeated. Maybe not the most eloquent reply.

"Oh, yes, it's true. People have nothing better to talk about than the imminent change in your domestic habits."

"People," I said, "are idiots."

"Be that as it may, I've had more than one offer of a gift certificate to a spa in exchange for some inside information about your tastes and preferences." Ellen held out a pink memo slip. "Usually," she said, "I don't even bother to take down the names and numbers, but in this case, I thought you might be amused."

I frowned, doubting I could ever find amusement in this situation, and took the slip of paper.

"I know this woman," I said, looking up at Ellen in disbelief. "She's sixty if she's a day. Is she kidding?"

"Oh, I think she's quite serious. In fact, I wouldn't be surprised if we get a delivery of daylilies sometime this afternoon."

"Daylilies?" I repeated stupidly.

"Yes. I told her they're your favorite flower."

"They're not my favorite flower. I don't have a favorite flower."

Ellen shrugged. "Well, she wanted to send you something. Besides, I like them."

"Good. Then you can take them home with you tonight. This is insane."

"Yes, it is."

"Wait a minute," I said. "How did word get out that I'm—that I'm changing my ways? I never said a word to anyone about—" Suddenly, I felt massively embarrassed. "About maybe, you know, wanting to get married."

Ellen looked at me with pity. "Women are highly perceptive, John. And the particular women who've launched this attack have been watching you closely for years. You miss a party, you leave a bar early, they know something is up. Once it's determined you're not having a torrid affair with a socialite holed up at the Ritz, the answer to your unusual behavior becomes clear. John Felitti is finished sowing his wild oats. He is, finally, bagable."

"Bagable?"

"Yes, able to be bagged. Just waiting to be dragged down the aisle."

"Oh, God." I rubbed my forehead. "Who else has called?"

Ellen recited the names of three women who until that moment had been, as far as I knew, as devotedly single as I. "And suddenly, they want to get married," I said numbly.

"They want to get married to a handsome, powerful, and, above all, wealthy attorney."

I cringed. "So it's not about me at all, is that what you're saying?"

"That's right."

"I suppose I should find that insulting. But I don't. I find it pitiful."

But not pitiful enough to turn down the offer of a date with Vanessa Lambert, a very successful, reasonably attractive tax attorney I'd met on a few occasions. I didn't remember much about our brief conversations, but neither did I have a memory of being bored by them.

I did hesitate for a moment before agreeing to meet her. I'd heard about Vanessa's romantic habits. She picked out the man; she picked out the restaurant. But when it came time to pick up the check, that's when Vanessa took a powder. Literally. The check arrived and Vanessa sailed off to the ladies' room.

But, I thought, what the hell? So she's got a thing about not paying for dinner. I usually paid for my dates, anyway. And I was absolutely certain there was no way that Vanessa, a woman who really did seem to have it all, would be interested in marrying anytime soon. I'd pass a few pleasant hours with her, maybe pick up a tax tip, and be home—alone—by ten.

The best-laid plans of mice and men . . . We were seated no more than a moment or two when Vanessa said: "I don't have to have kids, do I?"

"Excuse me?"

"Well," she said, her gaze frank and forthright, "I like everything to be clear up front. I think that's best when negotiating a deal, don't you?"

"Uh," I said eloquently, "yes, but—"

"Good. So, if we get married I don't have to have kids, right? I mean, that's not part of the deal, is it? Because if it is—"

I put up my hand, as if flesh and blood could hold back this craziness. "Part of what deal, Vanessa?" I asked. "What are you talking about?"

Vanessa gave me a look that seemed to say, *"Don't be coy, it's annoying"* and said: "Look, John, everyone knows you're in the market for a wife, it's all over town."

"It is?" I asked, though, of course, I already knew as much.

"Yes," Vanessa replied briskly. "And everyone knows there's no way you're going to settle down with some subpar woman with a poor education, a dead-end job, and a cheap haircut."

"Oh."

"So," she went on efficiently, "as the kind of woman everyone knows you're going to pick to be your wife, I'm asking: Kids aren't part of the deal, are they? Because I've never been interested in doing the mommy thing and I'm not about to change my mind at thirty-five."

Love? Wasn't love supposed to have something to do with marriage? Clearly, not for Vanessa. I was being interviewed for the job of husband; she assumed she was being interviewed for the job of wife. I was an unwilling participant in a very strange sort of corporate merger.

I cleared my throat. I didn't need to but I did. Vanessa was looking at me in expectation, hands folded on the table.

"Well, Vanessa," I said. "I'm sorry. I guess this meeting—I mean, this date—is over because you see, I do want kids. Lots of them, four or maybe five. And I've been considering the benefits of homeschooling. Of course, the mother would be in charge of that. And of getting dinner on the table for the kids by six."

Vanessa's face registered nothing, not even minor disappointment. "Negotiable?" she asked.

"No," I said. "I'm afraid this issue is one hundred percent nonnegotiable."

Vanessa absorbed this for a moment, then unfolded her hands and sat back. "Well," she said. "Okay. It's too bad, really. I could see us being married. We look good together, don't you think?"

Yikes, I thought. This woman brings shallow to a whole new level.

"That's irrelevant at this point, Vanessa."

"Yes, I suppose it is." Vanessa picked up her menu. "Let's order anyway. I've been dying to come here for ages. I hear the food is fabulous."

"You want to stay and have dinner together?"

Vanessa shrugged. "Sure. Why not? No hard feelings, right? It's just business."

I looked at her Botoxed face, at her lifted eyes and thought: *No feelings whatsoever.* But, I hadn't eaten since breakfast. "Sure," I said, "no hard feelings."

And if this really is just business, I thought, maybe there's a way I can expense this dinner.

* 18 *

Dear Answer Lady:

My son will soon be applying for admission at several private, prestigious high schools. His grades are decent but not what they should be to ensure he gets into one of these illustrious institutions. My husband and I have tried every method of coercion we can imagine to make our son achieve more academically but nothing has worked including intensive tutoring and physical punishment.

Recently, however, I began to volunteer at my son's school and discovered—never mind how—that I have access to tests before they are administered. Making copies of the documents is easy, as is sneaking them out of the school. Security, I am sorry to say, is appalling.

But for some reason I find myself hesitating when it comes to giving the tests to my son. It has occurred to me that giving him this advantage over his rivals for admission to the exclusive schools in our area, could, in fact, be considered cheating.

Please, assure me that I am within my rights as a parent to do whatever it takes to protect my child's future.

Dear Despicable:
   You know how they say that some people should not have children? Well, you—and quite possibly your husband—are one of them. Shred the tests thoroughly. Fire the tutors. Oh, and get ready for a visit from Child Services. Don't bother to try to cover your son's bruises, either. These people have seen it all.

JOHN

I stared up at the white ceiling. I put my hands over my face. I pulled my hair. I stared up at the white ceiling.

I felt as if I'd gotten involved in something almost sordid. I felt slightly disgusted with myself.

Listen to me. Almost sordid. Slightly disgusted. Why couldn't I come right out and damn my mindless behavior?

Here's the truth: By going home with this stranger named Cat—this woman next to me in bed—I'd proven that I wasn't in any way master of my domain. And if I couldn't do something as basic to maturity as control my appetites, sexual or otherwise—not my needs, but my desires—then how the hell did I expect to find and sustain a marriage, that ultimate commitment to something larger than the self: the union?

I snuck a peek at the body lying next to me. The sheets were in a tangle around her. Her mouth was open. Her hair was a mess. The small tattoo of a rose on her shoulder looked muddy in the weak, early-morning light.

Her name was Cat. I didn't know her full name. "My friends call me Cat," she'd said. As if I was a friend, or about to be one. As if friends were a dime a dozen.

Catherine. Kathleen. Something more exotic, like Catalina. I suppose I owed it to her to know her full name; I had, after all, had sex with her. But I just couldn't bring myself to wake her and ask.

Instead, I slipped out of bed and into my clothes, and left.
By lunch I'd made up my mind. After the disaster that was dinner with Vanessa (something I easily could have avoided) and my stupid one-night stand (ditto), I no longer felt confident in my ability to date wisely. It was clear I needed help. And—with some trepidation—I knew just where to turn.

* 19 *

Think of it this way: If lying was such a bad thing, why are there so many colorful ways to describe the act? Have fun with your lies—and enjoy "bearing false witness"!
—Sailing Under False Colors: The Creative Art of Lying

JOHN

"Do you know how many years I've been waiting for you to ask me to fix you up?" Teri asked.

"A lot?" I guessed.

"Since you were thirty. Mom's been dying to see you married. She's going to flip when she hears—"

"She's not going to hear anything," I said firmly. "Not until there's a ring on someone's finger and that might never happen."

Teri considered. "I suppose she could get all worked up for nothing. But knowing that you're finally considering marriage might really give her something to live for."

"She has Dad to live for," I pointed out. "And her grand-children. Come on, Teri, don't make this tougher on me than it has to be."

Teri sighed magnificently. "Oh, all right. I won't say any-thing. But I can tell Chrissy, can't I? She might know some-one, too."

"Okay," I agreed with some hesitation, "but make sure she knows what kind of woman I'm attracted to. I mean, she should be intelligent and well educated and, you know, pretty." Just like the woman Vanessa and her ilk are sure I'll be choosing. Assuming I can find someone who will have me.

"What are we, stupid? Do you think I'd set you up with a moron?"

"No, but . . ." Maybe, I thought, this wasn't such a good idea after all. "Look, don't go out of your way," I said. "It's really no big deal. Just, if you happen to meet someone you think I might like, you might mention me to her. Don't push it."

"Don't worry," Teri said wryly. "I do have a life, you know. I can't afford to spend all my time finding a girlfriend for my brother."

"Thanks, Teri. I appreciate your help. And I appreciate the fact that you haven't ribbed me about how pathetic I am, forty-two years old and asking his little sister to fix him up."

Teri laughed. "Oh, inside I'm ribbing away. Look, I've got to go. But I'll talk to you soon. We'll have you walking down that aisle in no time."

"Okay," I squeaked, imagining a groom's stiff white collar strained around my neck. "Okay."

* 20 *

Dear Answer Lady:
 I'm feeling kind of bad about something that happened recently. My wife and our neighbor, who is a
single mother, wanted to spend an afternoon together
without the kids so I volunteered to watch our son,
two, and her son, eighteen months. Everything was
just fine until Brooklyn, my son, pushed Bradley, the
neighbor kid, down the basement stairs. See, the
stairs are concrete and, well, Bradley got beat up
pretty bad and has been in a coma for almost a week.
Now, I know I shouldn't have lied but Brooklyn was
really upset and I kept thinking that our neighbor
would sue us for not having a safety gate, so I told
everyone that Bradley disobeyed my order not to go
near the stairs and fell down all on his own. His
mother believed me because Bradley often doesn't
pay attention and can be kind of clumsy. But just this
morning I found out that our neighbor's health insurance won't cover the kind of rehab the doctors say
Bradley is going to need. I feel bad. Should I offer her
some money? But if I do, won't she wonder why I'm
doing it?

Dear Morally Bankrupt Coward:

I've taken the liberty of notifying your wife of your perfidy and suggesting to her a counselor who will address your son's problem with aggression. This counselor will also attempt to eradicate the negative lessons you have imparted to your son by covering up his and your responsibility in this tragic situation. I have also contacted your neighbor with the name of a fiercely powerful lawyer with an unbroken record of success and he will be in touch with you shortly. Expect to be both divorced and destitute within the year. In the meantime, it might behoove you to childproof your home and to seek psychiatric counseling.

EVA

About a week after the baseball game and the dinner with Sophie and John, I stepped off the elevator and into the lobby of the building that houses the office of Caldwell and Company—to find Sophie's son leaning against a marble wall, legs crossed at the ankle, hands in the front pockets of his slouchy jeans.

I'm rarely caught off guard—sometimes I wonder if I've lost the ability to be surprised—but the sudden appearance of my friend's sexy son disarmed me. I continued to walk toward the big glass doors but felt a slight hesitation in my step.

"Hi," he said when I came within earshot. "Remember me?"

I stopped. "Oh," I said, as if just recalling our first meeting, "that's right, you're Sophie's son."

Of course, Jake didn't believe for a moment that he'd slipped my mind. "Uh-huh. Jake."

"What are you doing here?" I asked, innocently. "On your way to a job interview?"

Jake pushed off the wall and took his hands from his pockets. "In a way," he said. "I'm here to see you."

Oh, boy. This kid was good.

"You're cheeky," I pointed out.

Jake grinned. "It's one of my best qualities. Want to go for a drink?"

"Yes," I said, and then, "No."

"Is that a maybe?"

I looked again at his clothes: jeans, a T-shirt, and a relaxed, cotton blazerlike jacket. On his feet he wore a pair of Vans. Other than the shoes, the entire outfit probably came from Old Navy. "Where?" I asked.

"Wherever you'd like."

"You're a bit underdressed for the Oak Room," I said.

"My money," he said easily, "is as good as the stuff a guy in a suit carries."

"Money is the great equalizer," I agreed. Still, I thought, someone might see us at the Oak Room, someone I know, and then what? What would he, or she, think?

"How about J. P. Moran's?" I suggested.

Jake looked me up and down. Slowly. Damn. "I'd say you're a bit too well dressed for a pub," he said finally.

"I'm always the best-dressed woman in the room. I'm used to the attention."

"I'm sure you are."

There was nothing else to say. Together we left the building and mostly in silence—with an occasional glance and enigmatic smile—we made our way to J. P. Moran's.

"The bar okay?" Jake asked when we stepped into the cozy dimness of the traditional-style Irish pub.

"Yes," I said. "Down at the end." I led us to stools at the farthest, darkest end of the bar. Better, I thought, to play it safe. As far as I knew this place wasn't a hangout for any of the Caldwell staff, but habits have been known to change.

The bartender was a burly guy with Victorian mutton-chops. "Got some ID?" he rumbled to Jake, after taking my order of a martini.

"Sure." Jake reached into his back pocket for his wallet.

I cringed. I'm sure the bartender assumed Jake was out with his mother or his aunt or maybe even his boss. Certainly not—what was I? Not a friend. Not a lover. Not yet.

"I'm thinking of growing a beard. I think it will make me look my age."

When was the last time anyone had mistaken me for being underage? My parents and teachers used to say that I looked "mature" for my age. For a long time, I took that as a compliment.

"So, what do you think?"

"About what?" I asked.

"About my growing a beard."

"Oh, that." Had he mentioned growing a beard? "I'm not partial to facial hair. Of course," I said, with a nervous, flapping gesture of my hand, "it's your face. You can do what you want with it. Why should I care?"

When the bartender had placed our drinks before us, Jake looked at me intently and asked: "Are you uncomfortable? Being here with me?"

I took a bracing sip of the martini before replying. "I hate to admit this," I said, "in fact, I loathe myself for confessing—but, yes, I am a bit uncomfortable. Why are you here, Jake? Why are we here?"

"You chose to join me for a drink," Jake said matter-of-factly.

"And you chose to show up uninvited in the lobby of my office building. That's the burning question. Why? Why did you hunt me down?"

Jake turned to face me more completely. His knee touched mine. My body quivered. "I'd prefer to say that I sought you out. Hunting isn't a sport I can get into."

Oh, boy. "So," I said carefully, "you sought me out like a prize. Is that it?"

Jake nodded. His knee was still touching mine. "Well put," he said.

That's when I realized I was going to have to employ every ounce of my energy in order to resist getting involved with this sexy, impertinent, man/boy. I might not have been skilled at the game of friendship, but I wasn't ignorant of its general rules and regulations. My renewed friendship with Sophie was at risk should I get involved with Jake. Of course, if we kept our affair a deep, dark, secret, all might still be well. But if Sophie should ever find out what we'd been up to, I knew I could wave good-bye to the friendship.

The friendship I still wasn't sure I wanted.

"You're a man of considerable charms, Jake Holmes," I said. I wondered if my voice betrayed the dizzying effect his touch was having on my body.

Jake ran a finger down the length of my thigh. "I know," he said.

* 21 *

If you want to suffer killing pangs of remorse, un-
ceasing paranoia, and deep feelings of self-loathing,
go ahead and lie, cheat, and steal. You'll deserve
what you get.
 —A Guilty Conscience Needs No Accuser, or
 The Dire Consequences of Deception

Eva

He called the next morning. I'd given him my business
card but he could have gotten the number from information.
I was pretty sure that Jake didn't let little things stand in the
way of getting what he wanted. He was, after all, an only
child and I'd witnessed his mother's near-worship of her off-
spring.

He asked me to meet him for lunch. I told him that I had a
meeting. He suggested I cancel the meeting.

"You don't know me very well," I replied. "Nothing
comes before work."

"All work and no play dulls a woman's senses."

"Who said anything about no play? Really, Jake, you
shouldn't make assumptions."

"You're right," he said. "I shouldn't. But I'm human so I'll
probably continue to assume and make an ass out of you
and me."

"Cute. Anything else? Because I'm very busy."

"Not too busy to take my call," he pointed out. "I'm going to assume that's a good sign. I'm going to assume that you want to see me again."

I let him wait for my reply. I counted out a full sixty seconds, an eternity.

"Meet me at Hantman's at six-thirty," I said into the silence. "And don't be late."

"I won't be late," he said.

But he was, ten minutes late. I was just about to pay the bill and leave when I caught sight of him in the mirror over the bar. God, did he look good.

We had a drink and said little. When the bartender asked if we wanted another, Jake said, "No."

We went back to his apartment and had sex, immediately, without awkward preliminaries. It was fantastic.

Afterward, stretched out in Jake's rather comfortable bed (I later learned that Sophie had bought the expensive mattress for him "just because."), I felt a twinge of guilt about what I'd done; I did. But I defy anyone to resist the kind of sexual attraction that clamors to be fulfilled. Besides, Jake was of legal age, even if certain bartenders in this city didn't believe it without proof.

"Mom doesn't need to know," Jake said abruptly. "It's really none of her business, is it? What's happening here will be our little secret."

"There's one condition," I said. "Besides the secrecy thing."

"Okay."

"Maybe we can not talk about your—about Sophie, okay? At least, if you have to mention her, try to call her Sophie and not Mom."

Jake leaned on one arm and looked at me, his expression serious. "I can do that. I think."

"And no one else knows. No one."

Jake grinned. "I can't tell my friends I'm having sex with the hottest woman in town?"

I considered. A little free publicity never hurt anyone. "Okay," I said. "As long as your friends understand that your— that Sophie can never know."

"What about your friends?" Jake asked. "Besides my—besides Sophie, I mean. Are you going to keep me a secret from them?"

I didn't need to consider that question at all. Aside from Sophie, and possibly John, I didn't have any friends. And, really, I didn't even know Sophie and John all that well, did I? No one else would care that I was having an affair with a twenty-one-year-old graduate student with a fabulous butt.

No one would care.

That meant I was free.

"No," I said. "I'm going to enjoy you all to myself."

* 22 *

Dear Answer Lady:
   I think of myself as a good person. I send money
to several charities at Christmastime and I sometimes
offer to go to the grocery store for my neighbor who
is very old and walks with a cane. The other night I
was out with a friend at a bar. A really unattractive
woman sat next to us and we got to chatting about
the stuff you chat about with strangers. At one point
I complimented this woman on her outfit, which was,
in truth, hideous. She really seemed to appreciate my
kind words. After she left, my friend asked me why
I'd lied to the woman. I told her because I always try
to say something nice to people, especially when they
are ugly or poor. I mean, I have so much and they
have so little. My friend didn't understand; in fact,
she hasn't returned my calls. What could I possibly
have done wrong?

Dear Self-Righteous Snob:
   On the one hand, you are an ego-driven piece of
trash. On the other, I must admit that you have some
grasp of the social contract, in which white lies and
meaningless compliments play an enormous part. I
really have no advice for you other than to suggest
that when the end of the year rolls around you consider writing a check to my own favorite charity: me.

EVA

"You see those two at the table in the corner?" I whispered.

Sophie glanced ever so naturally at the painting on the corner wall. "The man with the silver hair and the woman in the red blouse?" she whispered back.

"They're having an affair. He's been married for over thirty years to the same woman. This one is his mistress. His latest mistress. He recycles about once a year."

Sophie's eyes widened. "How do you know that?"

"I did some work for his company once, about five years ago," I explained. "He attempted to recruit me for the job of prancing around town with him but I declined the offer. Though I must say he's known as a generous guy. I'm sure I could have scored some good jewelry."

"That's horrible!" Sophie leaned in. "I'm sorry, I didn't mean to talk so loudly," she stage-whispered. "What a creep!"

I shrugged. "He's actually a pretty nice guy. He gives a bundle to one of the city's most needy homeless shelters each year. And he set up a scholarship at his wife's alma mater."

"But still . . . He cheats on her!"

Poor Sophie, I thought. She sees life as black and white while I see it as entirely gray. "Practically every married person I know cheats," I told her. "Not all the time, necessarily, but when the opportunity presents itself. There's no harm in it, really. As long as the spouse at home doesn't find out. It can be very simple."

Sophie shook her head vehemently. "Cheating," she said, "is never simple. And it's wrong. It's insulting to the person being cheated on. Anyone can see that."

"I suppose that's one argument," I conceded. "It's just that I've seen so many functioning marriages that include affairs or the occasional fling it's hard to imagine a marriage that doesn't include some degree of illicit sex."

"Who are these people, anyway? Where do you meet these people?"

"Everywhere," I said. "At work, mostly."

"And they just admit to cheating on their spouses?"

I couldn't mistake the look of distaste on Sophie's face.

"Some talk pretty openly about their extracurricular activities, yes," I said. I thought about one of the senior art directors who regularly brought his latest mistress up to the office for a tour. "And sometimes, it's just rumor, but in most cases, the rumors turn out to be true. People leave a trail of clues, no matter how careful they think they're being."

Of course, as the words were leaving my mouth I was desperately aware of how they applied to my own situation with Jake. Was it only a matter of time before Sophie, before John, discovered our little secret? I felt uneasy and wished I hadn't steered the conversation onto the topic of behind-the-scenes sex.

Sophie snuck another look at the illicit couple in the corner. "How do these people reconcile being a good spouse with being an adulterer?"

"You're assuming," I said, "that they even try to reconcile the two. Plenty of people live two distinct lives and never, or rarely, feel the need to excuse or explain it to themselves or to anyone else."

"I could never live a lie," Sophie said.

I'm not exactly living a lie, I thought in my own defense. I'm not the same as an adulterer. But why should all these fine moral distinctions matter to me? Conversations with Sophie could rattle my usual complacency.

"No, you probably couldn't." My tone was distinctly mean-spirited.

Sophie, in turn, looked disappointed in me. "You make it sound like living an honest life is a bad thing."

"People have to live their lives in the way they have to live them," I said. "Who am I to judge someone else's behavior? I don't know what goes on inside the head of my colleague who loves his wife and kids but who's been having sex with someone on the side for years. As far as I can see, in terms of how he relates to my life, he's a nice guy. He's hardworking, goes to church, has a friendly smile. That's all that matters."

Yes, it sounded a little lame even to my own ears.

"Plenty more would matter to his wife," Sophie said indignantly. "And to his kids if they found out their father was a cheat!"

"Yes," I agreed, "it probably would matter to his family if they found out. But that's not my concern."

Sophie seemed to be thinking aloud when she said: "How can he go to church and stand before God and know he's living a lie?"

Didn't the Catholic Church preach that God forgives sinners? Maybe, I thought, the sinner has to repent of his bad behavior and promise never to do it again before he gets the good-to-go from God. I wasn't sure how it all worked but didn't want to drag religion any further into the conversation than I'd already inadvertently done.

"Sophie," I said, "I can't answer that for you."

"I'm not saying that I'm perfect, I'm not, but . . . It's just so hard to wrap my head around things like affairs and one-night stands. It makes me feel very confused."

"So," I suggested, "don't think about them. Focus on the stuff you can get your head around. Like . . . Well . . ."

"Real estate," Sophie replied promptly. "My job, I mean. My son. Taking care of my home. My parents. The fact that my ex-husband is dating someone half his age."

"How clichéd of him," I commented, annoyingly aware of my own clichéd situation with Jake. At least, I argued silently, I'm not cheating on anyone. Even so, on some very murky level my life was beginning to feel just a bit—well, murky.

Sophie laughed. "Well, Brad isn't always the classiest guy. He cheated on me, you know. Twice, maybe more. I know I denied it before, but now I want you to know the truth."

"Oh," I said. Wasn't that how friendships were supposed to be, ever more intimate? I shifted a bit in my seat. This friendship thing was a dangerously slippery slope.

"I never knew about his affairs until he asked for a divorce," she went on. "He didn't have to tell me at all. I'd already agreed to a divorce. But I think he needed my forgiveness."

"Or," I surmised, "he needed to hurt you for not begging him to stay."

"No," she said. "Do you think?"

"I don't know. But the male ego is fragile. It was stupid of him to tell you, really. You could have gotten furious and demanded a lot more in the divorce than I'm guessing you demanded."

"Maybe," Sophie said. "I was angry at first. But the more I thought about it the more I realized I didn't care so much. Back when I was happy—at least, back when I thought I was happy—I would have died if I found out Brad was sleeping around. But hearing about his affairs when I did just confirmed that the marriage was really over."

"Lucky Brad," I commented dryly. "He got off easy. Anyway, is that why you're so against adultery?"

"Really, Eva," Sophie said, as if scolding me. "Even if Brad hadn't cheated on me I'd still think adultery is wrong. Maybe it's understandable in some cases, I don't know, but in the end, it's wrong."

Just to play the role of devil's advocate I said: "Not if it's done with consent of the spouse."

"Of course. I guess." Sophie shook her head. "But that sort of thing puzzles me. I'm very straightforward when it comes to relationships. I believe they should consist of two people who are committed only to each other."

"No further restrictions?"

"No. What sort of restrictions would there be? Except of course that both people be consenting adults."

"Of course," I said.

"I know you think I'm a prude or hopelessly narrow-minded," Sophie said suddenly. "But I'm not either of those things, Eva. I like sex as much as the next person."

Sophie made this statement as if to convince herself, not me.

"I'm sure you do," I said.

Just then the illicit couple from the corner table walked past us. The man nodded at me, and winked. The woman raised a hand, ostensibly to pat her perfect blowout, but really to showcase the diamond ring she'd no doubt earned the hard way.

When they were gone, Sophie shuddered; I think it was for real.

* 23 *

A liar, storyteller, or dissembler might be described as someone with a Silver Tongue, but the man or woman who chooses against speech knows that Silence is Golden.
    —Give Them Nothing: Silence Speaks Volumes

John

I flung my tie on the bed. The shirt followed. Both would go to the dry cleaners in the morning. The suit could be worn once more as long as I gave the pants a quick press.

Yes. I am a man who irons. This interesting fact did not, however, seem to ensure successful dating experiences.

Take, for example, the dinner from which I'd just come. Teri had set me up with a friend of hers from college. Her name was Cheryl. She had a master's degree in education and worked as a public high school teacher. Needless to say, Cheryl was bright. Not brilliant but above average. She was also nice.

I would not be seeing her again.

I tossed my socks into the hamper and wondered if I was a horrible person. Was I just one of those Shallow Hal–type guys after all, completely focused on a woman's appearance rather than on her character and personality?

I revved up the electric toothbrush and dismissed the no-tion as ridiculous. There was ample evidence to prove otherwise. I was a nice guy. Pretty much anyone could tell you that. Just ask my mother.

Maybe it was the sting of the mouthwash that brought on the flicker of righteous indignation. Why, I thought, is it wrong for a nice guy to want to date—and eventually to marry—a woman he and every other red-blooded straight guy in the room finds attractive by the generally accepted standards of contemporary beauty?

Cheryl was smart and pleasant but she did absolutely nothing for me. Maybe if her wit had been sparkling I might have overlooked her bitten-down nails, might have found something charmingly quirky in her supershort, tightly curled hair, might have thought her diminutive size was adorable and not—well, a little weird.

The simple truth was this: I was way better-looking than Cheryl. I'm not bragging, just stating a fact anyone with eyes could verify.

And this bothered me. And it bothered me that it bothered me.

I imagined the whispers that would follow us whenever we entered a room together: Why in God's name did he marry her? She must be good in bed, dude, 'cause she's nothing to look at. Man, he could have gotten a model and he settled for *that?*

I know men. I know women, sometimes. I know people, and all of them, even the most upstanding among them, have moments in which they can be petty and mean and stingy with their kindness.

Maybe it's wrong but appearance and appearances matter to me. Not exclusively, of course. Consider Eva. Physically, she was fantastic. But her personality put a big damper on any feelings I might have for her.

I dabbed cream under my eyes and carefully stroked it in. I'm not trying to dodge old age, but neither am I courting it.

I want, I thought, to be turned on by the woman I'm going to marry. I want to be smitten with everything about her, and, yes, I want other men to look at me with envy and at my wife with admiration.

Evening ablutions completed, I stared in the mirror at my forty-two-year-old face. And there it was, the truth. I could pretend all I wanted. I could hold doors and pay for dinners and even fight for the neglected rights of neglected women. Nothing could change the truth.

"You," I said aloud, "are a pig."

* 24 *

Dear Answer Lady:

A friend of mine is studying to become a Catholic priest and while he hasn't yet taken his final vows, and therefore has not yet sworn to live a celibate life, he is currently dating a young woman. This woman knows nothing of his true situation. How exactly he misrepresented himself to her I don't know. What I do know is something about his motives. Never having dated much before becoming a novitiate, he feels this is the last chance he has to experience sex without breaking a "law" of sorts. Be that as it may, the young woman in question is being seriously misled. The other evening while at a bar with a small group— all of whom have been forced to keep our friend's secret—she confided in me that she's in love with my friend and expecting an engagement ring before long. I don't know what to do. I don't want to break my friend's confidence; I pride myself on being loyal. But what he's doing to this young woman is wrong and the longer he pretends to be someone he is not, the harder the truth will be for her to bear. Do you have any suggestion?

Dear Friend-Whose-Loyalty-Is-Sadly-Misplaced:

Send the young woman in question an anonymous note revealing your "friend's" treachery. Send an-

other anonymous note (no use in causing trouble for yourself) to the proper church authorities revealing your "friend's" unethical behavior. Be ready to comfort and support the disappointed young woman. There's a good chance that before long she will be wearing your engagement ring. Best of luck!

JOHN

"So, how was your date with Cheryl?" Teri asked. "Tell me everything."

"Well," I replied carefully, "there's not much to tell. We went to dinner. It was nice."

"What was nice, the restaurant?"

I moved the stapler to the left side of the phone. I moved it back to the right side. "Yeah, it was okay. Not my favorite place but Cheryl picked it, so . . ."

"So, what else? God, John, it's like pulling teeth talking to you. You have no gift for gossip."

"I wasn't aware," I said, "that gossip had become a good thing."

"Did you have a nice time with Cheryl?" Teri asked, ignoring my comment. Her tone brooked no more evasion on my part.

I shrugged to the empty office. "Yeah, it was okay, you know."

"What's wrong with her?" Teri demanded.

"Nothing's wrong with her. I just wasn't attracted to her."

Teri sighed magnificently. "Sex isn't everything in a marriage, you know."

"Yes, Teri," I replied patiently, "I know. But there should be some spark, at least in the beginning."

"Is it because she's so short? It's her height, isn't it?"

"Of course not," I protested. "What kind of a person do you think I am?"

"Right now, I'm not so sure."

"Don't you want your brother to be happy?" I asked rhetorically.

"Of course. It's just that Cheryl called me this morning and said she had a wonderful time with you last night."

My eyes widened in genuine surprise. I'd thought she was as uninterested in me as I was in her. God, John, I told myself, you're an idiot. "She did?" I croaked.

"Yes, she did. And she told me you said you'd call her. But now you're telling me you don't really like her!"

"I didn't say I don't like her," I argued. "She's very nice. I just don't want to go out with her again."

"Then why did you tell her you'd call her?"

Good question.

"Because, well, it's what you say."

"What who says?" Teri shot back.

"Guys. It's what guys say at the end of a date, even if they had a miserable time. It's just . . . easier."

"Not for the women you're lying to!"

"Come on, Teri, do women really believe men when they say they're going to call? What woman believes anything a man says?"

"Not funny, John. I am so mad at you right now. I want you to promise me you'll call Cheryl and apologize."

"What are you suggesting?" I asked stupidly. "That I tell her the truth, that I don't want to see her again?"

"That's exactly what I'm suggesting. No, I'm demanding it, John."

"But won't that be worse than my not calling at all?" I argued. "I mean, in a few days she'll probably get the idea that I'm not interested. If I call, if she sees my number on caller ID or the minute she hears my voice, won't her expectations be raised? And then I'll have to let her down again." The words sounded lame even to my ears.

"John. Call Cheryl tonight. But not too late," she added, "she goes to bed around nine."

"Most nights I'm just getting home from the office by nine. You see how incompatible we are?"

"Call her from the office, John." Teri was really angry. I did understand. Cheryl was her friend. My bad behavior might rebound on their relationship. "Apologize for leading her on."

"Okay, okay," I said resignedly. "If you really think it's the best thing, I'll do it. I'll call her. But it won't be easy."

"Poor you. I'm sure you'll survive."

"I can't wait until Mom and Dad get home."

"Why?" Teri asked.

"Maybe then you and Chrissy will stop bossing me around."

"You'd rather Mom boss you around?"

"Sure. She's the mother, that's her job. You and Chrissy are my little sisters. I'm supposed to be telling you what to do, not the other way around."

"Well, when you learn how to behave like a human being we'll leave you alone. Until then, you're fair game."

"Good-bye, Teri. I've got to work up the nerve to call Cheryl."

"Thanks, John." Teri's tone had softened. "I know this whole dating thing is hard."

"I hate it," I admitted. "I really hate it."

"Someday you'll look back on these days as just a bad dream."

"Promise?" I asked with a rueful laugh.

"I'm talking to God about it, John. He's working on it."

"Well, in that case, I'm golden."

"Not until you call Cheryl."

That's Teri—tough and tenacious. And she's got faith. If anyone is golden, it's my little sister.

* 25 *

Get your tail out from between your legs. Faithful is
for dogs. Opportunistic is for humans.
                    —Wake Up and Smell the Treachery

JOHN

"Cheryl, this is John Felitti."

"Oh, hi!" she said enthusiastically. "I was hoping you
would call."

My courage took a nosedive. "Is this a good time to talk?"
I asked, shamefully stalling.

"Oh, sure. I was just washing the kitchen floor but, here,
let me take off my gloves . . . Okay."

Could things get any worse? This woman was about to be
rejected while clutching a mop.

"This is very awkward," I said, then rushed on with my
miserable task. "I had a nice time with you last night, Cheryl.
A very nice time. But—I don't think things are going to work
out between us. I'm sorry."

There was an awful moment of silence before Cheryl said:
"So, you didn't call to ask me out?"

"No," I said, "I didn't. I'm sorry."

"You called to say you're not going to see me again?"

"Yes," I said, "that's right."

"You know," she said, not belligerently, "when a man says
that he'll call you, it's supposed to mean he'll call you for an-

other date. It's not supposed to mean he'll call you to tell you he doesn't want to see you again."

Oh, I was going to have a word with Teri. I'd been right all along. I should never have called. Eventually, my silence would have conveyed my disinterest. Or would silence really have been more hurtful, like Teri believed it would be?

"Yes," I said, "I know. Again, I'm sorry. I was just—I was just trying to be polite last night."

Cheryl laughed awkwardly. "Well, I guess that's that."

"Yes, I guess so. Good—"

"Wait," Cheryl interrupted. "What did you tell Teri?"

"What did I tell her?" I repeated stupidly.

"It's okay," she said and I thought I heard a catch in her voice. "It's fine."

No, it wasn't fine. "I told her I thought you were a very nice person."

"I am," Cheryl replied, with that little awkward laugh. I felt like a bum for being the cause of it.

"Yes, okay then . . ."

"Good-bye, John," Cheryl said, and then our mutual misery was over.

* 26 *

Dear Answer Lady:

I'm in big trouble. I forgot my stepmother's birthday. I mean, I forgot until I woke up that morning and realized that it was her birthday and that I'd forgotten to send her a card, let alone a present. So I called her that afternoon and asked how she liked the sweater and card I'd sent. What sweater and card? she asked. Didn't you get a package from UPS? I asked. No, she said. I acted all angry and told her that I'd get right on tracking the package. But then she said, No, I'll take care of this, I know someone who's a big shot at UPS and he owes me a favor so just give me the tracking information. Long story short, I got caught in my lie and finally had to confess that there was no package. Now I'm in deep doo-doo with my stepmother and with my dad. How could I have handled this differently?

Dear Big Mouth:

I suggest that you buy a copy of my latest book, entitled The Rubberband of Truth: How to Stretch It Without Getting Smacked in the Face. It is certain to guide you when encountering some of life's stickier situations. In the meantime, send your stepmother a dozen roses in her favorite color (even if it's plaid) *and a bottle of her favorite champagne (even if it sets you back a fortune) and eat humble pie until you puke.*

EVA

We always met at Jake's apartment. It was hardly a room at the Ritz but the place was clean and generally tidy. I tipped an imaginary hat to Sophie for having raised a boy familiar with the pleasures of a mop and a bottle of ammonia—until Jake mentioned that he hired someone to come in once a week and clean.

"I'm hopeless," he said with a shrug. "My mother did everything for me until I went away to college. I was lucky the campus was only an hour from home. Every Sunday afternoon I'd show up with my laundry and on Monday morning, I'd drive back to school with clean sheets, towels, and clothes, and enough food to feed me and my roommates for a week."

Unaccountably, I found this bit of information charming. See, I liked Sam as far as I was willing to, which wasn't very far; I had no interest in his life outside of the bed on which we were sprawled. But with Jake, things were different. I wasn't quite sure why and it worried me at first that I might be becoming emotionally attached. Why did I ask questions of Jake? Why did I listen to his answers with interest? Maybe it had something to do with Sophie, after all. As much as I didn't want her in bed with Jake and me, she was. Maybe I felt I owed it to her to know more about her son than the size of his penis.

On the other hand, I continued to guard my own privacy religiously. Jake might want to know all about me but he wasn't going to learn very much at the source.

About a week after our first tryst I asked Jake a question that had been on my mind since his performance in the lobby. I asked him if I was the first older woman he'd slept with.

Jake looked at me with some amusement. "Hell, no," he said.

His answer disappointed me. *I* hadn't drawn Jake's attention; my age had attracted him. Not my intelligence or my long legs but my experience and my crow's feet.

"So, you're in the habit of sleeping with women old enough to be your mother." I cringed at the foolish choice of words.

"I suppose it is a habit," he admitted. "Though it's not as if I have some rule about only dating women over forty. It's just that most often I find myself attracted to them."

"You must have been imprinted at an early age," I said, half-jokingly. I wasn't sure how deeply I wanted to delve into Jake's psychological makeup.

Jake propped himself up on one elbow and said, very seriously, "I guess I was imprinted. I lost my virginity at the age of sixteen to a twenty-six-year-old. She was a dental hygienist. We met at the dentist's office."

"Naturally," I replied. "So, did she seduce you?"

"No," Jake said matter-of-factly. "It was pretty much mutual. She knew I was sixteen but it didn't seem to bother her. I mean, neither of us was interested in anything long-term so what did it matter? It was all about sex. It was great."

"It was illegal."

Jake laughed and dropped back onto the pillow. "Yeah, I guess it was."

My young lover, I suspected, had quite a sexual history. Maybe that was to account for his prowess. And I'm not one to complain about prowess. "How did it end?" I asked.

"She met a guy around her own age. Last I heard, they were married and had a kid."

"And since then?" I prodded. "I can't believe you've been a heartbroken recluse since sixteen."

Jake looked at me with a mix of amusement and suspicion. "Why so interested in my romantic résumé?"

"No reason. Just curiosity."

"Can I ask you about your romantic past?"

"No," I said, a bit harshly. I softened my tone to say, "Well, of course you can ask but I'm not going to tell you anything. So, go on. What have you been doing with yourself since the hygienist?"

Jake wasn't put off. Young men like to talk about themselves. I suppose all men do.

"Well," he said, "since Gina I've been involved with several significantly older women."

"Ah, significantly older, not just older."

"I told you I must have been imprinted."

Or, I thought with sudden distaste, you're unconsciously in love with your mother.

As if he'd read my mind, Jake said: "I've always kept my choice of sexual partners from my mother. She wouldn't be cool with it. She's kind of old-fashioned."

Yes, I thought, she was. Or maybe naive was a better term to describe Sophie. Or, maybe, average. A person who lived comfortably within convention.

"Didn't she ever wonder why you weren't dating like a normal, red-blooded American boy?" I asked.

Jake laughed. "No. Every once in a while I'd show up at the house with a girl my own age to keep her from bugging me."

"What a little trickster! Did the girls know they were being used as a cover for your less ordinary sexual pursuits?"

"Of course not," Jake said, as if I was nuts to have asked. "I went out with them, too. I just wasn't all that into them. Girls my own age never seemed to have anything interesting to say, you know? Not like older women."

"Yes, yes," I said, "with age comes experience, if not necessarily wisdom. What about your father? Does he know you sleep with older women?"

"My father," Jake said with an air of mild criticism, "is into much younger, artificially enhanced women these days. He doesn't understand my interest in mature women—in real women. But he isn't bothered by it, either. He's always lived his own life and let me live mine."

"Does he know about your twenty-six-year-old?"

"No." Jake laughed. "I know when to keep my mouth shut. Let's go to your apartment next time," he said suddenly. "I want to see where you live."

"No."

"No?" Jake looked at me. "Why not?"

"There's another condition to this relationship besides secrecy," I told him. "No more showing up in the lobby of my office, okay? And we don't go to my apartment."

Jake's expression darkened but his tone was even. "I'm getting the feeling that you're embarrassed by me."

"No. It's not that." Oh, how I hated to excuse or explain my choices. "It's just that I need my space, Jake."

"That old cliché!"

"Don't laugh," I scolded. "Or, you know what, go ahead and laugh, I don't care. I require a certain amount of distance in a relationship."

"Eva," Jake said with the patience of a parent explaining a simple rule of social behavior to a lazy child, "relationships aren't about distance. They're about closeness."

We don't hit our friends, Eva, we hug them.

"Maybe your relationships are," I said, "but mine aren't. Come on, Jake, we don't even have a relationship, not really. We have sex. That's great, that's fantastic, but that's all."

I thought for a moment that I'd gone too far for Jake's delicate sensibilities. He shifted a bit away from me and didn't answer right away.

"That's a relationship in my book," he said evenly.

Oh, crap, I'd offended him. Poor kid. And poor me if I lost my incredibly gifted lover before I was done with him. So I made nice and we made up by having more sex. Sex works every time.

I watched as Jake slipped into the male postcoital doze. He

looked so very young and vulnerable. I knew he thought it was only a matter of time before he was curled up on my couch watching baseball and I was in the kitchen making dinner.

But he was wrong and he would learn that someday. But not now. Now, he was a young, sexy guy sure of his powers of persuasion. I'd let him enjoy the delusion—and the nap—while it lasted.

* 27 *

*We live in a crazy, out-of-control world where head-
lines routinely announce the most bizarre occur-
rences as newsworthy fact. Who's to say anymore
what's real and what's not real? The time has never
been so right for the flourishing of liars. History is
calling; stand up and be noticed!*
—You Can't Make This Stuff Up: When Fact Is
   Stranger Than Fiction

SOPHIE

There are two types of people: those who like to go to parties and those who like to give parties. I'm absolutely one of
the latter. I love being the hostess. I'm far less comfortable
being a guest. Aside from my own wedding (where I was, in
a way, the hostess), I can't think of one party I've ever enjoyed.

Knowing this about myself, you'd think I'd stay far away
from the singles "mixer" being held in the basement of the
local nondenominational church. You'd think that but in this
case, you'd be wrong.

I suppose it was news of Brad's impending marriage pro-
posal to Carly that propelled me out of the apartment and
into the church basement where about thirty other middle-
aged singles were gathered to talk about nothing while nib-
bling limp crackers and sipping flat soda out of plastic cups.

So, there I was, dressed, I hoped, appropriately (I'm sure Eva would have criticized the length of my skirt) in order to present myself to total strangers as a potential mate. My anxiety level rose the moment I crossed the threshold. But to turn around and dash away, especially when two women had noted my arrival with brief smiles, seemed cowardly and also, somehow rude. I walked directly to the table on which were laid out the meager refreshments (The church, I thought, must devote most of its money to family-oriented programs.) and reached for a cup of soda. My throat felt dry as sand.

Over the rim of the cup I surveyed the room. The women outnumbered the men. No surprise there. Two men in their sixties were deep in conversation; one wore a fishing cap studded with flies. And I suspected they weren't there to meet women as much as to hang out with a fellow sportsman. A few women looked to be near seventy. It made me unbearably sad to think of any person that age being "on the market," as Eva might say, for a companion.

One woman seemed much younger than the rest of us and I wondered why someone barely thirty and fairly attractive would need to meet a man in this depressing place. Had she simply gotten tired of the harshness of bars and the absurdity of five-minute dating? Finally, there were a few men in their forties and fifties, men I might consider eligible. But though each periodically surveyed the room, no one's eyes lingered on me. Feeling increasingly ridiculous (Someone had put on a tape of some old Billy Joel music, which seemed wildly inappropriate.), I was just about to leave when a tall, handsome man with an air of authority appeared at my side and said hello.

I wished he hadn't. With effort I looked up at him.

"Hello," I managed to say.

"I'm Ted." Ted nodded but didn't put out his hand. I was glad. My own hands felt uncomfortably sweaty.

"Sophie."

More silence.

"Do you—"

"I'm not very good at parties," I blurted, inadvertently cutting him off.

"Really?" Ted asked. His eyes wandered across the room, as if scouting a more interesting guest. I really couldn't blame him for wanting to move off. Anyway, I wasn't attracted to him. He reminded me of some of Brad's corporate buddies, a bit too perfect for my taste.

But maybe not for Eva.

"This might seem kind of odd," I said, "but I know someone I think you might like."

Ted looked back to me with some interest. I'm sure he was relieved I wasn't suggesting a date with me. "Well," he said with a charming smile, "it does seem a bit unusual. You don't know anything about me."

"So, tell me a few things." Now that the focus was off me, I felt almost relaxed.

He did tell me about himself and I told him about Eva, not the strange things or the inconsistencies, but all the good and impressive things, like how successful she was and how beautiful.

Ted handed me a business card. "I'd love to hear from her," he said. "She sounds fascinating."

"Great. I'll call her right away," I promised.

"Great. Well . . ."

"Well, I guess I'll be going," I said, suddenly awkward again. "I'm not much for parties."

"Yes, you mentioned that." Ted's eyes were already roaming.

I threw my plastic cup into the big trash barrel by the door and left. The night, I thought, hasn't been a total waste. I just might have found Eva's new Mr. Right.

28

Dear Answer Lady:
   Last week I got a ticket for ignoring a STOP sign. (I swear I thought it said SOAP.) Now I'm supposed to get an eye exam but I really don't want to wear glasses. A friend of mine works at the eye doctor's in the mall. I'm thinking of asking her to help me cheat on the exam. But I don't know. It sounds like maybe it's wrong. What do you think?

Dear Stupid:
   Sure, go ahead and cheat. Wait to get glasses until you're in jail for vehicular manslaughter. I hear prison-issue frames are very fashionable.

EVA

"Is this a good time to talk?" Sophie asked.
"No," I said, scanning the piles of paperwork on my desk.
"This will only take a minute, I swear."
I rolled my eyes. "What? I'm timing you."
Sophie spoke in a rush, as if she believed I was following the second hand on my watch.
"I met this wonderful man last night at a singles mixer at

the church down the block. Eva, I think he'd be perfect for you!"

First of all, no one perfect for me would be found at a singles mixer sponsored by a church. "No thanks," I said flatly.

"Oh, Eva, don't be silly. Let me just tell you a bit about him."

What part of "no" do perky people not understand? Why do they feel they're immune from dissention?

"Sophie," I said, a bit impatiently, "I mean it, I'm not interested."

"But why?" Sophie asked. "I thought you wanted to meet someone."

"I never said that. You made an assumption. And by the way, you've exceeded your allotted phone time."

"You won't even meet him once, maybe for coffee?"

"I don't like to be fixed up," I countered.

"He's very nice. And he's a doctor."

"I don't date doctors."

"He's very handsome."

"I prefer ugly men," I lied. "They work harder to please a woman."

"He has nice hair."

Then I did look at my watch. This conversation had gone on far too long. "If this guy is so perfect," I said reasonably, "why don't you go out with him?"

"I didn't feel a spark," Sophie admitted.

"Are you sure you didn't feel a spark, Sophie? Not just a little one? Why don't you meet him for coffee? I hear he's very nice."

"Okay." Sophie sounded hurt. "I get your point. I'm sorry. I was just trying to be—"

"Yes," I said, in a kinder tone, "you were just trying to be helpful, I know. Thanks. Really."

"Okay."

"Look, I've got to go."

"Okay," Sophie said again.

I disconnected the call. I'd been a bit rough with Sophie. I felt bad. Worse, I felt bad about feeling bad.

This friendship thing, I thought, turning back to my computer, is a hell of a lot of work.

* 29 *

Human beings are under no compulsion to reveal every thought or feeling or action to other human beings. We are entitled to hold close whatever personal information we care to, even when confronted by a nagging spouse or a nosy neighbor.
—The Privilege of Privacy

SOPHIE

"I thought you were going to bring your laundry?"

"Mom, I'm not a kid. I can do my own laundry."

I thought of Jake's weekly visits home during his four years at college, visits that were as much an excuse to drop off his laundry as anything else. "How often?" I asked. "How often do you do your laundry?"

"Often enough."

"Hmmm." Maybe, I thought, I'll use the key he gave me and surprise him one day. Who could complain about a drawer of clean underwear and socks? "So, how are classes going?"

"Good."

"Just good? Do you like your teachers? Do they give you a lot of homework?"

"Mom, it's grad school. Not third grade. It doesn't matter if I like my professors or not. And I'm there to work, not to slack off."

"Okay," I said. What did I know about graduate school? "Have you met anyone nice? A girl, I mean."

Jake opened the fridge and peered inside. "Actually," he said, "I'm too focused on my classes to have time for a relationship right now."

I sighed. "I don't understand people who spend all their time and energy on work! You sound just like Eva. The other day I tried to set her up with a very nice man and she wouldn't even agree to meet him for coffee!"

Jake closed the door and turned to me. "Oh? Did she say why?"

"She said that she wasn't interested in meeting anyone right now. I mean, coffee! How long could that take, half an hour?"

"Well, maybe she just wasn't in the mood. You can't force love, Mom."

"Oh, I know. I'd just like to see her happy."

"I'm sure Eva can take care of herself," Jake said. "But what about you, Mom? Why don't you go on a date?"

Why, indeed? Because no one had asked me.

I told Jake about the singles mixer and about how, in the end, all I'd gained from the experience was a deeper conviction of how I hate going to parties.

Jake reached out and hugged me. "Don't worry, Mom," he said. "There's a good guy out there for you. Of course, he'll have to pass my inspection, first."

I pushed him away playfully. "That's assuming I'm going to ask for your opinion!"

"You're getting my opinion whether you ask for it or not. End of discussion."

"You sound like your father."

"No way! Though I guess a commanding tone of voice can be useful."

"Speaking of Dad," I ventured, "did he ever ask for your opinion on his girlfriend? Carly?"

"Of course not," Jake said. "Has Dad ever asked for any-one's opinion on anything?"

"There's a point. Anyway, you never did tell me what you think of her. It's okay, I won't be upset if you tell me she's nice in addition to being a knockout."

Jake considered before speaking. "Mom, she'll never be you."

"You've become quite the diplomat," I said.

"Yeah, well, divorce will do that to a kid."

Oh. I reached out and took Jake's hand. "I'm sorry," I said. "I'm sorry for whatever trouble the divorce has caused you."

Jake squeezed my hand and let go. "Mom, it's okay. Really. I shouldn't have said that."

"And I shouldn't have put you in an awkward position by asking about your father's girlfriend. Subject over?"

"Yes, please."

Later, when Jake came back from the bathroom, he said he'd noticed that the overhead lightbulb needed replacing. I'd avoided dealing with it, even though it was a minor project. I showed Jake the kitchen drawer in which I kept extra bulbs and he hauled the step stool into the bathroom.

I stood alone in the kitchen and thought about how all my life I'd been reliant on men, specifically on my father, and then on Brad. And now, on Jake? Maybe, I thought, I shouldn't be in such a hurry to meet someone and get serious. Maybe it would do me some good to be independent for a while. It was an uncomfortable thought. I'd always seen myself as the kind of person who worked best as a partner. Brad might have earned the money and fixed the toilet when it broke—after some nagging—but the reality is that I raised Jake pretty much alone. And while Brad was taking meetings and doing lunches, I was taking care of the house and doing all of the cooking and the cleaning and the chores, like running Brad's suits to the cleaners and taking Jake to playdates and buying and sending Christmas and birthday gifts for the families. And I appreciated my responsibilities as much as I appreciated what I wasn't called upon to do.

Still, thinking of Jake replacing a lightbulb I was too—I don't know, lazy?—to replace, I couldn't help but wonder if I'd missed out on something by never having lived on my own.

"All done," Jake announced, joining me again. "Anything else need doing?"

I thought of the knobs on my dresser drawers that needed tightening and said, "No, thanks."

* 30 *

Dear Answer Lady:
My best friend loaned me her diamond necklace and I lost it. The thing is, I've seen the exact same style necklace for sale in cubic zirconia. She'd be heartbroken if she knew the necklace was gone. Should I replace it with the c.z. necklace and keep my mouth shut?

Dear Thief:
Are you sure the diamond necklace isn't tucked away at the back of your underwear drawer? Do your friend a real favor. Return the necklace and don't bother her ever again.

JOHN

"I hope this isn't a bad time," Sophie said. "I can call back."

"No," I lied, "it's fine." The middle of a workday is never a "good time" to chat. But I always manage to take the calls I shouldn't.

"Oh, good. I just wanted to confirm dinner on Wednesday at Marino's."

"Confirmed. Have you talked to Eva?" I asked.

Sophie sighed. "Yes, she's meeting us."

"Why the sigh?" I asked.

"I worry about her, John. She wouldn't even consider meeting this nice man I tried to fix her up with."

I'll admit this information pleased me. In spite of my better judgment and in spite of Eva's obvious lack of interest in me, on some level I still hoped I might have a chance with her. It was partly the thrill of the chase. But it was something else, too, something indescribable that drew me to Eva.

And then I remembered the vibe I'd caught when the three of us had had dinner. Somewhere, there was a man in Eva's life—or there was about to be. And I knew it wasn't going to be me.

"Maybe she's seeing someone," I ventured, trying to be rational.

"No," Sophie replied emphatically. "We're friends. She would have told me."

I wondered. Did Eva consider Sophie a friend? Even if she did, I wasn't sure Eva felt she owed anyone the truth about her life.

The reality was that after all the years of silence none of us really knew each other. What was Eva hiding? What was Sophie hiding? For that matter, what was I hiding?

"I just wish Eva would get over that guy who broke her heart. She's letting her past haunt her."

"What guy who broke her heart?" I asked, thinking immediately of the paragon Eva had gushed about when I'd seen her a few years back.

Sophie gave me the story in sum. The timing worked. The paragon was indeed the man who broke Eva's heart. According to Sophie.

I wasn't so sure Sophie's interpretation of Eva's emotional state was accurate. Maybe Eva wanted to be unattached. Maybe she liked being single. Then why did she hide behind the story of a broken heart? Was the façade of the tough, invulnerable woman really only a façade?

I dismissed the questions. There's no point in guessing

what's going on in someone's head. Ask them to explain and you still might never know the truth.

"It's good of you to be concerned about Eva," I told Sophie, "but I don't think she needs our help." Or, our interference, as Eva was likely to view "help."

"Maybe," Sophie conceded. "Anyway, I should go. I know you're busy. So, I'll see you on Wednesday at eight o'clock."

I assured her that it was penned in on my calendar.

* 31 *

When fabricating a fact or a feeling, stick to verbal expression. Never, ever put pen to paper—or, as is more appropriate for today's world, finger to keypad. Remember: The key to sustaining a successful lie, and then to being able to deny your involvement in it when convenient, is to leave no trail.

—Never Lie in Writing

JOHN

We stood on the sidewalk just outside the excellent French restaurant that Kelly had suggested. I knew when I met her at a one-day conference the week before that she had good taste. I know Tiffany's Atlas Collection when I see it.

I shifted, right foot to the left. "So, thanks for having dinner with me," I said. "The food was great."

Kelly continued to look at me expectantly. "You're welcome," she said. "So . . ."

"So . . . Well, thanks again." I stuck out my hand to shake hers. She kept her hand at her side and I let my own fall.

"That's it?" she asked.

Oh, boy. Teri hadn't coached me thoroughly; what was I supposed to do now? "Excuse me?" I asked.

Kelly gave me a significant look, the kind that mothers give their kid when the kid is supposed to be saying "thank you" for the slice of American cheese the guy at the deli counter just gave him.

"Am I going to see you again?" she asked.

I took a deep breath. This was not going well at all. "Well," I said, "you see, I had a nice time tonight." I paused. "But, well, I'm just not sure you're, uh, that we're . . . right for each other. At this point in my life."

Ah, the tongue-tied attorney! Kelly didn't find anything charming or even pitiable about my awkward explanation. She spoke her words carefully, as if not quite believing their meaning.

"You're saying that you're not going to call me."

"Well, uh, yes," I admitted. "I guess that's what I'm saying."

Kelly leaned toward me; I involuntarily took a step back.

"You bastard," she hissed. "You scumbag! How dare you insult me this way!"

Teri definitely hadn't prepared me for this kind of reaction. "What?" I asked, hands suddenly in the air as if to ward off the blow that I wouldn't be surprised was coming. "No, no, I didn't mean to insult you, I just—"

"Oh, just shut up," she spat. "What an idiot I am going out with a creep like you!"

"No, no, you're not an idiot," I said, though right then I was thinking, *Hey, this woman is crazy.* "I just thought . . . Look, please, my sister told me—"

"You told your sister about me!"

Oh, crap, John, just shut up and run for it. "Well, not about you in particular. How could I?" I pointed out reasonably. "This is our first date."

"And clearly our last!"

An older couple came out of the restaurant just in time to hear Kelly's pronouncement. The woman startled; the man looked at me sternly. I smiled feebly and the couple walked on, though the man looked over his shoulder twice before reaching the curb. Let me tell you, I didn't relish the idea of being arrested for "bothering" my date. I doubted it would help my reputation as a defender of abused and downtrodden women.

"Yes," I said, lowering my voice almost to a whisper, "well, be that as it may, could you please stop shouting? Please just let me explain."

Kelly folded her arms across her chest and the word that came to mind to describe her was "pugnacious."

"Oh, you'd better explain, mister. And it had better be good!"

"Okay. Okay. You see, I went out with this woman recently and, well, she was very nice, but I just didn't, you know, click with her." How to put this next part so as to avoid being the recipient of a mean right hook?

"Go on," Kelly urged, glaring up at me.

I did, but first I took another small step away from her. "Well, at the end of the night I hailed her a cab and before it drove away I told her that I'd give her a call."

Kelly made a sound like the bark of a small, pissed-off mutt. "Let me guess. You had no intention of ever calling her."

"Well, no," I admitted. "But I didn't know what else to say. I mean, I didn't want to hurt her feelings or embarrass her, so—"

"So, you lied."

"Well, yes. I guess I did. Anyway, I was telling my sister about it and she really lit into me. She told me that women prefer honesty. She said that women don't want to hear the white lies men tell at the end of the evening. She said that it was disrespectful. So—"

"So," Kelly interrupted, "you thought you'd try this honesty thing with me, is that it?"

"Yes," I said, grateful for her understanding, hopeful that I might yet make it home without blood oozing down my chin. "That's it exactly. But," I said, with one of my trademark charming smiles, "I'm getting the distinct impression that honesty wasn't the best policy in this particular situation."

Big mistake.

Kelly roared, "Don't try to make a joke out of this!"

My hands went up again. "I'm not, I swear! Look, Kelly, I'm sorry I upset you. Really, I am. But what was I supposed to do, tell you I'd call and then not call?"

"Well," Kelly said, "it would have been far better than telling me right to my face that you don't like me!"

God, I thought, I haven't prayed to you since grade school but if you get me out of this intact I'll write a big fat check to the old parish.

When I spoke, it was very, very carefully. "I didn't say that I didn't like you. You're a nice person, really. You have . . . great jewelry. It's just that—"

"It's just that you're not that into me, I know, I know, I've heard it before. It's not my fault—"

"It's not!"

Kelly bared her teeth. "Don't interrupt me! It's not my fault, it's all yours. It has nothing to do with me, I'm a fine woman, I'll make someone a lovely wife. God, I hate men!"

I spotted a cab. It was idling at a red light. If I ran really fast I figured I could duck in its backseat before the bullets caught up with me. "Maybe," I said, "I should just go—"

"Oh, you'd better go, mister!" Kelly shouted. "And the next time you're just not that into a woman, have the courtesy to lie to her, okay? When you don't call, we get the message. There's no need to humiliate us face-to-face."

"Okay," I said. "Again, I'm sorry—"

"Save your breath."

I did. I saved my breath for the dash to the cab. And once sprawled on its backseat I made a vow to never, ever take Teri's advice again. And when I dropped off that check with Father Imperioli the next morning, I just might inquire about becoming a monk.

* 32 *

Dear Answer Lady:
The lady next door is a real pill. Every time I have a party she calls the cops and just because I sometimes use her trash cans she thinks I'm some kind of a bum. Worse, she's got it in for my dog. Okay, so sometimes Buster gets out of the backyard and poops on her roses. I mean, he's a dog. His poop is probably good fertilizer. Anyway, the last time this happened she threatened to call Animal Control or whatever and have Buster taken away. What can I do to make this old biddy calm down?

Dear Menace to the Neighborhood:
Kick out your party guests at ten o'clock. Get your own damn trash cans. Make the fence around your backyard higher (consider barbed wire). Enroll Buster in an obedience class. And bring your long-suffering neighbor a box of expensive candies as an apology for your inconsiderate behavior. Have a nice day.

JOHN

I have to tell you. Being verbally attacked in public by a woman I've just bought dinner for is not my idea of a good way to end an evening. I can see if I had groped her or insulted her mother or done something objectionable like pick my nose. Sure, scream and yell all you want. Kick me if you need to. Go right ahead.

But all I'd done was to be honest.

For the millionth time (this is probably not an exaggeration) I found myself wondering what women wanted from men. Truth, lies, or an artful combination of both?

When I was just dating around through my twenties and thirties, with no intention of becoming serious with anyone, the rules were clear. I stuck to seeing women who didn't expect anything from me but a good time. Sure, there was the occasional woman who declared she didn't want anything serious and who then, after sex, morphed into a clingy creature, but they were few and far between and, frankly, I never found it hard to extricate myself from their desperate grasp.

Now that I was taking my love life seriously, I couldn't seem to do anything right.

I began to wonder if it really was too late for me to marry. Had I inadvertently become . . . the bachelor uncle? The guy with nowhere to go on holidays, the guy who depends on his happily married siblings to invite him for a home-cooked meal? The guy with no one to clip his ear hair, with no one to care if his nose hair grew offensively long, with no one to care if he took his Centrum Silver or developed prostate cancer?

One thing was clear. Men needed women. Let me be specific. I needed a woman. And preferably before I became a monster, the old man with no female companion to keep him from sliding in grotesquerie.

* 33 *

All writers, whether of "fact" or "fiction," are liars. And that's okay. But why should they be exempt from an ethical accounting? Why isn't it okay for the average secretary, say, to tell a tall tale when his boss asks what became of the one hundred dollar bill he left on his desk?
—The Creative Imagination and Its Dubious Relationship with the Truth

JOHN

"What do women want?" I asked. "I really want to know. What do women want? This is not a rhetorical question. I need an answer."

"Could you be more specific?" Sophie asked. "What do women want when? On a date, in a relationship, in general?"

I shrugged. "I don't know, in general I guess. From men, what do women want from men?"

"Sex."

Sophie rolled her eyes at Eva. "Respect. And love, of course."

"And sex. Unless they're lesbian and then women have no use for men at all."

"Eva!"

"Well, come on, Sophie. You can get respect from your assistant and love from a puppy. Sex, well, of course you can get it from a variety of sources, but I'll stick to men."

"You two," I said, "are no help at all."

Sophie reached across the table and patted my hand maternally. "I'm sorry, John. What's wrong? Did something happen?"

"Yeah, something happened."

I told them about the disastrous confrontation with Kelly. "I mean, one woman tells me that women want honesty from men. Another woman tells me that women want men to lie to them. All the time? Only in special circumstances? I tell you, I can't figure out you people."

"'You people'? Women can't be lumped into one convenient mass, John," Eva said. "I know it's difficult but you just have to take each one of us individually. Incredible concept, isn't it?"

I glared at Eva. "I know that, I'm not stupid. I'm just looking for some general guidelines, something I can actually use. But maybe it's ridiculous of me to even try to understand women. I don't know."

I became aware of Sophie eyeing me keenly.

"What?" I asked her.

"There's something else bothering you."

"Yeah, there is," I admitted. "But just forget it. I don't want to dump work stuff on you."

"No, John, tell us, please. Maybe talking about it will help."

Why not? "By now," I said, "you'd think I'd be used to watching women make lousy choices about their lives."

Eva raised an eyebrow. "Like men don't make lousy choices?"

I ignored her attempt to drag me into some stupid argument in which she would try to paint me as a misogynist slob.

"One of my pro bono cases," I said. "This woman's been her husband's punching bag for years. And every time I think we've convinced her to take the guy to court, every time we've got her all set up with temporary housing, every time we've got her emergency financial assistance and counseling, what does she do? She drops the charges and goes right back to the creep. It happened again and I swear, I'm tempted not to even try to help her next time—and there will be a next time. It's massively frustrating."

Sophie clutched my arm briefly. "You won't give up on her, John, I know you won't."

"Don't be too sure." I was aware of my voice having a sepulchral tone. "My time and resources are limited. I'd rather spend them on someone who'll actually accept the assistance and try to make a better life for herself. You don't give a new liver to an alcoholic who's determined to continue drinking when there's an otherwise healthy candidate waiting for one. You assess the risks and the chances of success and you act from there."

Eva nodded. "It makes sense. But assessing the winners and losers in a medical crisis isn't the same as assessing someone's capacity for emotional or psychological growth."

"Of course not," I agreed. "I'm not a psychiatrist. It's a big crapshoot for me to draw the line on a case. I don't walk away easily, believe me."

"I'm sure you don't," Sophie said, ever the encouraging one.

"By now," Eva said, "your instincts must be honed. I'm sure you can spot a loser more easily than when you first started out."

"Yes," I said, "but I don't use the word 'loser' when talking about victims of domestic abuse. Every client is of equal importance."

"Even the ones who can't pay?"

"Absolutely. It has to be that way." I waited for Eva to start slinging accusations of unethical tendencies, like she'd so enjoyed doing back in college. I really, really wasn't in the mood for that kind of thing.

But for some reason she dropped the argumentative tone

and said, "That's admirable." Maybe it was the look of apprehension on Sophie's face, her fear of an impending argument that persuaded Eva to back down.

"Does anyone want to share a dessert?" I asked, thankful for the peace. I might not have learned anything useful but at least nobody had come to blows. "Alberto's pastries are killer."

* 34 *

Dear Answer Lady:

I had to stay late at the office one night last week to finish a project. Just before I left—it was about nine o'clock—I went to the break room to put my coffee cup in the dishwasher. The lights in the break room were off. When I switched them on I found two of my coworkers making out. Someone screamed—I think it might have been me—and I switched the lights off and ran to the elevators as fast as I could. Since then, whenever I see the man he looks the other way. The woman, however, gives me a dirty look. I feel totally uncomfortable going to work. What should I do? By the way, both coworkers are married to other people.

Dear Unwitting Witness:

You are at no fault in this matter and it is entirely wrong that you should be made to suffer for the sins of these two adulterous people. I offer this advice: Ignore the man. He's obviously a coward. The woman, however, is a problem. The next time you run into her, smile brightly and offer a hearty greeting. Compel her to talk about the weather or some other neutral topic. And then, keeping the bright smile on your face, inform her that if she doesn't stop giving you dirty looks you will be forced to reveal a bit of infor-

*mation that might cause some distress to her and her
family. Offer a hearty farewell and be on your way.
You will then rightly have the upper hand in the matter. One further bit of advice: You work too hard.
The only people who should be in the office at nine
o'clock at night are illicit lovers.*

Eva

"What was Mom—I mean, Sophie—like in college?"

We were in Jake's bed. A bottle of wine sat on the floor
next to a cheap digital alarm clock and two torn condom
wrappers; Jake didn't see the need for a bedside table.

I took a sip of wine—a very good one, which I had
brought, as Jake kept only beer in his apartment—before answering. "You know you're not supposed to bring up the
subject of your—of Sophie."

"Oh, come on," Jake pressed. "I'm just curious about
what she was like when she was my age."

Well, I thought, it won't kill me to give the kid some information.

"Okay," I said. "My memory for details is pretty grim. But
what I do remember is that Sophie wasn't all that different
from the way she is today. Pleasant, sociable. Smart. Sometimes a little dull."

"Hey!"

"You asked a question," I pointed out. "Don't ask a question if you don't want to hear the answer."

Jake frowned. "Dull compared to you, maybe."

Most people, I thought, are dull compared to me. Or, at
least, dull compared to my public persona.

"So," Jake said now, "did she date much?"

"She went out from time to time. I don't think there was
anyone serious. And once she met your—once she met Brad,
well, it was all over."

"You make it sound so negative," Jake said. "Like her entire life was over when only her single life was over."

"Yes, well. I never much liked Brad. And he never much liked me."

Jake laughed. "I'm not surprised."

"Excuse me?"

Jake took a sip of beer before replying. "My father prefers women to be—how do I put this?—more docile. More malleable. That's why a twenty-four-year-old, not-very-bright restaurant hostess is perfect for him. She allows him to be everything he thinks he is: powerful, indispensable."

"Then why did he leave your mother?" I asked. I was too tired to correct my choice of words. We both knew about whom we were talking. "Didn't she play her part in his game?"

"You might find this hard to believe, but Mom developed a bit of a rebellious streak when it came to my father. She resisted him in subtle ways, but her plan—if it was even conscious—worked in the end. He left her alone. Now she can start over."

This was an interesting view of the situation. "Huh," I said.

"It was never in her to ask for a divorce," Jake went on. "I'm sure it never even crossed her mind. But in a slow and subtle way she forced him to the point of wanting out. And to wanting a woman more interested in playing the adoring, pampered wife of a rich and powerful man."

"How did you become so aware of your parents' relationship dynamic?"

Jake shrugged. "Most kids know a lot more about their parents' marriage than the parents think they do. Or would want them to know. And, I'm a particularly observant person."

"Oh, really?" I asked. Was Jake observant enough to realize that a large part of the time my attitude toward him was one of mild amusement? Did he realize that I saw him as in large part an entertainment?

"Really," he said, without a trace of defensiveness. "Still, I think if someone confronted my mother with this theory of mine she'd deny it. But I'd still say that I'm right."

"Sure of yourself, aren't you?"

Again, Jake was unfazed. "About most things, yeah."

About me? I wondered. How could he be? I thought of the call I was planning to make. Lately, I wasn't even sure of myself.

* 35 *

You've told your colleagues you attended the University of Michigan. You've referred to their winning football team as "we." For example: "The year we won the big pennant I was playing with a fractured foot." You neglected to explain that what you were playing was a trombone. Perfect! Now your colleagues assume you were a true hero for the football team! You've accomplished just what you set out to do!

—You Just Assumed: When Passive Lying Is Useful

EVA

I wasn't looking forward to making the call. But it had to be done and better over the phone than face-to-face.

I called Sam's cell, per my habit. There was no reason for his assistant to have any knowledge of me. He answered immediately; of course he did, my name showed on the screen of his phone.

"I have to cancel tomorrow."

Sam laughed dryly. "Hello to you, too. Okay. Let me get my Blackberry. How about Thursday? At one?"

"No," I said, "that's not going to be good, either. In fact, I'm not going to be seeing you for a while."

"Whoa. This is a surprise. What happened? Did I do something wrong?"

I laughed. "Everything has to be all about Sam. No, you did nothing wrong and nothing's wrong with me, thanks for asking. I'm just—we're just not going to be seeing each other for a while."

"Wait a minute," he said. I heard him get up from his desk and close the door to his office. When he got back on the phone he said: "Jesus, Eva, after all we've been through aren't you going to give me more of an explanation?"

Damn, it was going to be as exasperating a conversation as I had feared it would be. "Sam," I said, with exaggerated, false patience, "we've been through nothing together but a few hundred condoms. We're supposed to mean nothing to each other, remember?"

"Yeah, well, call me a romantic, but I like you, Eva." His voice sounded ragged. "I can't have sex with someone over and over and not grow to like her."

"You're just used to me, Sam, that's all." I fiddled with a pen. I am not a fiddler. I put down the pen. "You'll get used to another woman."

"There aren't many other women like you, Eva."

"By that you mean a woman who can divorce sex from intimacy." Except when she can't, I thought. Isn't that why I was ending things—temporarily—with Sam, because of some sense of loyalty to Jake? Or was it guilt about deceiving Sophie?

"You know that's not all I mean when I say that you're special," Sam replied, and for the first time since I'd known him, he sounded angry.

I didn't owe Sam an explanation, I didn't. But something made me give him one. "Look," I said in what I thought was a conciliatory tone, "if it makes you feel any better, I'll tell you the truth. I met someone a few weeks back and we got involved and, well, for now, while this other thing plays itself out, I'd feel more comfortable if you and I weren't having sex."

Sam's response was accusatory. "You're in love with this guy, aren't you?"

"No," I said, "I'm not, as a matter of fact. But I do like him, he's very sweet and that's all the explanation you're going to get."

Sam was silent for a long moment. I wanted badly to get off the phone and was just about to tell him good-bye when he spoke. "Eva, if sex with me means nothing to you, then why can't you keep sleeping with me while you see this other guy?"

Because . . .

"Look, Sam," I said, "I'm ending this conversation. I'll call you when . . . when this other thing is over and if you're still interested we can get together."

"Can't we even talk in the meantime?"

I sighed. "About what?"

"I don't know, about anything. So that I know what's going on in your life."

"Sam, you've never known what's going on in my life."

"Only because you won't tell me. You know I'm interested."

"And that's another reason I won't be seeing you for the duration. You're getting too attached, Sam. Look at how hurt you are. You need some time away from me."

"Why do you always assume you know what I need and what I don't need?" Sam shot back.

"Because," I said, "I usually do know."

Sam laughed bitterly. "Well, this time you're wrong, Eva. But I have no choice here, do I? You're breaking up with me and I have no choice but to accept it."

"You can't break up with someone you weren't dating in the first place, Sam. Now, don't be melodramatic."

"Right. Easy for you to say when—"

My stomach clenched and I disconnected the call. Sam didn't call back.

I suppose I'd half-expected him to. The silence left me feeling annoyingly unsettled. For a moment I doubted the wisdom of cutting Sam off, and the wisdom of allowing Jake an exclusivity he wasn't even aware he possessed.

What's done is done, Eva, I reminded myself. Besides, I knew I couldn't reverse the decision I'd made regarding Sam without losing the considerable power I had over him—and that prospect, the loss of power, was far too frightening to contemplate.

* 36 *

Dear Answer Lady:

Lately, my boyfriend has been spending a lot of time with my best friend, who everyone says looks just like Jessica Simpson. (She really does.) On more than one occasion my friend has told me my boyfriend is too skinny, so I know she's not attracted to him. And my boyfriend has said he thinks my best friend is too "perfect" and that he prefers someone "real" like me. But in the past week they've gone to a movie together (while I was at work) and met for dinner (while I was visiting my mom). I know I'm being ridiculous; I mean, it's not like they're hiding the fact that they've become friends. In fact, the only reason I'm writing this letter is because my sister is convinced my boyfriend and best friend are having an affair. Please, tell her (and me) that the two people who mean the most to me (outside of my family) are innocent.

Dear Painfully Ignorant:

The truth, my friend, is as plain as the nose on your face. You do have a nose, don't you? I wouldn't want to be accused of making an assumption here. Some people, I am told, do not have a nose due to accident or illness. Okay, then, assuming you do sport

said appendage, find a mirror and take a look at it
right now. See? There it is, your nose. As obvious as
the fact that your so-called best friend is fooling
around with your boyfriend. Dump the bitch and
send the bum packing. With friends like them . . .
Well, you know the rest. Or do you?

SOPHIE

"Eva? It's Sophie."

"Yes, I know. Caller ID."

"Oh. Right. Well, is this an okay time to talk?"

I always ask people that question. Almost always. Just in case.

Eva sighed. "Yeah, it's fine. I was just about to nuke some dinner but it can wait."

I made a mental note to have Eva for dinner soon. No one should eat frozen meals night after night. "I need your advice," I said. "It's about a man."

Eva's interest was piqued, as I knew it would be. "Ask away," she said.

I told her how just an hour earlier, when I'd been getting my mail from the boxes in the lobby of my building, one of my neighbors, a man who lived on the floor above, someone I'd only ever said hi to before, got off the elevator and stopped to chat.

"And?" Eva queried. "This is utterly boring so far."

"And then he asked me on a date. He asked me to have dinner with him Friday night."

"He what?" she barked.

"He asked me out for Friday. And I said yes. But I don't know if I did the right thing. I mean, he seems nice enough but I felt kind of pressured just standing there in the lobby, kind of like I was being ambushed. Am I being silly about this?"

"No," Eva replied emphatically, "you are not being silly."

I was relieved. From the moment he'd walked out of the lobby I'd doubted the wisdom of my decision. I mean, what if we went out and had a horrible time? Would I have to avoid the lobby entirely from that point on?

"Doesn't this idiot know the rules?" Eva went on. "You don't shit where you eat."

"Eva!"

"What? That's the saying. Anyway, I want you to call him right now and tell him you've changed your mind."

"Can't I just stick a note under his door?" I asked.

"No. He needs to hear the words from your mouth. Better yet, don't call him. Knock on his door."

"But what if he asks me why I changed my mind?" I asked. "What am I going to say?"

Eva considered. "If I were in your position I'd tell him straight out that he was an idiot for trying to date his neighbor. But you're not as tough as me. So what I want you to say is this: that you're not ready to date. You thought you were but you're not. And smile nicely for the man. You don't want your life in that building to be miserable. You don't want to be afraid of running into him every time you leave for work. What an ass. I'm really pissed at this guy."

You know, I thought, I'm pissed at him, too. How dare he put me in this awkward position!

I thanked Eva and let her get back to microwaving her dinner. And I spent the next half hour working up the nerve to follow through with her advice.

In the end I picked up the phone. (Thankfully, his number was listed.) I just didn't have the courage for what might become a face-to-face confrontation. I mean, what did I know about this man other than the possibility that he was, in Eva's words, an ass? I'm sure it would have sickened her to hear me apologize repeatedly for breaking the date he never should have asked for in the beginning. But my humility (faked, even though I hate playacting) seemed to work, and although he sounded mildly disappointed he didn't give me a hard time at all.

I settled in bed that night with a new mystery by one of my favorite authors, and tried to let myself be transported to another time and place—England in the 1920s, to be exact. But at the back of my mind the current world continued to intrude, and I couldn't help but wonder if my every experience with dating would be fraught with unforeseen complications and rules I would need a notebook to keep track of. Thank God, I thought, for a friend like Eva.

* 37 *

You neglected to call your mother on her birthday.
Maybe you forgot or maybe you consciously chose
not to call. Either way, some would call this a sin of
omission, i.e., not a good thing. Now, is it wrong for
you to omit this particular detail when your new
boyfriend, someone you're trying to impress with
your sterling character, asks how you spent your day?
Some would say that choosing not to tell him (or,
"forgetting" to tell him) about your poor behavior is,
in fact, the commitment of a sin. Face facts. No mat-
ter what you do or don't do, you're going to Hell.
             —Omission and Commission: A Trap You
             Can't Avoid

JOHN

"I married Marie because she's simple, you know?"

I supposed I was required to nod so I did. Gene nodded back at me and took a sip of his scotch on the rocks. We'd gone out for a drink after a particularly difficult day. Five minutes into the evening I was mentally slapping myself for having agreed to spend time with my disgusting colleague.

"Look," he went on—as if imparting information I hadn't already heard, information that for some reason he felt it vitally necessary that I possess—"she knows she's not a hottie.

Her self-esteem isn't great—you should meet her parents, they're crazy people, they really did a number on her—and she's not exactly a rocket scientist. She's a perfect wife for a guy like me, no trouble, stays at home, doesn't ask me where I've been when I come in late. And man, can she cook. Keeps a perfect house, too. I've got it made. Hey, maybe it's old-fashioned but so what? It works for me."

"And you're sure it works for her?" I asked, fascinated in spite of myself, as one is fascinated passing a car wreck. You see a bit of blood on the pavement and, repulsed, strain more closely in order to catch a glimpse of gore.

Gene made a face to indicate I was an idiot for even asking. "Of course," he said. "Marie never complains. Never. She's the ideal woman, except for the face and the body."

"I see," I said. I didn't see at all.

"I give her money to decorate the house the way she wants and she's having a kid, which she wanted more than anything, and once a year, on her birthday, I take her out for a fancy dinner and all that crap and she's satisfied. I tell you, John, if you ever get married, don't go for a looker. Go for someone like Marie, and you can have all the gorgeous women you want on the side. À la carte, man. It's the way to live."

Gene's absolute lack of shame was stunning. I've known plenty of guys who've cheated on their wives. And not one of them had ever spoken—in my hearing, at least—in so brazen a manner about their affairs. On the contrary, most cheating husbands I'd encountered kept a low profile and dealt with their guilt by saying nothing but good things about their wives to anyone who would listen.

Gene was one of a kind in my experience. From the beginning of our acquaintance I wondered if his bravado was real or some sort of act meant to result in his being found out. I wondered if he wasn't unconsciously hoping to get caught, for reasons I couldn't even begin to fathom.

I drained my glass—scotch, no ice—and stood. "I've got to be going," I said. "See you tomorrow."

"Stay for one more," he said. "Come on, the night is young."

But I'm not so young anymore, I thought. I lifted a hand in a wave and walked off.

* 38 *

Dear Answer Lady:

One of my friends is always getting compliments
on her hair, which is an interesting shade of red. She's
always claimed that it's natural but one day a few
weeks ago I was in a neighboring town on business
and what did I see? My friend in a hair salon, having
her hair colored! (I'm sure she didn't see me.) I can't
believe she's been lying all these years! Last night a
bunch of us were out and this really good-looking
guy came by our table and told her she had the most
beautiful hair he'd ever seen. My friend told him, of
course, that it was natural and he asked for her number. I could hardly control myself! I wanted to call
her on the lie right there and then, but I didn't. Now,
I regret keeping my mouth shut. Shouldn't she be
punished for false advertising?

Dear Woman-Who-Has-No-Life:

Three words: get over it. So your friend has some
bizarre need to sustain a stupid white lie about her
hair. Big deal. In the scheme of things, how does this
affect your life? Global warming, war, terrorism, an
escalating crime rate, growing unemployment—these
are the topics you should be pondering, not some
woman's pitiful need for attention. If you're so pissed

off, end the friendship. But for God's sake, let the poor woman live with her lie.

EVA

"I have to eat before we fool around," I said, kicking the door shut behind me. "I'm absolutely starved."

Jake stood in the kitchen, idly bouncing a pencil off the kitchen's peeling counter. "I don't think I have anything," he said.

"That's why I brought us lunch." I plopped a white paper bag on the counter and grabbed the pencil from his hand. "That drives me crazy," I said.

"Where were you last night?" he asked. "I called your cell a few times."

"I know," I said. "I got your messages. Do you have any clean glasses?"

"I thought if you weren't doing anything we could catch a movie."

"Well," I said, blowing a speck of dust off a drinking glass, "I was doing something. My company sponsors an annual charity auction. I didn't get home until after midnight, which means, of course, that I'm not feeling fabulous right now. Lack of sleep does nothing for my mood, not to mention my skin. I wouldn't be surprised if it breaks out by evening."

I handed Jake the chicken wrap I'd picked up for him. He took it, his expression openly hurt.

"What?" I asked. "What's wrong?"

Jake shrugged and fiddled with the paper around the wrap. "No, it's just . . . Did you go to this party with any-one?"

"I wouldn't exactly call it a party. These things are more like command performances. Nobody has any fun but everybody pretends to. Payment is in mediocre champagne and mushy caviar."

"But you didn't answer my question." Jake put his wrap on the counter. "Were you there with anyone?"

Ah, Jake was showing signs of his father's jealous nature. I wasn't impressed—and I wasn't going to make this little inquisition easy on my lover. "Yes, Jake. About two hundred of my closest friends."

"You know what I mean," he said, plaintively. "Why are you being so difficult, Eva?"

"Difficult? I'm not the one grilling his lover about her social habits."

"Why didn't you tell me about this auction?"

I folded my arms across my chest. Like a cat arching his back and running sideways at his enemy, this gesture makes me look particularly formidable. I know because I was told— by two employees on the day they quit their jobs and spilled their resentments. "Frankly," I said, "because it was none of your business. Come on, Jake. What possible interest could you have had in spending the evening in a hotel function room with hundreds of advertising types?"

"I would have enjoyed being there with you," he said stubbornly.

"No, you wouldn't have. Because I wouldn't have had any time to devote to you, Jake. And what could you contribute to a conversation about branding?"

"I'm a good listener. All my girlfriends have told me that."

Poor kid. He was lumping me in the girlfriend category. I uncrossed my arms. There was no real contest here. "Please, Jake, just drop it, okay?"

Before he could reply I took a bit of my sandwich and chewed enthusiastically. I'd eaten an entire half before Jake spoke again.

"I feel," he said, "that you don't respect me."

I wrapped the rest of my sandwich in its paper and sighed. Were all boys of Jake's generation so needy? And so articulate about their emotions? "Of course I respect you," I said carefully. "My decision not to ask you to come along had nothing to do with respect or lack of it."

"Are you embarrassed by me, then?" he pressed. "Are you ashamed of our relationship?"

I didn't answer Jake's accusatory questions. I couldn't answer them.

Jake shook his head. "I thought so," he said and he sounded deeply wounded.

"Look, Jake," I said, my patience worn thread-thin and my stomach still rumbling, "no one brings a spouse or a partner to these events. Hardly anyone. You would have been thoroughly bored. Trust me."

"I'd like the opportunity to decide for myself whether or not I'm bored."

I swear I thought the next words out of his mouth would be, "You're not my mother." Instead, he just looked at me and in his eyes I saw Sophie's emotional vulnerability. Poor kid, I thought again. Life is only going to be nasty if he doesn't toughen up.

"Well?" he demanded.

Well, what? Had he asked a question? I couldn't feel the slightest bit of sympathy for him. Frankly, I wished he'd just stop whining.

"Look," I said wearily, "I'm sorry you're upset but there's nothing I can do about it now."

"You could apologize."

"For what! I didn't do anything wrong. You're the first one to say that everyone is responsible for his or her own feelings. If you're feeling hurt, that's your responsibility, not mine."

"Even if you're the cause of the hurt?"

I grabbed my sandwich and stomped into the miniscule living room. "Jake, I just can't do this. I'm going back to the office."

Jake followed me. "Two people who care about each other

shouldn't walk away when they've reached an impasse. They should stay and work past the problem."

I whirled to face him. "Are you sure you're studying for a degree in engineering and not couples counseling? Good-bye, Jake."

As the door closed behind me, I heard Jake's voice, young and hopeful though still tainted with hurt.

"I'll call you tomorrow," he said.

The door clicked shut. I was spared the need to reply.

* 39 *

Remember: Everyone understands wrong assumptions. ("I thought you wouldn't mind if I ate the piece of cake with your name on it.") Everyone can relate to finding out that something she was told was real was, in fact, not real. (WMDs, anyone?) Everyone knows all about being duped by mistaken beliefs. (Santa Claus, The Tooth Fairy, The Easter Bunny— take your pick.) In short, everyone is well acquainted with prevarication, fuzzy thinking, and outright lies. What's the big deal?
—Don't Beat Yourself Up: Loving the Phony Within

EVA

That night, alone in my apartment, stretched in my one armchair (which I'd bought years earlier), feet propped on a box of books unopened since moving day, I recalled a similar situation with Ben.

I'd completely forgotten about it until that moment. This, as I've said, was not unusual. For years I'd been perfecting the art of selective memory. The ability to block out uncomfortable incidents . . . It's a fine skill to have. It allows you to get on with your life as if nothing at all upsetting had taken place.

Anyway, several months into our relationship my company had sponsored an event similar to the one I'd just attended. I mentioned the event to Ben. He asked if he was invited. I told him that no, he wasn't. He asked why not. I explained that it wasn't my habit to mix my personal life with my professional life.

Like Jake, Ben had been upset, though he'd been far less annoying about it. He said he felt I didn't take the relationship as seriously as he did. (It wasn't the first time I'd heard that remark, or the last.) I replied that I took the relationship as seriously as it should be taken. He asked what I meant by that, and—

And I had nothing.

Thinking back on this episode now I realize that the relationship had begun to fall apart right then and there.

What is it, I thought, about the way I relate to the people I supposedly care about that inevitably results in disaster, or, worse, in nothing, a dead end? Why, I wondered, do I claim to care about someone—my sister, Ben, Jake, Sam—but at the same time have the need to marginalize them?

The phone rang, mercifully interrupting these upsetting, revolutionary thoughts. I recognized the number as Sam's cell.

"What?" I asked.

"Eva?"

"Yes, Sam. Why are you calling?"

Sam wanted to meet with me. He'd had a tough day at the office. It looked as if heads might roll, one of them being his. "I'm still at my desk," he said. "Please. I really need to see you."

I hesitated. I'd ended things with Sam because of Jake. And now Jake and his unreasonable anger had tossed me into the depths of a bad mood. Too many disquieting thoughts were roiling around in my head.

"Eva?"

"Where?" I asked. "And when?"

* * *

Sam and I had a round of rip-roaring sex. There is nothing quite as mind-numbing as rip-roaring sex.

Afterward, I extricated myself from Sam's reaching hands and took a cab home. As I settled in the lumpy backseat I felt strangely unhappy, even near tears. This disturbed me. Why should I feel unhappy? Why?

And why, I wondered, should I be feeling anything at all? In the past weeks, things had gotten messy. People seemed to need things from me—things like conversation and commitment. In the past weeks, I'd found myself thinking far too much about things like trust, and truth, and, God help me, fidelity.

And everything had started with that first call from Sophie. The call I'd taken by mistake.

I gave the driver a lousy tip and went straight to bed.

* 40 *

Dear Answer Lady:

My husband and I have been having this ongoing argument for the past month. Out of the blue he announced there should be full disclosure between a husband and a wife. I immediately suspected there was something he wanted to get off his chest, like maybe that he'd gotten in trouble at work. So I said, "Of course," and asked him if he wanted to tell me anything. He said, no, what do you want to tell me? I honestly replied that I had no secrets from him. And he said, "I think that you do." And since then he's been on me like a crazy man to "confess" to some crime he thinks I committed. I got so frustrated that last night I demanded to know if he thought I'd had an affair. He gave me this weird look and said, "I don't know, did you?" Is he cracking up? Should I try to get him to go to therapy? Really, I'm starting to be afraid in my own home. Can you help me?

Dear Abused Wife:

I'll tell you what's going on here. Your jackass of a husband had an affair and is too cowardly to deal with the guilt like a man (i.e., to keep his mouth shut) or to confess his crime and ask for forgiveness. He figures if he harasses you enough you'll blurt, "Okay,

*fine, you think I had an affair, then I had an affair"
just to shut him up. Then, he'll admit to having had
his own affair in retaliation for your having had an
affair. At which point, you will cry out, "I lied! I didn't
have an affair!" To which he will reply, "But you just
said that you did. I'm out of here. Expect divorce papers in the mail." My advice? Beat the bum to the
punch. Serve him divorce papers and claim ongoing
emotional and psychological abuse. And when you're
free and clear of the imbecile, give me a call. I know
a nice doctor, very successful and newly single.*

JOHN

Why not? What harm could it do? I wasn't asking the
woman to marry me, just to meet for a drink after work.
Catch up a bit more on life since college. See where the conversation would take us.

Besides, the fridge was empty, I wasn't due to receive any
DVDs from Netflix for a day or two, and the book I was
reading—a history of the Spanish Civil War—was boring the
life out of me. (Not the topic, the writing.)

Okay, sure, Eva had twice turned down invitations, once
to dinner at my apartment with Sophie (who had come
alone), and another time to a small wine-tasting party I co-
hosted. But hey, maybe this time . . .

I punched in the number from the business card she'd
given me, expecting to reach an assistant or receptionist. Instead, Eva herself answered.

"Eva Fitzpatrick."

"Oh, hi, Eva, this is John."

There was a moment of silence.

"John Felitti."

"I know."

All right, I thought. What next?

"I wasn't expecting to get right through to you," I said.

"My assistant is out sick," Eva said without a note of sympathy. "Third time this month. It's getting old."

"Does she have something serious?" I asked, as a matter of course.

"What? I don't know. Can you get me the new layouts for the Penske account, please? I've asked you twice already this morning. I don't want to have to ask again."

More silence.

"Excuse me?" I asked. I could feel my face strained in an attitude that illustrated the slipping away of my patience.

"They send me a temp who can't follow the simplest orders. How do they expect me to work when I'm surrounded by incompetents?"

Clearly, my silence spoke volumes.

"What?" Eva demanded.

"To tell you the truth," I said, "I'm a little annoyed."

"Why?"

I shook my head. This so-called conversation was a ridiculous waste of my time. "Nothing. Forget it."

Eva laughed. "Oh, I get it. Just because you have the time to talk doesn't mean that I have the time to talk. God, John, you always were so self-focused."

"I just think you might be a little more pleasant," I said with a real effort to remain calm. "Why pick up the phone in the first place if you're going to be bothered by the interruption? Have your assistant take a message. Or," I said, remembering the sick assistant and the incompetent (and no doubt frightened) temp, "if she's not there, let the call go to voice mail."

"It could have been someone important," Eva replied. "The caller ID function isn't working."

Way to squelch a guy's ego. I said nothing.

Eva sighed as if dealing with a slow-witted child. "Look, John, I have to go. Oh. By the way, why did you call? Did you need something?"

"Never mind," I said. A bit disingenuously I added, "Have a nice day!"

Eva's reply was distracted, broken, something like: "Yeah, what? . . . okay . . ."

I hung up.

What happened to the person I'd known in college? That person—Eve, not Eva—was unfailingly polite and always had a sympathetic ear. She was the kind of girl who attracted the nerds and socially retarded types with her accepting manner; they trailed behind her like an entourage. I remembered Eve saying on more than one occasion that every person was interesting; you only had to pay attention to find out why.

There came a knock, followed by Ellen's appearance in my office. "Why the grumpy face?" she asked immediately.

"Bad clams."

"Don't want to talk about it, okay."

Ellen dropped something on my desk and turned to leave.

"Ellen," I said abruptly, "have you ever met someone you haven't seen in a long time and realized that she's nothing at all like how you remember her?"

Ellen perched on the edge of my desk. "Sure," she said. "Hasn't everyone?"

"I suppose. It's a lousy feeling."

"So, what are you saying, your memory distorted the so-called truth about this person?"

"I wish," I said. "No, in this case time distorted the so-called truth. This woman is completely different from the way she was in college."

"Judging from the scowl on your face, this is not a good thing."

A scowl, really? So much for my professional poker face. "Not in my opinion," I said. "I mean, she drove me nuts then and she drives me nuts now, but then, in college, I liked the way she got under my skin. Today, I just want to run."

Or ask her out for a drink.

"So the big reunion experiment has gone bust."

"No, I wouldn't say that. Not entirely bust. Sophie is pretty much who she was back in college. Likeable. Big-hearted. It's just this other one."

Ellen raised an eyebrow at me. "Does this other one have a name?"

"Get this. She changed her name from Eve to Eva. What is that about?"

"She had an identity crisis?" Ellen suggested. "She wants to leave the past behind? She wants to re-create herself anew? It's pretty obvious, don't you think?"

"I don't know what to think," I admitted.

Ellen got to her feet. "Well, there's nothing forcing you to be her friend now."

But what if I want to be her . . . friend? "Yeah, of course," I said, and then, "Do you have the file on the Adams's case?"

Ellen pointed a long, manicured finger. "I put in on your desk when I came in."

"Oh. Right. Thanks, Ellen."

Ellen gave me a suspicious look. Rather, a look of suspicion.

"Stay away from the clams," she said.

When she was gone I replied: "Noted."

* 41 *

Just as capri pants are not for the overweight and spicy food not for the sensitive of stomach, so truth (the telling or hearing of) is not right for everyone. Honestly identify your strengths and weaknesses before deciding such questions as: Do I really want to know if my husband is cheating on me with my best friend? Or am I better equipped to live in ignorance?
—The Truth: It's Not for Everyone

EVA

"So, what's been going on in your life?"

I shrugged. "Nothing much."

Sophie laughed. "Oh, come on, Eva. Something must be going on."

"No," I said. "Nothing."

John gave me a look of annoyance. What? Did these people have legal rights to the story of my life?

And what a story it was. No, under no condition was John to know about my strictly sexual relationship with Sam. I still wished I hadn't told Sophie; in spite of her protests I knew the information disturbed her.

And neither of them could ever, ever learn of my affair with Jake. I wasn't so morally bankrupt that I failed to realize Sophie and John would consider me a rat of a human being.

The really annoying thing was that a month ago, it wouldn't have bothered me to learn that someone thought badly of me. But a month ago I hadn't had friends. And friends, I was realizing (or remembering) were like moral guideposts. They helped to keep you walking the straight and narrow. They might love you even if you did trip off the road (i.e., if you failed), but that very misstep (i.e., failure) would cause enough embarrassment to make you try very hard never again to stumble.

All of which was a royal pain in the ass. Friends, I realized, were busybodies. Intruders. They weren't guideposts, they were moral police. And I resented the fact that they made me think badly of myself. If my mood was less than sociable that night, then so be it.

"Everything," I said with a careless wave of my hand, "is status quo. I'm sorry if this disappoints you."

"Oh. I was hoping that maybe you'd met someone. Maybe gone on a date."

Poor Sophie. Always the romantic.

"Yes," John said. "I for one was just dying to hear of your romantic exploits."

Sophie looked curiously at John.

"You men," I observed casually. "All you're interested in is sex."

"I said 'romance.' I said nothing about sex."

"But it's what you were thinking," I replied. Not that thinking about sex was wrong. I, myself, spent a fair amount of time thinking about sex. But I knew that John would never admit to such a preoccupation.

John smiled to himself, as if finding the patience to address a quarrelsome child.

"Let me go out on a limb here," he said. "Men do care about more than just sex. There are exceptions to every rule, of course, but most men want far more than sex out of a relationship."

"How would you know?" I challenged. "You're a ladies'

man, a stud, an eternally eligible bachelor. Obviously, all you care about is getting laid."

"I'm afraid," he said, "that I'm going to have to destroy your negative perception of me. For the past weeks I've been dating with the intention—well, let's say the hope—of meeting someone special. I finally came to the realization that I'm tired of being alone. I think that I would like to get married."

"John, that's wonderful!" Sophie exclaimed. "I think you'll make a fine husband."

"I don't believe you," I said. "I think you're working an angle here. And don't worry. I'll figure it out."

John sighed and excused himself to the men's room. I suspected the visit was less about the need to relieve himself and more about the need to get away from me for a moment.

"Why are you always so hard on him?" Sophie asked when John was out of earshot. She seemed genuinely bothered.

"I'm not hard on him," I said. "Well, maybe just a little."

"You're always insulting or contradicting him."

"He can take it."

"Shh, he's coming back already."

"That's one good thing about being a man, I suppose. All you have to do is whip it out and stuff it back in."

Sophie ignored my comment and smiled as John rejoined us.

"So," I said, "how's the quest for the wifey coming along?"

"Actually, and please note that I'm man enough to say this, things haven't been going so well."

Sophie pat John's arm. "Be patient. You can't force love. You'll meet someone special, I know you will."

And I just know that the new Miss Universe will be successful in her efforts to end world hunger.

"Show them your financials right at the start," I said. "You're bound to convince someone to marry you."

John laughed. "I'm going to give you a free pass on that insult," he said, "because there actually have been a few women who've come right out and asked about my portfolio. On the first date, mind you."

"That's horrible," Sophie said, her hand to her chest. "What did you do?"

"I told them—nicely, of course—to mind their own business and then I claimed a headache and went home."

"You've got to be kidding," I said. "A headache? How . . . feminine."

"What do I care what a gold digger thinks of me?"

"It takes a real man," Sophie said, "to admit a weakness."

"But his weakness," I pointed out, "his headache, is a lie. Do real men lie?"

"All men lie," John replied. "And all women, too. It can't be helped."

Sophie looked troubled. "I don't lie. At least, I try not to. What a depressing thought, that everyone lies."

"I think it makes life interesting." I shrugged elaborately, at which John scowled. "You never know what's true and what's not, what's been embellished and what's been left out. The uncertainty can be exhilarating."

"Yes," John said carefully. "But once you realize that someone is an inveterate liar, she—or he—ceases to be regarded as charming and simply becomes a bore."

Sophie's eyes darted between John and me.

"Are you implying," I asked calmly, "that I, perhaps, am a liar?"

John smiled falsely. "I've already said that everyone lies. Some are just more experienced at it than others."

"I think I need a coffee," Sophie said.

John and I each looked to Sophie, whose voice had been unnaturally high. She smiled a bit tremblingly, hopeful, no doubt, that John would stop provoking me.

"I'll have one, too," I said, though I don't really enjoy coffee after my morning cup. It leaves an unpleasant taste in my mouth, even after brushing. But for a friend, of course I would make the sacrifice. (I don't much care for sacrifice, either—I know I've mentioned this—but at rare times it is useful.)

John's expression, which had been hard and tense, now relaxed into its usual handsome calm.

"Coffee sounds good," he said, with a smile for Sophie.

Sophie gave him a grateful smile in turn. I'm sure she'd thought John and I would come to blows. Really, some people can be so dramatic.

* 42 *

Dear Answer Lady:

Recently, my husband brought home a colleague for dinner. From the second he walked through the door, I thought, "Oh, my God, he's so cute!" We had a very nice evening and since then have socialized a few times with him and his girlfriend. This man has never shown the least bit of interest in me in "that way" and yet I still have a bit of a crush on him. I would never act on it and I feel just terrible about finding a man other than my husband attractive. Should I confess to my husband? Do you think something's wrong with me? Help!

Dear Stupid:

Crushes are normal and almost always passing. Keep your mouth shut. Get yourself a hobby, but stay away from sharp objects. (This means that needlepoint is out.) Someone as dopey as you are might also consider wearing a helmet when you leave the house. Sheesh.

JOHN

To hell with Eva. First she was rude on the phone; then she was a pill at dinner with Sophie.

To hell with her.

That's what I was thinking when I decided to ask Jana to join me for dinner. Jana might not be Eva, but at least she wasn't Eva.

I'd met Jana months earlier at a party given by another partner in the firm. It was one of those command performance situations but it wasn't too painful. Stuart's wife goes all out with the food; her catering bill must be astronomical.

Anyway, I was introduced to Jana shortly after I arrived. We talked for a while, mostly about work. She told me she was an independent florist with a business supplying corporate accounts. At the end of the conversation she gave me her business card. I didn't promise to call. As a result I didn't feel too badly about so much time having passed since the party. Of course, first I had to find her card, which I did, finally, at the back of the top drawer of my desk, stained with ink from a leaky pen.

Jana remembered me and agreed to meet for dinner. Her pleasing voice on the phone brought back my impression of her as being an interesting combination of businessperson and creative type. True, I had only a vague recollection of what she looked like, which didn't seem like much of a promising sign . . . But a man needing to get a particular woman out of his mind is a desperate man.

We agreed to meet at a popular restaurant that specialized in fish. (Jana had told me that she didn't eat red meat.) I was on time. Jana was early. She waved to me from her seat at a small table in the bar. I nodded in return. I was pleased to note that Jana was rather attractive. Except for the being pregnant part.

I'm not sure when I've ever felt like such a massive idiot. And, let's admit it, a massive, slightly angry idiot. I'd been duped but good.

But there I was, towering over the little table at which sat my pregnant date, and someone had to say something.

So Jana did. "Hi," she said brightly. "It's good to see you again, John."

"Yes," I said stupidly. And then, "Good to see you, too. Our table is ready . . ."

Jana got to her feet with agility; she was very pregnant but not yet in the lumbering stage.

I swear I didn't know if I should come right out and state the obvious or wait for Jana to address the topic.

She did, as soon as we were seated in the main room and the waiter asked for her drink order. "I'll have a cranberry juice and seltzer," she told him.

I ordered a double scotch on the rocks. What did I care if Jana thought I was a boozehound? A man in shock needs a bracing beaker of the necessary (this, adapted from P. G. Wodehouse).

"I'm almost at the third trimester," Jana said when the waiter had gone, "and my doctor says then it'll be okay to have a glass of wine on occasion. But not yet."

I nodded. "Of course. Not yet." And then I thought, for God's sake, John, just spit it out. "So, I have to ask you Jana, at the party, when we met . . ."

"I was already three months along, but I wasn't really showing."

"No," I said, with a bit of laugh, "no you weren't. At least, not that I could see . . ."

"Yes, well, it's not like pregnant women should have to wear a sign around their necks announcing their condition." Jana's tone was unmistakably defensive.

"Of course not," I said. "I didn't mean to imply . . ." That you lied. I wonder if Jana could be considered guilty of false advertising. She was single; she hadn't misled me about that. But she did have a mini-me on the way. Still, full disclosure often didn't happen until the actual first date. And this was our first date.

"I guess you're wondering about the father," she said.

"Well, I . . . Yes, I guess I am."

Jana shifted in her seat. I've heard that many pregnant women suffer from hemorrhoids.

"Well," she said, "I was tired of waiting around for Mr. Right so I decided to take matters into my own hands. I went to a sperm bank, chose a donor, and, presto, I got pregnant. Well, it was a bit more complicated than that. But I'm sparing you the messy details."

Thank God for small favors. "Well," I said, "congratulations. I think you're very brave. I mean it."

"Very brave or very crazy." Jana looked down at her plate a moment before seeking my eyes again. "Look, John, do you think we can still enjoy dinner?"

"I think so," I said. I wasn't at all sure, but it would have been caddish to end the evening so abruptly.

I tried. I did. Jana was a gifted conversationalist. The fact that she had a great smile and eyes a compelling shade of gray-blue was like icing on the cake. Before long I realized that if it wasn't for the pregnancy, I would ask her out again.

If it wasn't for the pregnancy.

I need to clarify at this point. I'm not opposed to dating a woman with children from a previous relationship; in today's world, that would be a ridiculous standard to set.

But this particular situation didn't sit well with me. It bothered me that Jana was carrying a stranger's baby. And it bothered me that I was bothered. Was I, at heart, a moralistic, narrow-minded, prig? Was my liberalism only a façade?

And there was something else. Did I really want to sign on for the final trimester of a pregnancy with a woman I hardly knew? Did I really want to be there for the messy birth and the postpartum woes?

No. I didn't. And that bothered me, too. Of course, if I was in love with Jana . . . But if I was in love with Jana chances were good that I would be the father of her baby or that Jana wouldn't be pregnant at all, delaying the start of a family until after the wedding.

Too much. It was just too much for my suddenly disappointing self to take on.

We finished dinner. Neither of us ordered coffee or dessert. When the plates and glasses were gone, the emptiness was palpable. The distance between us seemed to clamor for attention.

"I'm sorry, Jana," I said, hoping for a kind reception but not expecting it. "I really am. I like you, I enjoy your conversation, I think you're attractive and obviously you're intelligent. It's just that—I don't think I can see you again."

"Because of the baby."

"Yes."

Jana sighed and folded her napkin. "Well, I won't lie, John. I'm disappointed. I like you, too, but I'm not entirely surprised."

"No, I suppose you're not."

"I made this decision," she said, almost as if to herself, "and it can be difficult, trust me. But I'm not at all sorry that I'm having this baby."

"Good," I said unnecessarily. "I mean, I'm glad."

We sat in almost companionable silence for a moment before Jana spoke again.

"It was good to see you again, John. And it was nice getting out of the house for something other than work and birthing classes. My social life," she said, with a trace of wistfulness, "hasn't exactly been exciting lately."

"It was good to see you again, too, Jana," I said honestly. "Again, I'm sorry I can't be . . . I don't even know the word I'm looking for," I admitted. "I'm sorry I can't be open enough to pursue a relationship with you."

"Maybe after the baby is born," Jana said. "Maybe I'll call you then."

The look on my face caused Jana to laugh. "Only kidding. Sorry. I guess it wasn't very funny."

I was immediately flooded with guilt. Strictly, I'd done nothing wrong. But you don't grow up in a Catholic home and expect to live a day without the nagging sense that you could have handled a situation with more grace or generosity.

I wondered if I should offer Jana assistance of some sort. Not money; that was something her family might offer, if she had any family. And what about friends? Maybe, like so many Americans these days, Jana had plenty of casual acquaintances but few real friends, the kind who would pick up her groceries or accompany her to the hospital or stay with her child for a weekend if she needed to be away.

"So," I said when the awkward silence had grown almost unbearable, "are your friends and family ready to rally around?" Maybe, I thought, I could stop by Jana's apartment once a week after the baby was born. Help out with the cleaning.

Jana laughed. "Don't worry, John. I'm not your problem or your project."

"I didn't mean to suggest that you needed my help," I said, though I suppose that's exactly what I had been suggesting.

"I'll be fine," she said, patting my hand as if I was the one facing the looming trial of single parenthood. "And I guess I should have told you about the pregnancy when you asked me to dinner."

"Yeah, it probably would have been a good idea."

"You probably wouldn't have gone out with me at all, though, would you?"

Why start lying now? "No, I guess I probably wouldn't have."

"I'm sorry," Jana said again.

"Don't be. It's fine." I looked at my watch. "But it is getting late. Let me get the check."

"Pregnant women need their sleep, huh?"

"Yes, and so do lawyers who have to be in court at nine AM."

Jana reached for her purse. "I want to pay for half," she said. "Please let me, John."

The look on her face convinced me that it was important to her.

"Okay," I said. "Thank you."

Jana and I parted amicably but once home and in bed, I felt a sort of sorrow descend on me. After a certain time in your life, you're no longer certain that things actually will look brighter and more hopeful in the light of day.

Fittingly, I began to wonder, and to worry, about my capacity for real intimacy. Maybe Eva is right, I thought. Maybe I'm really not the marrying kind after all. Maybe I will wind up living in a basement apartment of a niece or a nephew, hauled up to the dining room for Thanksgiving and Christmas. And if that was my fate, I had better get back to living large now, before it was too late and no woman would have sex with me unless she was well paid, in advance.

* 43 *

Start small, with simple flattery. For example, order what your boss orders for lunch, even if egg salad makes you nauseous. Remember: Imitation is the sincerest form of flattery, and often the most effective. A few revolting sandwiches and you'll be luxuriating in a corner office.

—What Lying Can Do for Your Career

SOPHIE

Mark had that shiny, just-out-of-the-shower look, and his clothes were always neat and pressed. Otherwise, there was nothing special about him; he looked like lots of fortysomething men, slightly balding and slightly fleshy, generally nondescript.

I'm not so beautiful that I would hold this against him. And Mark and I did have two important things in common. We were both divorced and both parents. Three things in common, if you considered the fact that we were both studying for our real estate license. Surely, we could find something interesting to talk about.

"Yes," I said to his offer of dinner one night during a break in class. "That would be nice."

We met at a new restaurant, one that Mark had chosen. Mark shook my hand. At least he hadn't tried to kiss me.

We weren't seated more than five minutes—the waiter had only had time to greet us and take a drink order—when Mark's cell phone rang.

I'd made sure to turn mine off before coming into the restaurant. Wasn't that the polite thing to do? I shot a nervous glance around the room, expecting to be met with annoyed stares. But no one seemed to notice Mark talking on his phone, not even the waiter. (Well, he must have noticed but clearly he didn't care as he set our drinks in front of us.) I took a breath and reminded myself that things were different now, that I'd been out of the social world for some time, and that it was normal for a man on a date to spend time on his cell phone.

The first call lasted over five minutes. It was from his daughter (Mark explained this after the call but I'd easily figured it out.) and seemed to involve a struggle over a curfew. In the end, Mark gave in. (How could I have helped but overhear?)

"My kids," he said, "live with their mom. It's a hassle keeping an eye on things at that house. I don't want to be one of those dads who aren't involved in their kids' lives, you know?"

Yes, I did know. I also knew that Mark hadn't apologized for the interruption to our date.

The waiter took our dinner order and call number two came in, this time from Mark's son.

By then, I was losing patience. Maybe this was the way people conducted themselves on dates these days. I could accept that as fact but I didn't have to like it. And I didn't have to like being virtually ignored.

Here's a sampling of the "conversation" that took place between Mark and me that evening:

Me: "My son is in graduate school studying for a degree in—"

Mark: "Damn, I just remembered . . . One minute." Mark

stabbed a key on his cell phone. "Tiffany? It's Dad, yes, again. Look, I forgot to tell you to use my AmEx and not the MasterCard when you order those shoes, okay?"

Me: "Jake plays on the university's baseball—"

Mark: "Trenton is a good kid, really, but sometimes he just gets overexcited. I mean, was there really a need for the teacher to file an assault charge on him? Okay, so he threw a piece of chalk at her. Come on! Boys will be boys, is what I say. Anyway, my lawyer is advising me to keep my mouth shut but I'm seriously considering slapping a harassment suit on her."

Me: "I'm finding our titles class—"

Mark: "Oh, wait, it's Tiffany again. Hi, honey, what's up?"

The evening wore on in this way until I was tempted to do something drastic like go to the ladies' room and not return. But I'm too trained in politeness so instead I sat and endured. And I ate. Mark's meal went largely untouched.

When the waiter finally asked if we'd like to see a dessert menu, I replied with a firm, "No."

"Coffee?" he suggested.

"No, thank you," I said. If Mark wanted coffee, let him get a cup at Dunkin' Donuts—on his way home to tuck his spoiled, violent kids into bed.

When the check came I sat with my hands in my lap. Mark paid with the air of someone very used to picking up other peoples' tabs—i.e., with the air of an abused father.

Once on the sidewalk outside the restaurant, Mark took a deep breath, as if relieved our date was almost over. And then he surprised me by saying: "So, when can I see you again?"

What kind of woman, I wondered, would sign on for such rude behavior?

"I'm sorry," I said. "We won't be going out again."

"But we get along so well," he protested. "We're both parents!"

And that, I thought, is the only thing we have in common: tuition bills. "What's my son's name?" I asked him.

Mark opened his mouth to reply and then he closed it. He had the decency to blush, but red cheeks weren't going to change my mind about a future with this man.

"I mentioned it several times over the course of the evening, but clearly, it wasn't important to you. Good night."

I began to walk away and Mark took a quick step after me. "No, no," he said, somewhat desperately, "it's just that I don't get out much and—"

I said, "Good night, Mark," and walked on. So much, I thought, for all the care I'd put into my outfit. So much for the fifteen dollars I'd paid for a blowout. So much for the predate jitters that had resulted in a last-minute visit to the bathroom.

I passed a small, cozy-looking restaurant. At the bar a woman sat alone, reading a book and sipping a glass of wine. For a fleeting moment I entertained the idea of stopping in as well. But I'd never eaten alone in a restaurant or sat alone at a bar. I tried to remember the last time I'd even gone to a movie by myself and couldn't.

I walked on, sorry that the date hadn't been promising, proud of myself for the way I handled the parting with Mark, and determined to work on my being-alone skills.

* 44 *

Dear Answer Lady:

Mine is a sensitive nature, easily offended by something as simple as a frowning face, and made anxious by everything from the use of a vulgar word or the employment of a harsh tone. My particular and immediate problem, however, lies with the excessively cheery counter person who works at the coffee shop I visit each morning on my way to my office (which, it should be said, is a private one). This person's greetings are offered in a singularly loud and grating voice (of which, I suspect, she is entirely unaware). Even more offensive is her habit of inquiring as to the state of my health. I ask you: What business is it of hers if I am feeling in robust health or suffering the ill effects of a restless night's sleep? On more than one occasion I have been sorely tempted to declare to this counter person that I no longer wish to converse about any topic other than my order, but each time the exceptional quality of the establishment's scones has prevented me from uttering a word. What, I wonder, would I do if I should be commanded to take my breakfast business elsewhere? Any advice you would be so kind to offer will be greatly and sincerely appreciated.

Dear Self-Centered Snob:

Maybe you should consider putting us all out of our misery by permanently removing yourself from general society by, say, becoming a recluse, or, better yet, by starving yourself to death in some freezing garret. Oh, and by the way: you might want to drop the lame attempt at writing like a nineteenth-century effete. It makes you appear even more of an idiot than I'm sure you already are. Toodles!

JOHN

Ellen was busy. I was busy. But the need to get my head back to someplace even close to the idea of marriage as a real possibility was overwhelming. So I decided to interrupt my hardworking assistant.

I never claimed to be entirely selfless.

I stalked out of my office and stood squarely in front of her desk.

"I know this is a ridiculous question," I said, "but I'm going to ask it anyway."

Ellen looked up from her computer. She smiled and swiveled a bit in the expensive, ergonomic chair I'd gotten for her the previous Christmas. "A ridiculous question is my favorite kind, Counselor."

"Good. Do you like being married?" At the look on Ellen's face that said, *"You're not coming on to me, I hope, because I will have to eviscerate you,"* I added quickly, "I don't mean do you love Austin, because I know you do. I mean, do you enjoy being married? As opposed to—er, not being married."

"First," Ellen replied after giving me a long and curious look, "that's not a ridiculous question. Second, yes, absolutely. I think marriage is a good thing. At least, it's a good thing for me. Which is not to say it sometimes isn't incredibly tough. Frankly, if it weren't for my admirable self-control, I'd be serving a life sentence for having stuck an axe in Austin's head. Several times."

"And Austin?" I asked.

Ellen waved her hand. "Oh, he'd have been executed years ago."

I perched on the edge of Ellen's desk and crossed one leg over the other. And I remembered with a wince that I'd strained a hamstring the previous day at the gym. "And yet," I went on, trying to ignore the pain, like a real man, "it's worth staying legally bound?"

"For me and, I'll venture to say, for Austin too, yeah. It is."

I thought about that for a moment before saying: "Okay, here's the real ridiculous question. Do you think marriage is a somehow . . . superior state to the other options?"

"The scary thing," Ellen said promptly, "is that a lot of people wouldn't find that question ridiculous in the least. And their answer would be a resounding 'yes.'"

"But not yours."

"No," Ellen laughed, "not mine. I don't believe that marriage is an inherently blessed state or that it's inherently superior in any way to being single or to having a life partner without benefit of a legal document. All that 'smug marrieds' nonsense angers me as much as it does a woman my age who isn't married. What's there to be smug about? Why is being married something to brag about?"

I shrugged and Ellen went on, warmed to her subject. "Just because you have a ring on your finger, and a piece of paper to prove that you're bound in the eyes of the court to another human being, doesn't infer any greatness on you."

"Witness the husband of our latest client," I said. The guy was a dirtbag. The one time I'd seen him, at a distance, down the hall at the courthouse, it was all I could do not to fly at him with a knife. Not that I carry a knife, but you know what I mean.

Ellen nodded. "Exactly. When you think of all the reasons people marry, it's insane to blanket the state of matrimony with sanctity. And when you consider all the reasons couples stay together, well, then you're even more lunatic to promote marriage as a State of Righteousness."

"Consider our esteemed colleague Gene and his long-suffering wife. There's nothing righteous about that union."

Ellen shuddered. "That's a travesty. Especially when you consider that there can be—can be, mind you, not necessarily—there can be virtue in hanging in for the long haul, but only if there's a sustained state of mutual love and respect."

I let my mind wander. Mutual love and respect. Easier said than accomplished, especially over years of daily wear and tear. I thought of my parents and wondered if I should ask them what makes their marriage work. No. I wouldn't bother. My father, embarrassed by such a personal question, would make a joke on the order of *"Keep saying, 'Whatever you say, dear.'"* My mother, on the other hand, would demur by saying something on the order of *"Don't be silly,"* and then ask me if I wanted something to eat.

Maybe the articulation of a marriage's secrets wasn't necessary to prove its success. Still, I appreciated Ellen's attempts.

I tuned back in as she said, "Marriage is a state of incessant vigilance. The slightest inattention can result in disaster." Ellen sighed. "Frankly, it's exhausting. And yet, its benefits can be worth all the effort."

"Sometimes," I said—finally approaching the crux of the matter, my reason for starting this conversation—"sometimes I wonder why I haven't taken the leap of faith. I've stumbled upon a few notions—"

"Like the fact that you enjoy sleeping with a variety of women."

"Yes," I admitted with a laugh, "like that, though in all honesty, it doesn't have the charge it used to. I actually find myself bored more often than not. You know what I mean. Or, maybe you don't."

Ellen nodded. "I do know. I was single for a long time. Too much of anything can be, well, too much. But back to you. Here's what I think: I think you're like the incredibly devoted kindergarten teacher with no children of her own at home. By choice."

"How is that like me?"

"Look, you spend hours each week giving your services free of charge to women in need. Right?"

"Okay," I agreed.

"You're a good brother and a devoted son."

"I try."

"You're a great guy to work for and I'm not angling for a raise. You have female friends. Clearly, you like women and they like you. So, why do you avoid the final act of intimacy? By which I mean commitment. Marriage."

"Yeah," I said, "that would be the question."

"So, I can't help but think that something about that ultimate act of selflessness—'Here, I'm giving you my days and my nights and in return I'm pledging to love and honor you until one of us dies'—I can't help but think that something about that vow scares the life out of you."

I laughed. "Doesn't it scare the life out of any sane person?"

"Of course," Ellen admitted. "But millions of sane—well, let's say healthy or typical—millions of people make that vow, some downright eagerly. Sure, about half of them wind up in divorce court but they give it a go."

"So, why not me? What's my problem? You haven't really suggested an answer to that burning question."

"It's not my job to. As your friend—and I'm assuming I can use that term—"

I nodded.

"As your friend it's my job to ask leading questions, to encourage you to think. Why do you give and give and give to women and yet not allow a woman—a wife—to give back to you?"

I considered before answering. "The giving I do to women—clients, friends, sisters, my mother—isn't as ultimate as the kind of giving a wife is entitled to. A wife has a right to everything. Maybe . . . Maybe I feel there's nothing left of me to give?"

"I don't know," Ellen said. "Is that what you feel?"

I laughed nervously. "I'll have to think about that."

"While you're thinking about that, think also about what you ask in return from the women in your life. Or do you ask for nothing in return? And if so, why?"

"That's something else I'll have to think about," I admitted.

Ellen smiled. "Your work is cut out for you, John. Now, we started this whole conversation by your asking what you called a ridiculous question: Do I like being married? Now, here's my own ridiculous question, but maybe it's not so ridiculous: Have you ever been in love?"

"Of course," I replied immediately, but I swear no memory came to mind, no name or face—except one, a possibility.

Ellen looked at me closely, as if sensing some ambivalence in my reply. "John," she said finally, "you can rest assured that if you don't marry I won't consider you a failure. I will, however, wonder what your life might have been like if you had tied the proverbial knot. And I'll be sorry that you never found out."

"Because you think I have husband potential?" I asked with a smile.

"Yes, but that's beside the point. Because I like and respect you and I suspect that being in a good marriage would bring you a lot of joy. But that's just my two cents."

"Your two thousand dollars," I corrected.

Ellen grinned. "You can always claim a meeting and walk

away. You can always fire me for butting into your personal life."

"If I fired you, who would rehash the latest episode of *The Daily Show* with me?"

"Oh," Ellen said with a smirk, "you'd find someone."

"I'd rather not take the chance." I got to my feet, hamstring twanging. "Thanks, Ellen. I'm a little shaken up by our chat but I guess that's a good thing. To be shaken up every now and then."

"It's human nature to grow complacent in our happiness or our unhappiness."

"Vigilance, right? Must be vigilant."

Ellen suddenly checked her watch. "Crap. I totally spaced on the time. I promised Austin I'd be home by seven so we could have a quick dinner together before he leaves town. He's flying to San Francisco tonight and won't be back until Friday."

"You'd better not tell him you were late because you were having a conversation with your boss about the sorry state of his personal life."

"That's exactly what I'm going to tell him," Ellen said, grabbing her bag and the jacket off the back of her chair. "When he hears my story he'll feel sorry for me and I'll be off the hook."

"So," I said, "honesty is the best policy here?"

"In some cases it doesn't hurt. Good night, John."

"Good night, Ellen. And thanks again."

Ellen stopped at the open door to the hallway and looked back. "Sure," she said. "Now, don't do anything I wouldn't do tonight."

* 45 *

If none of the above procedures appeals to you, you
could simply show up to take the test stinking drunk.
No one believes a drunk even if he is telling the truth.
And who would know if he is? Chances are you'll
just be sent home by the disgusted cop.
                    —How to Beat a Lie Detector Machine

EVA

"You know, of course, that this can't last. What we've got going here."

I didn't look at Jake when I spoke those words. Our legs touched under the sheets. My hands were folded across my stomach.

Jake turned to me; I could see him out of the corner of my eye. He sounded utterly surprised. "Why do you say that?"

"Oh, Jake, come on. Isn't it obvious?"

"Not to me it isn't," he said. Surprise had become annoyance, maybe confusion. "Besides, why do you want to talk about things ending when they've barely begun?"

I sighed, wondering why I really had to explain. "Because things—relationships—always end," I said. "It's foolish to pretend otherwise. I find it's healthy to acknowledge the truth right up front. Then you can enjoy the relationship while it lasts without loading it up with all these romantic fantasies and unrealistic expectations."

Jake sat up and there was no choice but for me to look at him while we talked. "How can you say that all relationships end? Okay, lots of marriages do end in divorce but enough of them don't. At least, until someone dies, but that's hardly the same thing."

"A relationship can be dead," I countered, "a long time before the participants pick up the smell of corruption. People live side by side in misery for decades, and to what purpose? At least some people have the sense to get out while they still have a life left to live. I just think it's easier to go into a relationship—of whatever sort—expecting eventual necrosis. It can," I suggested, "make the experience all the more poignant while it lasts."

"You're a pessimist, Eva."

"No, I'm a realist, Jake. You're a romantic."

"No," he said vehemently, "I'm a realist. I see the glass as half-full and getting fuller."

"And I see it as half-empty and draining all the time. I still think you're a romantic."

"Fine, you want to call me a romantic, then call me a romantic if it makes you happy. I believe that you should—no, I believe that you *have to* go into a relationship believing in its eventual success. That takes a leap of faith, sure. But otherwise, why bother make a connection with anyone at all? Why not just convince yourself that every person is an island and jump off the first high building you come to?"

"Do you see," I asked, "how ultimately incompatible we are? We could never sustain a relationship over time. We see the world in such very different ways."

Though once, I thought, I was a little more like you—or so my friends tell me.

Jake ran both hands through his hair. It really was fabulous hair. "Sometimes," he said, "opposing points of view can make the relationship more exciting."

"Not over the long haul," I said, with conviction. A united front is what makes life bearable. My parents had shared a worldview. If they taught me anything about romance it was that a true partner was someone who saw the world through the same colored glasses as you did. (Not that I had experienced that sort of romance or partnership. Not that I had ever looked for it. I shoved away the uncomfortable thoughts.) "Anyway," I said, "it's a moot issue, our becoming a real couple, for a million reasons. One big reason is that someday you're going to want to have kids."

And I'll be too old to bear them for you. For anyone.

"No, I won't," Jake stated defiantly. "I've decided I don't want kids."

"Jake, you're twenty-one, you have no idea of what you want. Someday you'll meet the right girl and next thing you know you'll be moving to the suburbs, buying an SUV, and saving for the kids' college education."

"How can you say that?" he cried. "How can you say I don't know what I want?"

I hadn't wanted to make him mad. I hadn't wanted to hurt him. I'd only wanted to educate him—and to prepare him for the end of us. I softened my tone and tried to show the . . . maternal-like concern I felt for my friend's son.

"Because I'm older than you are, Jake," I said. "I've been twenty-one and believe me, the person I was then is not the person I am now." A sharp needle of nostalgia pierced me just then; vague memories stirred and took on color. I actually gasped at the power of the sensation.

"Your point?" Jake asked sulkily. He hadn't noticed anything amiss with me.

"My point," I said after a moment, "is that things change. You get disappointed. Your energy becomes more focused on what you can accomplish and not on what you wish you could accomplish. You start shutting down certain dreams you had for your life because they seem ridiculous. Maybe your heart gets broken a few too many times. Maybe you break your own heart. Maybe your luck goes bad and for a while you're forced simply to survive rather than to live, and the habit sticks. Trust me, Jake, you have no idea what your life will be like when you're thirty, no idea what it will be like when you're forty. Absolutely no idea."

I lay there on Jake's bed, suddenly very tired.

"I have some idea," Jake said. "I know I won't be as bitter as you are."

I looked up at him, surprised. "You think I'm bitter? Oh, Jake, not at all. Just clear-eyed and clearheaded. I'm smart enough not to wallow in regret."

"You can call it what you want but I call it bitterness."

"Fine," I conceded. "But answer me this. Can you honestly say that when I'm sixty you'll still find me attractive? You'll be forty, Jake, still relatively young and vital. It's a lovely fantasy you've got harbored in your head, kiddo, but it's just a fantasy."

Jake didn't answer the question. Instead, he said: "Don't call me kiddo. I'm not a kid, Eva. It's insulting when you call me things like kiddo and boy."

"It's done with affection, Jake," I said, and realized that I meant it. "But I'm sorry, I won't do it again. At least, I'll try not to. I don't like to make promises I might not be able to keep."

Jake looked away. Quietly, I got up from the bed, dressed, and went home.

* 46 *

Dear Answer Lady:

Is it wrong to keep some things about yourself from your friends? See, I have these weird urges. I've never told anyone about them before. Like, sometimes when I'm waiting for a train I have the urge to grab the person next to me and fling him on the tracks. Sometimes I fantasize about torturing my lover. Things like that. Stuff, you know, that some people might find a bit odd. You're supposed to be honest with your friends though, right? Should I tell them about me?

Dear Psychotic Freak:

Unfortunately, it is quite normal for otherwise upstanding human beings to harbor the occasional violent or antisocial thought. In my opinion it is unnecessary to bring those rare thoughts into "reality" by discussing them with anyone other than a psychiatrist. That said, I have notified the proper authorities that there is a potential mass murderer in our city's midst. Expect a visit from The Men in White Coats shortly.

JOHN

She wore a blouse with a Peter Pan collar; it made her look an uncomfortable fourteen. (Note: You don't grow up with two sisters who are really into clothes and not know how to recognize a Peter Pan collar.) The short sleeves showcased her arms, which—and I'm being kind here—were not in the best of shape. The flounced skirt she wore only reinforced the appearance of an awkward young teen, someone who hadn't yet hit upon a style that was flattering and appropriate. Somewhere, Cathy had learned that when it came to makeup more is better, and almost every man will tell you that more is decidedly worse. I can't help but wonder about people who leave the house looking so—wrong. Is it an indication of a deeper inability to see the self as it really is and to improve upon it?

"So," I said into the deafening silence, "you know my sister Chrissy from church?"

"Uh-huh," Cathy said. "I'm on the altar guild. I iron the altar cloths. And wash them. Well, I wash them first and then I iron them."

I nodded. "Of course."

There followed a maddening silence as Cathy just looked at me placidly, waiting for the next question. The art of conversation was something she seemed unfamiliar with.

"So, what are you reading?" I asked dutifully.

Cathy's face clouded with confusion. "What?"

"What are you reading?" I asked again, this time with a pained smile.

There was another moment of confusion and then, finally, the light dawned and Cathy laughed. "Oh, like a book?" she asked. "I thought you meant, like, the menu, and I thought, why is he asking me what I'm reading when I'm sitting right here reading the menu!"

Murder, I thought, is too good for my sister. No, instead I'm going to devise a fiendish way to punish her for the rest of her life here on Earth.

"Right," I said. "I meant, what books are you currently reading?"

Cathy shrugged. "I don't really read books," she said. "I'm not really a book person, you know? I like the daily paper, I mean, I never miss the daily paper! And magazines. I like magazines."

"Really? Which ones?" I was beyond hope. I knew there was no way in hell my date was going to respond, "Oh, *The New Yorker, Vanity Fair, Atlantic Monthly.*" But I had to keep this so-called conversation going, as apparently Cathy was unable to generate questions of her own.

"Um," she said, "like those ones that show recipes and pretty houses. Those kinds are good. They sell them in the supermarket, by the—what do you call that?—the checkout."

"Uh-huh," I said, nodding like a madman. "I wasn't aware there was much writing in . . . in those kinds of magazines."

Cathy swatted my arm. "Oh, silly, there isn't! That's why I like them! I look at the pictures of those pretty houses and I think, maybe someday I'll live in a big house like that!"

Not on my dime, I thought. What in God's name had Chrissy been thinking, setting me up with this woman? We had nothing, zero, zilch in common, and we could hardly have a coherent conversation. I had to get out of that date and fast. But how?

Diarrhea? If I claimed a sudden and debilitating attack of diarrhea, complete with a graphic account of what was happening in my pants, would that turn her off so much that she wouldn't want a second date—and let me out of this first one?

I snuck a look at my date over my menu. Her too-red lips were moving as she read her own menu. Oh, yes, I thought miserably, she'll want a second date no matter how disgusting my behavior this evening. I felt my shoulders slump. It was going to be a long, long night.

* 47 *

Does your spouse really need to know that when you were twenty you had sex with your best friend's father? What purpose would that information serve in your marriage today?

—Full Disclosure: Is It Ever Worth It?

JOHN

"You're a snob, John. So the woman didn't go to college. That doesn't mean she's an idiot."

"I'm not a snob," I protested. "I've met plenty of people without a college degree who are intelligent and successful. But believe me when I say this woman was neither. She doesn't read, Eva. She doesn't read! How could anyone who knows me even a little bit set me up with someone who's idea of literature is the back of a cereal box? Maybe Chrissy was pissed off about something I said and this was her idea of revenge."

Eva grinned. "It is pretty amusing, picturing you stuck with an imbecile."

"Don't call her an imbecile. She seemed nice enough. It's not her fault she's—"

"Stupid?"

I frowned. "Let's just say less than brilliant. Really, Eva, you're the snob. What happened? Back in college you were all about equality. You were democratic. An egalitarian."

"Why does everyone always talk about how I was in college?" she asked angrily.

"Everyone?"

"You and Sophie. For God's sake, let go of the past already! I was different back then, we all were. Well," she continued with an arch of her brow, "maybe not you. You were full of yourself then and you're full of yourself now."

"Eva," I said, "you don't know me even a little bit. You didn't when we were eighteen and you don't now that we're in our forties. It's too bad. I'm an okay guy."

"Huh. Says who?"

"Plenty of people," I assured her. "But back to your being a snob."

"I prefer to think of myself as an elitist."

"Same thing."

"No, it's not," she argued. "And what's wrong if I do have high standards? I apply them as much to myself as I do to others."

Eva spoke in the challenging way I'd come to know too well. I considered the strikingly attractive woman seated across the table from me. Her clothes were expensive. Her style was immaculate. Her figure had to cost time and effort to maintain. Her career was flourishing. Who would this woman consider an acceptable mate? The role, I thought, would be an almost impossible one to get—and to keep. I felt both pleased and bothered by this.

"It must be tough to live with yourself," I said, "always striving for perfection."

"It's not as hard as you think," she replied smoothly. "Perfection and I are often hand in hand."

I found a moment's relief in a long sip of wine. While so occupied I wondered if Eva was exaggerating for my benefit, or if she really considered herself to have achieved perfection.

Sophie joined us just then and I was relieved not to be alone any longer with Eva.

"I'm so sorry I'm late," Sophie said, dropping into a seat between Eva and me. "I was at a class and it ran long and I didn't feel comfortable slipping out."

"Of course," I said. "Was the class interesting?"

Sophie's face brightened. "Oh, yes." And while she told us about the exciting topic of title insurance, I watched Eva as best I could without arousing undue suspicion. Her face was a barely concealed mask of boredom. She almost seemed to be asleep with her eyes wide-open. What, I wondered, would touch this woman?

* 48 *

Dear Answer Lady:

Here's the deal. I have this friend who's a single mom. About two months ago she got an invitation to a wedding out in Missouri. She asked me if I would stay with her three-year-old while she went to the wedding and I don't know what came over me but I said yes. My friend is totally psyched about this trip because it's the first sort of vacation she's had since she got pregnant. Okay, so my problem is, I met this great guy last week and he asked me to go with him to some island (I forget which) the same weekend I'm supposed to watch my friend's kid. I don't know what to do! If I say no to this guy I could blow my chances with him and I get this really strong vibe that he's The One. But if I say yes to the guy, my friend probably won't be able to find someone else to stay with her kid so she won't be able to go to the wedding. I know she'll be really upset if I tell her the truth about why I can't help her out, so I'm trying to come up with a really good lie, something that will make her feel bad for me. Any ideas?

Dear My-Word-Is-Worth-Less-Than-the-Gum-on-the-Bottom-of-Your-Shoe:

I'm guessing that the concept of shame is foreign

to you, yes? I'm tempted to point out in excruciating detail everything that's wrong with you, and scum— sorry, people—like you. But I've had a rough day and the only real energy I can summon is for thoughts of the martini that awaits me at home. So, here's my suggestion: Go away with The (Potential) One. Tell him or don't tell him about your broken promise to your friend, I don't care. Your single mother friend doesn't need scum—sorry, a person—like you in her life; it's already burdensome enough. As for the An-swer Lady? I'll be imagining scenarios in which you meet a gruesome and bloody end between the jagged teeth of a shark. Bon voyage!

SOPHIE

I kept thinking about that woman alone at the bar, the woman I'd glimpsed the night of the awful date with Mark.

And while I knew I wasn't ready to eat out alone, I also knew that I was perfectly capable of going to the movies on my own. Really, how hard was it to walk to a theater, buy a ticket and maybe some popcorn with that fake butter (I know I shouldn't eat it but I really like it; Brad always scolded me about it.) sit in a seat, and watch a movie?

I was feeling pretty good about myself as I waited in the lobby of the funky, independent art house that was showing a recent, British adaptation of *Jane Eyre*. The only disap-pointing thing was that the tiny concession stand sold only coffee and muffins. Not that I'm opposed to muffins but I'd had my heart set on popcorn and fake butter. Next time, I thought, I'll go to a cineplex.

While I was thinking about popcorn and fake butter and Brad's scolding, I became aware of a man to my right, also waiting to be let into the theater. He had a sort of Romantic look; maybe it was the long black wool coat he wore, and the way his hair swept off his forehead. I guessed he was about six feet tall. His features were fine but not small. And then I saw that his eyes were a startling blue-green. In contrast to his dark hair they were extraordinary.

I looked away, not wanting to be caught staring. And when a few moments later I casually looked back, I found the man staring right at me! Well, I can't say it was love at first sight because I'm not sure such a thing exists. But honestly, I don't remember ever having felt what I felt in that moment with this stranger. Everything tingled. Everything sort of lit up. It was as if I recognized him as someone I had been waiting for—though, of course, how could that be?

The man smiled. I smiled back. Then he came over to me. Whatever happens with this man, I thought, will be significant.

"Hi," he said. "I'm Ben. Ben Marin."

"Sophie Holmes, hi."

"I'm really looking forward to the movie."

"Me, too."

If the conversation was less than stimulating, the feelings that coursed through me made up for it. I don't remember what else we said; I do remember wanting very badly to kiss him. I also remember that he never looked away while we stood there. I felt—noticed.

Before long the theater doors were opened and people began to rush ahead.

I wanted to say, *"Let's not go in."* I wanted to say, *"Let's go someplace together."* But I couldn't.

"So," Ben said, awkwardly, "uh, enjoy the movie."

I nodded. I'm not sure I said anything.

Ben walked ahead of me. I followed; when I got inside I couldn't see where he'd sat. I walked toward the screen and took a seat on the aisle. And through the entire movie, I hoped desperately that he would wait for me afterward.

When the final credits began to roll I felt panicked. I wanted to rush back to the lobby in the hopes of finding Ben.

But I also didn't want to seem overeager. I hate games but I suddenly found I wasn't immune to the desire to appear—desirable. Anxiously, I waited until the lights finally came up. The theater was almost empty. Seven people walked ahead of me toward the lobby; none of them was Ben.

Maybe, I thought, I should have dashed out of the dark before now. But maybe that would have been a bad idea, as Ben might have simply walked off, leaving me feeling like a foolish high school girl who waits by her crush's locker for a glimpse of her idol on the slim chance that he'll finally notice her as more than just a nuisance.

And then I walked into the lobby and saw him standing against a wall of posters. I wasn't sure he was waiting for me until I came close enough for him to step forward and smile.

"Hi," he said. "I was hoping I hadn't missed you."

"Oh, hi," I said. Could he tell that I was elated?

"Did you like the movie?" Ben asked.

"Oh, I did, very much."

Ben nodded. "Me, too." He hesitated for a moment before asking if I'd like to get some coffee and talk about it. "There's a good little place right down the block," he said. "If you've got the time."

"Yes," I said. "I have the time." We walked to the coffee shop and sat at a table for two. Ben paid for the coffees and for an oatmeal cookie, which we split. I watched his hands as he neatly broke the cookie in two pieces. I hadn't noticed them before. They were slim and looked strong. Brad's hands had gotten chubby. All of Brad had gotten chubby.

We spent a very pleasant hour talking about the movie and exchanging bits of vital information—including the interesting fact that we were both divorced from our college sweethearts. I could hardly believe how much time had passed when Ben checked his watch and explained that he had to dash off for a class.

"I teach Romance Languages at Longfellow College," he explained.

"Oh," I said. "I'm afraid I don't remember much of my French. I haven't spoken a word of it since college."

"That's okay," Ben said with a laugh. "We'll stick to English."

Ben asked if I was going in his direction. We could ride the T together, he suggested. For a moment I was tempted to lie and essentially tag along, but I told him the truth, that my apartment was in another direction entirely.

Maybe Ben appreciated my honesty. In any case, he didn't take my no as a brush-off because he asked if I'd like to meet again for lunch.

"Yes," I said, "I would like that." But should I give a stranger my phone number? Ben didn't feel like a stranger, but he was, after all. I thought about the neighbor who'd asked me out and wished I could turn to Eva for advice.

"Would you feel more comfortable if I gave you my number?" Ben asked, as if reading my mind.

I hesitated. And in those few moments something else happened between us, something extraordinary. I felt overcome by a feeling of—rightness.

"No," I said finally. "I'll give you my number."

Oh, I know it sounds ridiculous, and maybe what happened in those moments happened all in my head. Even so, I felt extraordinarily glad to have begun this unknown adventure.

We parted on the sidewalk outside the coffee shop. I watched him walk away. At the corner, he turned and waved. I raised my hand in return.

49

*There's no doubt in this writer's mind that corruption
must be routed and that to do so requires the moral
fiber of a true hero. There's also no doubt in this
writer's mind that the average person lacks such
moral fiber. Therefore, this writer's advice to the average person is as follows: keep your mouth shut and
your head down.*
　　—Whistle Blowing: Do You Have What It Takes?

JOHN

"So, what are some of the good things about marriage?"

Ellen looked up at me as if I were an odd art installation or
something else problematic. "Didn't we just have this conversation?" she asked.

I perched on her desk, my usual spot. "We had a conversation in a similar vein," I admitted.

"I should charge you by the hour for my advice."

I reached for my wallet and withdrew a credit card. "Use
my corporate account and have lunch at M. Kaye's tomorrow. You know how to forge my signature."

"In that case," she said, closing the file on which she was
working, "I'm more than happy to answer your question.
But I'm afraid I can't tell you about anyone's marriage but
my own. What Austin and I have is unique to us."

"Yeah, yeah," I said, "I know every marriage is different.

But what are some of the things you like about your marriage? I don't mean to be too personal," I added hastily.

Ellen frowned. "Why all the questions? Are you taking a survey?"

"Something like that, for my own edification. So?"

"Okay," she said. "Here's a good thing: Austin and I both like to go canoeing. Being married, and liking each other, mind you, allows each of us to do something we like—in this case, canoeing—together."

I nodded. "The best-friend aspect, of course."

"Someone to bitch to about your horrible day at work."

"Not that you ever have cause to complain about your boss."

"Of course not," Ellen said, eyes wide.

I wondered. It was possible to be lonely in a crowded room. It was possible to be lonely all alone. But was it really possible to be lonely in a good marriage? Probably, I thought. But maybe not for long.

"Since you're conducting this informal survey," Ellen said then, "you might want to take a look at your parents' marriage, or at your sisters' marriages. What seems good about those relationships?"

"I never gave my parents' marriage much thought," I admitted. "Until recently. And I've come to the conclusion that food is their primary mutual interest. And, I suppose, their kids. But really, I think it's mostly about homemade pasta. They work together in the kitchen like a well-oiled machine. I'm not criticizing, by the way, when I say they're bonded by something as mundane as food. My parents are very close. Whatever they have works for them."

"Keep in mind that it probably took years for them to develop into that smoothly functioning team."

"Of course. And I'm not saying they never fight. My mother nags. My father doesn't listen. He says he doesn't listen because she nags and she says she nags because he doesn't listen."

Ellen laughed. "It's one of the realities of a male/female relationship. Mars and Venus and all that. In my opinion it's absolutely unavoidable."

Was it?

"My sisters," I said, "seem to have chosen well. Frank and Mike adore their wives. And they respect them. Of course, my sisters pretty much demand the respect, but, at least when I'm around, it's forthcoming."

"Ah, when you're around. There's the problem with forming opinions about other people's relationships. No matter how much you think you know, there are volumes more that you don't. And what you think you know, based on observable behavior, might be mostly an act for the benefit of outsiders."

"Which is why," I said, "that outside of my professional capacity I keep my mouth shut when it comes to making comments on other people's relationships. At least, I try to keep my mouth shut. I don't always succeed."

Ellen raised an eyebrow at me. "I've noticed. But you're right to try. Unless someone's bleeding from the eyes and the partner's knuckles are bloody, it's wise to keep your advice to yourself. If people need help, they'll ask for it."

"Unless they're suffering from debilitating low self-esteem or any of the other psychological or emotional problems we see every week."

"Of course," Ellen conceded. "I was talking about the average person, not some poor woman plagued by deep-seated insecurity caused by an abusive childhood, or someone manipulated into submission by an evil control freak. With a tiny dick."

"It does make you wonder . . ."

"About the tiny dick? Please. Any man who mistreats his wife or girlfriend has an issue with his penis. It's a no-brainer."

"You've conducted studies?" I asked.

"I've been around," Ellen said with an air of superior

knowledge. "And we women talk. Of course, not all men with tiny penises are demonic assholes. In fact, I remember one guy from college, he was awfully sweet and he had this incredibly small—"

"Uh, Ellen?"

"Oh." Ellen had the grace to look chastened. "Right. Okay."

"And all this started when I asked you what you liked about your marriage."

"Hazelnut gelato," Ellen announced. "I'm mad for it and whenever I feel blue Austin brings home a pint for me. He doesn't even ask for a spoonful. And most times I don't give him one. But he still continues to know when I'm down, even if I've said nothing specific—and to show up with the gelato. That's one thing I like about my marriage."

"That's a big thing." What, I wondered, would I like a woman to bring me when I felt blue? I'd never thought about it.

"You bet it is," Ellen agreed. "And here's another big thing. Whenever I ask Austin if a particular dress or pair of pants makes me look fat he replies immediately and automatically, 'Of course not!'"

"He's well trained."

"That, and he knows I don't mind being lied to about certain topics. See, I'm not really asking for his opinion when I ask about the dress or the pants; I just want to hear the answer I want to hear. Austin has learned to distinguish a real question from a—let's call it a phony—question."

"Some men might call it a trick question," I pointed out.

"Not once they've memorized the answer," Ellen countered. "And his reply isn't really a lie, is it? It's all part of a game, a routine, the "Ellen and Austin Show." Every couple has their own little variety show. Believe me, it helps pass the time—arguing about the same old same old, using the same catch phrases, repeating favorite quotes from *The Simpsons*. It's good stuff, routine."

And speaking of routine . . . I slid off the desk. "I'd better get back to work," I said. "Thanks for the chat. And don't forget to return that credit card tomorrow."

Ellen grinned. "I won't. But you might regret having given it to me in the first place."

* 50 *

Dear Answer Lady:
   Last night my husband and I had dinner at a cool little restaurant in the next town over. At the end of the night he went to get the car and asked me to pay the bill. Here's the thing. We ate at the bar and had gotten into a lively conversation with a bunch of people, so I wasn't really paying much attention when the bartender put the check in front of me. (I'd also had a few glasses of wine.) Anyway, this morning, I couldn't find the credit card receipt in my bag. I have this horrible feeling that I left the restaurant without paying! What should I do? I'm so embarrassed. Should I just forget about it? It's not like we ever have to go back to that restaurant. Besides, I know my husband will make fun of me when he finds out I spaced so badly.

Dear Alcoholic:
   Get yourself to the restaurant as soon as it opens this evening, apologize, and pay your bill. Then proceed immediately to the nearest AA meeting. Have a nice day.

SOPHIE

I met Ben for lunch two days later. His tousled hair, his startling eyes, his way of looking right at me when we talked—it was all there again, those feelings I'd had the first time we met. Not that I was surprised. When he'd called to make the date his voice over the phone had made me smile.

And as we talked, as I learned more about him, I couldn't help but notice the glaring differences between Ben and Brad. Ben's demeanor, his way of listening, it seemed that everything about the way he walked around in the world set him apart from Brad. It made me feel . . . hopeful.

When we'd decided on what to eat (Was it meaningful that we chose the same dish? Brad and I never did.), Ben told me that he owned an apartment in the Back Bay (not far from my own in the Fen) and that he had two cats, Rousseau and Cellini.

"Brad wasn't fond of pets," I said, wondering if I should be mentioning my ex-husband again. "When Jake was ten he wanted a puppy but Brad said no."

"That's too bad," Ben said, neutrally.

"I'm more of a cat person, though. I had a cat for a long time when I was a girl. His name was Rutledge. I don't remember why."

Ben smiled. "Are you thinking about getting a cat now that you're on your own?"

The question affected me like a good shake. "I hadn't even thought about it," I admitted. "How odd. I guess that I can get a cat, now that—now that Brad's not around."

"It takes time to get used to living alone. And to living not in relation to a particular person's particular habits."

"Yes," I said, "I suppose it does. It's only been a few months, since, well, since everything's been final."

"So, you're new to the horror that is the midlife dating scene."

"Yes," I said. And I thought: This is a date, isn't it? Maybe it's not—how would I know? Maybe Ben is about to give me advice about dating and if so, should I assume he just wants to be my friend? But do single men befriend single women only for the companionship? "It feels really weird," I blurted.

Ben laughed. "Of course it does. There's something wrong about being in our situation. You have to find the absurd humor in it or you'll sink into depression."

"I'm not the depression type," I said honestly. "So I guess I'd better find the humor right away."

"You will. There are a lot of . . . interesting people out there."

But I'm not interested in them, I thought. I'm interested in you. And I need to know some things about you.

"So," I said, "you were married only once?"

Ben nodded. "That's right. Since my divorce I've had a few relationships that lasted more than a year. But none of them worked out, ultimately."

"I'm sorry," I said, but I wasn't sorry at all.

"Fortunately, the breakups were civilized." His expression turned thoughtful. "Well," he said, "except for one."

I wasn't sure I should ask for details. I wasn't sure I wanted to hear details.

Before I could open my mouth to say whatever it was I was going to say, Ben said: "I suppose that after dropping that tantalizing bit of information I owe you a more complete explanation."

"You don't owe me anything," I said, but maybe he did.

"Be that as it may . . . What happened was that I ended the relationship after about eight months. To me, it was obvious we weren't working as a couple, but she didn't see it that way."

"Oh," I said.

"She often didn't see the obvious, at least, in terms of human relationships. Otherwise," he said, "she was very smart. She was quite successful in her career."

I nodded, not necessarily encouraging Ben to go on but not deterring him, either.

"Anyway, she was upset when I ended things. Finally, of course, she moved on."

"And you haven't heard from her since?" I asked carefully. Even a big city could be a small town. "You don't run into her?"

"No, our social and professional spheres are quite separate. I have no idea what's going on with her. I hope she found someone more suitable than I was."

"More suitable," I said. "In what way?"

Ben laughed. "A man who doesn't want a commitment."

I said with a smile, "I thought all women were supposed to want a commitment."

"Yes, well, not this one. She told me that she'd never been in a long-term relationship before me. It seemed a bit odd. I don't think she had any understanding of what a committed relationship requires."

"Sacrifice," I said automatically. "Negotiation. Communication."

Ben laughed again. "I'm exhausted just thinking about it."

"But," I said, watching carefully for his reaction, "the payoff is worth it."

"It can be, sure."

"So, that relationship is entirely over?" I asked.

"Oh, yes." Ben looked at me suddenly with some embarrassment. "Maybe I shouldn't have brought it up. But the fact is I still feel bad about how things ended. It never feels good to hurt someone, even if the wound is delivered unintentionally."

The waitress arrived just then. As Ben ordered for us, I wondered: When had I last hurt someone? I'd certainly annoyed Brad over the years of our marriage, but right then I couldn't remember the last time I'd had to apologize to him—by which I mean, I couldn't remember the last time Brad and I had had any important argument in which I'd said something mean or hurtful. Even our divorce and the conversations that led up to it were relatively bloodless.

Apologies arise when there's a sense of accountability. To say, "I'm sorry" to someone—for a deed more significant than an accidental bump on the elbow—implies that there's been some significant interaction. It implies that you recognize a relationship and respect it. An apology arises from a social contract; a rule has been broken and an apology is an attempt to fix it. It's also an act of recommitment to the relationship.

For the last ten years of our marriage, Brad and I had been living apart, though under the same roof. We'd been the proverbial two ships passing in the night, aware of each other's presence but only as a darker shadow in the general darkness.

But that relationship was over. Now I wanted the chance to make a mistake with someone so that I would also have the chance to apologize. I wanted to mean something to someone, to have an effect on that person. I wanted to matter.

The waitress moved off and Ben smiled at me.

"What are you thinking?" he asked.

"That I'm very happy to be here."

* 51 *

When telling a lie, look directly into the person's eyes and speak calmly and with conviction. Forget the histrionics. Your boss is far more willing to believe that your dog ate the report you were supposed to hand in that day when such information is delivered in a rational manner than when it's delivered with bulging eyes and garbled speech.

—Foolproof Fibbing

EVA

A framed photo of a little boy stood on a side table. The frame was decorated with blue and purple teddy bears. I picked it up to look more closely. "I assume this is Jake?" I asked.

Sophie had invited me over for a drink after work. With nothing better to do—I'd cut Jake back to only two nights per week—I accepted her offer.

Sophie poked her head out of the kitchen. "Yes, when he was almost three. Wasn't he adorable?"

He really had been a cute kid. Dimples, big eyes, the whole thing. "Yeah," I said, "he was."

"He was the spitting image of Brad at that age. It was only when he got to be about five that he started to look a bit like my family."

Genetics. Interesting stuff. I returned the photo to the side table and settled onto the very comfortable couch. Aside from the tacky frame, the apartment was furnished tastefully. I don't have the skills to decorate but I know them when I see them.

Sophie emerged from the kitchen carrying a platter of cold shrimp with three different types of cocktail sauce. I reached for a shrimp as the platter touched the table. Sophie perched across from me on a caramel-colored leather armchair.

"Jake was potty trained very early," she announced. "He was so proud of himself! I remember him announcing to total strangers in the supermarket that he could 'make' all by himself. It was so cute!"

I'll bet. I just love strange kids telling me about their bowel movements. "That's nice," I said. Really, what else was there to say? Luckily, talk of bathroom activities doesn't affect my appetite. I downed another shrimp.

"Oh, yes, Jake was early with everything: crawling, walking, talking." Sophie laughed. "He'd kill me if he knew I told anyone this, but I just can't help myself. Do you know what he called his penis?"

Oh, God, she had to bring up the subject of Jake's penis. I was inordinately fond of that organ but had no desire to discuss it or anything about it with my lover's mother.

I just shook my head.

"He called it his weepee. Isn't that hysterical!"

"That's hysterical, all right," I agreed.

Sophie popped off to the kitchen again and returned with a silver bucket in which a bottle of wine nestled. All those years that Sophie played the corporate wife/semiprofessional hostess were really paying off for me. The woman knew her wines and she cooked a mean roast beef.

When she'd poured us each a glass I attempted to introduce a subject other than baby Jake. But before I could suggest a discussion about the president's latest verbal gaff, Sophie launched back into her favorite topic.

"You know," she said, "Jake will definitely want to settle

down someday, get married and have a family. I just hope he marries the right sort of woman."

Meaning, I thought, a woman weak enough to be controlled by her mother-in-law.

"Oh," I said. "And what kind of woman is that?"

"Well, someone educated, of course. Someone kind and loving, that goes without saying. But also someone really—I don't know, cozy. Yes, that's the word I'm looking for."

Cozy? Well, I reminded myself, it's not like you want to marry the kid. Still, I was a bit disconcerted to hear that for her son, my friend envisioned a woman almost entirely different from me.

The doorbell rang. Sophie hurried to the door and peered out the peephole.

"It's Jake!" she announced happily.

Oh, shit, I thought. I should have known this was within the realm of possibility. I finished my glass of wine in a gulp.

Sophie unlocked and opened the door. "Jake, what a nice surprise! Come in."

Jake leaned down to hug Sophie and caught my eye over his mother's shoulder. Instead of a wink like he'd given me at the ball game, Jake gave me a wide-eyed look that said, *"Believe me, I had no idea you were here."*

"Oh," he said when he'd pulled away from his mother's fierce embrace. "I didn't know you had company. Sorry."

"Oh, don't be silly, it's just Eva. You remember her from your game, don't you?"

Jake nodded. "Sure. I remember. Hey."

"Hey," I said, my voice surprisingly even.

"To what do I owe this pleasant surprise?" Sophie asked brightly. "I wasn't expecting to see you until tomorrow for dinner."

"Uh." Jake pointed to the duffel bag over his shoulder. "I just thought, I mean—"

Sophie laughed. "Of course I'll do your laundry. Just put the bag by the machines and join us for a bit."

With a distinctly sheepish expression, Jake loped off into the depths of the apartment.

His mother was still doing his laundry? I found this both annoying and somehow embarrassing, for both Jake and me.

"Isn't this nice?" Sophie asked rhetorically.

What could I answer? *"No, actually, this is incredibly uncomfortable for me, as I am, in fact, having sex with your son."*

Jake returned and looked from the couch to an empty chair well out of my reach. As he bolted for the chair I bolted to my feet and excused myself to the bathroom. Maybe, I thought, we could spend his entire visit in separate rooms.

In the bathroom I checked my watch. A normal bathroom run shouldn't take more than two or three minutes. If I hid out for much longer than that I'd run the risk of Sophie knocking on the door in concern. When the second hand indicated that just over three minutes had passed I took a deep breath and stepped into the hallway.

Jake appeared from the direction of the bedroom. Before I could take another step he'd pushed me against the wall and his lips were on mine.

I pushed him back but he still held my arms. "Get off me!" I whispered fiercely.

Jake grinned. "Don't you think this is kind of fun?"

"No, I don't. Let me—Let me go!" I shoved Jake and his hold broke.

"You really do work out, don't you?" he asked with a low laugh.

I gave him a nasty look. "You couldn't tell before this?" Men can be such blind idiots.

I hurried back to the living room. Sophie was just emerging from the kitchen with a plate of something in puff pastry.

"Where's Jake?" she asked with no trace of suspicion.

I shrugged. Jake then appeared from the hall and made an excuse for running off, after promising his mother he'd be on

time the following night. I didn't meet his eye when he offered his farewell.

When Jake was gone, Sophie perched on a chair and, a
propos of nothing, she said: "I still can't believe you're in advertising. I swear I thought you'd have published, oh, a
dozen books by now. Or maybe be teaching literature in a
private high school."

I smiled stiffly to hide my annoyance. You'd think I'd
signed a contract back in college, pledging that I would pursue my stated goals, and that I'd broken that contract. What
did they want me to do—apologize?

"What does it matter that I'm not doing what I wanted to
do when I was twenty?" I said. "How many people get to live
out their dreams? Besides, those old dreams don't count anymore. I like my life just the way it is. Really." I looked Sophie
squarely in the eye. "It's perfect."

Sophie looked back at me doubtfully.

All right, not even I believed me. It was time to redirect the
conversation.

"So, how's the dating game going?" I asked. "Have you
met anyone?"

Sophie refolded the linen napkin on her lap. "Oh, no one
special," she said in a voice that said, *"I'm evading your
question."*

Fine. So we each had our little secrets.

I left after a second glass of wine. Sophie didn't press me to
stay for dinner.

* 52 *

Dear Answer Lady:
    My new boyfriend started using a brand of cologne my old boyfriend used. Now all I can think about is how much I miss my old boyfriend. Should I tell my new boyfriend what I'm feeling or just say nothing?

Dear Hung Up on the Past:
    Tell the new b.f. you're allergic to his cologne and ask if he would mind not using it. Say nothing about it reminding you of the old b.f.—unless the new b.f. refuses to switch fragrances. In this case, tell the new b.f. he's hung a lot smaller than the old b.f. and be prepared to move out.

JOHN

I just couldn't face another bad date, not without some time to lick my wounds.

But Eva? Was asking my prickly, insult-wielding old friend to join me for a night out really a wise thing to do, especially in my battle-weary state?

Maybe not. Probably not. But I had two free tickets to the new David Mamet play. And, I'll admit to a typical male stubbornness. It drove me crazy that I couldn't break through Eva's misconceptions about me as a person. Since college she'd persisted in seeing me as an unethical cad, and though almost everything else about her seemed to have changed, this one notion had remained fixed.

I wanted to change Eva's mind about me. I wanted her to see me as I really was: flawed, yes, but also good. At least, I wanted her to see me as someone who tried to be good.

Which brings us to the next million-dollar question. Why was Eva's good opinion of me so important? I'm not the type of guy who needs to be liked by everyone. I'm not the type who needs everyone's good opinion. Too many people are simply not worth my efforts to impress . . . the wife-beaters, the murderers, the people who don't pick up after their dogs. If that makes me a snob or an elitist, then, fine, maybe Eva was right in that regard.

Still, Eva was one of the people I wanted—needed?—to like and respect me. Maybe, I thought, just maybe, if she spent more time with me she might come to see that she'd misjudged me.

Hope springs eternal in the human breast. Sometimes, I've learned, hope should be blindfolded, gagged, and chained to a chair.

I made the call, pretty much assuming that Eva would say no, and unceremoniously at that. But she surprised me.

"Sure," she said immediately, "I'd love to go. Reviews of the show are great. Thanks."

"Great," I said, taken aback. "How about we have dinner first? Maybe at Donna Q's?"

"Sure," she said again. "I was there last week. The service is still working out its kinks but the food was fabulous."

We made plans to meet at the restaurant and hung up after a pleasant good-bye.

Well, I thought, sitting back in my chair with a grin and congratulating myself on my persistence, this could be the new beginning of a beautiful friendship.

53

Not every cheating partner is thorough in his or her attempt to hide the affair. Some cheaters want to get caught (for a variety of reasons, see Chapter Five), so discovering their infidelity is almost too easy. Don't give such a person what he wants, which is often a rapid divorce. Let him stew in anxiety while you collect the clues with which you will hang him.
    —Is That Lipstick on Your Collar? How to Tell If
      Your Partner Is Cheating

EVA

I was thrilled about the opportunity to see the new Mamet. The run was entirely sold out and so far, none of my clients had been of any use in digging up even one lousy, partial-view seat.

True, this did mean I'd have to spend the evening with John, and that prospect didn't excite me at all. I fully expected to be criticized, mocked, and subjected to tales illustrating how selfless and talented he was. But third-row seats! For third-row seats I could deal with an egomaniac for a few hours. And, as I'd told John, the food at Donna Q's really was amazing. The striped bass with roasted minivegetables in a butter sauce would help ease the pain of listening to stories about John's precious little nieces and nephews.

Really, I thought, it was a pretty good deal in the end. But sometimes, even I can be wrong.

He started in on me at dinner. I like to check my watch every once in a while. Big deal. But to John, it was.

"You've got somewhere better to be?" he asked, with a nod at my wrist.

"I just like to keep track of the time."

"You've checked your watch every ten minutes since we sat down."

I eyed him. "You've been timing my time checks?"

"Time flies when you're having fun. I sense you're not having fun."

"Maybe I would be having fun," I shot back, "if you stopped being so annoying."

John took a sip of his wine, then said: "Don't worry. We won't miss the curtain. I'm never late to anything important."

"How mature of you," I mocked, though didn't I share the same habit of punctuality, and wasn't I proud of it?

John frowned disapprovingly, something he's quite good at. "You've changed, Eva," he said.

"And you haven't changed one bit," I snapped.

But he did look good, even better than he'd looked in college. A woman would have to be dead not to find him attractive. This pissed me off.

"You used to be a lot less nasty."

"And you're still the same holier-than-thou, know-it-all you always were."

"Ah, yes, the one thing that hasn't changed is your lack of correct perception."

And then, the words came flying out of my mouth like bullets flying out of a gun. "I'm seeing someone, you know, and he's quite a bit younger, only half my age."

I couldn't quite read the look on John's face as he

processed this information. It was a mix of anger, disapproval, and maybe even disappointment.

And then, suddenly, his expression returned to its usual calm and he said: "Why are you wasting your time?"

"Wasting my time? Have you got a better way for me to be spending the nights?"

It was a challenge that I didn't really mean to issue.

John's expression remained neutral. "Of course not," he said evenly. "Why would I?"

"Are you implying," I asked, pressing him for a fight (but why!), "that I should be out looking for a suitable husband? Are you saying that my time is running out, that I'm getting too old to be single?"

"Of course not," John said again.

But I know a lie when I hear one. I'm sure he was thinking that my time would be better spent attempting a relationship with a man who was classified as suitable husband material. Someone, for example, like him?

"Are you saying that my lover is only having sex with me out of pity?" I persisted. There, I'd expressed the slight but nagging fear that Jake was, indeed, having sex with me out of a general sense of pity for single women over forty.

"No," John said with exaggerated patience. "That's not at all what I'm saying. But if the shoe fits . . ."

I didn't reply to John's nasty comment. Instead I gripped my fork and wondered what, exactly, Jake wanted from me, really. Just sex—or did he hope to get something more tangible and lasting from me, like a good job after graduation? Money? Was my twenty-one-year-old lover using me for material gain?

"Look," I blurted, "don't tell Sophie I'm seeing someone."

"Someone," John countered, "or someone her son's age?"

I felt sick. Had John guessed the truth? No. He was just being his usual superior self.

"Just do me a favor and don't tell her I'm seeing anyone," I repeated.

"Don't worry," John said, with an annoying little wink. "It will be our little secret."

"So," I said with a bright and phony smile, "how's the wife search working out for you?"

"Just fine," he said, but I wasn't going to allow him to dismiss the subject so easily with that obvious lie.

I laughed. "Sure. That's why you're sitting here tonight with me. Face it, John," I pronounced, "you're not the marrying kind. You're far too self-absorbed."

Again, John's usually placid expression darkened into a mix of black emotions. Well, I'd wanted a fight, hadn't I?

"That's entirely unfair," he said with barely restrained fury. "How can you call me self-absorbed when I'm trying to add meaning to my life by making a commitment to someone? What about you? Indulging in a strictly sexual affair is displaying an enormous amount of self-concern."

"What makes you think my affair is all about sex?" I demanded.

"Please, Eva. What could you possibly have in common with someone twenty years your junior? Unless, of course, you both share an avid interest in some arcane topic like, I don't know, the mating rituals of *Tyrannosaurus rex*. Then, well, I can see the mutual attraction."

It was useless to argue this particular point so I replied to another implicit charge against my character.

"Well, I'm not hurting anyone, am I?"

"I don't know," John said promptly, "are you? How's your boy toy going to feel when you toss him aside for the next new attraction?"

Another unanswerable question. I knew I would be the one ending the affair. And I knew Jake would be hurt. I knew these things like I knew my name was Eve. Eva.

God, John was a pain in the ass. I made a big show of looking at my watch again and announced, "We should get the check if we're going to be in our seats before curtain call."

54

Dear Answer Lady:
I'm getting married next month to a really great guy. The thing is, I don't really love him. I guess I got really excited when he gave me a big ring and then there were the parties and the gifts and all. I don't want to hurt his feelings—he really is great—so should I just go ahead and marry him?

Dear Nasty Bitch:
Do the poor guy a favor and end it. Now.

JOHN

What had I been thinking when I asked Eva to spend the evening with me? Well, I know what I had been thinking, but why hadn't I had enough sense to back away from such an insurmountable challenge?

Because you're an idiot, John. That's why you didn't have the sense. Idiots don't have sense. They're idiots.

Every conversation with Eva degenerated into a squabble. Back in college our repartee had been fun and good-natured, if sometimes a bit stinging. Underneath the elaborate insults had been laughter and a sense that, somehow, we were actually pretty much the same person, Eve and I. Or so I'd thought. Maybe I'd been wrong back then. Maybe Eve had never really liked me. Maybe I'd been under a delusion those four years, knowing for sure that she didn't want to date me but falsely believing she appreciated my friendship.

Well, there was absolutely no doubt in my mind that at this point in time, Eva hated me.

We sat moodily through the show. I tried to pay attention to the supposedly stirring dialogue but all I could think about was the furious woman sitting next to me in the darkened theater. At one point my arm accidentally, I assure you, touched hers on the armrest. She yanked her arm away as if my touch was poisonous. At another point I snuck a quick peek at her, in an effort to determine if she was at all enjoying the show she'd been so eager to see. Her posture was rigid; her profile betrayed a frown.

We parted that night with barely a nod and not one word. Eva hailed a cab and was off before I could raise my hand to hail a cab of my own. But then I decided to walk. Exercise can help work off frustration. So can alcohol. On the way back to my apartment I stopped for a nightcap at the Oak Room. But even a shot of smooth, one-hundred-year-old whiskey did little to budge the dark mood that sat heavily on my shoulders.

* 55 *

EVA

God, I can be an idiot. No theater experience could ever be worth the agony of spending time with that man.

* 56 *

Dear Answer Lady:
I think my husband is cheating. One night a week he works late, or says he is, and when he comes home he jumps right in the shower, before even kissing me hello. Should I confront him? Help!

Dear Hopelessly Naive:
Of course he's cheating. Unless he's out playing basketball at the gym with his buddies, there's no need for a late-night shower. Serve the bum divorce papers pronto.

SOPHIE

"It's official. I'm a licensed real estate agent in the state of Massachusetts. So, can I interest you in a ranch in the lovely town of Winchester?"

Ben laughed. "No, but thanks, anyway. And congratulations, Sophie."

We raised our glasses of Prosecco (Ben had brought a bottle for our celebration.) in a toast. I felt happier than I'd felt in ages. Okay, a bit nervous, too, starting out on this new venture, but also very excited.

"So," Ben said, "tell me all about your first day."

I did, every little detail. Ben was a good listener. And he asked questions. He wasn't dismissive; he didn't talk down to me the way Brad used to, as if he was an all-knowing father and I was his unknowing child. Ben's attention and respect meant a lot to me. That and the fact that his kisses made me weak in the knees.

"I really feel committed this time," I said finally. "There's nothing to stop me, is there? I can make this career as big as I want to."

Ben squeezed my hand. "I'm glad for you, Sophie. It's always good to set yourself a goal."

Yes, I thought, I guess it is. Moving back to the East Coast had made me realize that I needed to matter to someone other than my family and my friends. I needed to matter to me. I needed to have expectations of myself.

"Where do you want to have dinner?" Ben asked. "We have to continue the celebration."

Yes, I thought, we did. "How about we order in?" I suggested, sliding closer to Ben. "Let's celebrate, just us two."

Ben stayed over that night. He didn't have class until eleven so we spent most of the morning together as well. I learned that Ben had a banana and black coffee for breakfast every morning except Sunday, when he liked to go to a diner for a big, greasy egg feast. We made a date for the following Sunday at the diner of my choice. (I made a mental note to ask one of my new colleagues about local diners.) Before he finally left we shared another long and passionate kiss.

My life, I thought, is wonderful. Everything is falling into place. I have a lovely man (and getting him had been pretty easy!), a new career, a loving son, and two dear friends. The future, I thought, looks very, very bright.

57

Repeat five times, three times a day: Say one thing, believe another.

—Hypocrisy for Beginners

EVA

Really, the entire thing was my fault. Or, if fault is the wrong word, then let's say the entire thing was a result of my poor choice.

What made me say yes to Jake's suggestion that we go out to a club on a Saturday night? Where there was loud music and overpriced fluorescent drinks. Where there was bound to be a big, smelly splash of puke on the sidewalk outside. Where there was sure to be backed-up toilets in the ladies' room.

What, indeed? Maybe I was trying to prove that I could still stay up past eleven o'clock. Maybe I wanted to throw the kid a bone; after all, he wasn't allowed in my apartment and I wouldn't be seen in public with him during normal business hours or in places where I might run into people I knew. And, okay, I did feel a tiny bit bad about having "cheated on him" with Sam that time he was so hurt about my not taking him to my company's boring charity auction.

Whatever the exact motivations behind my agreeing to go to this club, they were wrong and stupid.

I didn't even go to clubs when I was of club-going age. Sophie would beg that I accompany her but I never relented. I just couldn't imagine a worse way to spend several precious hours of my life than being butted around by a drunken mob, most of whom—and here, I was English-major prejudiced—had probably never even heard of Thomas Carlyle.

"What are people wearing to clubs these days?" I asked Jake, ever so casually.

He shrugged. "I don't know." Jake might have his sensitive side but it didn't include a knowledge of women's fashions.

In the end I wore slim black pants, a white fitted T-shirt, and a black leather blazer. I don't believe a forty-two-year-old should dress in styles meant for women half her age. I don't believe in setting myself up for derision. If I turned out to be the only female not baring her stomach or her butt crack, fine. At least I would have my dignity.

The dignity of the middle-aged woman.

The evening was a disaster from the moment Jake and I, hand in hand (He took my hand; I tried to pull away; he wouldn't let go.) squeezed into the jammed, gyrating club. We made our way to the main bar and after being jostled and elbowed by guys who reeked of testosterone and girls who reeked of cheap perfume, we finally got our drinks. It was the worst martini I'd ever had.

We stumbled away from that particular throng and found a relatively safe space to stand. Real conversation was, of course, impossible in such a place, so we drank in silence until a slightly bulbous guy about Jake's age, wearing a baseball cap turned backward and a black T-shirt proclaiming I BRAKE FOR BABES, loped over and slapped Jake on the back hard enough to make him stumble.

"How's it hanging, dude?" the guy bellowed.

Jake looked distinctly uncomfortable. His eyes darted from the guy to me, and back again. Finally, he said: "Uh, Phil, this is Eva. Eva, this is my friend Phil."

I put out my hand. "How do you do?"

Phil looked at my hand as if it was covered in boils before taking my fingertips for a bare second.

"Hey," he said. He did not ask me how I was doing. He turned immediately to Jake.

"Dude, did you see that girl I was talking to over by the couches? Damn, she's hot." Here, Phil made a crude gesture that even I, jaded as I am, found offensive.

Jake froze. Really, it looked as if someone had injected ice into his veins he got so stiff and dumb. Even his pig of a buddy noticed.

"Oh," he said, darting a look at me. "Sorry. I, you know—"

"Of course," I said. "No offense taken."

Lamely, Phil patted Jake's shoulder and mumbled something and then he was gone.

Jake began to thaw, but slowly. I should have kept my mouth shut. But I didn't.

"What is his problem?" I spat. "He could barely look at me. He acted as if he were afraid of me, or like I had a giant open sore on my face."

Jake's tone was apologetic. Was he apologizing to me or for Phil? "He just doesn't get, you know, what we're doing."

"What is it, in fact, that we're doing?"

Jake's eyes darted around, as if what he was about to say was somehow shameful. "You know," he said quietly, "being a couple."

"Ah," I said. "He thinks I'm a heartless, powerful woman who is only using you for sex until an even cuter model comes along?"

"No, that's not it. He just"—Jake frowned and seemed to be searching for the right words—"he doesn't share my interest in older women. He's kind of turned off by the whole thing. It's like he thinks women over thirty-five are, I don't know, monsters or something."

"I see," I said.

I wasn't entirely sure I needed to be privy to Phil's extreme prejudice. What did Jake expect me to do with that nasty bit of information? Invite the kid out to dinner with us? Bake him a pie just like his mommy used to make? Or kick him in the nuts?

Then again, I had asked to know why Phil had acted like a jackass.

"I'm sorry about all this," Jake said when I'd been silent for too long. "This was a bad idea. Do you want to leave? We can go back to my place and hang out."

My pride, though shaken, would not allow me to retreat.

"Don't be silly, of course not. The night is young. Besides, do you really think I would allow a narrow-minded little prick like your friend Phil to bother me?"

I smiled falsely, brightly. Jake frowned. Maybe he didn't like his lover calling his buddy a prick.

I made my way back to the bar. Jake followed. I shouted to the bartender for another lousy martini. The bartender asked Jake if he wanted another beer. Jake shook his head. He had a test the next morning. Good boy that he was, he wanted to have a clear head.

"Hey." I looked toward the sound of the affected female voice. "You want to dance with me?"

Wedged between Jake and me stood a girl, her shiny head tilted up to Jake.

"I'm sorry," I heard Jake say. "I'm here with my girl-friend."

The girl turned. She looked me over from head to toe and back again. And then, she laughed. "You're dating her?" she asked, turning back to Jake. "I thought she was, like, your aunt or something."

She hadn't even tried to lower her voice. She probably assumed I was old enough to be hard of hearing.

Jake's face went ashen. I knew he would never hit a woman but I would have enjoyed watching him knock her off her candy-pink heels. But Jake just stood there, staring at nothing, and with another disbelieving laugh the girl walked off, her ass twitching in a pair of skintight stovepipe jeans.

Uncharacteristically, I could think of nothing to say. Neither, it seemed, could Jake. He mumbled, "I have to go to the men's room," and turned away.

When he was out of sight I grabbed my bag—a Hermes that little bitch could never afford—and pushed through the throng. At the door I waited impatiently for a gaggle of giggling girls to tumble in and then I bolted out onto the sidewalk.

Barely a second later, I heard Jake's voice.

"Wait, Eva, where are you going?"

I kept my back to him and strained to spot an empty cab.

"Home."

"But you can't go home alone."

"Why not?" I whirled around to face him. In the deep blue light of the club's marquee his face looked alien to me. "Because I'm a pitiful old lady who needs protection?"

Jake grabbed his hair close to his scalp. Who knew I could be so frustrating? "No, God, Eva—"

"Look," I said, suddenly immensely weary, "I know none of this is your fault. But I just—" I shook my head, unable to go on.

"I'm sorry about what happened back there, with that girl. I should have said something. I should have done something. Please, please come home with me." Jake's eyes were dark with concern. "Let me make it up to you."

A cab swooped to the curb and I grabbed for the door handle. "Not tonight, Jake," I said, tightly. He reached for my arm but I slipped into the cab before he could make contact. Jake stood there, waiting for something from me, but I kept my eyes straight ahead.

I gave the driver my address. He pulled out into traffic. And then the tears began to trickle down my face.

58

Dear Answer Lady:

Last weekend my girlfriend dragged me to some park for a "walk." Believe me, it turned out to be a freakin' hike. I almost broke my ankle on the roots of a stupid tree. Anyway, the signs said you had to "pack out" your trash. But there was no way I was going to carry around stinky sandwich wrappers and empty soda cans all day! So when my girlfriend wasn't looking I dropped our trash behind a big rock. But she caught me later when she went into my backpack looking for the trash that was supposed to be there. Man, she really reamed me about it. I think she's becoming some environment freak or something. But I'm like, what's the big deal about one lousy bag of trash? Can you talk some sense into her?

Dear Girlfriend of Nimrod:

Your imbecile of a boyfriend asked me to talk some sense into you so here goes: Dump him. If he's too lazy and unconcerned to follow a basic practice of environmental etiquette, he's never going to make it as a husband or father. Next time try meeting someone with a conscience.

EVA

To use a tired but apt expression, the bloom was off the rose.

This, of course, was inevitable. No relationship can avoid the introduction of reality, unless it ends with a tragic parting (I'm thinking of Romeo and Juliet here.) in its infant days. While the disaster at the nightclub was the defining moment, the turning point, the truth was that for weeks Jake had been getting on my nerves.

That ridiculous ambush in the hallway of Sophie's apartment! And I just couldn't stand how he always missed a few hairs when he shaved and how he never finished a cup of coffee without reheating it five or six times. I hated the fact that there were no wrinkles around his eyes when he smiled. None.

The truest words ever spoken: Youth is wasted on the young.

Still, the sex was great so I stayed on, in spite of Jake's faults, and in spite of the fact that I kept finding myself thinking of John.

Life can be cruel.

First of all, I felt bad about the way I'd behaved that night at the theater. There'd been no reason for me to be so obnoxious. After all, John did provide the tickets and did offer to pay for dinner (if throwing a credit card at the bill equaled an "offer"). As it turned out, I threw my card on top of his and we split the bill.

Another thing was bothering me: I couldn't figure out why I'd told John about Jake. I thought about my motives, I did, but couldn't come up with a plausible reason for "sharing" that bit of personal information. You would almost think I wanted to make John jealous but that was totally ridiculous.

Anyway, I wanted to apologize to John but the thought terrified me. I imagined his gloating grin and self-righteous lessons in proper behavior.

Maybe, I thought, it was best to simply go on as if nothing had happened. Eventually, the bad feelings would go away. I was sure they would. Bad feelings always go away. Sometimes you have to force them to leave but they do, eventually. Eventually.

* 59 *

Accuracy is for accountants. Approximation is for life.

—The Imprecise Nature of Truth

JOHN

One o'clock in the morning and I was staring at the ceiling of my bedroom, obsessing. Vanessa. Cat. Cheryl. Kelly. Cathy. The others not worth a mention.

And Eva.

Eva. Why had she told me about her juvenile lover? She'd thrown the information at me, like it was supposed to hurt me or at least make some sort of big impact. Could it possibly have been to make me jealous?

Ridiculous. But how had she wanted me to react? Just the way I had—with disdain and mockery? Or had she wanted me to pretend I wasn't bothered by the news that she was having sex with a kid?

I wondered: Had I tipped my hand by behaving badly? Did Eva suspect that I was interested in her, in spite of her being such a pain in the ass?

I threw off the covers and stomped to the kitchen. It was clear. I was spending way too much time with women. Look what had happened to me. I was lying awake at night desperately trying to analyze every little bit of a conversation, just like I'd witnessed my sisters doing throughout their teen years. "What do you think he meant by 'I like you'? Did he mean, like-like or just, you know, *like?*"

I stared into the fridge and wondered why the hell I was even in the kitchen. More adopted female behavior, late-night eating to dull the misery of a lousy love life. Clearly, I was becoming a disgrace to my sex. Somebody, I thought, should stage an intervention.

I slammed the fridge shut and stomped back to bed. I grabbed the remote off the nightstand and flipped madly through all nine hundred stations, looking for an old *Dirty Harry* movie, or maybe something starring Al Pacino, something masculine and gritty, a film in which guys took action instead of whining and worrying.

But all I could find was a Lifetime movie about a single mother with a violent five-year-old son and a boyfriend whose patience was wearing thin.

I turned off the television in disgust. Maybe, I thought, I should just scrap the idea of finding Ms. Right—and the idea of having any sort of relationship with Eva other than the purely antagonistic one we seemed to have now.

Being alone, I knew.

* 60 *

Dear Answer Lady:

My husband has a terrible habit of holding on to every piece of clothing he's ever owned. He insists on keeping T-shirts that are full of holes and covered in stains! The thing is, he doesn't wear these old things; he just likes to keep them around. And he keeps buying more stuff! His closet is stuffed to the gills but he won't let me throw out the old to make room for the new—which means that the new gets totally wrinkled the minute I put it away! As the one who does the laundry and ironing, am I justified in slipping a few ratty T-shirts into the garbage each week?

Dear Pathetic Housewife:

You are completely justified in tossing out your husband's crap. If he notices something missing—and I'm betting he won't—just shrug and deny any knowledge of its whereabouts. You won't be lying because said item could be at the bottom of the ocean or the top of a burning dump or wherever it is that garbage goes. The biggest concern here is that you felt the need to ask permission to take possession of your husband's personal items. Might I suggest a workshop on the topic of self-empowerment?

SOPHIE

Eva told me she was tired. John told me he'd been thinking of catching a movie.

"But we haven't seen each other, all three of us, in a while," I'd argued. "We won't make it a late night. Just a quick dinner."

Eva finally relented, but only, she told me, to stop my "whining." John, too, finally agreed, I think because he hates to disappoint the people he cares about.

We met at Marino's—John's favorite restaurant had become one of mine, too—at seven and I swear, it wasn't two minutes after seven before I noticed that something was up. Or different. Or—wrong. Both Eva and John were acting all awkward. Eva shot a glance at John; when he looked her way, she looked away. John shot a glance at Eva; when she looked his way, he looked away. Eva dropped her napkin, the kind of thing she never does. John spilled water on his silk tie, the kind of thing he never does.

Oh, yes. Something had happened between them, I was sure. But what? Sexual tension could account for the change, but not entirely. More likely, I thought, they'd had a particularly bad fight and hadn't gotten around to making up.

Well, I thought, I guess it's up to me to play good hostess and put the guests at ease. And maybe, in the process, one of them would drop a hint that would help me figure out what was going on.

But conversation was dull, no matter what interesting topic I introduced—Jake, real estate, the carpeting I was thinking of getting for the bedroom. "Oh," I said finally, desperately, "I saw this great movie on TV the other night. It was called *The Seducer*. And it was about this man who goes to these amazing lengths to seduce old rich women—"

"I wonder," John interrupted (unlike him), "if other primates keep secrets or employ deception in their social life. I'd like to know the answer to that."

My eyes shifted quickly to Eva, then back to John. I tensed, half-expecting a paranoid response from Eva and a cutting reply from John.

But when Eva spoke her tone was thoughtful. I relaxed just a bit.

"If humans are the only ones to lie, cheat, and steal—all forms of deception—does that mean that success as a species depends, at least partly, on the capacity for unethical behavior?"

"Of course not," I said. "That can't be right."

Eva shrugged, not convinced.

"I should ask my nephew Scott," John said. "He's really into animals. If he doesn't know the answer he'll make it a project to find out."

"So he can educate his old uncle." Eva smiled a bit to soften her words. John smiled back, though not exactly at her.

"Kids love teaching grown-ups. Jake would downright gloat when he knew something I didn't. Then again," I added, "so would Brad, so in this case maybe it's something he got from his father."

"People rely too much on genetics to excuse or explain their weaknesses," Eva said in her usual forceful way. "They say: 'My mom is overweight so of course I'm overweight and there's nothing I can do about it.' I say: 'Yes there is. Put down the fork and pick up the medicine ball.' There's a fatalism at work there I just can't stand."

"Fatalism," John said, "or laziness. Or, in some cases, maybe a fear of changing so much that you become unrecognizable to your family, even to yourself. Changing so much that you no longer belong in the world from where you came."

"You mean," I said, "that some people fall back on what they know—their family, for instance—because they're afraid of success?"

"They're afraid of outgrowing their parents' world, which was their childhood world. They're afraid of having to find a new life, a new tradition. They're afraid of cutting ties," Eva said.

I considered Eva's words. I'd tried to raise my son to be unafraid of challenge and change. Had I done enough? Too little? Well, I thought, time alone will tell if Jake will surpass his parents' achievements. Time alone will show the places Jake will go, maybe places I couldn't imagine myself ever going. That thought scared me. Someday I might lose my son to a world in which I was a foreigner.

"Change isn't always a good thing," I said. "Sometimes it's best to stay put."

Eva gave me her patented look of exasperation. I ignored it.

"It's true that some people let the past hinder them from growing," John said then. "But I like to think the majority of people want to transcend the limitations of their family and early environment."

"I certainly did. I certainly do." Eva paused before adding: "Sometimes I think my sister aspires to be less than what my parents hoped she would be. Can you aspire to failure?"

"Maura hardly sounds like a failure," I noted. "She's married and has a family."

Eva looked chastened (unlike her). "Yes, well, I didn't mean a 'failure,' exactly."

"You meant that you see more potential in her than she does in herself?" John asked.

Eva gave John another small smile. "Yes. Exactly."

What, what, what was going on? I wondered again.

"Brad's boss at one time was this superintelligent man with several degrees in business. He was nice, too, involved in the community, all that. And his wife was just as nice. She taught philosophy at the university. Anyway, both of their sons got involved with drugs and dropped out of high school."

Eva shrugged. "You can't blame the parents. Everyone is responsible for his own life."

"But what about children who fall apart?" I argued. "Legally, morally, they're the parents' responsibility. Are children really capable of making smart life choices? Anyway, my point is that these two boys had parents who were achievers and, really, I met them, they were lovely people. So, what went wrong? Maybe the boys had some genetic deficiency or something that made them, I don't know, more like an uncle who wound up on the streets."

"I'm afraid the nature/nurture argument is one neither side will ever win," John said. "And I, for one, am not qualified to expound on the subject."

I expected Eva to jump on John's last remark, to twist it into an insult, to say something like, *"You're not qualified to expound on any subject more difficult than twirling spaghetti around a fork."* But she didn't.

Yes, something had happened between Eva and John. Maybe, I thought, they need a few minutes alone.

"Excuse me," I said. "I'm going to the ladies' room."

* 61 *

Some people when lying will break out in a profuse and unusually odiferous sweat. Have the room de-odorizer at hand before confronting such a person.
  —Everyone Has a Tell: Learning to Read the
  Language of Deception

EVA

I hadn't seen John since the night I'd behaved like such a jerk. I'd been waiting for the guilt to go away but it hadn't gone anywhere. In fact, it had dug itself deeper in my brain, or wherever it is guilt resides. Now, sitting face-to-face with him, I knew an apology was necessary. An opportunity came when Sophie went to the ladies' room.

"I—"

"Look—"

John gestured for me to go ahead. I steeled myself for his mockery.

"Look," I said, "about that night at the theater."

"Yeah."

"I acted like a bit of an ass. I guess I was in a bad mood or something. I'm sorry."

John nodded. "Yeah, I'm sorry, too. I guess I wasn't in the best of moods, either."

I was shocked. John had apologized. His expression was sincere. Where was the gloating, the moralizing?

"Truce?" he asked when we had looked silently at each other for a long, strange moment.

"Yeah." My voice sounded a little wobbly. "Truce."

I'm not sure what might have happened if Sophie hadn't returned to the table at precisely that moment, because I had the odd conviction that I was going to lean across the table and kiss my old friend. Or that he was going to lean across the table and kiss me.

"I'm back!" she announced unnecessarily.

"There you are," I said stupidly.

"We missed you," John said ridiculously.

Just then, John's cell phone rang—well, it vibrated, John being the sort to always turn the ringer off in public places.

"Damn," he said, when he'd snapped the phone shut. "Sorry. I've got to go. Emergency."

"I thought only doctors got called away from dinner," I said lightly.

"Yeah, well, you thought wrong." John took a few bills out of his wallet and laid them on the table. "Let me know if I owe more."

"Poor John," Sophie said when he'd gone. "He works so hard."

"He likes it," I said. And then: "I admire him for it."

Sophie shot me a glance.

"What?" I asked. "I can say nice things about him, too."

"I've never heard you say anything good about John."

I shrugged in a way I hoped appeared casual. "Well, there isn't all that much nice to say."

"Well," Sophie said, reaching for her menu.

"I'm in the mood for a steak," I said. "You?"

* 62 *

Dear Answer Lady:
I live in an apartment building with a laundry room on each floor. One day shortly after moving in last year the machines on my floor were broken so I took my laundry to another floor. In one of the dryers I found this awesome T-shirt. It was so cute I took it back to my apartment. Since then, I check the machines on every floor a few times a week to see what other great stuff has been left behind. The way I see it, if you're careless enough to forget your stuff, then someone else deserves to take it. But when I told my boyfriend about it, he got all huffy and said that I was stealing. He's wrong, right?

Dear Crook:
Your boyfriend is right and you are wrong, end of story. Buy your own awesome, cute, and great stuff, you little bitch.

SOPHIE

"I think I'll have the cod," I said. "I feel bloated when I eat red meat."

Eva's eyes remained on her menu. "You should exercise. You'll feel a lot better. And you won't feel bad about treating yourself once in a while."

I caught myself before saying that Ben and I had talked about renting bikes that weekend. "Yes," I said, "I suppose I should exercise."

But my mind wasn't on my health. It was on Eva and John. I was sure something significant had happened while I'd been in the ladies' room, maybe a moment of reconciliation. Or maybe something more, something . . . romantic.

Of course, I couldn't just confront Eva. Can you imagine how she'd react? But I could dance around the topic. The waiter appeared and took our order. When she'd gone, I said to Eva: "I think John is looking well these days. I mean, better than usual."

"Really? I thought he looked kind of worn out."

"Well, he does work hard."

"Yes," Eva noted, "we've already talked about that."

We had, hadn't we? "Have you ever met his family?" I asked.

"I don't think so. Why?"

"I was just wondering. He's very close to his sisters. I read somewhere that men who are close to their sisters make great husbands."

Eva took a sip of her wine. "I wouldn't know," she said.

"Brad doesn't have a sister," I said. "Just one brother."

"Well, there you go."

I don't know where I was going but my attempt at getting Eva to talk about John was going nowhere.

Before I could think of another hopefully leading question, Eva asked: "So, how are things on your dating front?"

I laughed. "You make dating sound like a battlefield."

"Yes. So?"

I shrugged. "So, nothing much. Nothing worth talking about."

Eva lifted a doubting eyebrow. I shifted in my chair. I don't like lying of any sort, and I'm not very good at it. But I couldn't tell Eva about Ben, not yet. What, I wondered, is so scary about the idea of admitting to being in love? What, exactly, am I afraid of?

Maybe the same thing that Eva was afraid of when it came to admitting feelings for John (or, for anyone). Admitting to being in love is admitting to vulnerability. Admitting to being in love is admitting to being half-blind to reality.

No. I would keep my feelings for Ben my little secret for a while longer. Just as Eva was keeping whatever she felt for John, if anything, her little secret.

With all the deception in our relationship, I suddenly wondered if Eva and I had a real friendship after all.

"Our food," Eva said.

"Yes," I said.

The waiter placed our meals on the table and we fell to our dinners like people who hadn't eaten in a week. I think we were both glad not to have to talk.

63

Fib #27: While to all appearances you're a middle-class working gal, in reality you're a member of an ancient royal family from an unnamed European country, in hiding until your adored uncle is reinstated on the throne in a bloody coup that is sure to happen sometime in the next ten years. Note: Ten years down the line the people with whom you socialized as a single will have long since married and moved to the suburbs, having lost touch with you after the birth of their first child. No one will have any idea that you're still hanging out in clubs, stuffed into too-tight jeans, and telling outrageous stories to whoever pities you enough to listen.
   —Single and Loving It: Fabulous Fibs to Wile Away
      the Lonely Hours

SOPHIE

I let Jake into the apartment. He had my spare key but was reluctant to use it. Now, since meeting Ben, I appreciated Jake's respect of my privacy. How awful if my son walked in on his mother kissing her boyfriend!

"Thanks for being here tonight," I whispered as I hugged him. "It means a lot to me."

Jake handed me a plastic bag. "Sure, no problem. I brought some beer."

I took the bag and Jake followed me into the kitchen where Ben was chopping mushrooms and waiting for the big introduction.

I so wanted Jake and Ben to like each other, but I knew it might be hard for Jake to meet the man his mother was dating. I wasn't worried about how Ben would handle meeting my son; I figured Ben could take care of himself. But Jake might need my help in adjusting to this new person in our lives. Earlier, I'd closed the door to my bedroom. Jake, I thought, might see the bed on his way to the bathroom and imagine Ben and me together and get upset.

I'm happy to report that the meeting was surprisingly smooth. Well, maybe not so surprisingly. Jake was a mature young man, and for all his learning Ben was . . . uncomplicated. It was too early to tell for sure but I sensed that he wasn't prone to dramatics or unreasonable behavior.

Over dinner, Ben asked Jake questions about his graduate program. Jake replied in detail and I worried that he might be boring Ben, but Ben didn't seem to mind and even talked about some of his own experiences in grad school. Both discovered a mutual love of the novelist Carlos Fuentes and, in another area entirely, an interest in photography.

"You're interested in photography?" I asked Jake. "How come I never knew this?"

Jake shrugged. "I don't know."

I looked at Ben, then back to Jake.

"How long have you had this interest?"

"Mom, you make it sound like something dirty!"

"No, it's just that I—"

"Just that you thought you knew every little detail about me?"

"Well, yes," I admitted. "I guess I did. It seems kind of silly . . ."

"I bought an old Nikkon just before coming East," Jake told Ben. "I've been fiddling around with it whenever I have some free time. Which isn't often. It's a bit frustrating, actually."

Jake and Ben launched into a conversation that was mostly technical in nature. I half-listened, pleased that they were getting along so well, pleased that they were eating my dinner like men recovering from a fast.

"Sophie," Ben said as I cleared the table, "you are such a talented cook."

"Thank you." I know I was blushing, but pride in cooking can be excused.

I'd made an apple pie for dessert, the kind with raisins, another of Jake's favorites. I served us and poured the coffee—not for Jake; he has only a cup in the morning and it takes him hours to drink it. Ben mentioned that he'd invited me to a cocktail party at a colleague's house that coming weekend.

"Have you met Mom's friends yet? Eva and John?" Jake asked.

Ben shook his head. "Not yet, but I'm looking forward to it."

"You know," I said, "I had dinner with them the other night and I got a strange vibe. I think John and Eva might be attracted to each other. Although I doubt Eva's admitted it to herself."

"I think you're wrong, Mom," Jake said emphatically. "There's no way a woman like Eva would ever go for a guy like John. I mean, from what you've told me about her. And him."

"Why?" I asked. "I think they might be very good for each other."

Jake shrugged. "Nothing. Forget it."

"No, tell me," I pressed.

Jake took a long drink of water and deliberately wiped his mouth afterward. Finally, he said: "I have to get going. I have to get to the library before it closes."

I opened my mouth to protest but before I could speak,

Ben was saying: "It was great to meet you, Jake," and the two men were rising and shaking hands.

Maybe, I thought, it was best not to prolong this first meeting. Everything had gone so well; maybe it was best to "end on a high note."

Jake left. Ben helped clear the table and load the dishwasher. When we were settled in bed I said, "Thank you."

Ben smiled. "For what?"

"For being so good tonight. I was really nervous. It could have been a disaster."

"Jake's a good guy. I think he could see that I'm in love with his mother."

"You are?"

Ben kissed me. "I am."

I kissed him back. "Good. Because his mother is in love with you."

Could life, I thought, be any sweeter?

* 64 *

Dear Answer Lady:

A friend recently gave another friend a birthday party at her apartment. I was asked to bring the cake. But at the last minute I just didn't feel like going out. There was a really good movie on a pay channel and, besides, I don't even like parties. So I emailed the host to say I felt sick and wasn't coming. But now my friends are mad and say that I should have called and not emailed because the host didn't check her email until after the party and they spent all night wondering where I was because I wasn't picking up the phone (I hate to be interrupted when I'm watching a movie.) and if I really was sick (which they don't believe) I should have asked someone to come and get the cake (which, by the way, I ate while watching the movie). I mean, why is everyone freaking out on me?

Dear Clueless Wonder:

Your former friends are right in condemning your shabby behavior. I hope you get disgustingly obese eating other people's birthday cakes until the fire department has to hack your grotesque body out of an armchair so that you can be hoisted out through the window so that the department of health can fumigate the apartment you've become too disabled to maintain. Or something like that.

JOHN

Ever since the night I'd run out on dinner, the thought of kissing Eva had been driving me crazy.

It had happened just after Eva and I declared a truce, just before Sophie returned from the ladies' room. Suddenly, I'd felt an incredible urge to lean over the table and kiss her, long and slow.

The thought of what might have happened if Sophie hadn't shown up just when she did—well, it wouldn't let me rest. I reminded myself that I was an idiot when it came to Eva. I reminded myself that Eva's apology might not have been wholehearted. But the thought of the kiss that might have been . . .

"You're probably going to regret this," I said to my office as I punched in the number for Eva's office. Her assistant put me on hold while she announced my call. I was half-convinced that Eva would be "unavailable."

"Hey," a voice said, startling me.

"Hey," I said back. And then I froze.

"Uh, John? Are you going to tell me why you called?"

I got up from my desk, as if standing would bring back coherence. "Yeah, sorry. I just got distracted."

Eva laughed. "And you're always scolding me for being distracted on the phone!"

"True," I admitted. "Look, I feel bad about having to run out on dinner the other night."

"Don't give it another thought. We didn't miss you in the least."

Easy, I thought. Don't take it too seriously. Eva's default mode is flippancy.

"Nevertheless," I said evenly, "I'd like to make it up to you. Can I take you to dinner some night this week?"

There was silence on her end. Then, with an elaborate sigh that made me smile, she said: "Oh, all right. I suppose I can squeeze you into my schedule."

"Thank you. You can't see me but I'm bowing in acknowl-edgment of your generosity."

"But I pick the restaurant," she said.

"It's going to cost me, isn't it?"

"Please. It's not like you'll need to take a second mortgage. Besides, don't lawyers make oodles of money?"

"Ooodles? Some of them."

She mentioned a restaurant. I flinched. "Fine," I said. "Seven o'clock Thursday?"

"See you then," she said and ended the call.

I fell back into my desk chair. And with the fall came the reminder that Eva was involved with someone, if you could call having sex with someone young enough to be your child "involved."

I wondered if she was happy with this guy. I couldn't tell. Then again, I couldn't tell much about what Eva was really feeling. I mean, why was it such a big deal to keep the affair from Sophie? Sophie was Eva's only female friend. Correc-tion: Eva's only friend. I wasn't at all sure in what relation I stood to her.

But I knew in what relation I wanted to stand.

* 65 *

*Imagine waking each morning with an invigorating
sense of moral superiority. Imagine walking through
the day knowing without a doubt that you are more
ethically minded than every person you encounter.
Imagine going to bed each night secure in the knowledge that if, indeed, Heaven does exist, you will be
seated at the right hand of God.*
  —The Benefits of a Truthful Life or How to Build
  and Maintain High Self-Esteem

EVA

John wanted to "make it up to me" for having been called
away from dinner? It was a flimsy excuse for getting together.
Didn't he feel bad about having run out on Sophie, too?
Well, for all I knew he'd asked her to dinner as well. But I
doubted it.

I thought about wanting to kiss John. I'd tried to dismiss
the notion as silly and unappealing, a passing fancy brought
about by a fleeting mood, but I couldn't. I still wanted to kiss
him, days after the impulse. And now I was going to see him
alone. I could have said no thanks. But I hadn't.

Boisterous voices startled me out of my unhappy reverie.
Of course there would be a celebration. We'd just landed a
new account, a big one. A group of people would head out

for a drink before going home to spouses, boyfriends, girl-friends, and partners.

And no one would ask me to go along. In the past, the omission wouldn't even have registered. But now, listening to the excited voices of my colleagues I felt, unaccountably, lonely.

It was my fault that people didn't include me in their after-work get-togethers, in their Saturday afternoon softball games, in their lunchtime baby showers. I'd never made an effort to get along. My attitude was one of indifference. My presentation was off-putting. My nonprofessional conversation, such as it was, discouraged connection.

But hadn't that been the plan all along, to discourage connection? Yes, and I'd been quite successful in isolating myself from just about every person in my life, from dry cleaner to colleagues to neighbors. From Sophie, to some extent. From John, largely. I was unattached. I was unencumbered.

"Freedom is just another word for nothing left to lose." Right? Freedom can be a pain in the ass.

I looked up, my eye caught by movement in the hall. Three women from marketing were hurrying by. I couldn't recall the name of the shortest one. As the third woman passed, she glanced into my office.

I don't know what sort of expression she found on my face. Given the nature of my thoughts, it couldn't have been a pleasant one. Still, she stopped and murmured something to her companions now out of sight. Then she knocked lightly on the doorjamb.

"Ms. Fitzpatrick?"

"Yes?" I asked.

The woman—Traci was her name—hesitated before saying: "Well, some of us are going out to Churchill for a bit. To celebrate landing the Vargas account."

Maybe I nodded; I don't remember.

Traci smiled a bit. "You wouldn't want to join us, would you?"

Could there have been a more halfhearted invitation? I smiled a bit back. "Thanks," I said, "but I've got a previous engagement."

Maybe it was my imagination but Traci seemed relieved. Maybe it wasn't my imagination.

"Okay," she said, already walking away. "See you tomorrow."

I waited at my desk until I was sure I wouldn't run into any stragglers. Then, I left the office. At the corner I stopped in the grocery store and bought a preroasted chicken and a plastic tub of green beans. And then I went home.

* 66 *

Dear Answer Lady:

Recently I met a nice guy at the gym where I play racquetball. We talked for a while and then he asked me to have dinner with him. I said yes. Here's the thing. I'm a straight man and this guy is obviously gay. Should I let him know before our date that it's not really a date? Or should I just tell him when we're out together? BTW: This sort of thing has happened before.

Dear Closet Case:

Why the hell didn't you tell him you're straight when he asked you out? Oh, right, because you're not really straight, just a gay man in denial. Do the poor guy a favor and cancel. Then, get yourself a good therapist.

SOPHIE

What a week it had been!

I got my second client (!); went out after work one night for drinks with two of my new colleagues; bought a set of weights and an exercise video (which told me I also needed a mat and a ball and a whole bunch of other stuff, which I then went out and bought), and started working out (I wasn't even that sore!); and listened to some CDs I hadn't listened to in years. (Brad hated country music; I guess over time I'd just stopped playing it; now I remembered how much I loved it.)

On Monday the owner of the dry cleaners on the corner showed me photos of his new granddaughter—his fourth! He and his wife are such nice people. On Tuesday, I went to the museum and stumbled upon a docent giving a lecture about French Impressionism (my favorite). I didn't learn anything new, but it was fun, nonetheless.

On Thursday—I made a mental note to tell Eva—I chatted with a woman who lives down the hall, a retired teacher, and somehow the conversation led to other people in the building (which ones were odd, who played music too loudly, that kind of thing) and she mentioned the guy who'd asked me to dinner. It seems he hit on all the single women in the building! We shared a good laugh about that and made a promise to have coffee sometime soon.

But the highlight of the week was going to a book reading/signing with Ben at the college's bookstore. Ben knew the author, a poet, and introduced me afterward. I met several other people he knew, including some devoted students, and had such a good time. I bought a copy of the book, of course (the first book I'd ever owned signed by the author) and started it that night. I've never been much for poetry but I found myself enjoying the work and thought, not for the first time since moving back East: What other old assumptions about myself might be ready for the garbage?

My daily life was becoming rich in a way it hadn't been since college. I wondered if the change was more one of attitude than circumstance; I thought it might be. Brad hadn't been holding me back from getting "out there." I had. Brad hadn't told me not to play country music. I'd made that "decision."

But now, I thought, surveying my beautiful apartment, everything is different. Now, things just keep getting better.

* 67 *

The first thing to remember is that the verb "to per-vert" has an unfortunate negative vibe, what with notions of leading astray and distorting. Think in-stead of verbs like "to adjust" and "to improve" when "playing with" your presentation of the truth.
—Tweaking the Truth and Having Fun with It!

JOHN

"Oof!"

The sudden weight on my back made me stumble.

"Paul! I told you not to jump on your uncle like that!" Chrissy scolded. "He's getting old."

I dumped my sister's eight-year-old onto the couch. "And I love you, too, Chrissy."

Teri, passing through the living room from the dining room, grinned.

The football game that I was trying to watch with my brothers-in-law went to commercial. Frank hauled himself from his chair. "John, want a beer?" he asked.

"Sure, thanks."

"Mike?"

Mike nodded and Frank went off to the kitchen.

"Oh, I almost forgot." Chrissy's hand appeared before my face. "I got a postcard from Mom and Dad today. Look."

I sunk onto the couch next to my nephew and took the

card. Mom's terrible scrawl made me smile. "You can read this?" I asked.

Chrissy shrugged. "Enough to know they're having a good time but getting lonely for home."

I squinted again at the writing. "Amazing. I get nothing."

Chrissy took the postcard from me and brought it to Mike, whose reaction was close to mine.

Four-year-old Jean Marie sat on my right foot and grabbed onto my calf.

Paul turned to his sister, who had perched on the arm of the couch. "Why doesn't Uncle John have a wife?" he asked.

"Not all men have wives," Lucy said with all the wisdom of a ten-year-old. "Some men have husbands."

"Why?"

Lucy shrugged. "They just do."

"Can I have a husband when I grow up?" Paul wondered.

"When you're grown-up you can do anything you want. That's what Andrew told me."

Ah, yes, the twelve-year-old perspective. Andrew and his twin, Scott, displayed a lot of their mother's I-know-pretty-much-everything attitude.

"Can you have cookies for dinner?" Paul turned to me. "Uncle John, do you have cookies for dinner?"

"Sometimes," I lied. From across the room Chrissy shot me the look. "But not often."

"Well, I'm going to have cookies for dinner every night!"

"And ice cream!" Andrew and Scott shouted together.

"Personally," I said, risking another look from a sister, "I'm partial to pizza for breakfast."

Lucy wrinkled her nose. "Ew! Gross!"

Jean Marie let go of my leg and scrambled to her feet. "I like pizza," she announced. "It has cheese."

Teri reappeared at the entrance to the living room. "John," she said in a singsong voice, "could you help me in the kitchen?"

Crap, I thought. Frank appeared with the beers and

shrugged. Mike looked away from the TV to give me a grin that said, *"Ha ha."*

I followed Teri into the kitchen. Chrissy was close on my heels.

"So, Uncle John," she said. "Why don't you have a wife? What's holding you up?"

"Nothing's holding me up. I just haven't met the right person yet. Don't rush me."

"He's very particular," Teri said.

"He's fussy."

"I'm not fussy! I just don't want to make a big mistake."

"Nobody's perfect, you know."

I groaned. "Yes, I know nobody's perfect. Look, can we drop this interrogation and get back to the party? Please, I beg of you."

Teri sighed. "Oh, all right." She handed me a bowl heaped with guacamole. "Take this out to the table, will you? And don't put your fingers in it! Jeez!"

"I didn't put my fingers in it! Besides, my hands are clean."

"You were just down on your hands and knees in the living room," Chrissy pointed out.

Teri glared. "Are you saying my carpet isn't clean?"

I slipped out of the kitchen before my sisters could accuse me of having started the squabble. Family. Things would be pretty boring without them.

68

Dear Answer Lady:

I am terribly worried. I recently bought new holiday table linens to replace the ones I've been using for the past ten years. My husband saw me come home with the shopping bags and asked how much I'd spent. I panicked and told him the linens cost half of what they really did. When the credit card bill comes in he'll find out that I lied and confront me. What should I do?

Dear Misguided Soul:

Are you aware you're living in the 21st century? Are you aware you have the right as an American citizen to a life independent of your husband? (Unless, of course, you're a member of some backwards-thinking cult, but that's your problem.) Spend what money you want and never lie about it again. If he scolds you for your purchases, calmly point out the time he spent thousands of dollars on ski equipment he never used. (I'm guessing here.) If that doesn't shut him up, go out and spend more. Eventually, he'll learn.

JOHN

I'd done a lot of thinking in the days leading up to this dinner with Eva, a lot of thinking about the way I behaved with her, about the way she provoked me and the way I fought back.

And here's what I'd come up with: Maybe, I realized, Eva didn't really want to fight me but felt that she had to, for reasons only she could explain. Maybe she was struggling with some deep fear or unhappiness and if so, my combatative behavior in return was only proving her point—that I was an enemy, someone she needed to fend off, someone against whom she had to protect herself.

Maybe, I reasoned, the best way I could be of help to her—as a friend—was to listen uncritically for a change, to sympathize, to refrain from offering "solutions" to what I saw as her problems or her flaws. In short, to turn the other cheek when she lashed out, to keep quiet when she baited me. And, most importantly, to stop judging her against the standard of the young woman she once was, the young woman of my memory. Making that comparison and constantly pointing it out to Eva was entirely unfair. The fact that Eva had changed wasn't a fault. The fact that I was unable to accept it *was*.

Of course, grand determinations are easier talked about than executed. I was nervous; I doubted my ability to follow through. But with a skill perfected over years of having to perform in court, I wrangled the nervousness into adrenaline and, wearing a new tie bought just for the occasion, I walked through the door of DeMado's, Eva's choice, one of the five most expensive restaurants in the city, right on the nose of seven.

Eva, of course, was already at the bar. She looked . . . perfect. But when did she ever look anything less? Maybe, I thought, first thing in the morning. That was an Eva I would very much like to see.

"You were early," I said, stupidly, pushing aside bedroom images.

"And you were right on time."

"Do you think punctuality is a lost social skill? Half the people in my office wander in between nine-thirty and ten."

Eva shrugged. "Maybe we're the odd ones these days, but I refuse to give up the habit of being on time."

"Me, too. But maybe we refuse to give it up because we want to stand out from the crowd. If everyone suddenly became obsessed with punctuality, do you think we would start oversleeping and missing reservations?"

"Absolutely not! But I'll admit it's another thing we have in common, the habit of standing out from the crowd."

"Habit?" I said. "Or the need? Or the desire?"

Before Eva could reply the hostess appeared to lead us to our table. I was glad. I thought I might have gone over a line with that last remark, "accusing" Eva of a psychological weakness.

A waiter took our orders almost immediately. For such an upscale place, I noted, the service was a bit rushed.

"I'm starved," Eva said when he had gone. "I hope the food comes as quickly as the waiter did."

I refrained from voicing my opinion.

"I fired my assistant," Eva said abruptly. A challenge?

"Oh," I said, neutrally. "Do you have a replacement yet?"

"Of course. She starts next Monday. I just couldn't take the incompetence of this other one. And she always acted as if she was—afraid. Okay, I'm a tough boss but I'm not an ogre!"

"Of course not," I said. I could have pointed out that sometimes Eva was, in fact, an ogre, but I didn't. "Do you have a temp for the next few days?"

"Well, I'm not doing the menial stuff myself! Not anymore, anyway. That's how I started, you know. At the bottom."

I nodded. "And you've done quite well for yourself. You should be proud, Eva."

Our food came just then, another perfectly timed interruption, preventing the possibility of Eva's misconstruing my compliment as less than genuine. Well, at least postponing an attack based on her misperception. (Maybe, I thought, the quick service wasn't such a bad thing after all.) We ate for a while in a silence that felt almost companionable, speaking only to comment on our meals, which we both were enjoying.

"You eat too much red meat," Eva said, pointing with her fork at my almost-finished filet. "It's going to catch up with you."

"You're right," I replied. "I do." She was right, I did eat too much red meat; but only weeks earlier I would have fought her comment with a snide reply about her own eating habits. Or maybe about something else, because actually Eva did eat very well.

She paused, fork halfway to mouth, and looked at me funny.

"What?" I asked.

Eva seemed to consider, then shook her head and resumed eating.

When the plates had been cleared and we'd both declined coffee and dessert (I'd been considering the caramel tart, but after Eva's comment about my diet I thought better of it.), Eva asked: "So, you're not going to tell me I was wrong?"

"About what?"

"About firing my assistant for being incompetent? About not giving her a fourth chance? About not sending her to class for more computer training? About not treating her with kid gloves so she wouldn't be afraid of me?"

"No," I said, "I'm not. Even if I did think you were wrong in letting her go, which I don't—an office is a place of business, not a nursery school—I wouldn't say anything, because I'm trying to be a less . . . didactic person."

"Huh. Interesting. What brought about this decision for change?"

I shrugged. "Stuff. Things. You know."

Eva gave me a funny look. "What about the ability to articulate? Decided to lose that, too?"

"Obviously."

I laughed. She laughed. Pretty good, I thought.

"You wanted dessert, didn't you?"

I feigned shock. "Me? Whatever gave you that idea?"

"You could have had it, you know. I didn't mean the red meat comment as an insult. More as—a helpful warning."

"I know," I said. "I appreciate it."

The bill came then and I reached for it. My fingers had just lifted it from the table when Eva put her hand atop mine, holding it there. Her hand was beautiful, and warm. I looked up at her.

"Please," she said. "I'd like to split this."

"You don't have to do that, Eva."

She rolled her eyes at me, but her hand still covered mine. "I don't have to do anything, but I want to pay for half."

"I owe you for running out the other night."

"You don't owe me anything."

We sat there, hands touching, looking at each other, for what seemed like a long time. I wanted it to be longer. I considered arguing back, to keep us there, but better sense prevailed.

"Okay," I said. "Thank you."

Eva smiled and released me. "We should leave a good tip," she said.

"I always do. My mother waited tables for a few years. We needed the money. I heard the stories."

"I didn't know that about your mother, about your family."

"Eva," I said, "there's a lot you don't know about me and I bet some of it might just interest you."

She laughed. "Oh, really? Well, we'll see."

Possibility! Maybe Eva no longer regarded me as an enemy. Maybe she was beginning to acknowledge me as a friend.

I didn't kiss her at the end of the evening. I wanted to and I believe she wanted me to, but I didn't. Truth was, I was a little wary. Eva was still Eva, truce or not; I knew that she could sting.

But I don't think she hated me for it. I think that we parted with a sense of promise, with a sense of more to come. I know I did.

* 69 *

In this writer's opinion, the only time when complete and total honesty is proper, indeed, when it is required, is when not telling the truth will result in direct damage to the self. For example, your new mother-in-law places a pitcher of soured milk on the table. Your wife, careful of her mother's feelings, subtly signals that you keep your mouth shut and add the milk to your coffee. But I say that under no circumstances are you to drink the spoiled milk or refrain from announcing that in the interests of your health and the health of everyone else at the table, the milk must be poured down the sink. Note: Be prepared to spend the night on the couch. At least you won't be vomiting.

—Honesty Is (Almost) Never the Best Policy

EVA

Damn. I don't know how it had happened but it had. John had wormed his way under my skin.

And, I was fairly sure I'd wormed my way under his. But how could I be entirely sure? I couldn't just say, "So, John, I like you. Do you like me?" Please. What if he laughed? What if he acted all pitying?

What if he said, *"Yes, Eva. I do like you."*

The whole situation was ridiculous. I thought back to the

way it had been in college, when romantic relationships happened organically, sprouting naturally out of friendships. The transition from friend to lover had involved a minimum amount of awkwardness. At least, that's the way it seemed from this perspective.

Friend. Lover. I didn't even know what I wanted with John. Something more than what I had with Sam, something like what I had with Jake, or something else entirely?

No. A romantic relationship with John would be a disaster. Unless, of course, it would be the best thing that ever happened to me. But that's not the way my life worked. Good things didn't just happen to me. And love only meant regret.

Damn Sophie. It was all her fault. Life had been a hell of a lot easier before she barged into my life, dragging John with her. Then, I'd had no one to answer to but myself. Now, I was plagued with things like responsibility and accountability, duty and respect.

No. Things were already too complicated. I'd keep my mouth shut. This—whatever it was, an infatuation, a crush—would pass in time and life would be simple and orderly once again. As simple and orderly as it could be with friends in tow.

Still, I couldn't help but wonder what John's lips would feel like on mine.

70

Dear Answer Lady:

My husband is in a rehab facility after losing both of his legs in a car accident, which, by the way, wasn't his fault. He's due to come home next month. The thing is, one of the paramedics who brought my husband to the hospital asked me out. You know how tragedy brings people together. Anyway, since then he's been living with me. It's been great because he's been mowing the lawn and doing a lot of the dirty stuff my husband won't be able to do any longer, now that he's got two artificial legs. What should I do? I love my husband but my new lover is really useful.

Dear Piece of Trash:

What do you mean, what should you do? Throw out your opportunist paramedic and welcome your traumatized husband home with open arms. Then, get out there and mow the lawn yourself. And don't ever write to me again.

JOHN

I was falling in love with Eva.

Though I suspected she might have feelings for me in return, I was in no rush to approach her. I knew there was a very good chance that Eva might recoil from me. I knew full well that even if she didn't bolt, the road ahead wouldn't be smooth and that it might very well end in a ditch.

In fact, I wasn't sure I'd ever have the courage to tell Eva how I felt about her. My love for her might forever remain my little secret.

Still, I couldn't help but wonder what it would be like to hold her in my arms.

71

Absolute truth is for absolute idiots. If you think such a thing exists, you're delusional and should be put under the immediate care of a drug-wielding psychiatrist. (See the Index for a list of doctors in your area.)

—Absolute Truth: What, Are You Nuts?

EVA

"So, what do you think about this guy John? You know, your old college buddy."

I eyed Jake suspiciously. What could he possibly know about my troubling feelings for John? "Yes," I said, "I know who John is. Why?"

Jake looked up at the ceiling and shrugged. "No reason. My mother just mentioned him the other night."

Ah, Jake's inherent jealousy was once again rearing its ugly head. Sophie probably mentioned John's single status, and Jake put two and two together and came up with—well, with four. But he wasn't going to find out that his suspicions were in some measure correct.

Besides, I thought, weren't we just having fun in this "relationship"? Why would Jake care about my interest in other men?

Really, sometimes I sickened myself. Of course Jake would

care, whether he should or not. Suddenly, I felt distinctly guilty and in need of making amends.

"Did she mention that John is a jerk?" I asked with a laugh. "A woman would have to be nuts to get involved with him. He's completely self-centered."

Jake lowered his eyes from the ceiling. The boy was easily mollified. "Oh, yeah?" he asked, laughing, too. "She didn't mention the jerk part."

"She always had a soft spot for him. I've always seen him for exactly who he is."

Jake kissed my forehead (I hate when anyone does that.) and then went to the fridge for one of his specialty beers.

"Oh, I almost forgot," he said, after a swallow. "Mom's seeing someone. I met him the other night at her apartment. Some guy named Ben. He seems okay."

Ah, ha! I knew Sophie had been keeping something from me! But Ben, huh? I hoped that she would have better luck with her Ben than I did with mine.

"That's great," I said, though I wasn't sure I meant it. "Is she serious about him?"

Jake shrugged. "I think so. She looks at him all dreamy-eyed. It was a bit weird for me, but I've been through weirder."

I doubted that but didn't challenge the boy.

"Is he handsome?" I asked mischievously.

"How should I know?"

"What color are his eyes?"

"I don't know. Brown? Maybe blue."

Typical male inattention to detail.

"Oh, and by the way," Jake said, "don't tell her I told you about him. She wants to tell people in her own time. I don't know what the big deal is, but hey, if it makes her happy to dole out the information."

"It will be another one of our little secrets," I said.

Jake sipped his beer thoughtfully before saying: "I'm not sure you'd like him."

"Who—Ben?"

"Yeah."

"Why not? Is he a deadly bore?"

"No. I just don't see you two having a lot in common. But he and my mom seem really into each other. I can see them moving in together."

Really into each other. Suddenly, I was overcome with an intense feeling of envy. It was like a revelation of sorts: I wanted what Sophie had, a real relationship. Not the sex-only relationship I had with Sam or the pretend relationship I had with Jake. I, too, wanted something real and complicated and—

The troublesome thoughts fled as quickly as they had come and I was left standing there in Jake's miniscule kitchen feeling terribly empty and bereft.

"What's wrong?" Jake asked, obviously concerned by what I'm sure must have been my bleak expression.

I ran from the kitchen and grabbed my bag from the second-hand couch. Suddenly, getting out of that place was vital. "Nothing," I said without meeting Jake's eye.

"You're going? But we haven't even fooled around yet!"

"I feel a headache coming on."

"Oh. Well, stay here. I'll get you some ibuprofen."

I hurried toward the door. "No, thanks, it's best I go home."

Jake followed. He tried to kiss me good-bye. I gave him my cheek just long enough for his lips to barely touch it.

The first thing I did when I got back to my apartment was to check my answering machine. There were no messages. My cell, too, had been silent all afternoon. I flipped open my laptop. No e-mail, except for an ad from a mortgage company. I pulled the mail from my bag. Only bills and a solicitation from a singles dating service.

Pathetic.

Briefly, I considered calling John. But what excuse could I give for the call? How could I ever admit to him the bitter thoughts in my head and the depth of my loneliness?

But maybe I deserved to be lonely. Because on the way

home from Jake's it had occurred to me that all along I'd felt a bit superior to Sophie. I had a successful career. I had better clothes. I was in better physical shape.

But there had been something else, something that proved how inept I was at the art of friendship. You see, even though a part of me felt bad about keeping such a big secret from Sophie (felt bad about the nature of the secret, too), another part of me felt what one inevitably feels for the one being duped: a mixture of disdain and pity.

I lay down on the couch and put my arm over my eyes. Pity. It had become painfully clear that if anyone was the pitiful one in our "friendship" it was I.

* 72 *

Dear Answer Lady:

They say that necessity is the mother of invention. Well, recently I applied for a job that requires a master's degree, which, unfortunately, I don't have. But I really want this job so I made up the name of a school and got a friend who works in a printing shop to forge a diploma (in case anyone checks) and got another friend to let me use his phone number; if anyone calls him from the job he's going to pretend he's with the school and verify that I attended. Pretty smart, huh? The only thing that's bothering me is that my wife thinks I'm "morally bankrupt" (that's her term) and doesn't at all appreciate the time, effort, and creativity it took for me to set up this scheme. How can I get her to come around? She's really bumming me out.

Dear Deceiver:

Have you never heard of business ethics? Oh, wait, of course you haven't. You don't have a master's degree. Did you hear me? YOU DON'T HAVE A MASTER'S DEGREE! If I were your wife—and I am very glad that I'm not—I'd file for divorce now before another "necessity" compels you to "invent" a lie, the consequences of which land you in jail.

EVA

"Mrs. Holmes, hey. Jake's buddy. We met at his apartment? My name's Jerry?"

Sophie and I were having lunch when this Jerry person stopped by our table.

Sophie's face brightened. "Oh, of course, Jerry, how are you?"

Jerry shrugged like only skinny twenty-year-old boys can shrug, with an easy, rolling motion. "On the vertical. Can't complain."

"That's nice," Sophie said, ever gracious. "Oh, Jerry, this is my friend Eva."

Jerry looked down at me, his expression suddenly puzzled. Crap, I thought. Crap, crap, crap, he recognizes me from that horrible nightclub; Jake had waved to a group of friends and, yeah, Jerry had been one of them. With Sophie facing me there was no way I could signal this kid that he should keep his mouth shut.

Jerry's finger pointed at me and his mouth opened, but before he could say, *"Hey, dude, aren't you the woman who's doing it with Jake?"* I blurted: "We really should order now, Sophie. It was nice to meet you, Jerry." I stuck out my hand and gave Jerry a bright and artificial smile.

Jerry hesitated a moment and then took my hand. His grip was weak and he mumbled something like, "Yeah, well . . ." before letting go and walking off.

Sophie frowned, no doubt disapproving of my rude dismissal of Jake's friend. I returned her frown with one of my own.

"So," she said, aligning her fork and knife to be perfectly perpendicular on the napkin. "There's something I've been wanting to tell you since we sat down."

"Oh?" I asked, suspecting the news to come.

"I met someone," she said. "A man."

"I kind of figured the part about the man. How long have you been seeing him?" I asked.

Sophie blushed—blushed!—and admitted she'd been seeing this guy for a few weeks. "I wanted to keep it a secret at first . . ."

"What's the big deal?" I asked bluntly. "Is he a celebrity, is he in the witness protection program, what?"

"No, no, nothing like that." Sophie considered for a moment before saying: "I don't know. Maybe I didn't want to jinx the relationship. Or maybe I was worried what you might think if I went on and on about some guy and then it didn't work out."

"For God's sake, Sophie," I said, "why would I judge you about a failed relationship? Everyone gets involved in relationships that don't work out. Some people even make a career of it."

"Oh, I know," Sophie said, "but you're so sophisticated about relationships, Eva. I didn't want to sound like a schoolgirl with a crush."

How ironic. Just when I had begun to suspect that of the two of us Sophie might be the more sophisticated, at least, the more mature in the realm of relationships and I who might be the more . . . undeveloped. It wasn't a pleasant thing to suspect about myself, but I couldn't seem to avoid this new version of the truth. I mean, who was the one in an adult relationship and who was the one dodging twenty-year-olds ready to out me as a cradle robber?

"Well, I'm glad for you," I said, forcing a smile. "When am I going to meet this mystery man?"

"Oh, not just yet," Sophie replied. "I want to wait a bit longer before introducing him to my friends. It's a big step for me. I want to be sure he's going to be around for a while. You know?"

What I knew was that Sophie had already introduced her mystery man to her son. I wondered if Sophie subscribed to the notion of family being by definition more accepting and less critical than friends were.

"Sure," I said.

Sophie smiled. "I'm going to tell John this afternoon."

I'm sure, I thought, the news will make his day. And then I felt bad for having reacted, even silently, in such an unnecessarily snide way. Was I emotionally retarded? It was all too strong of a possibility.

"Where is our waiter?" I asked, flipping open the menu.

* 73 *

If you truly believe that other people want and/or need to hear your honest opinion on their clothing, child-rearing style, or their work habits, you are suffering from a massive case of hubris. Get off your high horse and concentrate on improving your own pitiful life skills.

　　—To Be Perfectly Honest: The Pitfalls of Sharing
　　　Your Opinions

EVA

Damn Sophie for falling in love. Damn her for telling me about it.

I called my sister. I would rather have sent her an e-mail but unlike the vast majority of Americans, Maura doesn't have an e-mail account at home. Something about the extra expense, I'm sure.

I suppose I should have reconsidered calling at seven o'clock on a school night. But is there ever a good time to call a mother of four kids who works three nights a week?

"What's wrong?" Maura asked when I'd said hello. Her tone was more impatient than concerned.

"Nothing is wrong. I just wanted to say hello."

There was a brief silence on the other end of the line. "Oh," Maura said, finally. "So, everything's okay with you?"

"Fine," I said. "Everything's great. I just thought I'd call. Uh, how's the weather been by you?"

I thought I heard the rumble of a truck in the background. Then the truck spoke words and I realized I was hearing Maura's husband asking for pretzels.

"In the bread drawer, where they always are," Maura replied testily. "Okay, you know. Weather is weather."

I'd have to think about that later.

"Everything okay with your job?" I asked.

Maura laughed. "I'm a cashier. How okay can it be? But, yeah, thanks for asking. At least I'm employed. One of my girlfriends just got laid off from SuperDuperMart. I don't know how she's going to make her mortgage this month." Maura paused. "But you don't want to hear about that."

Well, in truth, I didn't, but I said: "No, no, I'm interested."

Maura talked on a bit about her near-destitute friend and about how her own oldest, Brooke, was going to need braces next year (I made a note to get out the checkbook.), and about how Trevor's mother was coming to stay with them for a few weeks while the rotting foundation of her house was replaced.

I made the appropriate sounds of active listening and I waited for the usual question—"*When are you coming to visit your nieces?*"—but it never came.

I wondered: Had Maura given up on me?

A piercing wail followed by a voice yelling out: "Mommy! Britney got her hand slammed in the door of the fridgerator again!" ended our call.

Maura sighed. "I've got to go. Thanks for calling, Eve."

I didn't bother to correct her, as I'd done so often in the past. "Good-bye, Maura," I said.

Damn everyone.

74

Dear Answer Lady:
One of my friends is really overweight. The thing is, she doesn't seem to know it! She's got a good job and is always laughing and going to the movies and out to dinner with friends and stuff. Isn't it my duty to tell her she's fat? I mean, she should at least be on a diet!

Dear Jealous Bitch:
Clearly you are one of those nasty types who are only happy when someone else is miserable. Leave your friend alone and work on getting a personality half as good as hers. Then maybe you'll have a social life, too.

JOHN

"Really, Teri, I'm fine. I just—I'm just tired, okay?" I rubbed my forehead as if to prove the point. "It's been a crazy week and I just don't have the energy to go on another fixup right now. Maybe next week. We'll see."

The truth was that my heart just wasn't into dating. I was beginning to feel that if I couldn't have Eva I didn't want any woman. The dim possibility of love was exhausting me.

"I still think something is up, John."

My sister is like a dog worrying a bone when she suspects a secret. Still, I did manage to get her off the phone after another five minutes of intense questioning.

No sooner had I extricated myself from the call than Gene came bursting into my office.

"You got a minute?" he asked, tossing himself into one of the guest chairs.

"Uh, not really."

Gene leaned forward. "You have to hear this, man."

"Gene," I said evenly, "now really isn't a good time."

The self-centered don't understand no like we other-centered people do.

"This will only take a minute. You wouldn't believe what—"

I stood. Gene stopped talking, mouth open.

"I'm really not in the mood to hear about how you banged some chick last night, okay?" I said, with barely controlled anger. "I've got more important things to do with my time. And shouldn't you be in your office working instead of bragging about yet another infidelity?"

Gene scrambled to his feet. "Uh, yeah, okay, sorry. I'll just . . . Sorry."

Gene hurried out of my office. Slowly, I sat. My nerves were still tingling. My blood pressure must have leapt at least twenty points. I took a steadying breath.

Ellen, being a smart person, knocked lightly on the open door.

"Sorry about that," I said, assuming she'd heard my outburst.

Ellen closed the door behind her.

"I'm worried about you, John," she said. "Something's going on. You want to tell me about it?"

"Nothing's going on."

"You just lost your temper with one of your staff. Granted, if anyone deserves your wrath it's Gene but the anger was out of line. Not that you don't know that."

"It's nothing, really, Ellen," I said again. "Thanks for asking. I'm just tired. I need to get more sleep."

"Yes, well," she said, "sleep is restorative."

When she left she closed the door behind her, for which I was grateful.

* 75 *

Why should the right to fictionalize belong only to the artist? Everyone's life is a work of art; everyone is his own creator. So, lie as long and as hard as the masterpiece that is your life requires.
        —Creative License and the Average Person

EVA

It's said the real reason one should never eavesdrop is that one is likely to hear something one doesn't really want to hear.

And yet I just had to pick up the phone, ever so quietly, and put it to my ear.

Poor Jake. He thought he was speaking privately; he trusted his lover not to listen in on the bedroom extension. He was so naive. I pulled his shirt closer around me and with my eye on the door, I listened.

Jake: "Look, it's not like I'm going to marry someone old enough to be my mother. I mean, someday I'm going to want to have kids and then what? I'm going to want to marry— I'm going to have to marry—someone my age or younger. That's just biology, man."

So, I thought, Jake has changed his mind about wanting a family. Was I responsible for this change?

Phil: "Yeah, but how do you know some of these grand-mas don't expect you to marry them?"

Jake paused and when he answered Phil's incredibly naive question, his voice was unsure. "I can't imagine a woman in her forties would expect a twenty-one-year-old to propose."

"I'd be careful, my man," Phil warned. "You might find yourself hauling around a middle-aged ball and chain one of these days. Yeah, it's all biology. And the biological clock for forty-year-old women is ticking real loud. I don't know why you bother with anyone over twenty-three. Twenty-five, tops."

Jake lowered his voice, as if imparting vital information. "I told you, dude, sex with older women is more exciting, less inhibited. Besides, they're not drunk every night like some of the chicks at school."

Phil: "Yeah, but the body. Even Demi Moore, married to Kutcher—what's up with that? I'm sorry, man, but I just don't believe she looks so good when she takes off her clothes."

Jake: "Didn't you see her in a bikini? What was that movie, *Charlie's Angels* or something? She's got a great body."

Phil: "Airbrushing. Movie magic. I'm not buying it."

Jake (with a laugh): "Since when are you so obsessed with physical perfection? I've seen some of the girls you hook up with. That one the other night, the blonde? She was stuffed into those jeans. She was fat."

Phil: "She was stacked, not fat. Anyway, nineteen-year-old skin is sexy. Forty-year-old skin is not. That's all I'm saying."

Jake: "You're a pig, you know that."

Phil: "Whatever."

Jake: "Look, I have to go. So I'll drop off the CDs later, okay?"

I didn't wait for Phil's reply; I'd heard more than enough. I dashed under the covers, risking injury to my decrepit, wrinkly body in the process.

Jake found me there a moment later, just waking up—or so I let him think.

"Were you on the phone?" I mumbled, stretching elaborately. "I thought I heard your voice."

"Uh, did you hear—I mean, did I wake you?"

"Oh, no," I lied. "I just thought I heard the sound of your voice."

Jake looked somewhere above my head.

"It was just Phil," he said. "He's such an idiot sometimes."

"Yes," I said dryly. "I know."

Jake gestured feebly to the dresser. "I've got an early lecture . . ."

I tossed the covers aside and sat up. "I was just leaving," I said.

76

Dear Answer Lady:

My mother gave me ten thousand bucks to put aside for her funeral. Thing is, she's totally healthy and will probably live for another ten years. My wife said I shouldn't have but I spent the money on a new stereo and flat-screen, high-def TV. I figure, by the time my mother's funeral rolls around, I'll have made back the money from overtime or something. Was this wrong?

Dear Scumbag:

You are the definition of the "thankless child" and should be spanked severely. As for your mother, she's either hopelessly naive or afflicted with Alzheimer's. Why else would she trust a scumbag with her hard-earned money?

SOPHIE

I chose a little restaurant called The Bean for our lunch. Ben and I ate there about once a week. I hoped it would meet Eva's standards but I could never be sure what she would find acceptable. Eva could be a harsh critic, of places and people.

And I so wanted Eva to like Ben and Ben to like Eva. My anxiety about this first meeting was, I think, understandable.

Ben was five minutes late.

"So," Eva said, not too discreetly checking her watch. "Where's the Mystery Man?"

Before I could answer my cell phone vibrated and I grabbed for it. It was Ben.

"Hi," I said. "Where are you?"

Eva lifted an eyebrow at me. I looked away.

"Oh, that's too bad. No, of course I understand. Okay. Okay, I'll see you this evening."

"Are we being stood up?" Eva inquired archly when I'd disconnected the call.

"There's a bit of an emergency at work," I explained. "He didn't say what it was, exactly. Rats, I'm disappointed. I really wanted you two to meet!"

Eva shrugged. "Well, I guess Mystery Man will just have to remain a mystery a bit longer."

"Yes, well. I guess we can order now."

"Good," Eva said. "I'm starved."

I really don't know how she maintained her figure with all she ate. Ben liked my body, I thought, scanning the menu. Didn't he? I considered getting a salad instead of a burger. Then I wouldn't feel guilty about having dessert.

"So," I said when we had ordered, "has John told you anything more about his search for Ms. Right?"

"No, why? Is there something to tell?"

"Not that I know of," I admitted. "I mean, he hasn't asked me to help him shop for a ring."

"I doubt John needs anyone's help for that. Even I have to admit he's got good taste. I can't imagine it wouldn't translate into women's jewelry."

"You never know. Maybe he's never bought jewelry for a woman before."

Eva laughed. "John? He's had a million women. I exaggerate, of course. But maybe you're right. Men know that giving

a gift of jewelry to a woman, even something as seemingly in-
nocuous as a bracelet, can have the odor of commitment."

Our meals arrived. I'd never had a salad at The Bean before. It was disappointingly small.

"So, tell me," I said, watching Eva devour her whole
wheat pasta. "Have you met anyone lately? Anyone you're
interested in."

"It's an obsession with you, isn't it?" Eva replied, but her
tone was light.

I shrugged. "I just want you to be happy."

"And you equate happiness with a relationship."

"With a good relationship, yes."

Eva rolled her eyes at me. "But what if a good relationship
isn't my definition of happiness? What if my definition of
happiness doesn't involve any other person but me?"

"I don't believe," I said, "that anyone can be truly happy
alone."

"Fine," she said. "That's your belief but it isn't mine and I
think if you take a good look around, Sophie, you'll see that
a life lived outside the bonds—note that choice of word,
'bonds,' similar in meaning to shackles!—of matrimony or
long-term partnership isn't necessarily a wasted one. Or an
unhappy one."

"I'm sorry," I said. "I didn't mean to sound judgmental."

Eva gave a little laugh that let me know that while she
wasn't letting me off the hook she also wasn't really angry
with me.

"Well, you did. 'Single'—what a stupid term! No one is
ever more or less than herself; being in a relationship doesn't
make you, an individual, a double!"

"Of course not. I didn't mean—"

"A person who chooses not to make a long-term commitment to one other person can have a perfectly wonderful life.
She can have friends and family and a career, and, I don't
know, belong to a society of like-minded people, like a church
or a reading group or, a, whatever."

"I know," I repeated. "I'm sorry. Really. Forget I said anything."

"Even the promise to pay for my lunch?"

Had I said that I would pay for lunch?

Eva laughed. "I'm only kidding. We'll split it, okay?"

"Sure. But I want to order dessert first."

Eva gave me the once-over and asked: "What's your excuse for the calories you don't need?"

I considered. "Disappointment. I'm disappointed that Ben couldn't join us so I'm going to drown my sorrows in"—I glanced down the menu—"in peach cobbler."

"Can I get in on that disappointment?"

I looked at Eva, stunned.

"Don't look so shocked," she said casually. "Even I indulge every once in a while. Besides," she added, looking not at me but at her menu, "it's more fun indulging with a friend."

I ordered the peach cobbler and asked for two spoons. Eva had called me a friend.

77

Embroidery always adds color and interest to the hem of a skirt or the bodice of a dress. Why, then, wouldn't it bring a certain liveliness to the story of one's life?
                        —Taking a Life Lesson from the Arts of
                        Embellishment

EVA

It's said that a person is known by the company she keeps.

Before the reemergence of Sophie and John in my life, what company had I kept? Not much. Hardly any. How had I spent my "free" time? (Why free? Why, also, "spare"? Wasn't every moment of a life necessary?)

Here's how. Having sex without commitment with a variety of men about whom I knew very little beyond their approximate salaries and social position.

I kept, of course, the company of my colleagues, five days a week. But nothing could be said about me as a person by the presence down the hall of Jack Grossman, COO, or the presence at the reception desk of Marcella whatever-her-name-is.

And then there was Jake. His was the company I most kept right then, aside from the colleagues, random entities in my life. And yet I was forced to keep his presence from the two people who suddenly meant the most to me, the two people who'd barged into my life with the excuse of being "old friends," a title they seemed to think conferred rights and privileges in the present.

I couldn't tell Sophie or John the truth about me because the truth would make them hate me. I didn't want them to hate me.

I am a keeper of secrets; therefore, one might argue, I am a liar. Why, I wondered, would anyone want to keep my company?

* 78 *

Dear Answer Lady:

I'm going to ask my girlfriend to marry me. Problem is, I've been checking out the price of diamonds and whoa, it's like outrageous. Then I came across this store in the mall that sells rings with cubic zirconia. It's amazing; you can't tell the difference! I'm thinking of buying one of those and just not saying anything to my girlfriend. But how do I keep her from getting the ring appraised and wanting to see the certification papers?

Dear Cheapskate:

A diamond is forever. Clearly, if you proceed with your half-assed plan, your relationship is not. Take out a second mortgage, get yourself a loan, borrow the money from a friend, do anything you have to do to get this woman a real diamond—and not a tiny one, either. Do you hear me? I know where you live. (Nice fake-wood shutters out back. How much did that save you, twenty bucks?)

SOPHIE

"Sophie, sit down. I have something to tell you."
When Ben walked through the door of my apartment that

evening his expression was dark. I'd suspected something was wrong. Now, I was sure of it.

He's breaking up with me, I thought. Of course. And sitting down to hear the news was not going to help one little bit. Why is it, I wondered, that men expect women to faint at a moment of crisis? I've never fainted, not even when Jake fell off his bike when he was four and knocked out his beautiful little baby teeth. There was blood everywhere but I was perfectly calm and—

"Sophie?"

"I prefer to stand, thank you," I said, my voice a bit shrill.

"Okay. Well, I'm going to sit." He sank heavily onto the couch. "I really don't know how to say this, so—"

"Just say it, Ben."

Ben's face took on a ghastly look. And then I thought: Oh, no, he's not breaking up with me, he's going to tell me he has cancer.

I fell into the armchair facing him. Maybe it would be better to sit.

"About lunch today."

"Yes," I prodded, with a conscious effort to sound encouraging rather than defensive.

"There wasn't really an emergency." Ben's eyes held mine. "I lied," he said, "and I'm sorry."

"Why? Didn't you want to meet Eva? She's my friend. I was embarrassed." The last was a lie but what with the sitting and the standing and Jake's knocking out his teeth and Ben's having cancer I think I can be excused.

"I'm sorry. Really." Ben sighed and leaned forward, arms resting on his knees. "The thing is, Sophie, I did show up at the restaurant. I saw the two of you at the table, your favorite one in the corner, and, well, I just couldn't join you. Not until talking to you first."

The bad feeling in my stomach intensified and I thought I might have to dash to the bathroom. "Ben," I said, "this is very confusing. Please just tell me what you're trying to tell me."

Ben paused before saying: "Sophie, I used to date your friend Eva. For about eight months. And I was the one who ended the relationship."

"What?" I asked stupidly. "What do you mean?"

"Believe me, I had no idea that your friend Eva was the woman I once knew."

I sank back farther into the chair and put my hands to my head. "Oh, my God, Ben, this can't be happening!"

Ben got up from the couch and came to my side, where he knelt. He put his hand on my knee; it jerked reflexively away.

"But it is happening," he said gently. "When I saw the two of you there together I was stunned. Never in a million years did I suspect the two women were the same."

I let my hands fall to my lap and thought: Maybe it's not true. Maybe my Ben is not the horrible person who broke Eva's heart. Maybe my Ben was involved with Eva before that horrible person . . .

"When was this?" I asked abruptly. "When were you two involved?"

Ben told me. The timing was perfect.

"That man. I never, ever thought that you of all people could be the man who—"

A small, bitter-sounding laugh escaped Ben's throat. "What? The man who treated her like scum?"

I opened my mouth to say something, I don't know what, but Ben spoke first.

"It's okay," he said, rising to his feet and moving off a few steps. "You don't have to tell me. I can imagine the sort of tales she told about me. Eva was very good at blaming other people whenever something went wrong."

I felt angry. I didn't want to hear critical things about my friend. At the same time, reason reminded me that there are always at least two sides to a story. So I said nothing to Ben.

I just listened, as I'd listened when Eva had first told me her side of things.

"Every time I called her I felt as if I were bothering her. She mocked my profession and my friends at the college. After the first month I stopped inviting her to spend time with them. She never introduced me to any of her friends. Finally, it dawned on me that maybe she had no friends. By the end she'd only let me see her once a week. It was ridiculous. And insulting. So, I ended it."

"Yes," I said carefully. "You told me."

There were realities I would have to get used to—like the fact that Ben had wanted to be with Eva, that he'd had sex with her, made love to her . . .

"I'm sure I could have done certain things differently," Ben said suddenly. He was leaning against the dining table, talking to the far wall. "The failure of a relationship is rarely the fault of one partner entirely."

"Yes," I murmured.

Ben sighed and came back to the couch. "But in the end," he said, "I just didn't want to try any longer. I wanted to meet someone who would know how to be a partner, not an adversary."

We sat silently for what seemed like a long time. Finally, I said, "I guess I painted a picture of Eva that's not entirely accurate. But she's my friend. It's not in my nature to talk critically about my friends."

"One of the things I admire about you, Sophie," Ben said gently, "is your loyalty to your friends. And I'm sorry if it sounds like I'm criticizing Eva. I guess I'm just trying to help you to see the truth."

Ben's version of the truth, or Eva's?

"What are we going to do?" I asked. "We can't keep our relationship a secret from Eva. But it's going to be terribly hard to tell her."

"Neither of us has done anything wrong, Sophie. Eva won't like it but she'll come around."

I wondered. And the look on Ben's face betrayed that he, too, wasn't so sure that Eva would be able or willing to accept the news of our romance.

"I think," I said, "that I need to be alone tonight. I need to sort things out."

Ben began to protest. Instead, he picked up his bag and walked to the door. "Call me later if you want to talk," he said. "Please?"

I nodded. And Ben left.

79

*Relentless questioning under harsh lighting in a room
with poor air circulation and the distinct smell of cat
urine is almost guaranteed to produce results.*
— Let's Not Beat About the Bush: Getting to the
Truth Even if It Kills You

SOPHIE

"Jake, I have something to tell you."

We were in the kitchen. Jake had come by for his laundry.

"What's wrong, Mom?" he asked.

I took a deep breath. "Jake, Ben used to date Eva. They were together for about eight months. It was a few years ago but Eva still thinks about him. She told me he was the only one she ever considered marrying. And then he broke her heart."

Jake turned away and reached for a glass from the dish drainer.

"Jake," I said. "Did you hear me?"

He turned back. I noticed he looked a little pale. I hoped he wasn't coming down with something. When Jake caught a cold he was sick for weeks.

"She never told me about—I mean, you never mentioned some big love of her life."

"Well," I said, "Eva's love life is really none of your business. It's really none of mine, either. Only, of course, now it is . . . Oh, I wish she had never told me about Ben!"

Jake put down the glass he'd been holding. "When you met Ben did you know he'd gone out with Eva?"

"No!" I explained how Ben had seen Eva and me at the restaurant. "Eva never told me his name and even if she had, I never would have suspected that my Ben had been her boyfriend. Ben and Eva are so different. I just can't see them together!"

"Yeah. I can't see it, either."

"What?" I asked.

Jake cleared his throat. "Nothing."

"Oh, Jake, I'm so confused."

"What's there to be confused about? She's not involved with him anymore, right?"

"Right."

"And you trust Ben, right?"

"Of course I trust him," I said automatically, but I wasn't entirely sure that I did. Was Eva right after all? Had Ben left her for another woman? Had he really broken her heart? Or had Eva broken her own heart?

"So, what's the problem?" Jake asked. I noted that his color had returned.

"The problem," I told him, "is that I feel guilty for being in love with Eva's ex-boyfriend."

Jake laughed. "Mom, that's ridiculous. You've done nothing wrong. How can you possibly feel guilty?"

"Because I do. And I also feel guilty about keeping this from Eva. I hate secrets. I hate them. They always mean trouble."

I thought of the secrets Brad had kept from me over the years. And again I wondered: If I had known about his affairs at the time, would that knowledge have helped our flagging relationship or ended it more quickly?

"So," Jake was saying, "tell her. She'll understand."

"I'm not so sure she will, Jake. You didn't hear her talk about how hurt she was when she and Ben broke up."

"Mom, Eva is"—He stopped, folded his arms—"I mean, she seems like a pretty tough cookie. Maybe things will be a bit awkward for a while but everything will even out, I'm sure of it."

"Maybe," I murmured.

"Besides, maybe Eva has someone new in her life, someone who's made her forget about Ben."

I shook my head. "No, no, Eva has no one. She'd tell me if she was seeing anyone special, I know she would."

"Maybe she wants to keep him to herself for a while," Jake suggested. "You know, like you did with Ben."

I looked closely at my son. "Jake, do you know something I don't?"

"Of course not," he protested. "How would I know anything about Eva's personal life?"

I sighed. "No, I guess you wouldn't. But you won't tell Eva about Ben, will you?"

"Why would I tell her?" Jake sounded annoyed. "Anyway, I mean, I don't even know where she lives. It's not like I talk to her or anything."

I shook my head. "No, of course not, I'm sorry. I don't know what I'm saying. I guess I meant if you bump into her on the street sometime."

Jake came to my side and put his arm around me for a reassuring squeeze. "I'll keep my mouth shut, I promise," he said. "This thing will be our little secret for now."

"Secrets! They always seem to go hand in hand with lies!"

"Sometimes keeping a secret is a good thing, Mom," Jake reasoned. "You know that. Like when revealing something will hurt someone unnecessarily."

"Unfortunately," I pointed out, "in this case I have no choice. Eva has to be told about Ben and me. And I just know she'll be furious!"

Jake sighed and moved off toward the fruit bowl. I was glad to see that he was eating healthily.

"Jake," I asked suddenly, "do you have secrets from me?"

Jake coughed on a bite of banana. "Of course," he said when he'd recovered. "Everybody has little secrets, you know."

"Promise me you'll never keep anything really big from me? Promise you'll let me help you if you're in trouble or if I can advise you or be happy with you?"

"Mom, how can I—"

"Please, Jake, promise?"

Jake sighed and tossed the banana skin into the sink. Just like his father. I'm not sure Brad ever knew the location of the garbage can. "Okay, okay," he said. "I promise to let you know the important stuff."

I smiled. "Thank you, Jake. And thanks for listening." And then something else occurred to me. "Jake?" I asked. "You do like Ben, right? I mean, you think he's a good person?"

"Yeah, I like him. But Mom, you're going to have to trust your instincts on this one. You know him better than I do."

"Yes," I said, "I suppose so." But I wondered if Eva knew him even better than I did.

"Mom, look, I have to go. I've got a seminar at five."

"When will you eat dinner?" I asked as Jake grabbed his bag and headed for the front door.

Jake turned, kissed my cheek, and said, "Right after, I promise. Stop worrying. Stress will kill you."

And then he was gone. I felt bad for having dragged him into the whole mess. I'd always tried to keep my troubles from Jake but ever since the divorce I'd come to look upon him as a bit of a friend as well as my child. It was unfair of me, I know, especially when Jake had so much on his own plate with school and baseball and his friends. Of what importance could a romantic triangle—consisting of his mother, his mother's friend, and that friend's ex-boyfriend—be to a twenty-one-year-old?

I'd call Jake and apologize. Better yet, maybe I'd give his apartment that surprise cleaning. Or bake him some brownies. A young man shouldn't be worried about cholesterol!

80

Dear Answer Lady:

I just know my wife is cheating on me. Don't ask me why, just trust me, the signs are there. Just like they were two years ago when I accused her of having an affair with her boss. Of course, she denied it and when I confronted her boss things got a little out of hand and he called the cops and fired my wife. Anyway, to this day whenever I bring it up she denies ever doing anything wrong but I know better. And now it's happening again—and it's with her new boss! Problem is, she can't afford to lose another job because I'm out of work for some bogus "violation" of worksite conduct—so this time I'm thinking of hatching a plan to catch her in the act. You know a lot about this cheating stuff. Any ideas?

Dear Psychotically Jealous Husband:

You're right, I do know a lot about this cheating stuff. And here's my advice to you. Are you paying attention? Drop it. Your wife wasn't cheating on you two years ago and she's not cheating on you now. Keep up the suspicious attitude, however, and she will be cheating on you, I guarantee it. And another thing. Are you listening? You have way too much time on your hands. Use your temporary unemploy-

*ment to take an anger management class or get your-
self on some medication. NOW!*

JOHN

"This is not good," I said. "This is not good at all."

Suddenly, my appetite was gone. Thankfully, we hadn't yet ordered lunch.

Sophie's face fell even further. "I know. I feel just miserable about it. And it's put a strain on Ben and me, too."

"Sorry. I suppose I should try to be helpful."

"There's really nothing you can do. Except maybe give me some advice on how to tell Eva that I'm involved with the man she says was the love of her life."

The man she says was the love of her life. Something about Eva's claim had always struck me as . . . false. Maybe not entirely but it sounded too Romantic for Eva, even, in fact, for Eve, whose ideas about love had been, from what I could recall, less airy than earthy and solid.

"Yes, well, I'll try to think of something useful," I said lamely.

"I've asked Ben to join us. I hope you don't mind."

"Of course not," I said. As long as Eva doesn't happen to wander by, everything should be fine.

Ben showed up a few minutes after that. He greeted Sophie with a kiss on her cheek and a squeeze of her hand. She looked simultaneously pleased and embarrassed. Ben sat and Sophie introduced us. His firm handshake belied the overall delicacy of his appearance.

Ben spoke with precision; his voice was pleasing. His movements were graceful, almost elegant. He was deferential though not subservient. In short, it was ludicrous to imagine Eva with this man. It was like trying to imagine the Dahli Lama dating Carmen Electra, or Beverly Sills hanging out with Pete

Doherty. All right, the contrast between Ben and Eva wasn't quite that extreme but you get my point.

Eva, I was certain, needed a man more obviously dynamic, someone more like—me. She needed a man who could help her become the person she once wanted to be. She needed a man more like—me.

I'm not entirely unreflective. I wondered uneasily if I was again indulging in savior fantasies, imagining myself as the white knight coming to the rescue of the damsel in distress—even though the damsel wouldn't admit she was in distress. Then again, maybe that was part of my fantasy: convincing the reluctant damsel that she needed my help.

"Tell Eva as soon as possible," I said, interrupting Ben as he was saying something sotto voce to Sophie.

Ben nodded. "I agree. I think we need to tell her right away."

"And," Sophie said glumly, "I should be the one to do it."

* 81 *

In today's conscienceless society, where stubborn opinion masquerades as truth and "news" is more a creation of Photoshop than a balanced report of actual events, it is increasingly difficult for a decent person to maintain his or her ethical bearing. Recent studies show a marked increase in cases of extreme apathy and debilitating depression in people formerly devoted to conscientious social behavior and personal responsibility.
—Being a Person of Your Word in a Society
Dedicated to Fraud

EVA

I tasted the wine. It was something Sophie had introduced me to, a delicious Cabernet Sauvignon. John, I thought, will really like this.

John. When I'd postponed my "date" with Jake earlier that day, I didn't tell him that I was having dinner with John. By now, Jake knew better than to press me about my life outside his small apartment.

Not that it mattered. I was going to end it with Jake as soon as the right moment presented itself. The unpleasantness of keeping the affair from Sophie was wearing me down. I wanted it to be done.

And there was something else. Those feelings for John

were occupying more and more of my time. Not that I had any illusions of a relationship with him. I was still convinced that my feelings were temporary, a passing, aberrant thing. A whim. A fancy.

Still, it was time to walk away from Jake. He was young. Although his ego might get bruised, his heart would soon recover. And, I reasoned, he, too, might be ready to move on. He couldn't be happy with the narrowness of our situation. Youth is never content to be regulated.

I spotted John walking to our table and smiled.

"You look good," I said, when he joined me. "That's a gorgeous suit."

"You're not going to berate me for being late?"

I looked at my watch. "You are late. I didn't even notice."

"That excited to see me?" John grinned.

"No," I said. "My mind was just wandering. Anyway, you're not going to thank me for complimenting your suit?"

"Of course. Thank you. And I am sorry I was late. I don't know why I took the T. I should have just walked."

"Stuff happens. You're here now."

"You're in a mellow mood. Not that I'm complaining."

I shrugged. "I guess. Here, you have to taste this wine. Sophie recommended it."

John lifted my glass to his lips, then hesitated. "You're not afraid of my cooties?"

"I had my shot. Go ahead."

John took a sip. "That's great. Do you want to get a bottle?"

"Sure. It's a little pricey, though."

"But we lawyers make oodles of money."

"Oodles?"

"I'm quoting you."

I frowned. "I said oodles?"

"You did."

"Huh. Well, anyway, if you can afford that suit you can afford the wine."

John raised an eyebrow at me. "I can afford it? We're not splitting the bill?"

"I'm not in that mellow a mood," I said slyly.

John sighed, the long-put-upon man. "Well, all right. I'll live on Ramen noodles for the rest of the week."

"Just order the wine, you self-pitying wretch. And get us some menus while you're at it. I'm starved."

82

Dear Answer Lady:
My buddy is getting married and asked me to be the best man. I said yes; he and I have been friends since first grade. Problem is, I think I'm in love with his fiancée. I think about her all the time. It's driving me crazy. I want to say something to her but I'm pretty sure she barely knows I exist. Or maybe I should say something to my buddy. What do you think?

Dear Loser:
I think you should keep your big mouth shut and find yourself a woman who does know you exist. And start working on your best man speech now. Go!

JOHN

Eva liked my suit.

Eva was involved with another man.

I spent a good part of our dinner together trying to temper any hopes I might have regarding my relationship with Eva. It was exhausting, hope having a lot of energy.

I reminded myself repeatedly that Eva had given me no indication she was interested in me in a romantic way. True, she wasn't as disinterested or abrasive as she was when we first reunited, and she had apologized about her bad behavior the night of the show, and we had shared a good evening after that. And tonight—well, tonight was going nicely enough, though Eva seemed a bit distracted. Come to think of it, I'm sure I did, too.

Still, as I've mentioned earlier, I make mistakes but I'm not a fool. At least for the moment, at least until Eva learned Sophie's secret, at least until—sometime in the future—I would keep my feelings to myself.

Sophie's secret. I hated sitting across from Eva knowing I held a secret that when revealed—if Sophie was to be believed—would cause her a great deal of pain. But I wouldn't break my word to Sophie; the secret wasn't mine to tell.

I did wonder, though, if Eva would care so much that Sophie was involved with her ex; after all, she had that young guy now. But I knew Eva; at least I thought I knew her. Where once she'd been generous she'd grown stingy; where once she'd been reasonable she'd grown impetuous. The chances of her reaction being a mild one were slim.

Dinner over, we parted outside the restaurant. I hailed her a cab.

"I can hail my own cabs," she said. "But thanks."

I opened the back passenger door for her. "Yes," I said, "I know you can open your own doors, too. But, you're welcome."

Eva laughed. And then, just before slipping into the cab, she planted a quick little kiss at the corner of my mouth. But she made the mistake of lingering there a split second too long. I kissed her back. It was a bit awkward, not my best work, and then, with another laugh, she darted into the cab and was gone.

I hadn't meant to kiss her. But I wasn't sorry that I had.

* 83 *

This writer is tired of the bad rap the act of dodging has acquired. From Dickens's The Artful Dodger *to those who avoided the Vietnam draft (draft dodgers), the act of evading the law or one's so-called duty has been considered something of dubious moral value. In reality, the ability to successfully evade capture and punishment (just or unjust) is a skill that should be lauded.*

—Evasion as a Positive Life Skill

EVA

I wondered why I was even bothering to meet Jake, especially after John's unexpected kiss, a kiss that had made me want more, a kiss that had rattled a lot more than my body.

I checked my watch.

He was late again. I pulled out my cell and called my lazy, soon-to-be-ex-lover. The phone rang once, twice. On the third ring I scanned the area impatiently, half-expecting to see Jake loping his way toward me, an excuse on his lips.

But the street was empty except for a couple, a man and a woman. Something about them seemed familiar. They were holding hands. Coming closer, nearer to a streetlight. They stopped. The man pulled the woman to him and kissed her. They moved on, under the glow of the lamp.

Sophie. And Ben.

"Hey, Eva."

I was startled by the voice at my ear.

"Look, I'm sorry I'm late. I'm on my way—"

"I can't meet you tonight," I said mechanically.

"No, wait," Jake went on, "I'm really sorry, I'll be there in like, ten minutes."

I clicked the phone shut.

I backed into the shadows and watched as Sophie and Ben walked by.

84

Dear Answer Lady:
  One of my friends makes a lot less money than I do and it's really inconvenient. When we go out for dinner we have to eat at chains like Olive Garden or have a drink at a pub instead of cool places where they actually have good-looking bartenders. I like her and all, she's smart and funny and always remembers my birthday, but it's really getting old, hanging out in these dumps. I mean, it's not my fault she's support-ing her two kids since her husband ran out on her— did I tell her to marry the bum in the first place? Anyway, what do I do?

Dear Self-Centered Swine:
  You don't deserve a friend like the one you de-scribe. In fact, you don't deserve any friend at all. What you deserve is a swift kick in the butt and a life spent among other self-centered swine like yourself. Have fun rolling in the mud!

EVA

  Jake called twice that night. I didn't take either of his calls. I deleted his voice messages without listening to them.
  I saw, I felt, I knew only betrayal. Somehow, Sophie knew

when she met Ben that he had been mine. And yet she pursued him, maybe for that reason alone. And when Ben had learned the truth, he, too, had laughed and enjoyed the game.

It had been hours since dinner but I thought everything I'd eaten would come roaring up my throat. My head hurt. I tried to swallow two aspirin but gagged on them.

Hours passed. I remained painfully wide-awake. At one AM I was sure that if I spent one more minute by myself in that near-empty apartment I would shatter.

Sam. I reached for the phone. And then I dropped my hand to my side. No. Not that kind of help, not now.

John. His was the kind of support that made sense. Again, I reached for the phone—and again I withdrew my hand.

I wasn't used to asking for help. I felt frightened. What if John laughed at my pain or made light of my hurt? Sure, he'd been nice to me lately, but that proved nothing. Besides, I didn't fully trust myself around John, not after that kiss earlier. I knew that if something happened between us while I was feeling so vulnerable, it would kill anything real that might develop on its own. Maybe I'd grown smarter in the ways of the heart; maybe it was only self-preservation kicking in at a moment of great stress.

I sat heavily in my one armchair and looked at the opposite wall, blank of anything but paint. No desperate phone calls. No risk-taking. As I'd done since my parents' deaths, I'd weather this storm alone.

* 85 *

Consider carefully before you entrust someone with the fact that you're embezzling from the firm. Can you really trust this person? Didn't you see her in the supply room, stuffing pens into her purse? Do you really want her threatening to snitch unless you cut her into your scheme? And before agreeing to be the keeper of a secret, consider carefully the source. Weren't the police called to his house twice in the past month when neighbors reported hearing a woman screaming in distress? What kind of secret is this guy likely to impart? And do you really want to deal with his wrath when you decide his secret must be revealed for the sake of decent society?

—Don't Breathe a Word: The Delicate Art of
Imparting and Keeping Secrets

SOPHIE

"Coming!" I called. The bell continued to ring. I peered through the peephole and quickly opened the door.

I'd never figured Eva for the sort of person who would just pop in. But there she was, uninvited, looking almost disheveled.

"Eva," I said. "What are you doing here?" But I had a sinking feeling that I knew exactly what she was doing at my door.

"I know about you and Ben. I saw you so don't deny it."

No preliminaries, just the words I'd been dreading: *"I know about you and Ben."*

"I'm not denying it," I said, barely breathing.

Eva continued to glare and scowl. Crazily, I thought that her face must hurt from so much effort.

I stepped back into the apartment. "Come in, please. Let me explain."

"I don't want to hear any excuses," Eva snapped.

"I'm not making any excuses," I said with a pretext of calm. "I'm just trying to say how things came about." I took another step inside and this time, Eva followed. As I closed and locked the door I wondered if maybe asking her into my apartment had been such a good idea after all. I'd never seen Eva—I'd never seen anyone—so angry.

"Do you want something to drink?" I asked.

"This isn't a social call," she spat.

"Eva, look, I swear that when I met Ben I didn't know he was your ex! Please, you've got to believe me!"

"Well, then," she said, "how did you find out?"

I took a deep breath before answering. "Do you remember," I began, "when we met for lunch that time and Ben cancelled?"

"Of course I remember," she said and her tone suggested that I was an idiot for even asking. "And you wouldn't even tell me his name . . . Don't tell me you knew about us then and were going to spring him on me!"

"Of course not!" I cried. "What kind of a person do you think I am?"

Eva's eyes bored into me. She looked almost possessed with rage. "I'm not sure if you want to hear the answer to that question right now."

I felt sick to my stomach. I felt weak in the knees. Never in my life, not even during the divorce, had I experienced such a confrontation. "Eva," I said, my voice shaky, "please, just listen to me. Ben saw us at the table. He knew that the truth would come out the minute he joined us and that I would feel awkward and—"

"How nice that he cares about your feelings," Eva spat. "He didn't seem to care about mine when he walked out!"

Oh, God, I was making everything worse. "Eva, he didn't join us because he knew it would be difficult for both of us! Ben's not a demon, no matter what you say about him."

Eva laughed bitterly. "Oh, I suppose he's told you his version of our relationship, the version in which I star as the coldhearted, unnatural bitch."

"No, no, of course not," I said. It was partly the truth. Ben had never actually used the *B* word.

"What did he say?" Eva demanded. "I want to know. Don't lie to me, Sophie. I'm tired of being lied to."

"I never lied to you, Eva! I just—"

"You're just sleeping with the man who broke my heart! You betrayed me, Sophie! You betrayed our friendship."

"Eva, I swear, I told you, I didn't know that Ben had—that Ben was the one who—"

Who . . . what? Who ruined your life? Or the one who saved his own?

"—the one who broke up with you."

"And when you did find out?" Eva pressed. "When the truth came to light, what then? Did you dump the jerk who broke your friend's heart? No, you chose him over me!"

This isn't a contest, I thought. What is Eva thinking! "He didn't—"

"He didn't what, he didn't break my heart? Is that what you were going to say? You don't believe me? Why, because Ben told you his version of what happened?"

What could I say? Another shadow of doubt crept over me then. Was I, after all, just a dupe in Ben's game? Would he leave me with some vague excuse just like he left Eva? What, I thought, did I really know about Ben?

Then, again, what did I really know about Eva?

* 86 *

Dear Answer Lady:
I ate my roommate's last piece of leftover pizza. I denied it but my roommate knows no one else was in our apartment. Is it too late to come clean and apologize?

Dear Compulsive Eater:
Apologize immediately and get yourself into Over-Eaters Anonymous now.

EVA

I had to confront her. I had to. So the first thing the next morning I went to Sophie's apartment. She was still in her robe.

"Does John know about this?" I demanded.

She had the courtesy to look embarrassed. "Yes."

"Shit!"

"Eva," she argued, "he's my friend. And yours. I asked for his advice about how and when to tell you."

I imagined John enjoying the dark irony of this debacle. "And what did he say?"

"He said you deserved to know the truth right away."

"Right away," I repeated. Had that really been John's advice? Or was Sophie protecting him for some reason? "But you continued to keep me in the dark." I said. "When, exactly, were you planning on telling me?"

"Soon, Eva, I swear. We were—I was just looking for the right moment. Please believe me."

Why should I have believed her? Who knew what other secrets she was hiding from me? "Do you know what it was like to see you two together?" I demanded. "To be confronted like that? To see the person you once loved kiss the person you think is your friend?"

Sophie put her hand over her heart and gave me one of those obnoxious, pleading looks. "I'm sorry, Eva, I'm so sorry."

"An apology isn't good enough," I spat. "What does an apology do for me?"

"What do you want me to do?" Sophie asked. "Stop seeing Ben?"

I couldn't reply. I didn't know what I wanted from Sophie or from Ben or from myself.

Sophie shook her head as if she was beyond weary. And I left. But I didn't just leave. I stalked to the door of Sophie's perfectly appointed apartment and slammed it behind me in a magnificent huff.

How stupid I'd been! When Jake had told me that his mother was seeing a man named Ben, why hadn't I been the least bit suspicious? Because it had never occurred to me that a man who found me attractive could also be attracted to Sophie Holmes. Because I'd considered myself superior to Sophie, more beautiful, more stylish, more successful.

Stupid. I'd been an arrogant fool. And now I was being punished for it.

And John was witness to my humiliation! Every nerve tingled and my heart began to race. It frightened me, this overwhelming sensation of anger and violence. I wanted to attack. And I wanted to defend myself at all costs against any further pain.

* 87 *

The suppression of truth (suppressio veri) is a time-honored practice in every form of government including our own. As successful as this practice is in ordering the masses, it is equally as successful in ordering—or, in controlling—the individuals in one's personal life. Those skilled in the suppression of truth are inevitably those with the most material gain to show for their efforts.
—Various Methods of Playing Fast and Loose
with the Truth

JOHN

The door to my office was closed. Lately, I'd taken to keeping it that way. If it bothered the other partners they weren't bothered enough to complain.

Ellen buzzed me. "John," she said in a neutral voice, "an Eva Fitzpatrick is here to see you."

"Send her in, please."

My mood leapt in anticipation. Until the second I saw her face and knew she'd learned about Sophie and Ben.

"Do you want something to drink?" I asked lamely. "I've got water, juice—"

"Why didn't you tell me that Sophie was seeing my former boyfriend?" Eva stood squarely in front of me, her body rigid.

"Why don't you sit," I suggested.

Eva didn't respond. Oh, boy.

"When," I said, "did Sophie tell you?"

"She didn't." Eva laughed grimly. "I caught the two of them on the street last night. After our dinner."

One: Eva's choice of the word "caught" wasn't a good sign. One only "catches" an illicit couple, not a proper one. And two: Why the hell hadn't Sophie warned me of this?

"Does Sophie know you saw her?" I asked. "And Ben?"

Eva folded her arms across her chest. I find it odd when women do this; I don't know why. "Oh, she knows. I was just at her apartment."

Poor Sophie. I made a mental note to check in with her after Eva . . . After Eva, what? Calmed down? That was going to take some time.

"I only just found out myself," I said in the most reasonable, gentle voice I could manage. "And I promised that I wouldn't say anything to you. Sophie felt it was important the information come from her."

"You must have had quite the chuckle at my expense last night. Sitting across the table from me, keeping me in ignorance!"

"I hated not being able to tell you last night," I said urgently. "You've got to believe me, Eva."

Eva laughed again, unpleasantly. "Why should I believe you? Why should I believe anything anyone says? Aren't you the one who said that everyone lies?"

"Look," I said, beginning to despair, "I've kept your secret. Sophie doesn't know a thing about your lover. And I kept Sophie's secret. I thought I was being a good friend to the both of you."

"You're a jerk, you know that?"

"Maybe. But, look, Eva, I advised Sophie and Ben to tell you immediately. Short of breaking Sophie's confidence, what else was I supposed to do?"

Eva's jaw dropped. I know it's a cliché but people use the image for a reason. "You saw Ben?"

Had I been asked to keep that from Eva, too? That I'd met her ex? This whole thing was getting way out of hand.

"Eva, let's talk about this later, okay?" I asked. "I have a meeting in five minutes. I'll call you when it's over and we'll make a time to—"

"Don't bother!" Eva said angrily. "I don't care if I never see you again!"

She slammed out of the office, leaving me a bit shell-shocked and wondering if she could possibly mean what she had said.

A moment later there came a knock.

"Come in," I said miserably.

Ellen quietly closed the door behind her.

"She's very attractive."

"She's impossible," I replied.

"You wouldn't be interested in her if she was—possible."

Was that true? Disturbing thought. "Hmm," I said.

"Maybe," Ellen said calmly, "she's your cross to bear."

I looked up at my assistant dubiously. "Are you saying that Eva is my fate?"

"Maybe. Something big is at work. The energy between you two was crackling through the door."

"Is it that obvious?" I asked. "On my part, I mean?"

"Yes. But I'm guessing she hasn't entirely realized her feelings for you."

I rubbed my forehead before asking: "You think she ever will?"

Ellen shrugged. "Hard to say. I suppose coming right out and telling her how you feel is not a possibility."

"Are you kidding? That's probably the worst thing I could do."

"Yes, you're probably right. This is a tough one."

I laughed unhappily. "Well, Ellen, if you get an inspiration, feel free to share it. I'm out of ideas when it comes to Eva Fitzpatrick."

* 88 *

Dear Answer Lady:
  I'm not even sure I should be writing this letter. But here goes. My friend teaches math at an all-boys high school. Recently she told me that she's fooled around with a few of the boys. All except one are under eighteen, which I think is the legal age for consent. Or is it twenty-one? Anyway, if my friend gets caught she's going to be in really big trouble. I mean, she could lose her job and maybe even go to jail. I told her she should stop "seeing" her students but she just laughed and said that none of the boys will tell on her because they're having such a good time. What should I do?

Dear Spineless:
  Make an anonymous call to the police as well as to the principal regarding your friend's illegal and immoral conduct. Then dump said friend for being a predator and for involving you in a crime. Finally, get yourself into therapy and learn some assertiveness techniques. That's an order.

SOPHIE

"I'm just . . . I'm just having a hard time with this, Ben. I'm sorry."

Since Eva had stormed off that morning after our horrible confrontation, the living room had felt tainted. I thought I could still hear faint echoes of her fury. And now Ben was there with me and nothing felt right.

"You have nothing to apologize about," he said gently.

"Yes, I do. I'm sorry that my being upset is upsetting you. I'm sorry," I said, "that it's upsetting us. And I'm not sure what I can do about it."

Ben sighed, but it wasn't a sigh of impatience, more, I think, of sadness. "Sophie, I don't want my former relationship with Eva to destroy our happiness together. I'm afraid that's what's happening."

My happiness, destroyed. I got up from the couch and walked off a few feet. I stood with my back to Ben.

"I just need some time," I said. "Everything will be fine." But I didn't quite believe that it would.

Ben came over and put his hands on my shoulders. I stepped away.

"I'm sorry, Ben. Not tonight."

"I just wanted to rub your shoulders. It might help."

I turned to face him but could hardly meet his eye. "No, thank you," I said.

I watched the floor as Ben gathered his coat and bag. At the door he paused. "Sophie," he said. "Please look at me."

I did, but it was difficult. There was such pain in his eyes. But he was not a man to beg; he would spare me that.

"Take care of yourself, please."

I nodded.

"I'll call you tomorrow."

And then, he was gone. And I was left with the terrible feeling that Ben and I might never be happy again.

89

*Who cares that Dante committed the Neutrals to a
circle of Hell? Stop taking unpopular stands. Give up
making definite statements of belief. Reject devoting
yourself to popular causes. Life is a lot less troublesome when you disengage from public debate.*
    —Equivocate Now! – Avoid Committing Yourself
    and Start Living the Good Life

EVA

Alcoholics Anonymous teaches a Twelve Step program for
recovering addicts. Once, a long time ago, I came across
these steps in a magazine article I was reading while waiting
for the dentist. Though the religious aspect of the process
didn't appeal to me, some of the other steps seemed to make
sense. I thought they might be useful for the nonaddicted person, too.

So, I secreted the magazine in my bag—not that I'm a
thief—and once home, tore out the key page of the article,
and promptly forgot about it.

Until now. Though the page itself was long missing, I did
suddenly recall one of the steps, something about making
amends to people you've hurt. Maybe in this case my version
of making amends wouldn't count with AA. But it was the
best I could do.

First, there was Jake. I would break off the relationship

with as kind an explanation as I could find. And, maybe, I would also apologize; by saying yes to Jake's advances I'd allowed him to become a liar.

Then, there was Sophie. I felt bad about attacking her, first for the fact of her relationship with Ben and then for keeping it a secret. I had no rights to Ben and besides, I was keeping a big, damaging secret of my own.

Ben. I just might owe him an apology, too. For the first time I was able to think clearly about our relationship. Why now? I wondered. No matter. The point was that I finally understood that a large part of my anger about our breakup was just wounded pride in disguise.

And then I had to ask myself if I'd ever really been in love with Ben. The fact that he never raised his voice annoyed me. His cats made me sneeze. His habit of washing the rind of a piece of fruit before peeling it drove me nuts.

Why was I ever with him? Ben, I now realized, might have been more of a symbol for me than an individual. I believe I was drawn to him because in some way he represented my youthful self and the dreams that went with her. If I'd been in love with Ben, the individual, why would I have mocked everything about him? Why would I have derided him for loving me? Ben had functioned as a way through which I could work out my long-buried feelings of disappointment, resentment, and anger.

Poor Ben. A punching bag, not a person. How unfair I'd been to him.

I felt terribly tired. I don't remember ever having felt so tired except for the first few weeks after my parents' deaths. But there was still work to be done.

There was John. I would apologize to him for having thrown a fit in his office. John was guilty of nothing, except caring. What would happen after that, I had no idea. I hoped he would at least accept my apology. I didn't feel I deserved anything more.

90

Dear Answer Lady:

I'm a thirty-two-year-old lesbian in a committed, five-year relationship. A few months ago my partner and I started to discuss marriage and while we haven't made any firm plans, we've both been buying wedding magazines and talking about what kind of event we'd like. Then about six weeks ago my partner started a spin class at the gym and began to socialize with one of her classmates—a man I'll call "Bob." Bob is straight and single and even though he does nothing for me personally, I can honestly say that he's very handsome. My partner and I have been one hundred percent faithful since the day we met so at first it didn't even cross my mind that something might be going on between her and Bob. But lately, my partner has been growing distant; she hasn't wanted to make love for the past two weeks and she rarely engages in conversation with me. She makes no secret of the fact that she and Bob meet for lunch and sometimes even for dinner. I don't know what to do; I'm just sick about this. Should I ask my partner if she's attracted to Bob? What if she says yes? What if she says no but continues her unusual behavior? Please help me!

Dear You-Poor-Thing:

How to put this gently? There's a very good chance that your devoted partner is no longer so devoted. In fact, I would go so far as to suggest that she is about to have sex with this "Bob"—if she hasn't already. Now, take heart. Your partner's behavior might be attributed to a serious case of cold feet in light of your possible marriage plans. If so, all is not lost, as long as you are able to forgive her stress-induced lapse of fidelity and convince her to work through her fears about a lifelong commitment. On the other hand, the possibility exists that she has already "changed teams," much in the vein of the actress Anne Heche. If this is the case, relax! Has Ellen DeGeneres suffered from this defection? Have you seen Portia de Rossi? Listen to me: Talk to your partner; you have every right to know what the hell she's been up to.

JOHN

"It's your soul mate, line one."

I looked up at Ellen, momentarily confused. Then, "Oh."

"I'll close the door," she said, and slipped out of my office.

I wasn't at all sure what to expect. The last time I'd talked to Eva she'd declared she never wanted to see me again. I took a deep breath and plunged.

"Hey."

"Hi. Thanks for taking my call."

"Sure," I said.

"I want to apologize. I never should have gotten so angry with you for keeping Sophie's secret. I know you did nothing wrong. I'm sorry."

The words had spilled out, as if she'd rehearsed them, but they sounded genuine nonetheless. "Thanks, Eva," I said. "I accept your apology. I know it must have been a lousy thing to find out, especially in the way you did."

"Yes," she said, almost impatiently. "But there's something else."

"Okay."

I heard Eva take a deep breath. "I exaggerated to Sophie about Ben's importance in my life. I've spent a lot of time thinking about my motives for misleading her and, well, I think I understand a bit about . . . about a lot of things."

So, I'd been right about Ben all along. "I'm glad," I said carefully, "that you've worked things out. But I hope you're not apologizing. At least, not to me."

"No. I just thought you might want to know that—about Ben and me."

My heart—yes, my heart—leapt. But I warned myself to step with care. "Look, you want to get a bite to eat?" I asked, casually. "I know it's kind of early for dinner but—"

"Yes. Okay."

We agreed to meet at the bar at Morgan's, a rough-and-tumble Irish American pub. I was surprised by Eva's choice. But then again, there was so much I didn't know about Eva. Yet.

At the bar I ordered mozzarella sticks. It broke the ice, as I hoped it would. Eva scolded me for treating my body like a garbage can; I told her she was too uptight and dared her to eat one. "It's not going to kill you," I pointed out.

"Give it time. You keep eating all that fat and—"

"I work out! Do you see any fat on me?"

She eyed me up and down. "Your tailor does a marvelous job masking your physical defects."

"I've seen you eat crap."

"Everything in moderation. All I'm saying is that your fat intake is a little too high."

I sighed dramatically. "How about this. How about you let me eat this fried cheese without one more critical comment and starting tomorrow I'll go on a low-fat diet? For a while."

Eva grinned. "Deal." And then she grabbed one of my mozzarella sticks and bit into it with relish.

For about an hour we continued to spar about nothing and talk about mundane matters—everything, in short, except Sophie, Ben, and the meddlesome past.

"I need to get home," Eva said finally, looking at her watch (the fifth time that hour). "I've got work to do tonight."

"Sure."

"Hey. Thank you for suggesting this. It was fun."

I laughed. "But now I have to go on a diet."

"It's for your own good," she said. "But I know you. You'll cheat before the week is out."

"I will not!" And then: "Okay, you're right. I probably will cheat."

On this light note we left Morgan's. I walked Eva to her apartment in a Victorian mansion on Marlborough Street. I didn't ask her if I could or if she minded. I just sort of . . . went along.

"Thanks," she said when we stood outside Number Forty-Five.

"For what? The mozzarella stick?"

"No, idiot. For accepting my apology."

"Oh. That. Well, your reaction was totally understandable." It was mostly true, I thought.

"Do you want to see my place?" she asked suddenly. "It's nothing much, really, but—"

Down, big boy. "Uh, sure," I said, shrugging.

"Just for a minute."

If I wasn't going to be cautious, Eva was going to be cautious for both of us. Smart.

We climbed the stairs to the third floor in silence. Eva opened the door to her apartment—with a key on a Tiffany chain—and I followed her inside.

"Well," she said, with a nervous half-laugh, "this is it."

For a long moment I was without speech. And then: "It's, uh—"

"Yeah."

"I didn't expect it to be so—"

Eva laughed again; this time, she sounded more relaxed. "So like the apartment of a kid just out of college and barely able to make rent."

"Please tell me you're not sleeping on a futon."

"Of course not. I have a mattress and a box spring."

I gestured helplessly around the almost-empty living room. "Eva, why didn't you ever buy some furniture, hang a few paintings?"

Eva hesitated. "I don't know," she said finally. "I just kept putting it off. Eventually, I guess I just didn't care. I mean, why bother?"

"Too busy with work?" I ventured, though I was too busy with work, almost everyone I knew was, and we all had a couch in the living room and art on the wall.

"Something like that," she said. "There are weeks when I'm hardly here, when I'm working until ten and then I just fall into bed—okay, onto the mattress—for a few hours, get up and go back to the office. Decorating hardly seems worth the effort. Who would enjoy it?"

"You, for one," I said. "It's a good space. Big, lots of light. A cat would love to sit on that windowsill and watch the world go by."

"I'm allergic to cats. Besides, like I said, there are times when I'm hardly ever here. It wouldn't be fair to an animal."

"True, but it's too bad." And then I looked at my stylish, successful, difficult friend and said: "You could use a little companionship, Eva."

Across her face there passed a variety of emotions, only one of which was anger.

"Go ahead," I said, "jump down my throat, but I'm not apologizing for saying it."

"No," she said then, with a bit of a sigh, and looking not at me but out of the big living room window. "You're right. I could use some companionship."

Emboldened, I headed for what I supposed was the kitchen.

"What are you doing?"

"Looking in your cabinets. And the fridge." I turned to Eva, who had followed me. "Just as I suspected. No food worth mentioning. And"—I looked around, spied a likely drawer, and opened it—"no tableware worth counting. Don't tell me you use plastic utensils?"

"No, of course not," she protested. "Close that drawer, you've seen enough."

I leaned back against the counter and folded my arms across my chest. "So, it's safe to say you don't entertain often."

"Perfectly safe. In fact, you're the first person who's been here in—in a long time."

The first person? I wondered about the young man in Eva's life but didn't ask. I'd already taken some big risks; there was no good in pushing her too far too fast. "Oh," I said.

Eva leaned against the doorjamb. "I know that your home is supposed to reflect your personality. Your home is supposed to be your castle. But every time I try to think about how I would want to decorate, I come up blank. I just don't know where to begin."

"You'd begin," I instructed, "by thinking about what colors soothe or excite you, what style, Modern maybe, best suits your—"

Eva grimaced and raised her hand. "John, stop. I didn't ask you to solve a problem. And by the way, you've been watching too many home decorating shows."

"Actually," I said, "I have a natural talent for decorating. You'd know that if you'd ever come to my apartment."

"You never asked," she countered, with that Eva-like snappiness.

"Yes, I did. Twice. Once for dinner with Sophie, another time for a small wine-tasting party. Don't you remember?"

"Oh," she said, as if she really had forgotten until that moment. "Right. I must have been busy." Eva touched her hair in a gesture I hadn't seen since college. "What excuse did I give for not coming?"

"No excuse. You just said, 'can't,' which I took to mean 'won't,' so I let it go at that."

Her mouth twisted into her version of a thoughtful frown. "Well," she said finally, "if you ask me again, I'll say yes."

"Third time's the charm?"

"Just ask already."

"Okay," I said, cautioning myself to remember with whom I was dealing. "Eva, will you come to my apartment for dinner tomorrow night?"

"What are we having?"

"Does that mean you're coming?"

"I need," she said, as if talking to an idiot, "to know what kind of wine to bring."

"Prime rib. Be there at seven."

"More red meat? What happened to the diet?"

"We both knew I'd cheat."

"Okay. I'll have a small salad for lunch. Oh, one more thing. Where do you live?"

So like Eva not to know where her friends lived. She turned back for the living room and I followed. "Find me a piece of paper. I'll write it down."

"Just tell me," she said, reaching into her large bag. "I'll put it in my Blackberry. I can't believe you still use a date book."

"Paper and pen are a lot more reliable than an electronic device."

"But you use a computer."

"I didn't say I was a Luddite," I corrected. "And I'm not stupid. I just continue to appreciate the act of writing by hand. Don't ask me to explain or I will, in some detail."

"God, no." Eva smiled and opened her Blackberry. "What's the address?"

* 91 *

Specious reasoning, hollow arguments, circular logic.
Forget about clarity! It's the twenty-first century.
Time to get with the program!
    —The Century of Dissembling or, Don't Let the
    Truth Slow You Down

EVA

"Hi. You're on time."

John looked . . . good.

"I'm always on time," I replied.

John closed the door behind me, and locked it. "Nobody's always on time. Trains get stuck in tunnels, heavy rains cause pileups—"

"Yeah," I said, "I get it. How about, I try always to be on time?"

"Acceptable. Want the grand tour?"

John's apartment was beautiful, masculine without being clichéd; there wasn't a stuffed dead animal in sight. It had a welcome feel about it and yet it was as neat as a pin. Magazines were stacked neatly on the coffee table; the materials on his desk were perfectly aligned, just as they were at his office. (I'd noticed, in spite of my fury.) The bathroom was spotless. His bedroom was a refuge in dark blues and greens.

"You did this all by yourself?" I asked dubiously when we'd returned to the living room. "No help from your mother or a bevy of adoring single women just dying to leave their mark?"

"Fixing up an apartment to look like it's lived in is hardly rocket science, Eva."

"No," I said, "I suppose it isn't. Anyway, I love the couch. And that chair. And that print over the table."

"Sophie hates it."

I laughed. "I can see how it wouldn't be her kind of thing. Too depressing."

John squinted at the print in grays and blacks. "You think it's depressing?"

"I'm not an artist, John. As you've already pointed out. Nor am I an art critic. I think it's a little depressing, but that doesn't mean I don't like it."

"Sophie called it ugly. Only after I pushed her for an honest opinion."

I followed John to the kitchen. The smells were wonderful. He cooked, he cleaned, he decorated, he had a good job. Someday, I thought, John would make someone the perfect husband. I didn't say this to him. I wondered how his search for the perfect wife was going, but I didn't ask.

While John busied himself with final dinner preparations, I perched on a stool at the kitchen's concrete-topped bar.

"Maybe I should hire you to fix up my place," I said.

John looked up from whatever it was he was chopping, some kind of green, and frowned.

"No, I mean it," I said. "I could use the help. You've seen how I've been living."

"Friends don't let friends hire friends," he said. "Or something like that. I'm not eager to be your employee."

"Because I'd be such a lousy boss?"

I couldn't quite read the look in his eyes just then. "If you say so," he said, and went back to chopping.

I watched him work. I know I'd ribbed him about his lousy diet but he really was in fabulous shape, especially for a man in his early forties, when so many men tend to get dumpy. I crossed my legs; this was my body's silly attempt to toss aside carnal thoughts about my friend. "Can I help with something?" I asked.

Without looking up John said: "Can you dice?"

"No."

"Mince? Julienne?"

"No. And no."

"Then sit there and drink your wine."

Dinner was on the table before long: prime rib, salad, red roasted potatoes with herbs, all very simple and delicious.

"You and Sophie are spoiling me," I said. "I hadn't had a home-cooked meal in years before you guys reemerged."

John smiled and poured a sweet dessert wine. "It's not that hard to cook, you know."

"I know," I said. "I can cook. Not like you, but I can manage the basics." I paused, considered, wondered if it would be safe, realized there was only one way to find out. "I had to learn how to cook," I said. "After my parents died. Maura was only eleven. She couldn't live on peanut butter and jelly sandwiches."

John touched his glass to mine. I noticed the tiny wrinkles at the corner of his eyes. They suited him.

"Sometimes," he said, "I forget that you had such huge responsibility right out of college. It must have been very hard."

No accusing me of self-pity. Just . . . recognition of what my life had been like.

I shrugged, pretending his response hadn't pleased me as much as it had. "Yeah, that was me, in effect a working single mom. There was a distant cousin, an old woman named Vivian. She came around every month or so with a care package, but after about a year she moved to Florida. Which didn't bother Maura," I added. "She didn't like Vivian. Vivian smelled of mothballs."

"That old?"

"That preserved."

"If you know how to cook," John asked after a moment, "why don't you cook for yourself?"

"I don't know," I said. "Maybe . . . Maybe because it reminds me of those first years alone with my sister, trying to do everything, constantly feeling that I was letting her down, letting myself down. Or maybe because it feels too . . . lonely. Or maybe like too much effort just for one person."

"Three possibilities."

"Yeah. Anyway," I said breezily, a bit exhausted from having revealed so much, wanting to steer the conversation into brighter territory, "it doesn't matter. Now I can bum dinner off you."

"And Sophie?"

A good question, and we were back to the dark. "She hasn't called me back. I left a message saying I wanted to apologize for being so insane that morning."

"I'm sure she'll call," John said, with the reassuring tone I'd heard him use with our friend. "It's only been a few days."

I wasn't convinced but I smiled as if I was.

"I should be getting home," I said, rising. "Thanks, John. The meal was fantastic."

John rose, too. "Even though I served red meat?"

"Did you see anything left on my plate?"

John brought my coat and bag from a closet in the hall. "You are a devourer."

"Yes," I said, wondering if that was entirely a compliment.

"Do you want me to walk you home?" John asked at the door. "Or I could call you a cab."

I rolled my eyes at him. "John. I'm not a child."

"Did I say you were a child? You're a woman alone at night in a city. I'm allowed to worry."

"I'm a woman alone in a city every night and every day. Are you going to start escorting me to and from the office? The grocery store?"

"Point taken."

"But thanks," I said with a smile. "For the concern."

I kissed him good-bye. It was a quick and friendly kiss, on the cheek, close to the mouth but not there, not again, not yet.

92

Dear Answer Lady:

Last year I moved to a new city to help me get over a bad breakup with my long-term girlfriend. Anyway, about a month later I met a supernice guy and we started to date. I'd never had sex with a man before—I've always known I'm gay. Anyway, the sex did nothing for me but he was so nice that I kept sort of forgetting to mention that I was gay and whenever he asked about my past I was vague or made stuff up. Anyway, he asked me to marry him and I said yes because he's such a great guy and has a fantastic job. My problem is that I still want to sleep with women but I also really want to marry my fiancé. As long as I keep my lesbian life a secret from him, he won't be hurt, right? Sometimes honesty isn't the best policy, right?

Dear Turncoat:

Shame on you for sailing under false colors! After all gay people have gone through to achieve what dubious respect and rights they now own, your conduct is both insulting and cowardly. And on the matter of the poor fool you're planning to marry—shame on you again! Get back out of the closet right now— go!—and confess all to your fiancé. If he still wants

*to marry a declared lesbian, that's his choice—but
you'd better not let him catch you in bed with the
sexy new yoga instructor named Heidi.*

EVA

Not ever.
Because I couldn't let it happen to me. I couldn't fall in
love, not with John. Never with John. He would challenge
me, I knew it. He would raze my defenses, leaving me vulner-
able. He would love me no matter how hard I fought him.
Hadn't he already begun to prove that?
It sounded horrible. Wonderful. Horrible. Intimacy would
destroy me. It would save me.
I wasn't ready. I was afraid.
I didn't want to make the call. But I had to.
"Hello, Sam."
There was silence before Sam said, "Oh, hey. What's up?"
What's up?
"I thought," I said, trying hard to sound nonchalant, "that
you'd be a little happier to hear from me."
There was another disconcerting silence before Sam
replied. "Oh, well, yeah. You just caught me by surprise is
all."
"So," I said, loathing myself, "how about getting together
sometime this week?"
"Uh, right. Let me look at my schedule a minute . . ." And
then, abruptly: "Uh, no, sorry, this week doesn't look good."
"Okay. How about next week? I can do Tuesday after-
noon or Thursday evening."
"Uh, next week?" Sam coughed. "Next week doesn't, no,
I'm totally booked."
I took a deep breath. "Sam," I said, "what's going on?"
There was another moment of ominous silence before Sam
replied. "Eva, I can't see you."

"Either you're enduring an outbreak of herpes," I said, "or there's a woman."

"A woman. I met someone." Sam sounded apologetic.

"So?" Silently, I begged: Please, Sam, you've got to do this for me. You've got to help me erase him from my mind. "What's the problem?"

"There's no problem, Eva. I'm going to ask her to marry me." Whatever hint of apology I'd detected in Sam's tone was gone. Now, there was a hint of pride.

"Oh," I said, evenly. "Well, congratulations. I'll remember to send a bottle of expensive champagne."

"There's no need, Eva. In fact, you probably shouldn't."

"I know. I was only joking."

"Oh. Sorry."

"So, how long has this grand romance been going on?"

"Do you really want to know?"

No. But Sam had to know that I didn't care. "Of course," I said. "Everyone loves a love story."

"Well, to tell you the truth, I met her about a month before you called things off between us. When you wouldn't see me anymore because of that other guy, it kind of gave me an excuse to spend more time with her. She's really nice. I think you'd like her."

What made people say such ridiculous things? Of course I wouldn't like her. Of course I would loathe and despise her.

"Mmm," I said. "So, were you sleeping with her when you called me a few weeks ago, desperate to get together? You do remember that night, don't you?"

"Yes. But I regret it. I shouldn't have cheated on her. I mean, we didn't have an exclusivity agreement at the time, but still. If she knew about it now she'd be really hurt." Sam paused. "You'd never tell her, would you?"

"Of course not, Sam. Don't be ridiculous."

But I thought: What about me? My feelings didn't seem to

matter in this ménage à trois. Suddenly, I was fighting back tears.

"Thanks," Sam said. "I know you would never do something so mean, but . . ."

"So," I said brightly, amazed at my own acting skills, "what's the lucky girl's name? What does she do? Is she anybody?"

Sam laughed. "Eva, you're such a snob. Her name is Alison and she's working in a gallery on Newbury Street while she's getting her master's in fine arts."

"She's quite a bit younger than me, of course."

"Of course." And then Sam scrambled. "Wait, I didn't mean that in a bad way. It's just that, you know, I want to have kids soon so . . ."

"Don't worry, Sam. I never thought of you as anything other than a good lay."

"I know."

"Well then, I guess—"

"So," he interrupted, "how's it going with that other guy? I'm thinking maybe not so good, what with your calling me."

"Oh, that's over," I said airily. "It wasn't meant to be anything permanent. Besides, he was getting too clingy and you know how I hate clingy men."

Sam laughed ruefully. "Oh, I know. Sometimes I think you don't have any use for any sort of man."

"Don't be absurd. Look, there's no point in continuing this conversation. Congratulations, Sam. I'm sure you'll make a fine husband."

"Thanks, Eva," he said. "I'm going to try."

"One more thing, Sam. Is she as good as me in bed?" Like it mattered.

"No, Eva," Sam said mildly. "But we can't have everything, can we?"

"Speak for yourself."

"Besides," Sam went on, ignoring my flippant reply, "what

I'm giving up in passion I'm making up for in other ways. Alison actually likes to be seen in public with me."

"A poor attempt at levity."

"Sorry," he said. "Anyway, take care of yourself, Eva."

"Of course," I said, but I wondered if I had the slightest clue how.

* 93 *

You'll feel a lot better once you accept that fact that some damage is just too great to fix. Instead of wasting your time trying to make amends for having slept with your brother's wife (or your sister's husband), cut the family tie and move on. The pattern of repeated attempts at reconciliation followed by the rejection of such attempts will only wreak havoc on your psychological well-being.
—Repairing the Irreparable: A Study of Futile
Attempts at Reconciliation

SOPHIE

Juggling a plate of brownies covered in aluminum foil and a plastic bag stuffed with new shirts I'd picked up for Jake at Marshall's, I extricated my keys from my bag. Who wouldn't want to come home from class to find fresh-baked brownies and new clothing waiting for him?

I smiled to myself as I opened the door and closed it softly behind me. I hate loud noises. Brad was always slamming cupboards and letting the toilet seat drop and raising the volume on the TV. It drove me crazy. Jake was a much quieter person than his father, more like me.

I put the brownies on the counter and surveyed the tiny kitchen. Dishes in the sink, an open box of cold cereal on the counter, a half-empty bottle of energy drink. Well, Jake might be quiet like me but he hadn't gotten my neat-freak gene. I closed the box, emptied the bottle, and left the dishes for a moment. With the bag of new shirts, I headed for Jake's bedroom. The door was partially closed. That's another thing that annoys me. A house looks neater when doors are either fully shut or entirely open. I pushed the door open with my palm.

"Oh, shit!" Eva's hands flew to her face, as if covering it in shame. As if she could feel such a thing.

My boy, my son, lay on the unmade bed, naked but for a sheet around his waist.

The bag of shirts fell to the floor.

"Mom!" Jake cried, clutching the sheet to his chest. "It's not what you think!"

"Yes, it is," I said absurdly. "It's exactly what I think."

Eva, fully dressed, extended her hands toward me as if in supplication. "No, no, Sophie, you don't understand! I was just about to break up with him!"

"What?" Jake cried. "You were?"

"You're supposed to be in class," I said.

"Yes, yes, that's why I came over this afternoon, to break up with you!"

"I don't understand!"

"I'm paying a lot of money for tuition," I said. "Why aren't you in class?"

"Not now, Jake!"

Eva stepped closer to me, her face a mask of panic, and for the first time I noticed the lines around her eyes, a tiny skin tag on her neck. "Sophie, please—"

"You decrepit old bitch," I said, with amazing calm.

Eva froze, her ridiculously huge bag hanging off her shoulder, her eyes wide. And then she rushed past me, out of the room, out of the apartment. I heard the door slam.

"Uh, Mom? Could you turn around so I can . . ."

"Oh, God," I said and whirled to face the wall, hands over my eyes.

I heard some squeaking as Jake got out of the bed, then some muttering as, I imagined, he looked for his clothes. It seemed forever before he said: "You can turn around now."

"No," I said. "I don't think I can." And I dashed from the bedroom, through the living room and out into the hallway.

Jake called out but I didn't turn back.

94

Dear Answer Lady:

I know this is going to sound like I'm a whiny, ungrateful wretch, but here's the thing. I work for a woman who is a really great boss. She isn't married and has no kids so I think that in some way, her staff is her family. Well, every Wednesday morning we have "Group Breakfast," which is like an informal staff meeting, and my boss brings in something she's baked. She goes on and on about how she loves to bake so everyone feels compelled to eat something. Problem is, everything tastes like it's been baked in a vat of salt! It's freaking us out and I've decided to say something to her, in a nice way, of course. Any ideas on how to go about this?

Dear Whiny, Ungrateful Wretch (your words, not mine):

It's abundantly clear from your letter that you are unaware of what importance the "little white lie" bears to the social contract. In some situations, honesty should be damned and whatever bit of a honeyed tongue you inherited from some rogue uncle should start flapping. Next Wednesday, compliment your boss's baking with feigned gusto. Alternately, assuming you've kept your mouth shut to date, continue to do so as "Silence is golden"—another important concept you seem not to have grasped. A good boss is a rare thing in today's world; don't blow your lucky fortune just because she's not Betty Crocker.

EVA

Jake had been waiting for me in bed.

I hadn't even taken off my coat when Sophie appeared and everything blew up so spectacularly. Of course, she knew the truth immediately.

No point in telling her I hadn't planned on joining her son in his bed. That was the truth but she wouldn't have believed me. Besides, the damage had already been done.

John. Sophie would tell John and then I would really have no one. I was engulfed in shame. "What's wrong with me?" I cried to my empty apartment and I swear my words echoed off the blank walls, slapping me from head to foot.

I called Sophie at home, not expecting her to answer. She didn't. "It's Eva," I said, tremblingly, into the phone. "Please, let me apologize."

I called again later and left the same message. I called a third time and when I heard the automated voice again I hung up.

The silence of my life was profound.

* 95 *

In this writer's experience, the most effective way to
salvage an uncomfortable situation caused by a careless
word or thoughtless comment is to admit immediately
that you are, in fact, a jackass, and are prepared to
accept a right hook to your chin.
—Dislodging the Foot Crammed in Your Mouth

SOPHIE

"I just never thought . . . It never crossed my mind that . . ."

"Why should it have crossed your mind? It's absolutely outrageous."

"I feel so stupid."

"You're not stupid."

"I feel so betrayed." I looked up at Ben, sitting across from me at the kitchen table. Neither of us had touched the tea he'd poured. I hadn't eaten anything since finding Eva with my son the day before.

"Yes," he said, "you were betrayed. But I can't believe they acted with the intention to hurt you."

"It's not Jake's fault," I said, suddenly angry. What did this person know, this person who'd had sex with the woman who defiled my son! "He's young. He's not to blame."

Ben said nothing. I stood; my chair scraped harshly against the floor but I didn't care about the noise or the damage. Nothing mattered, nothing.

"I just can't do this, Ben," I said, looking down at this man who seemed alien to me. "I'm sorry. It's too weird. It's too incestuous. I can't."

Ben bowed his head. Oh, please, I thought, don't let him be crying, not that, or I'll start to scream. But when he looked back up at me his eyes were dry. Pained but calm, as if he was used to accepting disappointing news.

"I wish this wasn't happening," he said. "I wish there was something I could say or do to—to help."

"But there isn't." I didn't believe that there could be.

When Ben left I curled up in bed and sobbed for a long, long time. Eventually, I fell into a fitful sleep. I don't remember if I dreamed.

The next morning, groggy, my head aching, I climbed wearily out of bed. My once-lovely bedroom looked dreary. The thought of dressing and going to work was impossible. I climbed back into bed and reached for the phone.

The voice mail picked up; John must already have left for his office. In a mechanical way I told him that our friend had been having an affair with my son since just after our reunion at Marino's—the night we'd toasted our friendship.

"One more thing," I said, my voice ragged. "Ben and I. It's over."

96

Dear Answer Lady:

My husband Bob's sister Lara's husband, Chet, is a recovering alcoholic. He's been sober for almost two years now, which makes my sister-in-law very happy, as when he was drinking he was highly abusive. Here's my dilemma: We're having a dinner party next week and I'm planning this wonderful meat dish that requires braising in red wine. Now, I know that Chet isn't supposed to have any alcohol at all, but the dish just won't be as tasty if I don't use wine and besides, the alcohol content will be mostly burned off by the time the dish gets to the table. I suppose I could cook Chet a separate dish but that might make him feel awkward, like he was being singled out. Is it okay if I just serve the dish and not say anything?

Dear Shallow Gal:

Your selfishness is almost beyond comprehension. You're willing to risk your husband's approbation, your sister-in-law's safety, and your brother-in-law's health all for a plate of tender meat? Choose another dish, one that doesn't require the addition of alcohol, and say your prayers that your family never sees this letter. (P.S. Hint for the future: Don't use real names.)

JOHN

Acquaintances in adversity, two people brought together by disappointment in love. This was what Ben and I were, as we sat hunched over coffees a few days after I got Sophie's shocking message.

"I'm in love with her," I told him. "I don't always admire her behavior. I don't always agree with her choices. But I love her. I think I might be insane."

Ben smiled faintly. "You're not insane. There's something compelling about Eva. And there's a lot more to her than she lets on. It's just—"

"Just what? That she's a challenge only a glutton for punishment would take on?"

"Well, yes."

"Assuming," I said, "that Eva would allow me to try. How pitiful is it to be my age and suffering a case of unrequited love for a woman who eats men for breakfast and makes soup out of their bones for lunch?"

Ben gave me a reproving look. "She's not all that bad, John. I think she's more frightened than frightening. Of course, that's easy for me to say, from this safe distance."

"I know," I said. "About her being frightened. I realize that now. But, Jesus, what was she thinking having an affair with Sophie's son!"

"I'm not so sure she was thinking."

"I don't want to be judgmental but I swear, she drives me to it. Then again, it's not hard for me to be judgmental. I'm not proud of it, but there it is."

"She was wrong," Ben said, "there's no doubt about it. But Jake was culpable, too. Not that Sophie's ready to admit that. She thinks the boy walks on water. And she's not doing him a service by idolizing him."

"Not that you can point that out to her," I said unnecessarily.

Ben smiled ruefully. "Especially now that I'm the ex-boyfriend."

We sat in brooding, moody silence, sipping our ridiculously overpriced coffees. The companionship felt good.

"About whom was it said that he was 'mad, bad, and dangerous to know'?" I asked.

"Lord Byron, by Lady Caroline Lamb. She became one of his lovers. Actually, the words could have been used to describe her, too."

"Huh."

Ben frowned. "Wait a minute. You're not thinking of Eva, are you?"

"Well," I said bleakly, "it had occurred . . ."

"Don't demonize her, John."

"I'm not. I'm just being an ass. I'll get over it." But when? And when would I be able to see Eva again without thinking of her with Jake, without wanting to shake her, without wanting to kiss her?

"I'm going to get another coffee." Ben went up to the counter of the pretentious little shop and suddenly I wondered if he knew about my brief fling with Sophie back in college. If he did know, the news didn't seem to be troubling him. And if he didn't know, there was no point in my telling him. Sharing that information was Sophie's right. That is, it had been her right. Back when she was in a relationship with Ben.

"What are you going to do about Sophie?" I asked when Ben returned with a fresh cup of coffee. "I could talk to her if you think it would help."

Ben shook his head. "No, but thanks. Sophie needs to work things out on her own. But she means a lot to me, John. I am going to try to talk with her again. I am going to ask her to reconsider our relationship. I have to. I can't just let her slip away. Some people you just can't give up without a fight."

"Yeah. And the key to success is to fight smart. Pick the right strategy and employ it at the right time."

"Yes," Ben said with a half smile. "That would be the challenge."

"Sophie might come around on her own, you know," I said. "It's possible. Anything's possible."

Ben shrugged, uninspired by my lame remark.

"I think we should be drinking something stronger than coffee."

Ben checked his watch. "Six-fifteen. The bar at The Grille just opened."

"Let's go."

97

Let's face it, ugly people are just not that pleasant to be around but the fact is that ugly people are human, too. So when you find yourself in a social situation with such a person—say, with a colleague's big-nosed wife or your sister's obese fiancé—do the kind thing and lie. Compliment her hideous ensemble (Note: Many ugly people are born with poor sartorial taste.); assure him you'd kill to have his clunker of a car (Note: Many ugly people lack the skills to make a decent wage.); and by all means, avoid making eye contact when you do. Ugly people are used to being lied to and will see the deception in your eyes.
      —When Lying Is the Kindest Thing

JOHN

"John?"

I looked up from the brief I was reading to see Ellen at the door. She'd closed it behind her. "What's wrong?" I asked. "You look weird."

"Uh, thanks. And what's wrong is that Gene's wife is here to see you."

"Gene's wife?"

"Her name is Marie, in case you've forgotten."

"I haven't forgotten. What does she want?"

"I don't know, she didn't say. I'm assuming she's here—actually, I have no idea why she's here."

"Okay, well, send her in."

"Right."

"Oh, and Ellen? Don't eavesdrop. I'll tell you everything—if I can."

Ellen lowered her voice to a whisper. "Wouldn't it be fabulous if she wants to hire you as her divorce attorney!"

"Leaving aside the conflict of interest, yes, in one way it would be . . . fabulous. Not that I like to see a pregnant woman dragged through a nasty court battle, and you know any divorce involving Gene would be nasty."

"Maybe not. Guys like him are usually cowards at bottom. Notice I don't say 'at heart' because guys like Gene don't have hearts. I bet—"

"Uh, Ellen."

"Oh, right. I'll send her in."

The word that came first to mind in describing Marie Patton was plain. Nondescript came next. She wasn't unattractive as much as she was . . . not noticeable. Of course, standing next to Gene she was virtually invisible. She was exactly the foil Gene required to satisfy his insatiable need for attention.

I asked if she wanted anything to drink. She said no. I indicated a guest chair and she perched on the edge of its seat.

"I know that Gene isn't in the office this afternoon," she said. "He told me he'd be in court."

"Okay." I was glad Gene hadn't lied to her this time. More than once I'd heard him on the phone, telling his wife he'd be working late when I knew full well he was meeting one of his girlfriends. And spending money on booze that he should have been spending on decorating a nursery.

"I didn't want him to see me talking to you."

"Marie, why don't you tell me why you're here?"

"I remembered," she said. "I remembered how nice you were to me at the Christmas party last year."

"Oh," I said, "well, I enjoyed talking to you. It was my pleasure."

"Mr. Felitti—"

"You can call me John."

"Okay. John. I . . . This is very hard for me."

Her eyes were pleading. I nodded sympathetically for her to go on.

"Mr. Felitti—John—I think my husband is cheating on me. I've thought this for some time now but, well, I've kept my suspicions to myself."

Oh, crap, I thought. This is going to be bad.

"Go on," I said, and my voice cracked a bit.

"I . . . I know my personal life is none of your business. I know it's not your job to get involved with the home life of your employees . . ."

"Only if problems in the home life are affecting performance in the office," I said, more to buy time than for any other reason.

"Yes, of course. I wouldn't know about Gene's performance here," she said. "He doesn't tell me much about his work." Marie looked off, as if embarrassed. "You see, Mr. Felitti, my husband doesn't consider me very bright."

I didn't correct her this time. Maybe the formality of my surname offered some degree of distance from or protection against the terribly personal nature of her visit.

"I'm sorry to hear that," I said. I wanted to say more, about how Gene was a jackass, but I didn't.

Marie sighed and the weight of her sorrow and humiliation were in that sigh. "I wonder," she began. "I guess what I mean to say is that—I need some advice. I don't know what to do, Mr. Felitti."

"Have you confronted Gene?" I asked, though of course I knew the answer to my question.

Marie laughed uncomfortably. "Oh, no. He's quicker than I am. He'd prove in about a minute that I was an idiot for doubting him. And I'd believe him. You see, Mr. Felitti, that's how things have always been between us."

Lovely. An emotionally abusive relationship. But maybe the fact that Marie was aware of her situation was an indication of a change to come. Maybe. I'd seen too many victims ultimately succumb to their tormentors, even after several bold attempts at liberation.

"Marie, do you want a divorce?" I asked bluntly.

"No! Absolutely not. My parents—a divorce is impossible."

"Would you go to counseling? If Gene would agree to go?"

"I would have to keep it from my parents," she said. "But yes, I would go to counseling—if I could convince Gene to go with me. But he would never agree." Marie looked at me squarely. "You know Gene, Mr. Felitti. You know what he's like."

"Even men like Gene," I said, "if faced with the possibility of the end of a marriage, have been known to agree to counseling."

"You have more faith in him than I do," Marie said.

"Marie, I'm going to ask you a very important question. Do you love your husband?"

"In spite of everything," she said promptly, "yes. I do."

That moron, I thought. He has no idea how good he has it.

"But you want things to change?" I asked.

"Yes." Marie's voice took on a note of urgency. "Things have to change. Not so much because of me, because I'm unhappy—"

That, I thought, is your biggest problem right there. It should all be because of you.

"—but because of our baby. I don't want to raise our child alone, Mr. Felitti. I want our child to be proud of his father. For the sake of our family, I want Gene to stop seeing other women. If he's seeing other women!"

"You still have doubts," I said, in disbelief.

Marie looked at her lap as she answered. "I can't help but think that maybe I'm making it all up, that all the little signs I think I see really mean nothing at all."

Yes, I could see how years with Gene could compel an already doubt-riddled woman to consider her sanity. I withheld a sigh and asked: "What, exactly, do you want me to do?"

Marie looked up. "I want you to tell me the truth. If you know Gene is seeing other women, I want you to tell me, please. Then, maybe, I'll have the courage to confront him. If I have proof then he can't tell me I'm wrong."

"My word," I said carefully, "wouldn't be proof. Gene could claim that I was lying. My word would only backfire on you."

"Oh." Marie rose abruptly from the chair. "Well, thank you, Mr. Felitti, for your time. I'm sorry I bothered you."

This is ridiculous, I thought. Why am I protecting this bum at the cost of his wife's sanity?

"Marie, wait." I reached for a piece of notepaper and wrote out the name and address of Gene's favorite nightspot. "Tuesday, at seven. There's a good chance Gene will be here. He probably won't be alone. If you want proof."

Marie took the paper with a surprisingly steady hand. "How can I thank you, Mr. Felitti?"

"There's no need for thanks," I said. "I wish I could do something more. In the future—"

"I will."

At the door, Marie turned. "One more thing," she said. "There's no need to tell Gene about our talk, is there?"

"Absolutely not. It will be our little secret."

"Our little secret."

"Take care of yourself, Marie."

Marie smiled a bit. "I'm trying."

When she had gone I sat alone with my guilt at having ratted out my colleague. And I sat alone with my pleasure at having helped my colleague's deserving wife.

"You got involved, didn't you?"

I looked up. Ellen.

"You could be a cat burglar, you know?" I asked.

"Stealth is useful. What just went on in here?"

I told her what Marie had said. And I told her what I'd done.

"You interfered," she accused.

"I had to," I explained.

"I understand. I just hope your good intentions don't lead Mrs. Patton straight to hell."

"For just one moment can I please enjoy the fact that I screwed Gene?"

"One moment. And then you'd better start praying things don't blow up."

98

Dear Answer Lady:
   My best friend told me a secret about herself and made me promise not to tell. The very next day I told another friend of ours! I don't know why; the words just seemed to pop right out of my mouth! Now I feel just terrible. I can't eat, I can't sleep, I just don't know what to do. Can you help me?

Dear Big Mouth:
   Go assuage your guilty conscience with a good bout of self-flagellation. When done, drag your bloody body to your best friend, admit all, and ask her never to tell you another secret, as clearly you are untrustworthy in the extreme. No doubt she'll never talk to you again but at least you'll be able to eat.

SOPHIE

The phone rang six times before a male voice answered groggily.

"Brad," I said, "it's Sophie."

"I know. I have caller ID."

There was no point in wasting time with pleasantries.

"I have terrible news, Brad."

"What?" he demanded. "Did something happen to Jake?"

"Only that he got his heart broken!"

There was a moment of silence and then Brad laughed. "Is that all? Jesus, Sophie, I thought you were going to say that he was in an accident and broke a leg or something."

"Brad! How can you be so callous? A broken heart is far worse than a broken leg."

There was another moment of silence before Brad said: "Sophie, please. I'm sorry for Jake, but in the scheme of things, a broken heart isn't the worst thing that could happen to him. In fact, it's probably a good learning experience."

"What!"

"Jake hasn't experienced much disappointment in his life," Brad said matter-of-factly. "He needs to learn that life isn't all about winning. Besides, he's young, he'll get over it."

"Not this time," I predicted. "Not for a long while, anyway."

Brad sighed dramatically. "Could you not be so enigmatic? I haven't had a cup of coffee yet. You are aware there's a time difference between California and Massachusetts?"

"Of course I'm aware! I've been waiting for hours to call you. It's"—I checked the clock over the sink—"it's five minutes after seven on the West Coast. You're always up at six thirty."

Brad sighed again. "Sophie, we haven't lived together for over a year. Habits change. For future reference, I'm getting up at eight o'clock these days."

"Oh," I said. It had never occurred to me that Brad's daily habits might have changed. Why?

"Carly's on a late shift at the restaurant and doesn't get to bed until after midnight so I've adjusted my schedule to fit better with hers."

I heard Brad murmur, "Thanks, honey," and a moment later he said, "Ah. The first sip. Like magic. Okay, my brain is functioning now."

I wondered if Carly was sitting at the kitchen table with Brad, listening to his side of the conversation, rolling her eyes at him, mocking his annoying ex-wife. I wondered what she was wearing. Did she sleep in a loose cotton nightgown, like I did?

"Sophie? Are you there?"

"Brad," I said, "Jake was—seeing—my friend Eva. My college friend, the one I looked up when I moved back East."

I heard Brad take another long swallow of his coffee before he said, "Whoa. That is big. Wait, how did you find out about it? Did Jake tell you?"

"No," I said, "he didn't. I—I walked in on them in Jake's apartment. I have a key."

Brad whistled. "First question: What were you doing breaking into your son's apartment?"

"I didn't break in! I told you I have a key!" Brad could be so infuriating. "Anyway," I went on, "it was horrible, the worst experience of my life."

"I would think so . . ."

"The . . . affair was wrong, terribly wrong."

"Well, I agree that Jake and Eva might have shown better judgment. But I don't think what they did was wrong."

"She's twenty years older than Jake!" I argued. "My God, Brad, the whole experience might have really damaged him! Emotionally, psychologically—"

"Sophie, calm down. First, Jake isn't twelve, he's twenty-one. Second . . ."

"What?" I demanded. "What's second?"

"Look, Sophie, Eva isn't the first older woman Jake's been involved with."

"What do you mean?"

"I mean that Jake likes older women. He's had several relationships with women at least ten years his senior."

I stared at a corner of the fridge until my eyes almost crossed.

"Sophie? You okay?"

"No," I said finally, "I am not okay. Why didn't you tell me this before?"

"I didn't see any reason to upset you," Brad said matter-of-factly. "See, now you know and you're upset. Sometimes it's best to keep certain things a secret. Jake and I agreed a long time ago that we should keep our mouths shut about this."

My husband and my son had conspired against me. I felt betrayed and humiliated.

"Why does everybody think I can't handle the truth?" I demanded. "Does everybody think I'm a child?"

I heard some muted noise from Brad's end of the line—maybe Carly shuffling off to take a shower?—and then Brad sighed. "Look, Sophie," he said, "be reasonable. If Jake had come to you in the beginning and told you he was involved with your friend, do you think it would have made a difference to how you feel? Of course not. By keeping quiet they were just trying to protect you."

"Eva used my son," I said. "She left a message on my voice mail claiming that Jake pursued her but I don't believe it for a second. She just doesn't want to take responsibility for her disgusting actions."

"What did Jake say about it?" Brad asked.

"That's Jake's version of the story, too," I admitted. "He says he showed up at her office building one day and well, asked her out."

"See? Jake knew what he was getting into. He'll be fine." It annoyed me that Brad sounded so smug and triumphant.

"But of course he'd say that," I argued. "He doesn't want his mother feeling sorry for him. More importantly, he doesn't want to look like a failure to his father, a man who's dating someone more appropriate for his son!"

Brad didn't reply right away. I knew he was counting to ten. For all of Brad's faults, a fiery temper isn't one.

Finally, he said, calmly: "Carly isn't Jake's type. She's into murder mysteries and you know how Jake feels about detective fiction."

I felt somewhat chastened but not enough to apologize.

"You know what I mean, Brad. She's a lot closer to his age than to yours."

This time, Brad only counted to five before saying: "Speaking of romantic entanglements, how are things going with Ben?"

"Fine," I lied.

"Not according to Jake. He says you broke things off."

Jake, it seemed, might be skilled at keeping his own secrets but he wasn't very good at keeping other people's. True, I hadn't asked him not to tell his father about my leaving Ben, but still.

"Ben was Eva's boyfriend," I said. "He had sex with her. I—I just can't get past that."

"Look, Sophie, I know you think I'm the last one to be offering advice on matters of the heart, but—"

"Yes, I do."

"But I'm going to, anyway. Jake tells me this Ben seems like a good guy. He says you seemed very natural together. I just think it would be a shame to let a chance at happiness escape because of something that happened in Ben's life before you even knew him."

I let Brad wait for my reply. "Sophie," he said finally. "Did you hear what I said?"

"I heard. I was just wondering if you were finished offering your wisdom."

"I know you, Sophie. A good marriage will make you happy. There's always going to be someone's past to accept and—"

I interrupted fiercely. "Eva was with Ben and then she was with Jake . . . And then I was with Ben! It's all feels so incestuous!"

"Your dating Eva's old boyfriend is simply coincidental," Brad said. "Try to keep that fact separate from the Jake and Eva issue."

I had tried to keep it separate. Hadn't I? No. Since discovering Eva's affair with my son I hadn't thought clearly about anything. "Mmm," I said, unwilling to commit to taking Brad's advice.

"And by the way," he went on, "while you're being so furious with Eva, why don't you direct some of your anger toward your son? He lied to you, too, in a way."

My reply was spontaneous, involuntary, the mother protecting her child from any sort of culpability or blame. "He wanted," I said, "to protect me from the truth."

"I thought you resented people trying to protect you from the truth."

"I do, it's just—"

"Has Jake apologized to you?"

"No. Why should he?"

"You might want to ask him for an apology. He's not a kid, Sophie. He's accountable for his actions. Again, I'm not saying he did anything wrong, technically, in getting involved with your friend, but he should be made to understand the effects of that choice."

Interesting, I thought. Suddenly, Brad is offering advice on child-rearing, the one area of responsibility he'd left almost entirely to me. "Good-bye, Brad," I said.

"You spoil him, Sophie. You let him off the hook too easily. You always have."

"I'm not talking about this again, Brad. I have to go."

"All right. I'm sure Jake will be fine but I'll check in with him later."

Oh, I thought, I'm sure your call will fix everything.

"Good-bye, Brad."

"Good-bye, Sophie," he said and then he was gone, probably off to take a shower with Carly.

* 99 *

If you assume that everyone is guilty of some form of misconduct, you'll soon find there's no need for the sordid details. Does it really matter if you know the name of the woman your husband slept with on his last business trip? Are you really going to feel any better knowing her name is Karen rather than Gail?
    —Ignorance Can Be Bliss: Asking Only What You
        Really Need to Know

EVA

"I wasn't sure you'd take my call," he said. I heard in his voice a trace of self-pity.

I'm not sure why I did take Jake's call. A nagging sense of guilt, I suppose.

"What do you want, Jake?" I asked evenly.

"I think I left—I mean, I think you left a CD at my place."

"I never brought a CD to your apartment, Jake."

"Oh. It must be Phil's. Or someone's."

"Yes," I said, "I'm sure it's someone's. Look, Jake, is that all? I really have to—"

"Did you know," he interrupted, "that my mom had a thing with John back when you guys were in college?"

The words didn't register for a moment. And then, they did.

"By 'thing,'" I said carefully, "I assume you mean a sexual affair?"

"Yeah. I think it went on for a few weeks."

"No," I said. "I didn't know. Frankly, I wouldn't have cared then and I don't care now."

Jake made a sound of disbelief, something like a snort.

"Why did you tell me this?" I demanded.

"I just thought you might want to know."

"Well," I said, "you thought wrong. Good-bye, Jake."

Jake said nothing. I disconnected the call.

"Idiot!" I hissed to the walls of my office.

But it wasn't Jake I was angry with. Jake was just a kid who'd had his ego busted up. He'd needed to restore his self-image by hurting the one who'd done the busting.

No, I was angry with Sophie and John. For all these years they'd kept their relationship a secret from me. And while withholding information isn't exactly the same thing as lying, it's close and I, if anyone, should know. I felt betrayed, much as Sophie must have felt—

Oh. Much as Sophie must have felt when she came upon her friend in her son's bedroom.

Of course. Sophie was hurt so deeply by our affair because she loved Jake, and maybe even me. At the very least, she cared about me, which is why our betrayal wounded her so deeply.

Sophie cared about me like I cared about or maybe even loved . . .

I took a few deep breaths and tried to think reasonably. Sophie had had sex with John. Fine. Their brief relationship was in the past, and the past, as I'd so often told myself, just didn't matter.

Except for when it did.

What a fool I'd been, and for so long. I hated myself at that moment, hated myself for my stubbornness and stupidity and utter lack of emotional courage.

Jake would never know just how effective his retaliating phone call had been.

100

Dear Answer Lady:

About a month ago a family moved in next door to the house in which my husband and I have lived for the past twenty years. The parents seem like nice people (though they never acknowledged the muffin basket I gave them as a welcome to the neighborhood), but they have a fifteen-year-old daughter who—I can hardly say it!—who has been flirting with my husband whenever he leaves for work or comes home or goes out for the mail . . . It's like she's always there! Also, when I run into her in the grocery store (which has happened so many times I'm beginning to think she's stalking me!), she gives me a nasty smirk and I feel my face flush and I look away. I don't know what to do! Please, can you help me?

Dear Candidate for Therapy:

The truth about your slutty little neighbor is as obvious as the roll of fat around your middle. And I'm guessing you have quite the belly, which might account for your self-esteem issues. But back to Lolita and her blatant attempts to drag your unwitting husband into a disgraceful affair—and to humiliate you in the process. Put your foot down, NOW. Next time you "run into" Lolita at the grocery store tell her right out—do NOT look away!—that if she doesn't *cease and desist in her quest to screw your husband, you, and your marriage, all for her own, shallow amusement, you will rip her eyes out and feed them to her beloved cat, Princess (I'm guessing here). Trust me, a confrontation is the last thing this spoiled little brat expects. Call me when it's done; I have a great diet plan you should definitely try!*

SOPHIE

As the days slipped by, days without Ben and days without Eva, my feelings about Jake's part in this mess began to change. I began to think that Brad was right. Jake was a man, not a boy, and should be made to realize the consequences of his selfish, careless actions.

Since that awful moment in Jake's bedroom I'd spoken to him only twice. The first time, later that night, he called to explain that "we never meant for you to find out" and, somewhat self-defensively, that "we didn't hurt anyone." The second time he called, a few days later, he bragged that he was the one who had initiated the relationship with Eva. And then he asked if he could come for dinner sometime that week.

Just like that, as if nothing traumatic had happened to me. And that's when my mind began to change.

Jake showed up around seven. Our kiss on the cheek was awkward. I wanted to hug him like I always did—but I couldn't. Maybe later, I thought. Maybe after he apologizes to me.

Jake followed me to the kitchen.

"It smells great in here," he said. He opened the door to the fridge. "No beer?"

"No," I said. "I must have forgotten." That was a lie. My hand had been on a six-pack of an expensive beer Jake liked, but I'd taken my hand away. For the first time in my life I wasn't in the mood to cater to my son's whims.

Jake frowned. "I guess I could have a glass of wine."

I nodded toward a bottle on the counter. "The corkscrew is in the drawer," I said. Do you know what it cost me to stand there and not open the bottle for him?

I'm sure Jake knew that I was going to confront him. Or maybe it had never occurred to him that I would.

"I want," I said, "to talk about what happened."

Jake sighed. "Mom, look, it's over between Eva and me. Let it go."

A small, dry laugh escaped my mouth. "No, Jake, I won't let it go. I can't, not yet."

Jake popped the cork on the bottle of wine and sighed again. "What is there to say?" he asked.

"You damaged my relationship with Ben," I said evenly, amazed at my courage. "My head was so confused, what with finding out that he'd dated Eva and then"—careful, I thought, about how you word this—"with finding out about you and Eva."

Jake looked puzzled. "That was your choice, Mom. You were the one who broke it off with Ben."

Could he really not sympathize, not one little bit?

"But your actions contributed to my pain," I said. "Now I've lost Ben and I've lost Eva." No, I thought, I never had Eva. She'd only liked me for the proximity to my son. "It's not all your fault," I said, "but I do think I deserve an apology."

Jake said nothing.

"What were you thinking when you asked out my friend?" I pressed. "Didn't you have any idea of what trouble you might cause?"

"She didn't have to say yes." Jake's tone was defiant. He took a long drink of wine—the wine I'd paid for—and returned the glass too loudly to the counter.

"No, she didn't," I agreed. "She acted selfishly. You both did."

Jake folded his arms across his chest and a look of petulance came to his face. I knew that look well, though I hadn't seen it for some time.

"I'm twenty-one, Mom," he said. "I can see anyone I want."

"Of course," I said. "But can't you see any fault in your actions?"

Again, silence, as Jake considered how to get out of the conversation.

I waited. I had no place to go and no one to meet. I was very alone just then.

Finally, he unfolded his arms and stuck his hands in his front pockets. "Yeah," he said. "Okay, I'm sorry. I just—I guess it was just lust."

I felt so deeply disappointed in Jake right then. The enormity of what he and Eva had done to me made me feel almost sick with anger.

"Lust!" I cried. "I am so sick of the whole subject. I am so sick of hearing about husbands cheating on their wives and women having meaningless sex and middle-aged men marrying girls half their age!"

"Stuff happens," Jake said with a shrug. "Nobody's perfect."

His studied indifference infuriated me. "I'll say," I shot back. "And what about you? When are you going to start being normal and date women your own age!"

I'd never raised my voice to Jake, even when he was little. And I'd never said anything so hateful, so hurtful, to him—to anyone.

"That was uncalled for," he said, his voice wavering. "I'm perfectly normal. I resent your saying otherwise."

I didn't apologize. I didn't want to. "Maybe," I said, "your father is right. Maybe it's all my fault. Maybe I did spoil you, maybe I did smother you. Maybe that's why you're fixated on older women."

"I'm leaving now." Jake grabbed his bag off the kitchen table and turned for the door.

"Fine," I said to his back. "I have nothing more to say."

The door slammed shut.

101

No matter how well you cover your tracks, no matter how deep your secret is buried, remember this: The Truth Will Out in the End. Repent or not, it will make no difference when the Lord sorts out His people on Judgment Day.
　　　　—Eternal Damnation and Your Undying Soul

SOPHIE

I waited another few days before making the call, just to be sure. Just to be sure I was free of wasteful notions of what was acceptable and what was not. Just to be sure I was free of the need to rely on my ungrateful son for the semblance of a life. Just to be sure I still felt for Ben what I'd felt for him before Eva and Jake tromped in and sullied my happiness.

He answered after several rings.

"Ben. It's Sophie."

"Oh, hi," he said. "I almost missed your call; I just got in from class. I'm glad I didn't."

"Ben, I'd like to try again. I'd like us to forget everyone else but each other. I'd like us to be together."

"No preamble?" he teased, gently.

"No. I'm tired of wasting time. I miss you. I love you."

"I love you, too, Sophie. I wish you could see the smile on my face."

"Come over," I said. "I'll make dinner. And you can show me your smile."

"I'm on my way."

102

Dear Answer Lady:

I've hated my wife's best friend from the first minute I met her nine years ago. I don't know why. Anyway, she saw me the other night with a female colleague from out of town. We (the colleague and I) were kind of drunk and kind of making out. Anyway, the second I saw my wife's friend I pushed my colleague off my lap (she's okay, just a sprain) but just as I was about to run over to her (the friend), she ran out of the restaurant. Should I contact my wife's friend and offer her money not to tell my wife what she saw? I mean, she loves my wife and won't want her to be hurt, so I have some chance of keeping this all a secret, no?

Dear Shithead:

I've already called your wife. (Don't worry about how I found out your real identity; that's my business.) You'll be receiving divorce papers at your office this afternoon. By the way, I've urged your injured colleague to press charges of battery. Thanks for writing.

JOHN

"Counselor?"

Gene was standing just outside my office. I have to remember to keep that door closed, I thought. And where the hell is Ellen?

"You don't look so good," I said blandly. There were dark circles under his eyes and his face was unevenly shaven. "Late night?"

"Yeah." Gene gestured for permission to come in and I nodded. "But not in the way you think," he said, sinking into a guest chair.

"You mean, carousing 'til all hours with a woman not your wife?"

Gene shook his head, like a man just waking from a nasty dream.

"She found out," he said. "Somehow, she found out I'd be at Muse last night. She caught me red-handed, man. It was bad."

"I can imagine," I said without a trace of sympathy.

A flicker of something like suspicion crossed Gene's face. I decided to speak with more care. Gene didn't need to know I'd acted in collusion with Marie.

"No," said Gene. "I don't think that you can imagine. Do you know how embarrassing it is to be out with a gorgeous, sexy woman and look up to find your pregnant wife standing over you?"

"You're right, Gene. I can't really imagine. What happened?"

"Nothing much. Marie just looked at me. I don't think I even said good-bye to Heather. I just followed Marie out to the parking lot. She got in her car and I got in mine. It was when we got home that the shit hit the fan."

Good for you, Marie, I thought.

"Somehow she knew where to find me," Gene was saying. "But how?"

"Maybe Marie isn't as dull-witted as you've claimed she is," I suggested. "And maybe you're not as crafty as you've claimed you are."

"You mean, maybe I got sloppy?"

"Yeah," I said, "maybe."

"I thought I had it all worked out. I never thought she'd suspect me of cheating. Even if she did, I never thought she'd have the nerve to confront me. Man, she's been talking to someone. Someone's been giving her ideas."

"Hmm," I said.

"My in-laws are a big problem. You don't know these people; they still treat Marie and her sister like they're eleven-year-olds. If they get word that the marriage is in trouble—and that it's my fault—I'm in for a world of pain."

"I gather," I said, "that you're not taking advantage of Marie's discovery to file for divorce."

Gene looked stunned. "No way! Marie's family has money. And besides, it's not really bad at home. It's just . . . dull. I mean, Marie's a fabulous cook. I swear, if I didn't go to the gym every day I'd be as big as a house. How many guys these days can say their wives have dinner on the table for them every night?"

"You're preaching to the choir, Gene. I've been telling you for the past few years that you don't appreciate your wife. She's smart, loyal, and clearly a lot tougher than she appears. You don't deserve her and maybe now you know it."

Maybe, I thought, but I doubted it. In my experience men like Gene don't change enough for the better to make being married to them worth the trouble.

Gene's reply to my last remark was to say, almost as if talking to himself: "I've got to tow the line for a while, at least until the baby is born. It's going to be rough." Gene paused, hands gripping the arms of the chair. "But I know Marie. Once the baby is here she'll be all wrapped up in it. She won't care if I start coming home late again. Everything will get back to normal. I just have to be patient."

Gene's words were hopeful but his expression was that of a defeated, bewildered man. I almost felt pity for him.

"I've got a client meeting in a few minutes," I said.

For a moment, Gene continued to sit, hands tight on the arms of the chair. Finally, he rose to his feet. "Maybe," he said, "I should bring Marie some flowers tonight."

Like putting a Band-Aid on a cancerous tumor. "It won't hurt your cause," I said. "Oh, and Gene? Close the door behind you."

103

Evasion is sexy. People are far more attracted to the mysterious than to the obvious. Before you tell your entire life story on the first date, think twice. Consider eluding certain questions and giving only tantalizing clues to others. A second date is sure to follow.
—How to Navigate the Winding Road to Marriage

EVA

Almost two weeks after Sophie found me in Jake's bedroom I finally worked up the nerve to call John.

I knew he might recoil from me. I knew that any feelings he'd had for me might be dead, killed by the news of my despicable actions. I could only hope for his continued friendship, nothing more, though I was terribly afraid I would be getting something much less.

He agreed to meet me for dinner at Marino's, the place where it had all started, our botched reunion. I almost cried when he walked into the restaurant. I was so relieved he'd actually shown up, so glad to see his familiar face.

"Thanks for meeting with me," I said when we were seated at the corner table I'd requested for some degree of privacy.

"Why wouldn't I?" he asked easily, but his expression was guarded.

I trembled with the possibility that I'd lost him. "Please,

don't pretend ignorance. I know Sophie must have told you. And you haven't called so I know you've been angry with me."

"Oh," he said. "That."

"Yes, that. I want to clear the air between us, John. I need to."

"Okay."

"I'm sure there's something you want to say to me. I promise I won't get mad." I attempted a smile. "At least, I promise I won't punch you in the nose."

"Okay," he said, with a weak smile of his own. "Here goes. First, I'm not mad at you. More . . . disappointed. And I didn't call because I thought maybe you needed some time alone. Maybe I was wrong."

"I don't know what I needed," I said. "I was a wreck. But, what else?"

"It bothered me from the beginning that you were seeing someone so much younger."

"So much younger than me or so much younger than you? I don't mean to be antagonistic."

John hesitated. "Much younger than me," he said finally. "It drove me crazy."

I replied archly, out of habit. "I suppose I should be flattered."

John flinched.

"I'm sorry. I didn't mean to sound flippant. I'm just—I guess I'm still a wreck."

"It's all right. Forget it."

We sat in awkward silence for a few minutes, John staring down at his fork, me surreptitiously watching him. "Weren't you worried that I'd get hurt in the affair?" I asked finally.

John looked up. "As long as we're being honest," he said, "and as long as you keep your promise not to punch me, then no. I wasn't worried about your feelings at all. I suppose I assumed you were invulnerable to heartache."

"A coldhearted, self-serving bitch?" I suggested.

John smiled. His expression seemed less cautious. "Those are your words," he said, "not mine. Look, I know it was stupid of me to think of you as beyond emotional reach but I did. I figured you could take care of yourself. I figured you knew exactly what you were doing. Of course, I also thought you were wasting your time dating a kid."

"You made that very clear," I reminded him.

"Sorry. In spite of my being an attorney, I've never been very good at dissembling."

No. And that was one of the things about John I'd come to appreciate.

"Do you think I'm a horrible person for sleeping with my friend's son?" I asked. "Because I do. I think I'm a horrible person."

"No," he said readily, "I don't think you're a horrible person."

"Then what?" I pressed. "What am I? What kind of person does what I did?"

"A fallible human being. Who did something deeply stupid. Look, I'm not passing judgment on you, Eva, really. We're all—most of us, anyway—helpless when it comes to sex. Not all the time but every once in a while."

"It wasn't just sex," I said honestly. "Not after a while, anyway. If that helps."

John smiled. "You don't have to make anything easier for me, Eva. I'm a big boy. I can handle it."

"I know it was wrong of me, John. I did think about Sophie's feelings, I did, really. And yet . . . I let Jake persuade me because I wanted to be persuaded. I suppose—"

Where, I thought, am I going to get the courage to admit the depths of my vanity?

"You suppose what?" John asked. "We're being honest here, right? And we don't seem to be fighting or hurling insults."

And there was the courage; it came from John's willingness to listen.

"I was flattered," I admitted. "It's ridiculous, I know. Lots of men my own age find me attractive. And yet, this . . . kid's interest in me . . ." I shook my head. "God, what an idiot I was! I let vanity win out over respect for my friend."

"Don't beat yourself up, Eva," John said kindly. "It's in the past, it's over."

"But it's not over, John," I said, "not really. Do you think Sophie is going to forget that I slept with her son? Not for a long time, maybe not ever. And as long as she remembers that . . . betrayal, our friendship is finished."

I felt tears threatening. I sipped a bit of water, hoping for distraction, and it dribbled down my chin. John handed me the napkin I'd neglected to unfold and put on my lap.

"Okay," he said patiently, "there are consequences to your actions. But try not to overdramatize, Eva, okay? You didn't commit a crime. You didn't break a vow, not technically."

"Why are you being so nice to me?" I asked with a bitter laugh. "I don't care about technicalities. Suddenly, all I care about are the results of my bad choice. I hate the fact that Sophie hates me."

"She doesn't hate you."

"How do you know?"

"I don't think Sophie is capable of hate, not in the way you mean. She's angry and hurt but she'll get over it."

I hoped John was right. And I wondered: What about me? As a result of my affair with my friend's son, my life had taken a definitive turn onto a new path, but I had no idea of where that path would take me. Forever after, my life would be divided into two phases: Pre-Jake and Post-Jake. Just as my life had also been divided into the time before the death of my parents and the time since then. That first defining moment I hadn't courted. This one, I'd called down on my head.

"Thanks," I said, voice wobbly. "For being so . . . supportive."

"It's what friends do. Help each other through bad times."

Friends. Thank God, I hadn't lost John's friendship. Anything else he might offer would be icing on the proverbial cake.

"Oh," he said then, "here's news that will cheer you up. Ben called me last night. He and Sophie are back together."

"I hadn't even known they'd broken up!"

"It was Sophie's decision to end the relationship. She was having trouble accepting—everything."

"Oh," I said, miserably. "I see."

"But all's well that ends well, right?"

I smiled weakly at John's attempt to make me feel better after having so badly disrupted Sophie's life.

"Hey," he said, "are we ever going to order? The waiter's been hovering."

I hadn't even noticed. And suddenly, for the first time since that awful day in Jake's bedroom, I had an appetite. "Yes," I said. "Let's start with some appetizers, okay?"

An hour later we stood outside Marino's. "Thanks, again," I said.

"For paying?"

"For listening. And for paying, yeah. It's on me next time."

"Deal," he said. And then, before I knew what was happening, John's arms were around me.

"You're supposed to hug back," he said against my head.

I lifted my arms around him. It was the first hug I'd shared in—in a very long time.

John was the first to pull away. I felt bereft of his touch. I wanted him to kiss me but I knew it was wanting too much.

"Friends?" he asked, smiling down at me.

"Yes," I said. "Friends."

104

Dear Answer Lady:

Recently a guy I befriended in a local bar pitched what sounded like a great business deal. We talked about it for a few weeks—I must have seen him six or seven times—and finally, I was convinced to go in on the deal to the tune of ten thousand dollars. I'll spare you the details, but in the end, the guy made off with my money. The phone number and e-mail address he gave me are bogus and no one at the bar has any idea where he is. I can't help but feel that I'm partly to blame for getting duped. Am I the one at fault?

Dear Too-Late-Now:

You must learn how to hit on the truth before it hits on you. In the future, keep your eyes open for the ugly signs of fraud, your ears open for the dull roar of deception, and your nose perked for the sickening stench of corruption. The next time someone tries to take advantage of you, you'll be able to avoid being made a fool. Oh, and one more thing: Don't make business deals in bars, Stupid.

Eva

Please don't let it be cookies.

That was my first thought when I brought the package from my sister into my apartment. When Maura was a kid she was an enthusiastic but lousy baker. For all I knew her baking skills hadn't much improved.

I reached for the box cutter that sat on a cardboard box unopened since I'd moved in to my apartment. What I found in Maura's package wasn't cookies at all.

I felt light-headed, almost as if I was going to faint. Before I could fall on the open box cutter blade I put it on a high shelf behind me. Then, I breathed deeply and reached for a folded sheet of paper with the words "Aunt Eve" printed wildly in a kid's hand.

I unfolded the paper. Maura's handwriting was difficult, just like our mother's. The note began:

> *Dear Eve:*
> *Just after Mom and Dad died, when we—well, really, you—were cleaning out the house so it could be sold, I found these notebooks in the garbage. I remember wondering why you'd throw them out because you really loved to write. Anyway, I took them out of the garbage and I've kept them ever since. They got kind of warped along the way, so I'm sorry for that.*

I picked up one of the notebooks. It looked as if it had been left out in the rain but the handwriting (mine) was still legible.

> *Remember how Mom used to say she was psychic? Well, I don't know, but maybe I got some of her gift. Since your last phone call I've been thinking about you a lot and then, the other day, I got this funny*

feeling that you might want the notebooks back. That maybe this was the right time. Anyway, they're yours so you can do with them what you want. Oh, I thought you might like to know that Brooke takes after you. She's always scribbling stories. Her teacher says she has some talent. She certainly doesn't get it from me! Call when you can.

Love from us all,
Maura

I refolded the note and put it on the table next to my old notebooks. Carefully, I picked up and opened another. Wow, I thought. I really was a terrible artist. But the words . . .

And suddenly I couldn't stand being alone for another minute.

I grabbed my cell from my bag and pressed the button for his cell. He answered on the second ring.

"It's me," I said.

"Eva, are you okay? You sound out of breath."

"I'm fine," I lied ridiculously. "Just—could you come over? Now? I want to show you something."

"I'm on my way."

I shut my cell and waited for John.

I didn't have to wait long. He was at the door, then in my living room. And that's when the tears came, a ridiculous flood of them, like they'd been dammed up for years and someone had poked a hole in the dam.

John reached for me but I turned and pointed to the pile of old notebooks. He strode over to the table and then looked back at me.

"Where did you find them?" he asked.

"My sister."

I watched as John picked up one of the notebooks and carefully opened it to a page, then to one more. When he put it back on the table and reached for another, I walked over to him and put my hand on his.

He looked at me, a question in his eyes, and then, the answer.

"Eva," he whispered and took me in his arms.

I buried my head in his shoulder. I leaned my body into his. I was so tired.

"Eva," John said softly. "I hope this isn't the wrong thing to say right now. But I can't help it. I love you, Eva. I love you."

The words I had been waiting to hear. "It was the right thing to say," I whispered.

We kissed frantically, desperately, and the whole time I continued to cry. Finally, John lowered us onto the floor—because I'd never bought a couch—and held me. I don't know how long we sat there. I think I might have fallen asleep a bit and maybe began to dream, because suddenly I found myself saying: "My left foot drags when I'm tired."

"I'm prone to athlete's foot."

My shoulders began to shake. John held me tighter. But I pushed away. The laughter burst out of me.

John frowned. "What's so funny?"

"I don't know," I gasped, wiping my eyes, now full of laugh-tears. "Just the way you said it, the athlete's foot. It was—cute."

"Cute, huh?" John grinned. "Well, I'll take it. It's better than being called an egomaniac."

"I have called you lots of things, haven't I?"

"And none of them nice. Except for friend."

Yes, my friend. "I love you, John. There. I said it. God, that took a lot of nerve."

"Thank you, Eve. I mean, Eva. Crap. I really didn't do that on purpose."

I laughed again. "For once. Every other time was to make me angry, wasn't it?"

"Yes. But I'm through with making you angry. At least, on purpose."

"I really was a horrible artist. Those sketches are awful."

"At least you tried. Maybe you could take a drawing class."

"Maybe," I said. "But let's talk later, okay? Now . . ."

So, it was finally time. Best friends with benefits.

105

Is it really worth losing your medical license because you haven't quite met the required hours of yearly reeducation? After all, you intended to take the CME courses; you've just been busy. What's the big deal about swearing in writing that you've completed the work? You know you'll register the first moment you get a chance. It's the spirit of the truth that counts here, not the "actual fact."
—The Truth Is Relative; Getting What You Want Is Divine

SOPHIE

I miss Eva. I wish none of this had happened—but what do I mean by "this"? I wish Ben had never met Eva; I wish I had never gotten back in touch with Eva; I wish I had never known that Ben and Eva had been involved—what? And if it's this last, am I saying that I would have preferred to live with Ben in ignorance, that I would have preferred he and Eva share a secret and because of that, remain bonded?

I wish that Eva hadn't had an affair with my son. That I know for sure. I know I'll never forget what Eva did. I wonder if I'll ever be able to forgive her.

Oddly, I continue to feel Eva's betrayal of my trust more deeply than I feel Brad's betrayal of our marriage vow. Maybe because Eva was my first real friend. And even though she'd changed so drastically since college, I still loved her—even at those moments when I didn't much like her. I still wanted her in my life, as a witness to my past; as a participant in my present; and, hopefully, as a part of my future.

But that's all over now.

Ben and I are getting married next autumn. His semester will be in full swing so we'll put off a honeymoon until the following summer.

I'll invite Jake to the wedding, of course. But after everything that's happened, his presence doesn't feel essential. It hurts to admit that, but it's the truth. I love him but right now I don't much like him. I hope that in time our relationship will improve and that we'll be close again.

But for the moment, I'm concentrating on me.

106

Dear Answer Lady:

A particular coworker was in direct competition with me for a promotion. I'd always liked her so when she asked if I could do her a favor last week, one that involved my being out of the office to meet with one of our lesser clients, I was happy to help. (She said that her daughter had an important doctor's appointment that afternoon.) When I got to the client it turned out he wasn't expecting me. Instead, he had planned on mailing a document to our office. As I was there, I took the document and returned to my office where I discovered that my coworker had cleverly orchestrated a meeting with a huge new prospective client, a meeting at which my absence was glaring. In short, she got the promotion and I got a reprimand from our boss. I'm furious. This woman sent me on a fool's errand. I want to report her but if I do, then the entire office will know that I fell for her ridiculous ruse. What should I do?

Dear Hoodwinked:

The public's opinion of you is worth far more than you realize. If you ever want to be promoted, keep your mouth shut and don't disabuse your colleagues of the notion that you are a person of intelligence.

*And the next time someone asks a favor of you, say
no. It's not as hard as you think.*

EVA

I love John.

And I will never tell him about Sam or about the other
meaningless affairs I had over the years. John's not dumb.
I'm sure he has his suspicions about the way I lived certain
years of my life. Why do I need to confirm such ugly truths
about myself?

It's said that a guilty conscience needs no accuser. And
while I didn't break any laws or commit any crimes of a legal
nature, some of my actions—like having sex with married
men—weren't exactly ethical. I hurt people and I feel bad
about that. I know I hurt Sam and though he seems to have
recovered nicely (he's married now), that doesn't erase the
fact that I treated him as somewhat less than a human being.

My old habit of selective amnesia should come in handy
when the guilt gets too loud. Because revealing a past crime
isn't a way to ease guilt. Revealing a past crime just creates a
mistrust that will follow you forever, no matter how exem-
plary your behavior.

Some might argue that a couple should engage in full disclosure if their relationship is to be strong. I disagree. Which
is why I've also decided not to tell John that I know about his
brief affair with Sophie. By doing this I'm allowing John his
privacy in addition to guarding my own. Though I have learned
to love, I am, at the core, deeply self-protective, deeply wary.
I will do my best to keep the door to myself open, but only
partway.

I hope John will understand.

107

Instead of quibbling over the truth of what happened just before the champagne bottle broke over your boyfriend's head, agree that both of you were stinking drunk and place all blame squarely on the booze. This way, you're both winners!
—The Fine Art of Passing the Buck, or It's Not My Fault!

JOHN

I love Eva.

I remember Ellen saying once that maybe Eva is my cross to bear, that if she was "possible" I wouldn't want her the way I do.

Eva challenges me to be a better person by pushing the very buttons that result in my being the worst I can be: a judgmental know-it-all.

I hope that I challenge her to be . . . if not a better person, then a happier, more fulfilled person. Only time will tell.

After getting the box from her sister, Eva enrolled in a graduate program. She's working toward a master's in creative writing. It's not like her to do things partway, to audit a class to see if she's still got her academic chops. No, she had to dive right in and, honestly, she seems happy. At least, content. And though her schedule is more hectic than ever, she manages to spend a lot of time with me without complaining that I'm interfering in her life or keeping her from more important things. Eva's transformation is a bit of a miracle, really, even though she hasn't changed entirely from the woman I first had dinner with a few months ago.

But that's okay by me. I love her for who she is and not for who I thought her to be or who I wanted her to be. Or something. This love thing—this big, serious love thing—is new to me. I don't really know how to talk about it so maybe I'll just shut up and get to work. Eva's coming over for dinner and I'm hoping to persuade her to spend the night. I've got a pretty good shot; my apartment is so much more comfortable than hers that she doesn't need much coaxing to stick around until morning. The other day I even found a toothbrush stashed under the bathroom sink. It made me smile to see that little by little she's allowing our lives to mesh.

Now, if only I can talk her into meeting the family, all eleven of them. But I'll be patient. And I'll try to believe that all good things will come in time—like our marriage.

108

Dear Readers:

After much consideration and three failed suicide attempts, the Answer Lady has decided to retire. Don't try to find me. I'm going into deep seclusion in a concerted effort to erase from memory my horrifying experience with you, the general public. It's time for you morons to clean up your own messes. Or not. Go ahead, lie, cheat, steal—what do I care? You're not my problem anymore. Au revoir!

EVA

Some time had passed since I'd last attempted to talk to Sophie about my affair with Jake. Maybe it would have been easier just to let it go, but I couldn't. I wanted to apologize. I hoped Sophie was finally ready to listen.

I called her one weekday evening. I realized there was a chance that Ben or Jake would be at her apartment. I just prayed that neither man would answer the phone.

"Hello?" It was Sophie's pleasant voice.

"Sophie," I said, "it's Eva."

She didn't reply immediately. I thought she might hang up, but after a moment she said, "Oh. Hello."

"Do you have a moment?" I asked.

"I suppose."

Her reply wasn't encouraging but I hadn't expected open arms.

"Sophie," I said, the words rehearsed, "I'm sorry about what happened with Jake. I never should have gotten involved with him. It was hurtful to you. And I'm sorry I got so mad at you about Ben. You did nothing wrong. I guess I was just—surprised."

"Thank you for apologizing," she said evenly.

Maybe I should have ended the call there. Instead, I asked: "Can you forgive me?"

"I don't know."

"Okay." What else could I say? You can't force someone to forgive you. You can only get them to lie about forgiving you so that you'll shut up and go away.

"It's all right about Ben, I guess," Sophie said suddenly. "I really didn't want you to find out the way you did. I felt bad about that."

"Thanks. I appreciate your understanding." And then: "And about Jake?"

"You used my son."

Me and my big mouth. Never content to leave well enough alone.

"He pursued me," I said. "We were consenting adults."

"But he cared for you," Sophie argued.

"He thought he cared for me. But he didn't."

"How do you know?" she demanded.

How to explain my experience with Jake? Finally, I said, "I looked into his eyes."

Sophie laughed bitterly. "As if someone like you could look into someone's eyes and know what they're feeling! You understand nothing about real intimacy, nothing."

The force behind her words stunned me. Still, I tried very hard not to answer in a defensive way. After all, I was the first to admit there was room in my life for improvement.

"I'm not evil, Sophie," I said after a weighty moment. "I just had to learn how to take care of myself. I was alone at

Jake's age. I had virtually no family. I discovered I had it in me to fight for success so I did. I have some regrets but I'm also proud of what I've accomplished. You can judge me all you want; I can't change what happened."

Sophie said defensively: "I don't judge you."

I asked how Jake was faring.

"He's fine," Sophie said, almost as if she begrudged her son his happiness. Had she really been hoping—for her own complicated reasons—that Jake would fall apart after our breakup? "He's seeing someone named Lisa." After a pause she added: "She's a few years older."

Of course. A few years older but of childbearing age. Perfectly acceptable for all occasions.

"I'm glad he's happy," I said.

"Ben and I are getting married."

I felt for any feelings of jealousy or pain. There were none. "Congratulations," I said. "That's great."

A note here: John thought that telling Sophie about our being a couple might help heal the rift, might humanize me a bit in her mind, but I didn't agree. I thought Sophie would see our being together as another betrayal and I feared her anger. John argued that my refusal to tell Sophie about our relationship compelled him to secrecy, too. I sympathized, but held my ground.

"Well," Sophie said then, "I have to go."

"Okay. Thanks for listening. I appreciate it."

"Okay." She paused. "Look, maybe someday we could have lunch or something."

"Sure," I said. "That would be great. Give me a call sometime."

It was a comfortable fiction. We both knew that the friendship had suffered a deadly blow. We knew that we would see each other again only by chance.

"Good-bye, Eva."

"Good-bye, Sophie," I said.

And another part of my life was over.

109

Note to the General Public: The Polidori Publishing Company, long the leader in self-help books, has declared bankruptcy due to the fact that its founder and president "made off" with the company's every asset. Devoted readers of such titles as *Just Forget It Ever Happened: How to Repress an Unpleasant Truth* and *It's the Truth If You Believe It, or Life as a Sincere Liar,* can, for a limited time, purchase products at drastically reduced rates, both in bookstores and on the sidewalk outside company headquarters.

EVA

"How is she?" I asked. "I mean, was it awkward?"

Six months or so after my call to Sophie I finally agreed she had a right to know that John and I were a couple. John was the obvious one to tell her; he'd stayed in touch with Sophie and Ben via phone and e-mail, though he rarely saw them socially.

John took off his coat and sank onto his gorgeous, plushy couch. I joined him there.

"Let's put it this way: I don't think I'll be hearing much from either of them, at least for a while."

"I'm sorry," I said. I took John's hand in mine. "I know how much Sophie's friendship means to you."

"You were right all along. She didn't come out and say it,

but it was clear she sees my being with you as just another in a long line of betrayals, her reunion scheme gone bust."

"But we couldn't keep it a secret much longer," I said. "What if Sophie stumbled on us one night like I stumbled on her and Ben?"

John lifted my hand in his and kissed it. "Oh, we did the right thing, telling her. Anyway, you and I being together is the least of Sophie's concerns right now."

"What do you mean? Is she sick?"

John smiled. "You do have a flair for the dramatic, don't you? No, she isn't sick. It's about Jake. Your former paramour. Your boy toy."

I took my hand from his but kept my tone calm. "John, I'm asking you again not to 'remind' me—not to 'remind' us—of what went on between Jake and me. Please. It's important to me that you not keep bringing it up. I'm embarrassed enough without—"

"Hey, I'm sorry, Eva, really. I was being an idiot there for a moment. And I promise not to bring it up again."

I couldn't stay mad at him. Someday, I thought, I'll be furious with him for days on end. But not now. "I'm keeping you to that promise, John," I said, taking his hand again. "I mean it. Now, what about Jake?"

"He's engaged to a twenty-seven-year-old grad student in anthropology. Seems she just left for Africa on a field trip, but when she comes back they're tying the knot."

"But he can only have known her for a few months," I protested.

"What can I say?" John shrugged. "Sophie's not thrilled but Jake swears it's true love. He's an adult, so she can't prevent the marriage."

"What about Brad? What does he think about Jake getting married?"

"According to Sophie, Jake's news barely registered with Brad. He's engaged to some twenty-five-year-old actress/

model/waitress. She'll be pregnant a few months after the wedding, I'd lay money on it."

"Poor Sophie."

"She'll be fine."

"She does have Ben," I conceded. "And a career. If she sticks with it." And then it struck me. "John, maybe you could talk some sense into Jake."

John frowned. "Why do you care so much?"

"Because I can't help wondering if I'm responsible for his rushing into this marriage. Sophie told me that I broke his heart. I thought she was just . . . being Sophie, but maybe I did hurt him badly when I broke things off."

"Maybe, but don't get any ideas about marching over to his apartment to apologize."

I had to laugh. "Don't worry. That would be a huge mistake."

"Yes, it would. Jake's life is his own to make or break. Besides, his parents' divorce probably had a deeper influence on him than his fling with you. And I don't mean that as an insult."

"I know. And I hope you're right. It's terrible knowing you've messed someone up."

"Welcome to the human race. Membership is all about saying you're sorry."

"It's a lousy club with lousy rules."

"You have an alternative in mind?"

"No." I moved closer to John and lifted his arm around my shoulder. "I like how humans kiss. I could never let that go."

"Ah, yes. The kissing. That is a good thing. And it leads to even better things."

I shimmied away from John and got up from the couch. "Better things will have to wait," I said.

"What? Why?"

Poor John. He looked so bewildered.

"Your sisters are coming over, remember? Girls' night in, poker, wine, no men. Don't tell me you forgot."

John groaned and got to his feet. "I suppose I'm making food for this event?"

"Of course. Now, get to it. They'll be here in half an hour."

I watched him leave the room, knowing he wasn't in the least angry about cooking for the women in his life. His groaning and my bossing were part of our dynamic, part of our unique routine, our version of the daily stuff that keeps people together. Who knew the mundane could be so valuable, so productive?

"Eva!" John called out from the kitchen. "Where's my big spoon?"

I rolled my eyes. "Where it always is," I called back.

"I don't see it."

"I'm coming!" And I headed for the kitchen to find my fiancé's big spoon.